First Published Worldwic

Books by Luke Smitherd:

Novellas

The Man On Table Ten

Hold On Until Your Fingers Break

My Name Is Mister Grief

He Waits

Do Anything

For an up-to-date list of Luke Smitherd's other books, his blog, YouTube clips and more, visit www.lukesmitherd.com

The Physics of the Dead

By

Luke Smitherd

For Angela

"Though the days are long
Twilight sings a song
Of the happiness that used to be.
Soon my eyes will close
Soon I'll find repose
And in dreams you're always near to me."
—Gus Kahn

"You don't have to stay anywhere forever."
—Edwin Payne

Has anybody here seen my old friend Abraham?
Can you tell me where he's gone?
—Marvin Gaye

"Do you remember the good old days before the ghost town?
We danced and sang and the music played inna de boomtown."
—The Specials

"Monotony, boredom, death. Millions live like this (or die like this)
without knowing it. They drive a car. They work in offices...They picnic with
their families. They raise children.
And then some shock treatment takes place, a person, a book, a song,
and it awakens them and saves them from death."
—Anais Nin

Table of Contents

Part One:

Checking In

Chapter 1: In Which We Meet the Dead, Learn About Flyers and Blueys, and Discover How the Guests Survive Life In the Invisible Foyer

***

On days when Hart looked back at it all—looked back at the days when he and Bowler were still together—he remembered to focus on the positives. At the very least, he would have to say that they got what they wished for. At least things *happened.*

And then he would remember what happened to Bowler, and how it ended, and would then pause in whatever he was doing as he sighed and went through, once again, the list of regrets in his head. Undoubtedly, the worst of it—the physical pain—all happened to poor Bowler.

Hart missed him very much.

***

Taken from *Hart's Imaginary Guide to Being Dead, 'Television'*

For the dead, the watching of television is vital for staying sane.

To understand this, imagine: you never sleep. You never get the rest so badly needed by the human brain. You can't pick up a book to escape into its pages.

Now add to this the fact that you can only travel within the boundaries of The Foyer. You can't go to new places to see new things. You can't find change. So how do any of us ever let our minds switch off? How do we pass the time without irretrievably losing our minds?

We stand behind the living and watch with them. They think they're alone, in their rooms filled with reminders of the recent past. But we are there too.

***

The year 2000:

Mary grunted in her sleep, and Bowler jumped in his seat reflexively. Some things were harder to unlearn than others, Hart noted. He thought he'd probably been the same when he first arrived, but he was sure he'd picked things up a lot quicker than Bowler had. When Hart died, he'd been older than Bowler, to be fair, and from a far less mollycoddled world, but were he given the choice, Hart certainly wouldn't change that. These days, they knew *nothing.*

Bowler glanced sheepishly over; Hart gave him a brief wave of the hand. *Don't worry about it.* The younger man ran a hand nervously through his shortish hair and tried to resettle in his seat. Hart thought it would still be some time until, even unseen and intangible, Bowler was completely comfortable in other people's houses. It occurred to him how very human— how very *English*—it was to have the need to know you'd actually been *invited* somewhere.

Mary carried on dozing. She always tended to at this time of the day, and it was another reason Hart preferred to watch TV in her apartment than elsewhere. Mary was a creature of habit, and therefore easy to predict. Better for Bowler and, to a lesser extent, for Hart. Plus, Mary's place made him comfortable. The décor was definitely to his taste. That which he called classic (and Bowler called old fashioned) style was strongly in evidence.

Brown, floral patterned wallpaper and dark, dirty red carpet, with iron framed, yellowing photographs adorning the mahogany effect cabinets and side tables, as chipped and faded as Mary herself. Hart liked it. Bowler wasn't a fan, but Hart knew Bowler would never complain about it. What was the phrase he'd heard? *Wouldn't be seen dead in it.* Hart sneered bitterly at the irony. And then, right on schedule—it hadn't spoken up for a good five minutes—the voice in Hart's head spoke up again.

You've got to get OUT of The Foyer. You can't last much longer. What are you DOING, why are you wasting time?

As always, Hart blocked it out and focused on routine. Monotony. The safety net.

Mary's snoring began to drown out the tick of the large, seventies-style clock in the corner, which sat extremely awkwardly with the rest of the bric-a-brac. As the sound became harder to ignore, Hart fought extremely hard not to envy her. It was a feeling bordering on hate, made worse by the maddening drone. Once, back when he'd first arrived, he would have had to leave the room to calm down, driven to a nearly uncontrollable, jealous rage. *Sleep ...* Hart closed his eyes, as if to simulate it for himself. Of course, he felt no change in his state of mind, nor would he ever. Blessed, blessed sleep ... the temporary respite—no, the *sanctuary*—of rest. The living had absolutely no idea how good they had it. To hear her snoring so heavily was like a child's taunt to Hart's ears, *nya—nya—na—nya—naaa. Look what I've got.* Nowadays he could control his emotions better, though it had taken a long time to learn how to do so. More than anything since he'd come here, Hart had learned the importance of self control. It was the difference in this place between survival and ... the alternative. Hart had promised himself, long ago, that he would *not* end up like the others. He would remain intact. He realised he was gritting his teeth, and relaxed his jaw.

He forced himself to look back at Bowler, who was sitting and squinting at the glowing screen, trying to keep up with the goings-on in Albert Square. Soaps were an absolute lifeline for them, and he was glad he no longer had to give running commentary to his friend. Simple vision over distance was a major problem for the new arrivals, who had to learn how to master it just as they did with so many other aspects of their new physical existence, aspects that had been effortless in their former lives.

Hart sometimes thought the younger man wouldn't even *begin* to adapt, and Hart had even wondered if Bowler might end up being more trouble than he was worth; that Hart had made a large mistake. But now Bowler seemed to be ticking away nicely. Just a late starter.

"Who's the guy in the jacket?" asked Bowler peering intently, trying to focus.

"David," answered Hart, glancing at the screen. "He's new."

"When did he turn up? We never miss this."

"Last episode, must have been. Mary turned over for that film, so he must have been in the bit we didn't see. He was reintroduced at the start of this one. You missed it because you were late coming back from your ... walk."

The elephant in the room. One of the many open secrets they never talked about.

It was a deliberate, probing jibe, a childish act on Hart's part, but he was feeling annoyed and needed to vent. To his mild satisfaction, Bowler winced almost imperceptibly, and reddened, but kept a straight face. Hart knew Bowler hadn't actually done anything wrong—hadn't broken his promise to not return to his old ways—but just the mention of the subject was enough to goose Bowler, to unsettle him. There was nothing jumpier than a tempted man.

"I wasn't—" he began, but Hart closed his eyes and held up a hand.

"Yes, yes, I didn't say anything. Anyway, he's thingy's brother. The car chap."

Bowler nodded, glad of the change of subject.

"But wasn't he sleeping with—"

"Bowler," Hart theatrically sighed, "I'm quite certain that, at some point in the future of this programme's plumbing of the depths of morality, we'll be treated to the characters' *pets* having intercourse with one another behind their loved ones' backs. So I really wouldn't express any surprise at who has jumped into bed with whom," Hart said, finishing with a folding of his arms.

Bowler smirked, rolled his eyes, and turned back to the TV. Hart smiled despite himself. Shortly after, the drumbeats sounded that signified the end of the show. Bowler stretched and turned to his friend.

"So are we staying to watch the news, or are we going to the Polish Guy's for something else, or ..." When Hart didn't answer immediately, Bowler raised his eyebrows and his hands. "Or what?" he finished, good-naturedly.

Hart had to think about it for a second. As with every day, this was a legitimately important question. *What are we doing next* was to them, in this place, as food and water had once been. Their sustenance was entertainment, and survival depended upon activity. Without it, Hart knew too well, they would ... *change*. End up like the others. And that was too terrible an idea to even consider.

You've got to GO. You've got WORK to do, you've got to GO—

"News," Hart said, finally, and Bowler turned back to the screen.

"Spot the Blueys?" he asked, back to squinting.

"Spot the Blueys," Hart replied, already staring at the ceiling, his mind miles away.

***

7

He's aware that he exists, and this is progress. Before, there was a brief time when he didn't exist at all. He doesn't know where he physically begins and ends, but he knows that he used *to. And wait, wait ... he used to have a name. Currently everything is black, more than black, nothing ... but he doesn't know if it is his surroundings, or if he's just unable to see; he has no way of checking, no hands to check for eyes that aren't there. But he does have a sensation of moving, of surfacing, a sense of moving* through *and* into *something, and he knows there has been an incredible change, the biggest change there could possibly be. He tries to remember who he was before now, what he was, even what his shape was, but he can't, though he feels that this knowledge will come. After a time that may have been five minutes or five years, there is a sensation of touching down, landing, settling ... developing weight. A feeling of arriving somewhere. He thinks he can hear someone and vaguely is aware of wondering how that is possible without ears ... it's a voice. A voice that is breathing hard. Desperate.*

"Come on ... oh, please... *oh, for goodness' sake, please, please ...* work *..."*

***

"One!" shouted Bowler triumphantly, pointing, but Hart was actually more interested in the TV report about local redevelopment. You never knew; a change of the physical landscape around them, it might make a difference if it came close enough ... it could maybe mean something *(escape,* freedom*)*, but this thought was fleeting, as he knew it to be untrue and foolish.

Even so, he couldn't help but glance at where the smiling twenty-nine-year-old pointed; he had to admit, Bowler had done well to spot it with his limited vision, especially as far back in the shot as the Bluey was.

It was a shot of the city centre that they knew too damn well, knew it like they knew the only smell of whatever it was that filled all the space in their enclosure (it certainly wasn't air). The report was about the people of the city's responses to the redevelopment; one red-faced Coventry gentleman was suggesting that Hart's opinion of the people was right; even though the exact place this man was suggesting the council could stick said redevelopment was edited out, Hart thought that he could guess where the man meant.

Bowler's cry had come after that. On the screen, they'd been watching as a blue-shirted reporter filled two-thirds of the screen, with the shot over his shoulder revealing throngs of Saturday shoppers. If Bowler's sighting had been made within this group, it would have been less impressive, but he'd managed to catch a glimpse of the Bluey as it passed through the small gap between the reporter's right shoulder and the top corner of the screen.

This particular Bluey was a middle-aged black man, bearded and wearing a shell suit. He was walking slowly with the slight, awkward smile reserved for those wanting to appear on TV, but trying to appear nonchalant while simultaneously checking that they're in shot.

And, of course, covering his outline from head to toe was a pale, translucent blue glow.

Hart looked at Bowler and cracked a small smile, wagging his finger at him approvingly. He was genuinely pleased.

"That was impressive, you know. You couldn't have spotted that a month ago."

Bowler shrugged.

"Ta. First one for a while, too. What is that, three weeks?"

Hart thought, and nodded.

"About that."

Bowler's brow furrowed in response.

"So frustrating though, aren't they ..." he said quietly, gently shaking his head, and Hart scowled.

"I'm not in the mood for the discussion, Bowler. Just ... it means nothing for us. Speculation is pointless. Accept it, and please stop bringing it up." Hart stared at Bowler until he looked away and fell reluctantly silent, a slight scowl on his face.

The younger man sat quietly, and again decided that Hart's way, on this at least, was best. Hart had a *lot* more experience in The Foyer than Bowler had, and if Hart didn't know the best way to handle things, then who was Bowler to argue? Bowler got that sense again of how lucky he was, and his anger faded; he even shuddered as he thought about the alternative. He'd seen the other inhabitants of The Foyer … seen how he could have ended up. He relaxed for the first time that evening.

Hart watched his friend and felt a twinge of guilt. He couldn't blame Bowler. Once he'd have been the same. Bowler had been here for the blink of an eye compared to Hart's time, and he hadn't been through the things that Hart had been through. Hart had to remind himself what it was that Bowler gave him, just by being present. And for all of Bowler's persistence, his *hope* … as dangerous as it was, as unchecked as it was, he didn't deserve a dressing down all the time. Hart sighed, and again reminded himself to be patient with his companion. He needed time … which was just as well, here. Hart tried for an olive branch.

"Although …" Hart ventured with a theatrically arched smile, raising a finger towards the screen. "D'you think that he looked like the chap from the news?" he finished, raising his eyebrows.

Bowler brightened. Lookalikes. Their favourite game, and one of their bonds. Funnily enough, it had been Hart's invention.

"Trevor MacDonald?" he replied.

"That's the one."

Bowler thought about it and laughed.

"Trevor MacDonald in a shell suit. Welcome to Newsnight."

"News at Ten."

"Yeah, that."

It was all right now, and they went back to watching a report on underage drinking. The teenagers ... their behaviour never ceased to fascinate and horrify Hart, while Bowler just seemed to accept it.

***

Taken from *Hart's Imaginary Guide to Being Dead, 'Eyesight, New Arrivals, and Physical Adjustment'*

In my experience, new guests in The Foyer—or Check-ins, as I call them—take some time to command full control of their physical faculties. Having a complete body is the first challenge. Then speech. Then eyesight. Then being able to stand on the ground beneath them without passing into it. Once the basics are in place, a relatively normal existence—in terms of physical movement—can then begin. However, the eyesight takes a little while longer to reach whatever standard the viewer enjoyed in life. I do not know the reason for this, but I have found with Bowler that, with training and practice, this process can be expedited.

***

Getting heavier, becoming more ... solid. The voice is crackling in and out, like a badly tuned radio.

"You see, if this is actually going to work ... if I'm RIGHT ... I've got to keep talking, I think. I think if I keep talking all the time, then maybe we'll calibrate together, you see. That's what I'm trying to do. So ... I'm just going to talk about anything. I wish I could have a book; I'd just read to you from that. I wouldn't have to think of something to say. I've got no idea how long it takes, you see ... you're the first one I've been able to find at landing point. You know, to actually follow you to where you came down and landed ..."

There's a pause, as if the speaker is lost in thought, gone into his own head. When he speaks again, it's hurried, not only because he has caught his own silence, but because he's scared.

"Actually, you're only the fourth I've ever seen check in; not a Flyer, if you know what I mean. And I don't even know if you can hear me. It's a complete shot in the dark ... so ..."

The voice trails off like that of an uncomfortable dinner party guest. This is not a socialite. This is someone trying, and failing, to be chatty. This is someone uncomfortable when placed in a one on one situation with a stranger.

"Are you a man or a woman?" *the voice continues.* "You'd think I'd care—I'D think I'd care—but you'll be surprised to hear that I don't, really. No one does, here. I actually hope you don't remember this. I'm not used to ... anyway." *There is a short, embarrassed, angry silence. Then the speaker continues, forced, and angry that things are this way.* "I HATE being like this ... it's all probably a waste of time ..."

And the thought comes to Bowler's reforming consciousness, Please, don't stop. Don't ever stop. Don't you understand I *need* it?

***

"What about them? Can you see them, Bowler? There?"

Hart pointed at a group of young men, laughing and eating kebabs as they walked up the street. The city centre was unsurprisingly deserted tonight; a Tuesday. In other, major cities, maybe this wouldn't be the case these days (according to Bowler, at least; Hart had to take his word for it), but in Coventry, a Tuesday night was always quiet.

It was dark early, November nights (Hart hated November) coming in quick and cold. Bowler and Hart wouldn't have known about the latter, were it not for the people around them every day changing their attire over time from T-shirts and jeans to thick layers and winter jackets, shorts and sunglasses exchanged for scarves and gloves. The men before them had done the same. The streetlights were on, but the group was walking along the side of the road where the pavement was overhung by shop awnings. The angle made it difficult to see them as they slowly crested the rise, with their thick clothing destroying any sense of figure—and therefore making it harder to identify their sex—along with the shade created by the awnings. Hart knew that all of these elements would make picking out details quite a test for Bowler.

The younger man squinted, leaning forward; the effect was comical.

"Five guys ... wait, six. Eating something. Am I right?"

For the second time in one evening, Hart was impressed. He'd hoped for their number and their sex, but not what they'd been carrying.

"Bowler ... I had no idea you'd taken such a jump. You've gotten so much better."

Bowler shrugged.

"I haven't been doing anything different. Maybe it's just, y'know, time."

Hart shook his head, sadly.

"Not the case. Not everyone gets it, even after being dead for years. You know that Guest in the red coat, the one that looks like a rag? Have you seen him? You can tell he can't see a thing. You can tell by the way he jumps sometimes when he catches sight of things by accident."

"Well, points for me then. Result," Bowler said with a shy smile. Compliments did not sit easily with Bowler. It wasn't in his nature to enjoy attention, even here. However, the visual effort been extremely difficult for him. He now had a headache, but it had been worth it to hear Hart's approval.

He hated headaches. When he was alive, he would have just killed it with a Neurofen. That wasn't possible here. In The Foyer, headaches were a total fucking pain in the arse. He sighed and said nothing.

They went back to the conversation, except it wasn't a conversation; as usual, it was a debate. Debates were better. They fired the imagination, and that was important. Plus they were the few times Hart saw Bowler get animated, and that was always pleasant for him to see. However, Bowler could be beaten down most of the time, acquiescing, which Hart found frustrating. Tonight, it was about The Polish Guy, and like always, Bowler found Hart maddeningly out of touch.

"Even if you're not BORN here, y'know, but say you like England and are proud to live here, and, like, are like ... proud of everything England is ... then, y'know, you're welcome," Bowler reasoned, hesitating every few words. Though he was far from stupid, he didn't like to get caught saying the wrong thing, or to have his point lost by rushing it. He took his time. Plus, he'd learned the hard way that Hart would ruthlessly take advantage if he tripped over his own sentence and sounded like he was fumbling. "It's the ones that don't, that aren't interested, that don't help ... what's the word ..." he snapped his fingers repeatedly.

"Integration," said Hart, firmly. "And I don't believe that. Come here, live here, be welcome here, become a citizen, by all means, and I shall shake your hand and call you my neighbour and my friend. But you can never truly be called English. You can never be called an Englishman."

Bowler shook his head to disagree. He opened his mouth, but Hart cut him off, holding up a hand and looking away. Bowler wanted to slap him when Hart did that, but Bowler never would.

"That's not 'racist.' You know I'm not 'racist,'" Hart sniffed, "I'm just ... they're different. Different culture, yes? I was there when they first arrived. They're *welcome*—are you hearing me, they're more than welcome, welcome to stay here and raise a family and put down roots—and respectable and perfectly jolly nice and everything else, and they deserve all the freedoms that everyone else has ... but don't tell me they're English."

14

Bowler didn't agree—in fact, he disagreed quite strongly—and he knew the words were there, but he just couldn't do it when he HAD to, when he NEEDED to ... there was some sort of blockage. But swallowing everything back felt bad, too. Hart had repeatedly impressed upon Bowler the importance of looking after the mind.

And then all thoughts were blasted from his mind as he looked up.

"Hart ... HART ..." Bowler's mouth went dry, and it took all he had to stay upright. His skin felt light.

Hart saw, and his eyes lit up for a brief moment—he believed it as well for a second—and then dimmed. He shook his head.

"No," he sighed. "Not coming for us."

"You can't see it properly! You can't say for certain!"

"Bowler, I can. It's dark, and you've clearly improved vastly, but I can see it better than you can. It's a Flyer."

Bowler sagged. He stared off to his right, looking at nothing for a second. *Shit ...* He'd been certain. Knowing it was fruitless, Bowler looked back at the sky. He was, of course, desperate.

"Are you sure?"

Hart shrugged.

"I've seen four Check-ins during my time here—of which you were one, of course—and several Flyers. The Check-ins look very different. They're bigger, for starters."

He realised he was being rather blunt, and thought for a moment. He drummed his fingers on his thigh, sighing.

"It's an easy mistake to make, Frank. It's all right," Hart said, quietly.

Bowler cocked his head in Hart's direction. It wasn't quite a shrug, but the gesture said *it's all right*. He continued to peer intently up at the fuzzy object in the sky, resigned to the truth now, but still fascinated. He'd been here only two years, but had still seen a few Flyers; it wasn't the first time he and Hart had had a similar conversation. Yet the disappointment was still just as strong. *Why, though?* whined a voice in Bowler's head. The voice was wheedling, petulant, and Bowler didn't care. He'd earned the right to think that way. Nothing changed here. They both knew it, and that's what made survival so hard.

Hart knew that too, and Bowler had seen that brief glimmer in his eyes when he first looked up. Bowler knew what it would mean for Hart if it *was* another Check-in. It would mean more protection. Bowler smirked, in spite of himself; he knew the way his companion thought. And Bowler wasn't daft, or at least not as daft as Hart thought he was. What Hart didn't know was the other reason *Bowler* needed a Check-in so badly. How it might mean that Bowler was more than just protection for someone.

The Flyer crackled with a warm energy as they watched.

The object in the sky was cloud shaped, but slightly transparent, ethereal. It was here one second, gone the next, then back again, flickering like an old film. It was about nine feet long by four feet across; a glowing, white, airborne piece of elongated popcorn, lit from within. Bowler tracked its progress across the sky, still holding onto a glimmer of hope despite Hart's words and his own knowledge (*it wouldn't really make any difference in the long run ... but please let Hart be wrong on this*), a glimmer that died the closer the Flyer got to the edge of The Foyer. Even though his belief was tiny, Bowler's heart sank as the Flyer began to shift trajectory, and started the all-too-familiar inexorable journey upwards.

It *wasn't* a Check-in. It was a Flyer. Another dead person, but not one that was coming to join them in The Foyer. It was going wherever the hell all the others went, and the sight of it doing so, as ever, made Bowler ache in a way he never had while alive.

As it ascended, it made the low thrumming sound that Bowler knew painfully well, the one that sounded like someone despairing. It was a sound that perfectly matched the feeling in the pit of his stomach.

They stood silently for a few minutes, watching it until it ascended completely from view. Bowler continued tracking it in the sky long after Hart had stopped watching; the older man had begun an inspection of his fingernails, despite there being no dirt under them and no chance of there ever being any. Hart caught himself, and noted again that some things were harder to unlearn than others.

Hart waited until Bowler's gaze also returned downwards, and watched his companion for a few moments. When Bowler didn't move, Hart sighed, hesitated, and stepped only slightly closer to him. He knew the way Bowler was feeling all too well. It was only two years ago that he had finally stopped feeling that way himself—stopping once he'd gotten what he wanted in the form of Bowler's arrival—and the memory of that time was still strong enough to move him to a kind of pity. He was not an unkind man. He was just one who had never been given much reason, when he was alive, to learn how to discuss anything that was deeply rooted. He wasn't even consciously aware that he was going to try and comfort his friend.

He gently put an arm around the young man's shoulders, barely touching him, and guided Bowler slowly forwards. Bowler allowed him to do so.

"Come on," Hart muttered gently, but awkwardly. "Let's go and see what the Polish gentleman is watching tonight.

***

There's a sudden snapping sound, and everything rushes into Bowler's head; memories, knowledge, identity, and the strongest memory of all is one of great pain. Not the greatest pain he will ever know—that will come from the Train, of course—though he doesn't know this yet. That will be a physical agony so great and so lasting that he will brush against madness, and he will discover why madness is to be feared above all else here.

17

The next thing he's aware of is the voice again, the voice that hasn't shut up, that blessedly hasn't shut up, and he's more grateful than the voice's owner will ever know. The voice is breathless and desperate now, almost shouting. Its owner has seen something.

"Can you hear me? Can you hear me? I can see you! I can see you properly now! Hello? Hello? Do any kind of gesture, anything!"

And he nods in response, and with that he realises he has a head now, and with this knowledge comes the sensation that the rest of his body has also arrived. He still can't see, but he thinks that will come very soon. He stretches his hands and realises something isn't right, but he can't tell what yet ... he's lighter, lighter than he should be, but it's a sensation that he can't understand. He'll later realise it's because there's no gravity. No air. No breeze.

The voice gasps and continues tremulously.

"Have you been able to hear me ... all this time?"

He's still figuring out what's going on with his body, but he nods again, even though it makes him feel sick. He owes the voice that.

The voice sighs, and there's silence, and then he realises the voice is laughing with relief. When it speaks again there are reluctant tears in the laughter.

"Well ... well. I didn't think ... heh ... d'you know, I didn't believe for one solitary second that that would actually ... bloody ... work."

***

Taken from *Hart's Imaginary Guide to Being Dead, 'Guests, Communication, and Cruelty'*

You will be amazed by the abundance of cruelty in The Foyer. Everything in life that ever made one stop and say *surely not* is nothing compared to the many, many perfectly placed mental tortures here.

For example: even for those of us that preferred their privacy in life, it turns out that Satre was wrong. Hell is not, in fact, other people, although I remain convinced beyond all doubt that this place is not Hell. I imagine Hell would be far worse. Along with sleep, I find the cruellest restriction in The Foyer is an inability to communicate with other Guests verbally, or words coming across as silence to the listener. To those that don't avoid us, anyway. Those that remain, for now at least, sane. The vast majority are not.

Some—meaning Bowler—take this as more proof of a guiding hand behind all of this. A deliberate device to prevent us coming together and solving the puzzle of The Foyer. I disagree. I think it is further proof, if any were needed, of the abundance of cruel coincidence in all planes of existence.

***

Wednesday morning, the shopping precinct. Hart always liked this time of day; he liked the hustle and bustle. People rushing, talking on mobile phones—Hart desperately wanted to try one of those, despite himself—late for work, shopping, kids skiving, sitting on the edge of the large fountain set in the middle of the crossroads, the heart of the city centre rush.

Bowler liked it too, but for him the reason was being able to see the people more easily. It wasn't as hard in the daytime, and he didn't have to strain. Today, George had joined them.

George was the Guest—out of the three that they associated with, the three that would actually come near to them and "talk"—that they hung around with most in The Foyer. This was because George was the one Hart tuned in with the most frequently—which was still extremely rare—meaning that communication was actually possible, but also because he was so damn likeable they couldn't *help* but hang around with him. Even so, Bowler had noticed something odd about the way that George and Sarah and Mark could keep finding each Hart and Bowler—most of the time—when they wanted to. The Foyer covered an area of roughly one square mile, full of buildings and other visual obstacles. All the Guests obviously moved independently of each other (apart from Hart and Bowler) and so it would be expected that the "friends" would run into each other a lot less than they did ... and yet somehow, that wasn't the case. Hart and Bowler had many discussions on the matter—Hart holding court with Bowler left trying to get a word in—and the general theory that Hart held, and one that Bowler agreed with, was that it was all to do with energy. Perhaps they sensed each other subconsciously, heading towards each other half the time without realising it. It was the thing that seemed to make the most sense, despite the eventual physical discomfort that would begin after spending time in each other's presence; after a short while, they would have to part until it passed and their bodies returned to normal.

They sat quietly, people watching. George, of course, was totally silent to their ears. Bowler knew very little about George, struggling more than Hart with the "gestures only" conversation. Hart knew more of the man, partly due to his being better practiced at both miming it and reading information, but mainly due to his ability to occasionally tune in with George, which Hart (of course) proudly took as proof of his theory about frequencies. In the past, whenever he tuned in, Hart had used the brief period that it lasted to ask probing, experimental questions about how George felt, what he'd been thinking at the point that they suddenly could hear each other, et cetera, in an attempt to crack the trick. Over the years he'd cycled through to personal questions out of curiosity—inescapable even for the ceremonial Hart—but he'd now exhausted those and so it was back to the science of it.

Bowler had to admit, Hart's frequency and energy theory was a good argument. Regardless, he liked George because of his easygoing nature, and though he'd never say it, it was nice not being the quietest one every now and then. He also liked how George tried to speak to him, and didn't just rely on Hart. He felt like George made an *effort* with him. And George was doing so at that very moment, tapping Bowler on the shoulder and gesticulating.

Bowler looked at George, a man in his late sixties who was portly but still with a full head of grey hair. He looked jolly where Hart looked severe; round faced, whereas Hart's features were sharper, thinner. It fascinated him to see that George still had thread veins here in The Foyer, while Hart's skin was still quite healthy. Hart, visually at least, radiated robustness, hard in a wiry way. Slim but tough, corded like his suit. George seemed to suggest cuddles, based on both his nature and appearance.

In the latter element—although he was "physically" older than Hart—George wore more modern clothes, an acrylic jumper and trousers compared to Hart's brown corduroy suit. Even Hart's hair was more old fashioned, a slicked down side parting compared to George's crew cut, an interesting look for a man of George's age (Bowler assumed using clippers at home was a more appealing option than the barber in George's former life.) But then, George hadn't been here anywhere near as long as Hart, so it all made sense.

George began his charade, and Bowler watched intently. It was a good game with a practical purpose, and Bowler loved being on the receiving end of it. He pieced it together as George went.

Gesturing over his shoulder; Bowler knew this one. *Yesterday.* Now hands to eyes. *I saw.* Fingers to the back of the head, head thrusting downwards and forwards, growling face ... though it looked very funny, Bowler got the impression George was actually being deadly earnest. Bowler couldn't get it, and threw his hands up, putting on a confused face. George looked at Hart, who had been watching, and pointed at Bowler. *Explain to him.*

21

Hart looked at the crowds around him with a slight sigh, and answered, not taking his eyes off the people milling around.

"He says saw The Beast yesterday, Frank."

Bowler drew in his nonexistent breath dramatically, looking at George with wide eyes even though it was a false expression put on for the older man's benefit. Bowler thought George was lying. If the old man had seen The Beast at a close enough range to be story-worthy, he very much doubted old Georgie would be healthy enough to be sitting here telling them about it. But he knew what old people were like. They made things up, didn't they? His Gran had been the same. She once had claimed that she'd won five grand in the lottery and lost the ticket. He'd watched his mum making a big show of shock and dismay, rolling her eyes at the rest of them to do the same and keep Granny amused. He'd been annoyed by it.

Mum ...

Bowler pushed the thought away. He'd gotten good at doing it. He looked at George and drew his palms close to each other. *Close?* George furrowed his brow with a smile and shook his head. *Come on, of course not.*

This was interesting. Maybe it *was* true then.

Bowler thought about how best to express it. He just couldn't do the charades, though he had gotten better over time. Deciding, Bowler held his hand above his head, shaking it rapidly, then slowly lowered it to his waist, reducing the shakes as it lowered, until his hand was at waist height, and still. Then he raised his eyebrows. Internally, he was pleased with himself. It was a good mime.

George got it, and shook his head, screwing up his face emphatically, then mirrored the low-hand action. The Beast hadn't been raging, he'd been calm. That made sense. If The Beast was in the maddest of his many personalities, you literally ran as far as The Foyer would allow. George must have seen him from a good distance away, but it was safer to watch if The Beast wasn't raging. He seemed like he could *sense* you when he was like that. The consequences if The Beast caught you in that mind were unthinkable. He'd never seen an actual attack himself—though he had only seen The Beast raging once, by chance, before Hart had grabbed him, screaming to run, *run*—but had never seen him catch someone. He'd heard Hart's version of when he'd seen it though, and the way his face had gone pale, the way his hands shook ... he knew enough.

Bowler held his hands up and cocked his head. *What was he doing?* George made a serious face and cast his hands about, looking this way and that. Bowler understood. On the occasions he'd seen The Beast himself, he'd been doing the same thing; walking around, quietly inspecting things. Again Hart had appeared, yelling, had physically thrown Bowler over his shoulder and ran him away, pale faced and shrieking.

All in all though, George wasn't telling much of a story, but Bowler appreciated the thought. George was just making conversation, and letting Bowler know that he didn't just communicate with Hart. Bowler made an impressed face and nodded. In the distance, he saw another Guest emerge through the wall of Boots. It was the one he always thought of as Horse Guy, due to his rather long face. Like all the other non-communicating Guests, Horse Guy was in his normal state of undress, and he was one of the most mentally gone. As usual, he was talking to himself animatedly, and today, the mess of self-inflicted welts across his chest seemed worse than usual. Bowler watched him go without mentioning it to the others. Other, long-resident Guests were no longer of any interest. They were all pointless.

Hart leaned forward as a lady shopper walked past.

"Five past eleven," he said, sitting back. "It's starting soon."

They stood, and George remained seated, raising his eyebrows at them. Hart tapped his wrist, and George nodded, standing. It was time to go.

***

Bowler tries to speak and can't. He wants to ask why he's naked, but the man seated on the floor opposite him seems to already know what he's thinking.

"If you're wondering about clothes, they come very soon. Mine did, anyway; maybe a couple of hours. They come by themselves, as far as I can ascertain. My theory is we form them ourselves here, out of our unformed energy. I think we do it without thinking, from our state of mind. They're the only ones you get, and I've no idea how they're decided. It's not a case of getting the ones you wore the most, anyway. Take mine; I only wore these for special occasions, but it can't be that either as I'm the smartest-dressed Guest here. Easily the smartest, and I'm not talking about fashion, I mean in terms of neatness. I think it's just random, whatever's in your mind when clothes first pop up. But I can't say for certain. It must be something to do with your mind, regardless. How you look, I mean. Just look at The Beast … ah, not that you would know. How do you feel? All right? Just nod if you do."

The clothes that man is talking about, the clothes the man is wearing, are an old-fashioned, slightly ill-fitting brown corduroy suit. They look like something from the 1940s. Bowler hopes he doesn't have to wear those.

He nods anyway, and starts to panic as it suddenly strikes him that he's sinking into the floor, incredibly slowly, but sinking nonetheless. It takes a second to register, and he almost doesn't comprehend it, but now he realises that his body is dropping into the concrete as if he were lying on quicksand. As he lies on his side, two inches of his thigh have already sunk into the concrete of the street. It's the most terrifying thing he's ever seen, even after everything that's just happened; this is (the pun vaguely registers) concrete evidence that everything he's going through is real. He starts to thrash, but the man in the suit calmly holds up a hand.

"That's not going to help," he says. "Just imagine, just picture in your head, that you're lying on the surface, and you will. After a day or two it'll be automatic. You won't even need to think about it."

Bowler can't hear the man properly, however, as panic has taken hold, but the man in the suit begins to shout.

"Imagine you're lying on the surface!"

Somehow it penetrates, and Bowler does as he's told. Slowly he begins to raise back up; now he thinks about feeling the concrete, feeling its textured surface, but he knows he won't, as he knows, somehow, that he will never properly feel another surface again. He panics and gasps for air, and it dawns on him that he can't feel any in his lungs. He'd never notice it if it were there; but he can feel it now it's gone.

There's no town smells, no street smells, no car smells, no drain smells, no smells that he recognises at all. As he takes in his surroundings, he realises that he's in a car park, an empty car park at an unidentifiable hour of the night. There's a sign saying LEVEL ONE, and arrows on the walls telling pedestrians that aren't there which way to go, strip lights on the ceiling covered by plastic cases that are full of dead flies and moths, their bodies inexplicably on the inside. He realises the only thing he can smell pervades everything. Everything smells of one thing only; a faint, unpleasant odour, that makes him think of the word Electrical. Were he more experienced, Bowler would realise the smell is ozone.

The man in the brown suit stands.

"That's better," he says with satisfaction. The man on the floor knows that the man in the suit doesn't mean he's pleased that the situation is resolved, or is feeling glad that the man on the floor is feeling better. The man in the suit is pleased with the other's progress. The man in the suit is seeing exactly what he wanted to see here, and when he speaks next, what he says hits deeply, harsh and hard, damning and burying.

This isn't just because of the words spoken, but because of the manner in which they are delivered. Blunt, direct, frank, just like his name (his NAME ... Frank. Frank ... BOWLER, yes!) and by this, the man in the suit lets Frank Bowler know a number of things without saying them directly; that the man in the suit will not provide what Bowler's mother gave, what Bowler's lovers have given. No comfort, no unconditional affection; there is none of this here, none in this man, and what he says makes Bowler ache uncontrollably for it and tells him that he will never have it, never again.

"All right," the man in the suit says, "I believe in straight talking; so here it is. It really is the best way, to get it out of the way now, you see." He pauses, taking a breath, not looking Bowler in the eye. He looks like he's steeling himself. And when the man in the suit looks up, it is the face of a police officer, one who comes to your house to deliver some highly unexpected and unpleasant news, the worst news, thinking, This is the part of the job I hate, delivering news to these good folks, but I have to do it.

"But please remember the good news," he continues. "The fact that—and I still can't believe this has worked—I've managed to fix it this way … that fact means you've actually got it better than everyone else that's ever arrived here. You really have. But anyway …" Pause. Deep, deep breath, and Bowler suddenly knows what's coming, but it's too late. And he is stunned as he actually sees the man in a brown corduroy suit smile, albeit in an embarrassed and apologetic way.

"All right. Look here … I mean … I'm sorry … but you're dead. And as far as I've been able to tell in all the time I've been here … this, well. It certainly isn't heaven."

And Frank Bowler begins to sink into the floor again, faster now.

***

Hart looked across at Bowler and was not at all surprised to see the rapt expression on his face. The cinema still had the same effect on him, even now; it was an escape over all others, when the lights went down and the screen lit up. It was a cliché, but for a few hours, they were alive again.

George was the same, but more serious looking. George *really* got into his films. If the bad guys were being bad, George's faced showed anger. If the good guys were winning, George's eyes were like a child's, enthusiastic and delighted. But Bowler ... Bowler's face showed nothing but delight all the way through. For Bowler, Hart thought, it was more than just an escape. It was a way of forgetting that which burned constantly at the back of his mind. Hart sometimes wondered just how hard it was for Bowler, sticking to the deal they'd made ... But he'd made Bowler agree to it for his own good, hadn't he? As well as for *his* own good? The thought reminded Hart that it was good he was here for the young man. As vital as Bowler was to Hart, good lord, he knew Bowler needed him too.

On screen, Bond dispatched another villain. This Bond was good, but Hart wasn't sure he liked him. Bowler did, of course; it was Bond. That was enough for Bowler. But for Hart, it was just another example of how different things were now. He remembered Moore, and the raised eyebrow, and the puns, and thought the modern version lacked some of the fun of the past. Hart sighed. He was getting bitter. He needed to keep an eye on that. He knew where it might lead.

He leaned over to say something to Bowler, but George glared at him fiercely and made a shushing motion. Hart was taken aback. He frowned and slumped back in his seat. He wasn't used to being told off.

"You can't hear me anyway, idiot," he murmured, scowling.

Some habits *were* harder to break than others.

***

Bowler is clothed now. He can't remember the way his getup arrived, the same way he can't remember the movement of hands on a watch; he just suddenly realises they're there, on his body. To his surprise, his outfit is a pair of blue jeans, black shoes, and his old white Nike T-shirt. He only wore it about

27

five times, and wasn't a particular fan of it, so he doesn't get why this is the top he's ended up in. He doesn't know it yet, but this outfit will change over time, and he will not notice that either, any more than he will remember which outfit he started out with.

Hart isn't giving him many details; every time Bowler manages to ask a question, in stammering, half-formed words (he can't understand why it's so hard to speak), Hart says it's best to continue getting physically orientated first.

"Because," as he reminds him for the tenth time, pacing up and down, "you're going to get to learn in a few days—because you'll actually be taught—what everybody else here has to learn for themselves over several years. You're already walking, while most new arrivals spend several weeks wedged into the floor up to their waists until they figure it out, as far as I can gather. Let's get the basics down, while you get your head around your situation. Too much and you'll just overload, and that can lead to … well … you just don't want to do that."

Another burst of memory suddenly floods into Bowler's mind. This is the third time it's happened, but Bowler feels like there's still SO much more to get. His mouth glues up as he tries to express it.

"Ah," he says, stuck. Hart sees this, and waits for him. "Ah. Ah."

"Go on," Hart urges, excited and patient. He's seeing progress.

"Mech. Mech."

"..."

"Mechanic."

"Good."

"I. Mechanic. I like … bikes."

"Racing?"

"Mmm."

"Good. Keep going."

***

George, Hart, and Bowler were standing outside, Bowler's eyes still adjusting to the sunlight. They'd seen everything else that was on at the cinema, and Hart made them ration their visits, at least as a threesome, saving them as something to look forward to. Hart knew the importance of having something to look forward to. George was excitable, partly from movie buzz, and partly from the frustration of not being able to articulate fully what he thought of the film. Hart had told Bowler that George used to be a taxi driver when he was alive.

They watched George patiently as he moved, his current charade a complicated one; hands higher and lower, flitting around his head, then thumbs up. It was difficult to understand, but for once, Bowler saw it and got in there first.

"He liked it better because there were more special effects."

Hart shook his head, pulling a dramatic scowl for George. Bowler wondered if Hart wasn't really hiding annoyance; Hart's mime interpretations were rarely beaten to the punch.

George looked shocked with Hart's disagreement. His hands became flicked up. *Why on earth would you think that?*

"Yeah, are you for real, man?" said Bowler, agreeing. He'd loved it too, had thought it was exciting. Hart looked sharply at him, and Bowler reddened.

"Not as good as the old style. Bond is fun escapism, but still with *some* element of realism," said Hart, after a moment more of staring at Bowler. "Not close enough to the style of the books," he continued loudly, anticipating Bowler's response as he opened his mouth to protest. "Bond is Fleming, and once the books ran out, they shouldn't make any more." Bowler frowned.

Hart looked at George, doing the Moore eyebrow and pointing at it, then giving a thumbs-up. He then pointed at the cinema and gave the thumbs down. George laughed silently, waved Hart away, and then proceeded to act out a bit he'd liked, mainly for Bowler's benefit. George's mouth worked silently as he gave a running commentary neither Hart nor Bowler could hear. It wasn't that George was childish. It was that he was old enough to know better and not care.

Hart scanned the street absentmindedly, listening to Bowler laughing with George in the background. He felt restless today; this was always the downside to coming out of the movies. His usual fear was intensified during the comedown. They needed more than TV today. They needed real drama; a good couple's argument to sit in on, a parking dispute, a fight, anything. They could go and find it. A *safe* little hunt. Now they had a job for the afternoon, and, as always, the thought made him feel better. They had a task. He breathed easily as he turned back to the others, not realising he was smiling as he watched them. He loved them both, even if he was no more aware of it than they were.

He turned to Bowler to explain, just in time to hear George's voice tune onto their frequency and say "—ills the first fella, boom, and then ... what? Bowl? *Bowl*, have you got me? *Have you got me?*"

He'd seen Bowler's face change, but as usual, in moments that needed action, Bowler had frozen, not speaking. He gaped dumbly at George and then quickly turned to Hart, but the older man was already there, grabbing George by the shoulders and turning him so they were face to face. They'd *both* tuned into George this time, and as Bowler's paralysis broke they both started talking hurriedly over each other; this usually happened when they tuned in with someone. Both of them had their own things to try, their own experiments, frantic, but it was George himself who got there first this time.

"Quickly, how can you both hear me together, how does Bowl get it—"

"I've told you, it's Bow*ler*, and I caught him when he arrived so we're tuned on the same frequency, it was an experiment, it worked—"

"Frequency?! What the hell, how, how did you—"

"It doesn't matter, listen—"

"If you've worked it out, tell me! I can have—"

"Shut up and listen! What were you thinking just now, what was different?"

"You said that last time, there was NOTHING—"

"I want to try this, this, does it help if I touch you? Is it louder?"

"No, what were YOU thinking?"

"Nothing new—"

"Well don't move, let's, let's, I don't know—"

"Is it easier if I'm closer?"

"No, well, you're louder, but then you're closer—"

"Can you hear me? Over here?" Bowler blurted out, trying to contribute in some way. George nodded at him frantically, and went to speak, but Hart snapped his hand out, waving Bowler silent.

"Listen, listen, now this. Your mood, are you happy? Actually, wait, you were quite energetic just then—"

"Nothing new, I've been like this before and it hasn't happened—"

"Well, HELP me, think!"

George then did his usual darting-eyed, mouth-moving, gasping bit as he tried to think under pressure.

"Well ... well ... oh, look, I don't think there *is* a reason!" he said, shoulders slumping. *He gives up so easily,* thought Hart. "How many times have we been here before?" cried George. "You always try this, that, and we've tried everything, the forehead thing, *everything.* Now tell me h—" and then cut off suddenly. His mouth carried on moving, but no words were coming out, the sound gone as quickly as it had arrived. Hart flung his arms down.

"*Shit!*" he yelled, and as ever, whenever he swore, he immediately straightened himself up afterwards, closing his eyes and taking a deep breath as he regained his composure. Bowler never said so, but he always observed this and found it quite cool. *Proper old school,* he thought.

George was shrugging apologetically, and Hart was fighting back his anger, despite a deep suspicion that George was probably right. He motioned for George to sit down, as he knew what was coming next, and indeed the colour had already started to drain from George's face. Hart felt a stab of guilt that he knew was irrational; he hadn't asked George to tune in—not that he could do anything about it anyway—and as ever, it had just happened. And, as ever, it was George who paid the price, and not Hart. It was like the Blueys; Hart, Bowler, and George just didn't have a clue as to what it was all about.

George nodded, got two steps, and started to buckle slightly at the knees. The other two were already there, catching him and guiding him gently to the floor, where he lay down and began to breathe heavily, even though there was no air to take in.

They waited there for a while in silence, Bowler not wanting to provoke Hart in his current mood, Hart frustrated and speechless. People passed by; lunchtime shoppers hurrying to get as much done before returning to work. Bowler practiced his sight as Hart observed the crowds, not saying a word. Eventually, Hart nudged George gently with his foot, who feebly looked up. Hart made walking gestures with finger on his hand, then pointed at himself and Bowler. George nodded, eyes closing, and waved them away gently with his hand. George would be there for some time, Hart knew, and today he couldn't face the wait. George would be okay.

"Come on," he said, tapping Bowler's chest with the back of his hand. "Let's go."

Bowler was still standing, looking at George.

"We're lucky to have the Odeon here, aren't we," he said, without looking up. It wasn't a question.

***

All of this had happened during the days before Hart and Bowler had been torn apart.

And *that* had been Hart's decision. Though an indescribably hard choice to make, Hart had never been a man to shy away from difficult decisions. Or accepting the consequences of those choices.

***

Chapter 2: In Which More Bad News Is Relayed, Bowler Lies—Poorly, Theories On Time and Punishment Are Exchanged, And We Hear of the Many Escape Attempts of Sarah Boss

✳✳✳

"Do we ever sleep?" Bowler asks, with a pleading edge in his voice. They are walking—Bowler shuffling awkwardly, and the other striding slowly—along Gosford Street. For the first time in several days, a question from Bowler is not met with a rebuke, or a dismissal, because "he needs to get the basics first." Bowler wonders if his improved speech is taken as a sign of being ready for answers.

"No, we never sleep. You should have realised that by now. We've been walking and talking for three days, and I'm betting you don't even feel slightly tired." Bowler nods at this, glumly. He realises that he wishes he DID feel tired. The idea of never sleeping …

"How do we rest, you know … reset? How do we not go crazy?" asks Bowler. To his surprise, Hart laughs, but it is dark and without humour. There is a long pause as they walk, and when Hart finally speaks it is as if the question had never been asked, his tone deliberately breezy.

"How's your vision? Seeing the people clearly, and so on … any better?" Bowler squints, and although there is no improvement, he can still see the thin outlines of the multitudes doing their shopping.

"No better than when … at the start," he answers, struggling both to find the right word and avoid saying it. "I mean, in terms of seeing the people. The buildings and that, they were easy straightaway. But at least I can see something. You told me that at first you couldn't—"

"Yes, I understand, Bowler," says Hart, looking at something Bowler can't see. Bowler thinks he's just doing it to make some sort of point, but says nothing. He needs this man, and he's coming to realise just how much.

"You need to keep working on that," Hart continues. "If you can't see them, you can't see TV. And if you can't see TV, then you're in an enormous amount of trouble, as awful a thing as that is to rely upon."

They walk in silence a moment longer, past the university theatre building. It's Saturday night, dark already, and the drinkers are starting to emerge; young-to-middle-aged men and women, dressed in their finest and looking for booze, company, and intimate warmth. Things forever taken from Frank Bowler. And yet he is surrounded by the potential for it and a million miles away at the same time. Something that will weaken him terribly is born inside him, and begins to grow.

Also, he could murder *a pint.*

The Gala bingo down the road will be packed, and this is the pair's destination. Bowler will be able to see the tickets relatively easily, they don't move, and he and Hart will be able to get close enough both for Bowler to make them out and to see the whole ticket at the same time. It's the people *that are still like ghosts to his eyes for some reason, people and TV screens and cinema screens and LCD readouts. They will pick a ticket each, play over the living players' shoulders, and enjoy it far more than they would have done if they were alive. A release.*

Bingo as a release. Fuck ME, *thinks Bowler.*

Hart had said the Gala is as far as they can go; they can't go past it. That is their limit. He hasn't said why. There is a heavy sigh, and Hart speaks, staring up at the stars as he walks.

3

"To answer your question, of course *there's some that go crazy. Look …
to be perfectly honest, apart from you, I, and three others … as far as I know,
everyone … well. There are those here that are already gone fully Loose—
that's the word I use for it—and some who* almost *have, who are pretty much
there. You can always tell by the hands. Shaking, you know." He walks on,
staring ahead now, and Bowler watches him closely. Hart's face is showing a
kind of very practiced blankness.* He's trying to look like he's casual, *thinks
Bowler.* He's trying to look like he's not that bothered by this, but this is
what bothers him more than anything. Doesn't he know how obvious that
is?

*Hart pauses for a second, then suddenly stops walking and turns to the
younger man. Bingo is forgotten in Bowler's mind. He'd been surprisingly
excited at the idea, and now isn't even aware of it.*

*"It's the single most important thing to worry about here, Frank. Not
going Loose. Do you understand? Everyone here—apart from the other three I
can spend time with—is insane. They are all insane." Bowler stands, open
mouthed, not wanting to break Hart's flow. Here are answers.*

*"You see, it's incredibly easy to end up that way. I think you'll realise
that by the end of the week. You'll realise it properly, and yes, you'll realise
that quickly. That's how prevalent it is." Neither of them know it for certain,
but Hart is right. Bowler* will *realise by the end of the week. "And if that
happens … and I don't mean even ending up as bad as the worst of us …" he
trails off, lost and thinking about something that makes his face grow that
much more pale. Bowler wants to ask what he means, but to do so might
mean the end of this information. He waits.*

*"If that happens," Hart continues, coming back, "then you'll never stand
any chance of getting out. So you have to keep it together. It's the most.
Important. Thing. Here," he repeats, stepping close, looking into Bowler's eyes,
wide and intense. Hart never stands this close. There is such urgency that*

Bowler realises that there's something Hart isn't telling him, some extra reason. He's too scared to ask what it is.

"So ... so ... how do we get out?" he says, not realising that he is shaking. "I mean, you call this place The Foyer, the lobby ... when do we get to, you know ... get to the main ..." he trails off, for once not because he is lost for words, but because he is almost unable to complete the sentence through fear. He forces himself, pushes.

"... the main building?" he finishes. He can't hide the tone in his voice, so much so that even Hart has to look away. When no answer comes immediately, Bowler continues, terrified now and not trying to hide it. He steps in himself, their faces almost touching, faces that would be nose to nose if Hart was looking at him.

"How many ... how many have gotten out since you've been here?" Still no answer, and worse, Hart's head is now hung low. Bowler's eyes are blinking rapidly. He raises his hands to Hart's shoulders, trembling, but doesn't touch him; he balls his hands into shaking fists, held just inches away from the older man's sides, digging his nails into his palms, biting his own lip.

"How long have you been here?" he whispers.

***

Taken from *Hart's Imaginary Guide to Being Dead, 'Looseness'*

Self-control is paramount. Indulgence leads to carelessness. Your sanity is *always* ready to break. If it does, you are lost. Therefore you must be very, very careful if your loved ones are still alive in the area that you inhabit.

Will their presence comfort you? Or will the uncrossable distance drive you insane?

***

Hart realised Bowler wasn't walking alongside him anymore, and turned to see the younger man standing with his hands in his pockets, pretending to look at something on the floor, as the few people wandering about this part of town walked by. Hart took in the surroundings, and realised which street corner they were on.

Blast. Not again. Shouldn't have taken this route. They could walk through walls if they felt like it; even after all this time, he still preferred to take the proper pathways. Walking through walls was unpleasant to Hart. Bowler thought it fun after his initial wariness, but to Hart it was a painful reminder of both where and what they were. He liked to pretend that they *were* part of the world around them, or to be reminded that they *weren't* as infrequently as possible.

The other reason he didn't like it, though, is that he thought it lazy, too easy. Not only did that suggest a distasteful lack of self-discipline, but to him, that would always be the first step towards going Loose.

He strolled casually over to Bowler, looking at the sky, as Bowler snuck glances at Hart from under his eyelids, like a child that'd been caught out. As good hearted as Bowler was, he had his sly side.

"What have you stopped for?" asked Hart, kindly. He got the sly glance in return, once again.

"I fancied a bit more of a walk. It's a nice day. If you want to go ahead, I'll meet you at The Polish Guy's. We'll catch Millionaire, he loves that," he said, forcing a smile, that faltered and disappeared altogether when Hart said nothing. The older man's brow furrowed. This was pathetic. The first time Bowler had tried this in the past, Hart had actually been fooled for a moment. Maybe this was progress? Maybe by trying less hard now, Bowler was making it so Hart *could* stop him? Because Bowler certainly couldn't stop himself.

"Frank," Hart said gently, after a pause. "Come on now. Please give me more credit than that."

Bowler started to try again, but Hart just raised his eyebrows and Bowler closed his mouth, head hanging slightly. He looked defeated. What was going on here? This had come out of nowhere. Not for the first time, Hart wondered how much went on in Bowler's head that he didn't express. He had to learn to stop that, and Hart made a mental note to work on that with him. Goodness knew it had been hard enough for *him* to learn, and even now he struggled. If Bowler went Loose because of that, of all reasons, it would be so ... *stupid*. Not to mention disastrous for Hart.

"I just want to ... check," said Bowler, and he began to fiddle with his fingers, suddenly finding them interesting. Hart was surprised. Bowler had his childlike moments, but never like this. Was this some sort of breaking point? Had he been thinking about this since they first decided to go to the cinema? Hart didn't think so ... Bowler had been fine once they'd left. Did George's turn set this off? That felt a bit more correct.

They stood in silence a moment, deadlocked by their own internal battles, until the spell was broken by a Japanese man dressed in a sharp suit walking straight through them both. Neither of them liked it when this happened, despite it being as painless and devoid of physical sensation as walking through a shaft of sunlight. It was the eyes. It was when their eyes filled your own, or went half through the top or bottom of yours. Plus, it was worse seeing it happen to someone else, turning them into a live special effect. It just was *odd*.

Either way, it loosed Hart's tongue again.

"Frank ..." he said, with a slight, but audible, weary sigh. "We agreed." Bowler nodded in silence, still staring at the floor. "You know what it could mean ... yes? You ... well, you know. You could end up ..." Bowler looked up, and Hart saw he was fighting back tears.

"But ... are you ... are you sure ..." he snuffled, and Hart gave a slight smile despite himself, charmed by Bowler's lack of front.

"You know I am. You don't want to be ..." He waggled his finger round his ear with a smile, trying to make light of it and failing. Bowler didn't return the smile, and his face creased as he looked back to his shoes.

"Yeah ... okay," he said, and Hart realised Bowler was fully crying now as he saw the tears dripping round the younger man's feet. He wondered again if this was good or bad. He hoped it was good. Some sort of release.

Hart hesitated, unsure what to do. It had been a long time since he had cried. It suddenly struck him just how long. Years, he thought. Years and years.

***

"Sixty years?" Bowler gasps, and after a moment, he collapses onto his buttocks, sinking slightly into the floor, all now-instinctive control lost for a moment.

"Give or take. It's slightly more, maybe. I remember ... oh, very little about the early years. They were an extremely tough time," says Hart, tapping the side of his head, but Bowler doesn't see it, staring blankly ahead.

Bowler tries to take it in. Sixty years. More than twice the length of his entire lifespan. Spent here. It strikes him how he never even left England in his lifetime, and with that comes stomach cramps, then vomit, except nothing comes out because you don't eat in The Foyer. Sixty years. And in that time, Hart must have tried everything to get out. While Bowler walked the streets of Coventry, growing and changing, living his life, Hart was nearby, unchanging, always there. Hart must have been here, wandering around the city centre, while Bowler went shopping and got drunk and embarrassed himself in front of girls. Hart would have seen the place change and develop and grow before

Bowler was even born; might have even seen Bowler being led, whining and complaining, around the shops as a child. The thought was too big. Too big.

In his shock, Bowler blurts out a question he'd been shy to ask; as if asking it here, in The Foyer, was somehow taboo, like asking how the tricks were done at a Magic Circle dinner. You just didn't.

Or maybe it was because he knew that if someone asked him the same question, he wouldn't know the answer, and maybe hearing someone else give their *answer would mean he'd suddenly remember too, and he didn't know if wanted that, didn't know at all, as he had a feeling it was pretty bad ...*

He finds himself remembering a time when he'd been an apprentice over in Binley, standing out the back by the bins with the others as they had their fag break. Warren talking about some lass he'd banged in Nottingham, and everyone laughing at the story, Bowler too, though he had a feeling that Warren was talking out of his backside again. Warren, who looked ten years older than he really was, and had a leer instead of a smile. Bowler knew he was better looking than Warren, and although he wasn't the loudest guy in a crowd, he knew a lack of confidence—never attractive in a woman's eyes— was preferable to a wealth of unhygienic sleaze. And so if Bowler *was not a ladies' man, then Warren's many tales of dramatic female conquest seemed highly unlikely to be true, to Bowler's eyes at least.*

But he wouldn't say that here. He was the new guy, and still fitting in; the young man who let himself be "fooled" into going to find a left-handed screwdriver or tins of tartan touch-up paint, knowing full well what they were trying to do and doing it for them anyway. That way, they'd laugh both at him and with him, Bowler paying his dues to get into the work social circle. He knew how it was supposed to go, and that was fine by him. One day he'd do the same to his *new guy, and looked forward to it. Bowler looked forward to having respect.*

And then Carlo came rushing out, both panicked and angry, and told Bowler breathlessly that he needed to come into the workshop right now, and

Bowler knew something very bad and expensive has happened, and it was all going to be his fault. He knew it was going to be really bad, and all of a sudden more than anything he didn't want to know, he'd pay for anything that needed paying for, but he didn't want to know any more.

And here is that moment again, but even after everything he's already heard, this is so much worse. Infinitely worse.

Hart hears the question, and sighs. "I don't remember." He scuffed the bottom of his shoe on nothing. "I don't think I ever knew. Do you remember? You don't either, am I right?" Bowler slowly shakes his head. He does remember pain, vaguely now, from somewhere before he was a Check-in, but he remembers very little about that time at all, and certainly nothing immediately before that.

Hart hunkers down and puts his hand on Bowler's shoulder. Bowler almost flinches. It is the first time Hart has touched him. His hand is too heavy, forced, like he has to pin it there.

"You'd think it'd be the one thing you would *remember," Hart said quietly. "But some things are odd here. Which actually brings me to ... while we're on hard subjects ... we should really cover all this now. Now you're ready. The sooner the better, I think. It'll hurt, and push you a bit, but you'll bounce back quickly. It needs to be out of the way. Needs sorting. Don't you agree?" Hart continues before Bowler can answer, keeping an air of briskness that does a very bad job of hiding how much he's struggling.*

You coward, *thinks Bowler.* You fucking coward. You've sucker punched me, and you're unloading when I'm down. You sneaky, cowardly bastard. *But he can't even think about talking now, and lets Hart's words wash over and through him.*

"This might even make you feel a bit better. You know George? You met him yesterday?" Bowler remembers George. George couldn't talk to them, but Bowler had liked George.

"I see most of George. The three that try to talk, or communicate, or socialise, and spend time with us ... there's that odd discomfort that comes in after a while of being near to each other. I've told you about that. Perhaps you even felt it slightly with George earlier, yes? That tightness in your lower back, that vague ache throughout your bones that starts to creep in after a while. And the silence between us ... it gets too alien to handle. Does that make sense? It's just unnatural. Even for me, even now; after all the time I've been here. And I'm no talker." Hart pauses, and absentmindedly adjusts his tie. Bowler is glad he didn't end up in a suit here. *"When we very briefly get on the same wavelength, about once or twice every year or so, it always takes it out of old George for some reason. Not me. It makes me think that* he *drops into* me *rather than me into to him, I don't know ... but before you came, it got me thinking."*

Hart sits properly now, taking the weight off his knees, and now while he talks he doesn't look at Bowler once.

"I'd been wondering about the talking thing for a while. If George can calibrate with me like that, at random every now and then ... well, if everyone is on a different frequency—that's how I think of it, frequencies—then it stands to reason that maybe we find our own frequencies when we're Check-ins, as we settle ... we find our frequency as we materialise, if you like ... so I began thinking ... what if that could be influenced?"

Hart is clearly impassioned about this bit, about his scientific talk, and it is odd for Bowler to watch how Hart's fingers and hands work as he speaks, his face still turned to the concrete. He looks like a religious follower struggling to explain something to the Almighty, all the while respectfully facing the floor to avoid looking directly into the face of God.

"What if I could make it so a Check-in is on the same frequency as me?" he says. *"And how would I do that? Of course, this was about twenty years ago; bear in mind you're only the fourth Check-in I've seen in my whole time since I've been here. I actually missed one about ten years ago. I couldn't find*

where it came down. Incidentally, that turned out to be Sarah. It took me around two years to get over missing that chance."

He chuckles slightly, then waves his hands as if to say ignore that bit, it's not relevant, I'm rambling, *and continues.* "But then ... a long *time later* ... *you arrived. And my big experiment, my big idea, was just to babble at you until you fully arrived. You might vaguely remember that. Making sure you were hearing nothing but my frequency, trying to guide you in. Just talking rubbish, saying anything to help you attune to me, that all you would hear, all you would* experience *while you got yourself together here was me. After years thinking about it, believe it or not, that was the plan that made the most sense, the plan that sounded the most plausible. I never thought it'd work, or that it hadn't been tried before." He is smiling as he finishes, shaking his head in delighted disbelief. Or is it relief? Hart lifts his head, chuckling now, lost in his own thoughts. He turns to Bowler, taking him in, looking him over like he doesn't even know that Bowler is watching him. After a moment, he registers Bowler's actual presence and grins again.*

"But it must never have been tried," he continues, shaking his head again, and laughing as he speaks, clearly revelling in the recollection of his own discovery. Bowler has never seen Hart laugh openly before. He won't see it very often in the years to come. "As I've never seen another pair of people that stay together! You know, without the discomfort, or that can talk all the time," *he finishes.*

In a moment of sudden rapture, he grabs both of Bowler's shoulders, hard. Bowler stares into eyes that are now moist and showing alarming traces of what is going on inside.

"Don't you understand?" says Hart. "Don't you SEE it? You're the luckiest Check-in there's ever been. D'you have any idea how much safer I've made you? D'you have any idea just how lucky you are?"

All Bowler can think is, But ... doesn't that mean *you* get to talk to *me* as well?

Instead, what he says, in short, stammering gasps as he finally gets his glued-up mouth to work is, "There ... must ... be ... a way ..."

The light in Hart's eyes rapidly dies, as he says nothing in reply, and his gaze drops away again. It's hard to believe that just a few moments ago this man was so passionate and—for want of a better phrase—alive. Hart sighs and stands, putting his hands on his hips, exhaling nothing.

"Aaahhh ... Bowler ..."

He squints off into the distance, all energy gone. He is thinking, and weighing something up, and it suddenly reminds Bowler of someone preparing themselves to put a pet out of their misery. And he suddenly remembers his earlier fear, and knows that the cause is here. What he was fearing. What he could sense under the surface. There was bad news, and this was bad news of a different kind. He knows that this means pain. This means a lot of physical pain.

"Right," Hart says finally, and looks down at Bowler, his face set like he's summoned up everything he has to get through this. At least you've found your balls, thinks Bowler, but Hart is already speaking.

"I suppose we'd better get this out of the way now. You'll try it eventually. I think everyone does, as they all think they can hold on a bit longer than everyone else. That the only reason everyone else failed is because they couldn't take any more. That they can take more than the others. But they don't realise that it doesn't make any difference. You will too, eventually, so best do it now, so you know. False hope ... it'll get you in the end. It's always worse when it turns out it was nothing. It can break ... but anyway. We've got about a mile walk now. Typical that we're totally on the wrong side of The Foyer ... Can you stand?"

Bowler managed it.

"Where ..."

Hart looks sad. Not, not sad. Hart is pitying him. Bowler can see it. And Bowler now knows for certain that whatever is coming is going to hurt a very great deal indeed.

"You're going to catch a train," Hart says.

***

Taken from *Hart's Imaginary Guide to Being Dead, 'Friends and Influences'*

Some people have many friends and few acquaintances. Some have few friends and many acquaintances.

Here, one has very, *very* few acquaintances, and that's all. But they are more precious than could ever be expressed.

***

"The guy, the guy with the nips."

"The *what*?"

"Sorry, the nip*ples*. Triple nipple!"

"I haven't the *faintest* idea what you're talking about."

"He was in *Lord of the Rings*, too."

"Ah, I liked those. Who was he in that?"

"I can't remember … Dracula. He was Dracula."

"Bela Lugosi? I'm sure he was dead by the time they made *Lord of the Rings*."

"No, Dracula in the sixties or whenever. And that film with him out of *The Equaliser*, the weird one with the hippies."

"*The Wicker Man*."

"Yes! Lousy, it was."

"I liked it. Very disturbing."

"Anyway, he was the head hippy."

"Ah … Christopher Lee."

"Yeah … I think that's his name. Anyway, him. He's my favourite."

"*The Man With the Golden Gun.*"

Bowler rolled his eyes, but so Hart couldn't see.

"Well, obviously, but that's easy. I mean his actual name. Scatter, Scamma …"

"Scaramanga."

"Yes! You didn't get that from Triple Nipple? How many movie bad guys have triple nips?"

"Mmm. I'm sure I wouldn't know."

"So anyway. Him."

Hart considered it.

"Yes … he was a good one. A good rival. That's what these new ones are lacking. No decent antagonists."

"Baddies."

"Yes."

They were sat in a pub, watching a game of darts. It had been Bowler's idea originally, and Hart had to admit it had been a good one. Pick a local team and follow their exploits week by week. Learn about the people. Listen to their conversations. And if they said anything that interested them, they could follow them home and see how it all panned out, providing their activities were within the boundaries of The Foyer. Although it was rare that they were, it was always an exciting taxi ride along with them to see if they did indeed live inside the perimeter, to see if they could get a payoff to the beginning of the story. And, of course, they liked to watch the games and support the team. Maybe they'd feel a part of it after a while, Bowler had reasoned.

Plus, Hart liked the pub. It was one of the few remaining in the town centre that still had brasses on the walls and carpet on the floor. Pubs should always have carpet, Hart thought. And absolutely, categorically, no TV, or at least TVs switched off unless there was some kind of event being televised. Pictures on the walls that actually had some relevance to the building, and that weren't just there for the sake of it. Music that wasn't at eardrum-splitting levels. Clientele that weren't all seventeen. People that actually had conversations. There were even sometimes people playing dominoes. This was Hart's kind of place, and he took pride in that fact for some reason. Pride in himself.

Yes, it was all fine by Hart. Yes, he and Bowler had to sit on the floor; there were never any empty seats, and generally any that were empty in the darts room invariably got taken. That meant being Passed Through when someone sat on you. So they sat in the corner, wedged half in and half out of the back door. It was a fire escape, so no one used it, no one leaned on it, and no one really came close enough to Pass Through them. Hart had been doing this sort of thing for years, and although Bowler had found it highly odd at first, he was used to it now.

Bowler turned back to the board. Will had just got his first win of the season, shouting for joy as the rest of his team cheered. Bowler thought that, of course, they'd managed to pick the shittiest team in the league, as evidenced by their sheer delight every time they won something, but they had the best pub in his opinion.

"Brian doesn't look happy," sniffed Hart, nodding in the team captain's direction.

"He's knackered," replied Bowler. "He was up all night with Sherry."

Hart shrugged.

"Well, if you booze all night, don't complain when you're tired."

Bowler looked at him blankly for a second, and then burst into raucous laughter. Hart was shocked at first, then confused, and as he watched Bowler breathlessly slapping the table—his hand passing through it as he lost control—while trying to compose himself, it occurred to him

16

how long it had been since he'd heard the younger man laugh even slightly. Even so, Hart couldn't help but smile at the tears streaming down Bowler's face, as he wiped them away and leaned forward to explain through hiccupping breaths.

"Sh ... Sh ... aha ... Sherry is ... is his daughter ... she's teething ..." Then he was off again, and now even Hart had to laugh with him. It felt good for them both. The next game began behind them, the players unaware of the two spectators who sat in invisible hysterics on the other side of the room.

By the time they'd got their breath back, their boys were 2–0 up, with eight more games to go; nothing to get worked up about. Defeat somehow always seemed to find them.

And that was the moment when Sarah Boss walked through the wall to their right, unaware that they were there, on her way through the building and on to wherever she had in mind. Bowler saw her first.

"Hart! Sarah's here!"

Hart had been watching Shaun—his favourite player—try to claw back a one-leg deficit, and looked where Bowler pointed. His brow knotted, and he licked his bottom lip absentmindedly.

"Hmm ... not seen her for a while." He watched her a moment as she made slow, and notably shaky, progress across the room, strangely avoiding the tables when she had knowingly just passed straight through a concrete wall.

She was, as ever—not that she could ever change her clothes— dressed in her thick woollen jumper and stonewashed black jeans, sensible flat shoes ("*Lezzer shoes*" as Bowler had called them once. Hart hadn't got it, but didn't like the tone, and had told Bowler so. Hart liked Sarah) and her straight black hair tied back in a ponytail. Hart had always assumed the hair tie had materialised along with her clothes, accessories being rare amongst the Guests. He kept meaning to ask her about it.

But as he watched, he realised that it really *had* been ages since he'd seen her, let alone "spoken" to her. Why was that? They crossed paths with the other three Talking Guests all the time. What had she been doing? Hart stood up.

"Quick, if you're going," urged Bowler, not taking his eyes off her. He was right. Sarah had nearly cleared the room, not even glancing at the players surrounding her. She looked very focused, leaning forward slightly as she went, like a gun dog intent on finding its master's quarry. Hart stood and moved after her.

As he reached her, and raised a hand to tap her on the shoulder, he realised that doing so would scare her out of her wits. She would have heard the room, the background music, the players and the banter and the bleep of the gambling machine, but not the Guest coming up behind her. They weren't tuned in, and *very* rarely were. He thought he'd only heard her voice as little as twice in the last ten years, but it was hard to say.

He accelerated and overtook her, coming around her left-hand side, trying to make his movements as big as possible to give her enough warning, and hoping a flash of hand or leg at the edge of her peripheral vision might catch her eye and turn her gently to him. It didn't really work, as she still jumped considerably.

When she saw who it was, her initial shock disappeared. She put a hand to her chest and smiled, holding her other one up, her shoulders moving as she chuckled lightly. *Hi, you made me jump!*

Hart smiled back, shrugging. *Sorry.* She waved him off. She wasn't a particularly attractive woman, in Hart's opinion (he knew this, despite no one in The Foyer, himself included, feeling or displaying any sexual urges whatsoever for some reason. One thing, at least, that nobody there ever had to worry about. They could still love, though. Bowler was testament to that), but she had a natural charisma that Hart responded well to. In his old life, he was never really comfortable around women, but he did feel at ease with

Sarah. He couldn't put his finger on why, but he considered her a friend. Not just because she was one of the three Check-ins he'd ever seen, and one of the Talking Guests. Mark was one, and Hart didn't consider him a friend. He'd not really had any female friends when he was alive—in Hart's day, you were friends with your friends' wives and that was roughly it—but with Sarah it was just the same as it was with Bowler and George.

He waved his hands around and pointed outside with a confused look on his face. *Where are you going?*

She grinned, pointed one way, then the other, then did a swirly motion with her finger. *Here, there, everywhere ...* the grin was cheeky, but forced. Hart smiled at the attitude, but something was off. He didn't think this was just teasing; something in Sarah's eyes said she was being secretive. It wasn't the usual thing she came out with. In fact, she was normally quite blunt, which was one of her traits that appealed to Hart. No messing about with this one. But this was different.

He decided to keep it light. He put his hand on his chin, and made a comedy-calculating face. *Really ...*

It got a reaction. She smiled and threw her hands up and out wide, comic innocence. *Wha—a—a—at?* But again, it was an act. She wasn't comfortable, and it radiated off her. Out of ideas, Hart dropped the pretence and gave her what he hoped was a winning smile. He bobbed his head from side to side and raised his shoulders, moving the hands around once more and doing the confused face again. *Come on, Sarah, where are you really going?*

Sarah's smile stayed, but her shoulders dropped slightly. She was going to tell him, then, but she didn't want to. She was embarrassed. Hart relaxed slightly. Nothing serious here. It was interesting, all the same; Sarah wasn't the type to get embarrassed. She put one hand on her hip and straightened up defiantly with a smile, pointing at him. The question was obvious: *Where are YOU going?*

Hart pointed at Bowler (who waved; Sarah returned it) then at his eyes, then to the board, then at a number on the wall clock, then the walking fingers, then a little box in the air. *Watching this, then about nine we're going to watch TV.* He added a gesture between the two of them. *Want to come?*

This was a test, and an obvious one, and she caught it easily. She raised her eyebrows, amused, and shook her head with a smile. She sighed, and then raised a finger, looking at him—*because*—another sigh, hesitant now ... then held her palm out flat, and put the tip of her finger on it and drew a circle. She then added another fingertip and made comical skipping motions with her fingers along the line of the invisible circle she had drawn.

Hart saw what she meant, and also saw how she'd attempted to make light of it, as she knew exactly what his reaction would be. So he tried to catch himself as he breathed out in a heavy sigh, tried to avoid shifting his weight on his feet as his body language betrayed his annoyance, and didn't try hard enough. He knew what *her* reaction would be to this; defiance.

In fact, it was already happening. She was still looking at him, which was good, but the eyebrows were up petulantly, in a come-on-then-what's-wrong-with-that expression and the arms were folding. He held his hands out wide, so she could see that he wasn't trying to engage her, and it was true; he really wasn't. Hart could argue with men all day long—had made a career out of it—but arguing with a woman just made him squirm.

He repeated her walking gesture back to her, and then looked at her kindly, shrugging his shoulders. *Walking the perimeter? Why?* Then he scrunched his eyes up slightly and smiled. *Come on now, Sarah, why?* He was trying to appeal to her sensible side, and it was meant to bring out a realistic Sarah, one he knew could laugh at her own actions. He thought they were still at the stage where that Sarah could be brought forward.

If he hadn't have added the last gesture, the conversation would have perhaps have gone a lot better for him, and he knew straight away what a mistake it was. *Idiot*, he thought. *You just looked like you were laughing at her.* He almost winced physically as she scowled, and made hammering gestures with one hand onto another, then shoved her hand through an imaginary small hole and expanded it to freedom. *Weak spots.*

She then suddenly slapped the side of her head—hard—and stuck her tongue forward underneath her bottom lip. The move was sudden, overly aggressive, and violent, its intention clear and at an uncalled for intensity for the conversation. *Obviously, you idiot!* Sarah had stepped it up a gear out of nowhere. He'd expected, and had felt, the coming strop, but nothing like this.

He decided to continue on the same tack, ignoring the insult. Hands pushing slowly downwards—*Easy, easy*—and not saying what he was thinking (*What the blazes is wrong with* you? *Weak spots? You know there are no weak spots!*). Instead he did the walking circle gesture several times, quickly, then counted on his hands. *How many times, Sarah? How many times have you been doing this?* She started to protest, but he held up his finger with a wincing expression and she actually stopped; he had her attention.

He didn't want to make this point now, but she was ready for a fight and he had to take the opportunity while she was listening. He pointed out the window, in several directions, as if picking out individuals. He then did the circle-on-the-hand gesture lightning fast, over and over and over, then looked at her and did searching hands, face looking here and there, and then straightened up and twirled his finger around his ear slowly, looking her straight in the eyes, deadly serious.

Bowler sat watching this surprising conversation from the other side of the room and was impressed. It was a good mime, and clear—he could see what it supposed to mean, even from over here—showing an impressive amount of imagination from Hart. It was good to see.

Sarah didn't move. Her lips were tight and she was breathing nonexistent air heavily through her nose—Hart could see her nostrils twitching—as she then dropped her head to one side. Hart waited.

When she still didn't say anything for a few more moments, Hart carefully and slowly raised a finger. He'd pushed his luck, and it appeared to have paid off. So now was the time to try and wrap this up, while he could. They'd talk about it later, find out what was up, but he needed to get her out of here and relaxed, first. Not for the first time, he inwardly cursed himself for not knowing more about women.

He pointed at himself, at Bowler … then at Sarah. Then a little circle in the air. *Us three.* Then the little box, and fingers to the box-space and to his eyes. He ended all this with a smile, and cocked his head slightly in the other direction. The gesture was friendly and warm, and Bowler noted it. These always stood out with Hart, as when they happened they were rare, but genuine. *What do you say?*

Her lips remained set, but her bottom lip tightened up a bit more. He thought about putting a hand on her shoulder, and at that moment he happened to look down and saw something that shocked him. Later, he would think that he shouldn't really have been surprised.

He looked away quickly, but she'd caught him. Her eyes widened, and she opened her mouth to say something, then obviously realised it would be pointless. She hesitated, then suddenly smashed Hart across the face with the flat of her hand. Across the room, Bowler jumped to his feet.

Hart actually fell over, stepping backwards in surprise and tripping over his own feet. He was temporarily stunned, not physically but mentally. Her attack didn't hurt—even though it had been a VERY long time since he'd been struck here—but it had shocked him. He fell through the floor slightly, passing through it an inch and halting as his subconscious caught him. He looked up to see Sarah fuming, shoulders set, frantically gesturing at him, cheeks shaking as she breathed furiously. He tried to get his thoughts together and understand what she was saying, but it was hard; he'd missed the start and her hands were all over the place because ...

She cut it all off by suddenly throwing her hands and chin up in the gesture he'd anticipated at the start—there it was, *we're done, you're a waste of time*—and she then turned back very briefly, eyes blazing in a way he'd never seen before. Then she was gone, storming out through the wall.

Hart felt Bowler behind him. He'd come over, kneeling now, but Hart waved him off—no fuss—and instead just pulled himself up on Bowler's arm.

Bowler stood back and gave Hart a moment. He knew talking to the older man right now was pointless. Hart's dignity had been ruffled, and in a moment of softness, no less. He knew he had to give Hart a moment to rearrange his suit. He looked away and discovered that their boys were 3–0 up. Bowler smiled, but shook his head. The idiots would still manage to lose.

"What was she blathering on about?" Hart said, turning to him, everything back in place. "At the end there, I didn't catch it. Did you see?"

Bowler scratched the side of his head. He'd seen it, all right. It had been tough, but he'd gotten better at this.

"Yeah ... she wasn't happy ..." he said, shifting his weight onto a chair back and folding his arms. "She basically asked who the hell you are to call her crazy—"

"I didn't call her crazy!"

"And said that ... just because you're a coward and have given up doesn't mean that *she* should." Bowler said this with a sigh and raised his hands to his face, shrugging. "I'm the thingy, messenger. Don't shoot."

Hart reddened. There was an awkward pause, during which a spectacularly well-timed cry of disappointment rose from the team as they dropped to 3–1, and the inevitable weekly downward slide began.

Hart raised a finger and nodded sharply.

"She's going Loose."

Bowler shrugged again. He couldn't disagree, at least. It certainly didn't look good for Sarah. Hart straightened his tie and muttered something.

"What?" asked Bowler, leaning forward.

"I said did you see her hands?" said Hart, staring into the distance. His jaw was set, his face still crimson, but less so already. Bowler told Hart that he hadn't. He'd been too far away.

Hart readjusted his cuff links, stiffly, even though he'd already done them.

"Her hands, Bowler. They were shaking. She had the Shakes." Bowler looked up, surprised.

"You sure?" Hart closed his eyes and nodded, sighing, composure flooding back.

"Yes ... I'm afraid so. Just before she struck me, I saw. She noticed me noticing, too. There was nothing she could say." He looked up and raised a finger again. "False hope, Bowler. False hope." He pointed at the wall. "Right there. You saw it. You remember me telling you?"

Bowler did. Hart stared at the patch of wall that Sarah had exited through.

"Are you okay?" asked Bowler, trying to think of something to say. Hart continued to look at the wall.

"She's getting like Mark," he said. Bowler slowly nodded. Not so much at the comparison, but thinking about Mark.

"How long do you reckon he's been here, Bowler? Mark. Take a guess."

The younger man chewed his bottom lip and thought.

"Mark? Ten years? Fifteen, maybe?"

Hart smiled, satisfied, and shook his head.

"Try thirty-five."

Bowler looked shocked.

"No way ..."

Hart started to respond, but hesitated, as a voice in his head whispered *You never found out how long* Simon *had been here though, did you? Because he didn't tell you. But you think that he hadn't been here much longer than you. I wonder what* he's *up to now, eh?* Of course, Hart shut that voice off quickly.

Simon was dead to him, as much as he literally was to the world of the living. Simon was firmly in the past and was to be forgotten.

"Definitely," said Hart, brightening up, to Bowler's surprise. "I was here when he checked in. Imagine that, Bowler," he said, stepping instinctively out of the way of Craig as he came past carrying four full pints. "Thirty-five years, spending so much time alone. Even if he does talk to us."

"I thought you said you two used to talk a lot?"

Hart curled a lip slightly and sighed.

"We did at first; spent quite some time together actually. Almost as much as George spends with us. He was quite annoying really, some funny opinions, but as you know … you'll take what you can get here. But there are limits." He folded his arms, hugging himself, and leaned back slightly, reminiscing. "So when he buggered off, I wasn't desperately bothered. Even here."

"What, when he started going off by himself?"

"Yes … it wasn't the end of the world for me, if you like," said Hart. "Funny fact of life, Bowler, or in our case death; even in a world where no one can talk to one another, when ninety-five percent of the inhabitants are insane, and your only available company is four other people … sometimes even some of those people are just too much of a damn pain in the backside to put up with." Hart smiled a little at his own witticism. "But Mark, yes. Off he went, and each time I saw him after that he was always that tiny, tiny, little bit worse. But what do you expect when you go off alone? Never knew why he did; he wasn't a particularly independent character. He must have been more disturbed by the usual physical proximity problems than most, as well the close silence that comes with it. Now you can see the Shakes on him. Definitely. So much so that I try and stay out of his way, really. I can't stand it when he goes off on his rants. I certainly don't like him hanging around with George these days, but what can you do? And now he tunes with us a lot more. Have you noticed that?"

Bowler had. George managed it rarely, but Mark was doing it much more often. Most of the time he wouldn't do it when you were actually talking *to* him; you heard him elsewhere. It was very rare he struck up a conversation, being a loner, after all, but you'd hear him rabbiting to himself as you passed him on the street. No headaches afterward either, it seemed, not like George. Mark just came in and out, with no ill effects. Bowler made a link in his mind and was about to express an opinion on that, when Hart got there first.

"That's just proof to me that he's definitely going. Because you hear The Beast, don't you? When he tunes in? From streets away, even, and that's the best way to have it. And The Beast is obviously the most Loose, by far. Yes ... it's not just the Shakes. I think it perhaps plays with your frequency, makes it wider, or something like that. I think the Loose ones tune in more often."

"I spoke to Mark last week," said Bowler, quietly, thinking of Mark; big ears and tall. Thickset. Swarthy skin, a bear of a man, middle-aged enough to be at his most solid and tough. Young enough to stay fast. Not someone you wanted to go Loose. That was a good term of Hart's, he thought: Loose. "He was tuned in, and did you know, he didn't even seem to realise."

Hart huffed at this slightly and raised a palm as if to say "there you go."

"He wanted me to go with him," said Bowler, and as he saw Hart's expression change, he carried on quickly. "I made my excuses, though, and then he said it didn't matter anyway ... as he was going to try the Train again that afternoon. For the fifth time," Bowler finished, looking at Hart through the bottoms of his eyebrows.

Hart took a slow and deep breath, and then let it out, puffing his cheeks.

"Well ... that explains why we haven't seen him around for several weeks," he said. "And of course, that's the icing on the cake. That absolutely seals it. Once, everyone does it. Twice, still common-ish. To ride it not just three, but five times ..."

Hart looked at Bowler, his face actually a little pale now.

"He's definitely gone completely and totally insane."

***

Chapter 3: In Which Bowler Considers Taking the Train, Theories On Being Bad People Are Discussed, and An Important Deal Is Made

***

Taken from *Hart's Imaginary Guide to Being Dead, 'Boundaries'*

Boundaries are a problem for everyone in every existence. In life, global wars and personal battles are fought for years over such things, and for the most part they are due to one party's encroachment—or perceived encroachment—on the other's space. In death, boundaries do damage in the opposite way. The inverse synchronicity is startling. The dead are *kept* apart, and we fare no better as casualties of the resulting wars inside our own minds.

We are kept apart from one another by the physical laws of our existence, which makes us ache for those times when our loved ones were within arm's reach to be grasped tightly. And, of course, we are kept apart from the rest of the planet, this lush and verdant world that we are still somehow bound to but forbidden to explore. The Wall may stop us from going any farther than this small city centre, but it doesn't stop us seeing the horizon beyond it. We can see through The Wall.

Believe it or not, that isn't a good thing.

***

It's not a big train station, nor is it an impressive one, but it's busy. At first Bowler tries to avoid being Passed Through, but after watching Hart making his way through the crowd for a minute, he realises there's not much point. It's next to impossible. So the trip has started unpleasantly enough, but it is nothing—nothing—compared to what will come on the Train.

Hart is stony faced. He hasn't even looked at Bowler since they set off. Bowler tries to imagine it's just because he's concentrating now, trying to focus while wave after wave of people Pass Through him, but he knows it's because Hart is about to lead him to something horrible. Some rite of passage, maybe.

Bowler hurries to catch up as he realises it's getting harder to see Hart ahead; as the distance between them increases, it's more difficult. His vision is still not as sharp as it will be in the future. Why isn't Hart keeping an eye out for him? Hart knows Bowler will struggle here, but the older man is still striding ahead, not even turning around.

"Hart. HART." Hart glances over his shoulder, but doesn't break stride. For the first time since they've set off on their way here, Hart speaks, his face blank and pale, and he speaks flatly.

"I'll tell you on the platform," Hart says. Bowler can wait the remaining seconds it will take them to finally get down there, but his annoyance is growing along with his fear, one fuelling the other.

Platform four. Hart is there several steps ahead of Bowler and stands at the foot of the stairs waiting for him. The edge of the platform is lined with people, staring ahead and trying not to catch each other's eye. The only things of visual interest in their view are two billboards advertising books, a vending machine, and a tiny cafe in the middle of platforms two and three. There are just four platforms here at this station, the others accessed by overhead walkway. All here is grey, and all is at least twenty years old. To say the surroundings were completely bleak would be an exaggeration; however, it would not be much of one.

"You remember how I told you about The Foyer? The size of it?" Hart says, turning to Bowler and talking more loudly than necessary. Pushing himself. Bowler nods. "About a mile across, give or take," continues Hart. "And if there's anything for us beyond it—any more people like us, perhaps—we can't see it, or them. All we see is more city. We only see what they *see," says Hart, gesturing towards the people now crowding on the platform edge.*

"But you can certainly feel *the edge of The Foyer," he says. "Not hard, like a wall. Spongy. You can push against it. It gets harder and thicker as you get nearer, and eventually you hit the very edge, and it's like taut cling film. You can't push through." Bowler nods again. He'd wanted to feel it for himself, but had been content to play it Hart's way for now, assuming that sooner or later they'd take a trip out to it. The wind is quicker on the platform, he realises, as he sees a crisp packet whip past on the tracks. He wonders if the walkway above and the steps leading up to it are creating enough of a tunnel to speed the wind up. He remembers that from a school science lesson; it's one of the few things he remembers from school full stop. The living people are tucking their chins in. It must be cold for them, Bowler thinks.*

"You'll reach the same conclusion that everyone does *here," Hart continues, looking out along the track now, watching. "That it* must *be breakable, and someone just needs to find out how to do it. And you'll think about how it could possibly be done. And the answer will be obvious." He turns back to Bowler, and Bowler thinks about how it could be done. And the answer* is *obvious, especially given their surroundings. He realises Hart is waiting for a response, and gives him it.*

"You'd ... you'd maybe just need enough ... force," says Bowler. "More force than you could get by running or walking." Hart nods, slowly and sadly. Bowler carries on talking, already knowing the answer, but explaining his thinking. "And it'd need to be big, as well. Heavy. Something big and fast and heavy, bigger and heavier than a car." He sighs. "A train."

"Go on."

30

"But trains come through here all day long, and The Foyer wall isn't broken ... but it's not the Train that would break it, it'd be you, if you could ... anchor into it, or something. You'd take on the weight, and, and the force, and the speed of the Train ... and maybe you could push through."

"That's the thinking, yes."

"But it doesn't work."

"No."

"So why are we here?"

Hart sighs again, and Bowler has to resist an uncharacteristic urge to smash him in the face, to just keep hitting him, as for a moment he's certain all of this is Hart's fault. And in the same moment Bowler remembers what this place would be like without Hart, and so he clenches his fists and listens. As he does so he catches a glimpse of bright headlights down the line. They are very far away, but they are getting closer, and Bowler realises that he is seeing a train in the distance. A train on the track, bringing with it everything Hart is talking about, and getting closer every second. And Bowler begins to feel truly afraid.

"I told you," says Hart. "We're here because eventually you'd end up here anyway."

"But I know it doesn't work. You told me."

"It won't make a difference, Frank."

"What the hell are you on about?!" Bowler shouts, raising his voice in anger to Hart for the first time, though many years later it will be much, much worse. Right now, he is tired of Hart's all-knowing ways, telling Bowler what he will do no matter what. How the fuck does this old bastard know what he's going to do when he's only got a fraction of the answers? He talks like he knows everything, when he's just as lost and confused as everyone else. Fuck you, asshole! "Why would I fucking bother!" Bowler shouts.

Hart winces slightly at the language, but is otherwise unfazed.

"Because eventually, when it all gets too much, you'll convince yourself that everybody else just didn't do it right. You'll come here because after a while, when you've exhausted all your options, no matter what I tell you, here is something you haven't tried for yourself. *You'll decide that everyone else just couldn't anchor in hard enough. Or that they couldn't take the pain and gave up, that they just couldn't handle it. Or that, in some way, you're different to everyone else. And you'll do it because you will need to know."*

Bowler realises something, and stops for a moment.

"So it hurts," he says. Hart stares at him, and when he speaks it is slow and deliberate.

"Frank ... it hurts more than anything you've experienced in your entire life. You can't even imagine it, because it hurts in a way that nothing hurts when you're alive. This body here ... it's not the same as a living one. And this pain goes deep in a different way; like your very ..." Hart trails off, trying to find the words. "... your very SELF is being hurt, is the best way I can put it. It tears at everything that makes you, you," Hart says, taking a step closer.

"And that's not even the worst part. The worst part is afterwards. And that's the other bit you really need to go through. To truly understand what's the most important thing here. You need to know that to appreciate how things work, to stand a chance of being okay. It won't be as bad for you, I hope, as I'll be here to help. You won't have to do it on your own ..." And Hart straightens up, stopping abruptly. Bowler points at him, finger wagging madly.

"You. You've done it."

"Obviously. I said everyone does it," snaps Hart, "I'm talking from experience, Bowler. If I thought for one second that you wouldn't in the long run, then we wouldn't even be here. But you'll always eventually make your way onto the platform." At that moment, Bowler realises that while they've been talking, the Train in the distance is no longer in the distance. They've been that lost in the conversation, and the Train is that fast—frighteningly

fast—that even when it's in its slowing-down phase, it's already reached the platform, is now drawing alongside the end and slowing down, and Bowler can see its green and yellow colours and hear the steel wheels squealing lightly as it tries to slow down to a stop. And to Bowler it seems impossibly huge, so much so that for a moment he is amazed by the nonchalance of the people, who even now are shuffling gently, pretending they can't see each other jockeying for position, pretending that this is all totally civil.

Bowler is very afraid now, afraid that what Hart says is right; that he will *go through this, that he should go through it right now. That it will be better to get it done in the long run. That he will learn from it, and not spend years wondering. He remembers a safety guy coming to their school. From the trains. Talking about not playing on the tracks.*

"The wheels are like scissors," *he'd said.* "The metal wheel coming together with the edge of the track as they move forward are like giant scissors. And they will slice your legs clean off. *Snip!" And they'd all gasped, horrified and excited by such a gruesome thought, giggling and glancing at one another. But Bowler had just been terrified.*

He turns back to Hart, raising his voice now over the bladelike squealing of the Train, and realises as he speaks that even if it's not today, Hart is right. Eventually, he will need to know. And that means that he is sentenced to pain, and that it will definitely, definitely, definitely happen. It is already hanging over his head.

In a world where sanity is to be prized above all else—at least, according to his mentor—can he afford to have that above him, waiting? Bowler finds himself looking for a way out of the pain, a way to do it, learn it, yet not have the pain. *A thought process of avoidance which, as Hart was trying to tell him, will lead Bowler right into it. Trying to prove that he might not have to feel it.*

"But … you don't know … if I'm different. You … you don't know …"

And Hart looks at his shoes as the Train screams to a halt, and ominously, in the way that every living person on that platform wants to happen to them—as they would love *to happen to them, meaning they could get on first, get first dibs on seats, their biggest worry in that moment—the entrance to one of the carriages pulls up perfectly in line with Bowler and Hart, and clunks forward, and slides sideways, and the carriage is open. The choice laid out, just like that, right before Bowler. He looks back to Hart who is still staring at his shoes and saying nothing.*

It hurts more than anything you've experienced in your entire life ... you'll always eventually make your way onto the platform ...

And Bowler is rooted to the spot in terror, unmoving, uncertain, and hating himself as he still can't help but think—can't stop the fear from making him think—"But maybe ... I am *different* ... "

The Train is now full, and is about to leave.

***

"For goodness' sake, woman, take the money!" growled Hart, as Paula from Swindon dithered over walking away at £16,000 despite clearly not being the brightest and having no lifelines left. The Polish Guy was muttering away angrily in the seat opposite, thrusting a hand at the figures onscreen, and very much seemed to be in agreement with Hart's position. Though they couldn't say for certain, of course, as they had never heard him speak a word of English. They still hadn't even been able to ascertain his name, as they had never seen any post arrive addressed to him, though they'd certainly tried—Bowler's idea—and had never heard him offer his name in conversation; when he was with his friends they all spoke the same language, and although he was very friendly with the customers in his Polish restaurant, he didn't seem to have any regulars that spoke English and knew his name. He was lively and eccentric though, and they both liked him. His manner was the opposite of Mary's, and they liked variety. More than liked it. Although they weren't so keen on it the time that they walked in to find him standing in front of a mirror in his living room and wearing nothing but a pair of women's panties, high heels, and a great deal of crudely applied makeup. It had taken Bowler nearly six months to get Hart to go there again.

The contrast between this place and Mary's was stark; it was neat, modern, and full of expensive audio visual equipment. The Polish Guy liked his home theatre. The flooring was laminated wood, the walls were painted magnolia, and the seating was leather. The Polish Guy made his money and liked to live in a modern fashion, and although it wasn't Hart's way, he couldn't criticise him for it. After all, he knew you couldn't take it with you. Expensive canvases hung on the walls, and as Bowler had pointed out, it was more like a bar than a living room.

Not that he was pointing it out now. The younger man hadn't said much since they'd left the pub. He seemed deep in thought. Hart left him to it, knowing he'd finish working it out and say what was on his mind once he'd done so. Plus, he'd been doing some thinking of his own, despite his better judgement. He was thinking about what Sarah had said.

Had he given up? *Was* he a quitter? The thought was surely ridiculous. Sarah didn't know how many times *he'd* walked the perimeter. How he'd had hope dashed over and over. How he'd seen what happened to those who kept doing it. No ... Hart hadn't given up, he just knew better. *So if that's true, what have you done lately to get out? When was the last time you even tried anything?* said the voice.

He was waiting, that's what he was doing. The most important thing was keeping everything level, being sensible. It had to be. Plus, he had Bowler to watch out for. If he went Loose, then Bowler would definitely follow. Had to look after Bowler, had to ... but like most things that hurt, even when we know they're wrong, Sarah's words would not go away. Hart bristled, and waited for either Bowler to say what was on his mind, or to see what Paula's next question was, having finally decided to play on.

"I think you should be nicer to Sarah," said Bowler finally, in an airy manner. His eyes hadn't left the TV. "I think we need to do more to get her onside."

Hart was already irritable, and this just made him plain angry. Which conversation had Bowler been listening to? Be *nicer*? Not only bad grammar, but utterly wrong. His sole intention *had* been to be nice to her.

"Are you trying to be amusing?" said Hart, red faced. "In case you didn't notice, the whole subject of the conversation I had with her, before she flew off the handle, was me trying to get her to come with us, out of concern for her well-being. I—" and his voice faded, as he saw Bowler shaking his head and waving his hand, cutting him off. Hart fell silent in both compliance and surprise.

"Bad choice of word," Bowler said, "Not nicer, just ... more considerate. You're not going to get her onside by telling her off—however good your intention—" he added quickly, seeing Hart's reaction. "Or by saying that what she's doing is daft. She's stubborn. Stubborn people don't like that, do they?"

Hart didn't say anything. Bowler had a point.

"See, I think we need to spend more time with her. With everyone, really."

Hart slowly settled back in his chair, a suspicious look on his face. He had a feeling he knew where this was going. It had been a while since they'd had this one out, and Bowler was picking a *bad* time to attempt it. In his current mood, Hart almost relished the coming storm.

"And why is that?" he asked, looking at Bowler with catlike eyes, his narrow features glaring.

Bowler didn't see this; he was deliberately talking towards the TV, where Paula was crashing predictably out on £32,000.

"Because ... well ... maybe it's what we're supposed to do."

"Explain. Because this sounds like what we've talked about before, and you know my thoughts on this."

"Not this idea, we haven't."

"It all adds up to the same claptrap."

Bowler turned to him. He was angry, and Hart could see it. It was a surprise to him.

"Are you not even going to hear it?" Bowler asked. He paused for a moment, shaking his head slightly, incredulous. This was more than anger. This was hurt anger. "Do you ... do you have that little respect for me?"

Hart was caught short here, and it showed. More new behaviour from Bowler. He began to get a strong sinking feeling—one that would progress over the years ahead—that things were going to change, and that they would not be good for Hart. Possibly for neither of them. Hart stood his ground though, and pointed a slow finger at Bowler.

"Well, do you have that little respect for *me* that you would try to change my mind on something I have made absolutely clear that I don't want to discuss?" It was a good response, and it worked; some of the fire in Bowler's eyes died, and when he spoke again, the familiar uncertainty had crept back into his voice.

"It's not that ... well, not really that," Bowler said. "Well maybe it is, but this is a new idea, and I think you should at least listen to it. It's just something I've been thinking about, and whether you agree or not, you should at least listen; you want me to keep it in? You're always saying about looking after your head, but I have to keep in all the thoughts, the big thoughts, that you don't agree with?"

A good comeback from Bowler, and harder to combat because it was completely genuine. Bowler wasn't trying to win anything; as ever, he simply meant what he said. *Ideas, ideas, always with crazy ideas ... just like*

Simon, eh, Hart? said the voice in Hart's head. He silenced it, and flounced back in his chair irritably.

"Fine, fine. Spit it out," Hart said, looking past Bowler now to the screen.

Bowler sighed—*why is he always so difficult?*—and began.

"It just strikes me that, in this place … there's so few of us. How long has this place been here? Is the first person to be here still here? We don't know. And I think they're not, as we'd know in some way, like we'd have found out by now—"

"How would we know if they were mad? Or The Beast?"

"Well, yes, but someone else would know—"

"Not if they were also mad."

"*Anyway*, that's not really the point. My point is, if it was just a case of everyone who died within The Foyer's boundary ending up living, or existing, I mean, in The Foyer as a result, and being stuck here forever, then it'd be full to bursting, right?"

"Nothing new there, we've always assumed that."

"So it's either that dying within the boundary of The Foyer has nothing to do with coming here—"

"Hard to ascertain, seeing as none of the Three Talkers remember exactly how they died. Or you, or myself."

"Or that it does, and people have been getting out somehow—"

"All right, though very hard to believe that hundreds of people have been coming and going under my nose for sixty years."

"Or that, as we've talked about before now, that The Foyer reaches some kind of maximum …"

"Capacity, Bowler. And yes, that's been one theory."

" … and then everyone gets out. Or—"

"Let me guess. God turns up and says we've all learned our lesson, and tells us we now get to go to a wonderful heaven and live on a cloud, is that about right?"

Bowler turned red, and Hart saw it was both embarrassment and rage. But he didn't care. He was ready for this. If Bowler wanted to have a shouting match, he could have one. But he wasn't going to be the one to start it.

"Hart," Bowler said after a moment, looking directly at Hart, talking quietly and dangerously, trembling gently with anger, "go fuck yourself, you rude fucking twat."

Hart leaned forward in his seat now, too, eager for his turn. Debate— the great cut and thrust!—he loved it at the best of times, but now he was angry and knew he could pick apart Bowler all day long. It felt good in a way only the dead could understand, feeling such a delicious rush that was so, *so* rare in The Foyer. He was going to enjoy this, and knew it was wrong, and unfair—Bowler was not any kind of debate expert, while Hart used to do it for a *living*—but the sweetness of it was too much. It was like being alive. He was chipping away at his friend, and a small part of him was screaming at him to stop, but damn his eyes, he couldn't help himself.

"This is all nonsense really, though, isn't it, Bowler?" Hart said, with a wicked grin. "Come on. What are you *really* thinking?"

"What?"

Hart chuckled unpleasantly.

"I know you. What are you really thinking, when you talk about this daily meeting?"

"I just fucking told you—"

"No, no. I know what you really mean." Hart leaned closer, smiling cruelly, now lost totally in the juicy pleasure of malice, something which he rarely permitted himself; such things can be addictive in The Foyer, incredibly so, and any addiction there was disastrous. It *gripped* you there, and in that moment Hart was smothered in it.

"Let me guess. Your get-together idea? Something like … if we all get together regularly … then we all learn about each other." His voice took on a simpering, singsong tone, mocking and cruel. "And then we learn to *love* each other. And the power of our love breaks down the walls of The Foyer, and we all go off to heaven together holding hands, singing hymns and weeping as we remember our past wickedness … something like that? Am I on about the right lines? Hmm?"

Bowler stood and seemed to be biting his tongue for a moment, even in his rage. His fists were clenched, and his jaw was locked. Hart stood, too, and carried on.

"Because we were all bad people, weren't we, Bowler?" he crowed. "That was your theory, correct? And when we learn our lesson, off we go. Even George, despite the fact that he wouldn't hurt a fly, he must, no doubt, have been some sort of notorious serial rapist in his past life, something like that? And me, the man who never even got as much as a parking ticket, hardly ever even drank, why, I must be some sort of a murderer, right? So what's *your* lesson to learn then, Bowler?" he asked, stepping in closer, his own heavy breathing matching Bowler's. Bowler matched his gaze, not dropping his eyes, also breathing hard. "To grow up and realise your situation? You've been here a year now. Any idea when that might happen?"

"Where do the Flyers go, Hart?" asked Bowler, quietly. The sound of it was like a child's question. Hart snorted.

"Different frequency. Higher frequency. That's why they go up, my friend, and *not* because that's where *heaven* is. Because we're energy, Bowler, *energy*. We're leftover energy from our lives, something that can't be snuffed out. Hell, maybe we're not even us, maybe we're just our memories, or something that *thinks* we're us, the ghost of an *idea*. But either way, we're just *energy*. That which can be neither destroyed nor created, just converted into different states. That's *science*. Not souls, not *chi*, not ghosts, just *energy*. That's all. The Foyer, here, it's not because we're bad people, or because we're being punished, this is just where we ended up. If we'd died on a Tuesday, if we died wearing blue, if we died having a big steaming *shit* maybe we wouldn't be here, who knows? This is how our deaths fired us off, how they set up our afterlife, and it's no more influenced by the way you live your life than the colour of your hair or whether you're double jointed; it's just the way it is. It's just what we happened to *get*."

Bowler looked him slowly up and down, jaw locked, bottom lip tight. Contempt.

"Sarah was totally right about you."

Hart's index finger came up, the smugness temporarily rocked. Bowler had stung him with that one, hit him on a sore spot. But he'd been trained in this. Trained to think on his feet. He rallied magnificently.

"Far from it, my friend. I just don't take the fairy position on this. You know what *really* causes the madness here, Bowler? What really makes the madness the biggest threat?" He had his finger right by Bowler's face, but Bowler didn't even notice it. He was staring at Hart with undisguised hatred. This was probably the moment, Bowler would think later, when he truly began to see Hart as a coward.

"It's the boredom," Hart continued hotly, letting go, releasing, *unloading*. "It's the *boredom*. Frustration comes from hope, so you can watch that. It's hard, but you can do it. But boredom has to be challenged, has to be taken on and beaten, and you have to be able to initiate *change* to do that." Hart was actually curling his top lip as he spoke. He looked like a snarling dog. It looked repulsive. "You have to be able to change things, to have some influence. And we have none here, Bowler, none. Despite your hippy pretensions, you'd better learn that fast." The finger wagged closer to Bowler's face, and Bowler reflexively whipped up a hand and slapped it away. Some part of Hart's brain registered this with a small amount of surprise—and Bowler actually jumped slightly at himself—but Hart himself carried on regardless.

"Sarah doesn't realise that I *do* want to get out of here, but I'm being smart about it," Hart said. "I'm avoiding the frustration. But I'll tell you why I want out of here, Bowler. It's not to get to heaven; this place proves beyond a doubt that it doesn't exist. It's for that *change*." Hart's finger lowered as he lost himself in his vision, eyes widening, and, it seemed to Bowler, Loosening.

Later, Bowler would think that not only had he never heard Hart talk about what he actually *did* hope, but how it was the only time he'd ever heard him do so. The change in Hart's demeanour was so odd, so clearly visionary, and so utterly at odds to the Hart he usually saw. Even through his anger, Bowler found it fascinating to see.

"It's to find the way out of here," continued Hart, eyes darting around as he spoke. "So we can go to the *next* Foyer. And in there, maybe we can find others on our frequency, and then show *them* how to get out too. So we spread it, and we can keep moving. So we can keep having constant change. No more frustration. No more boredom. *Change,* Bowler. That's the best we can hope for! New things. That is the very best we can ever hope for, and you need to know that." He was back in the room now, attention focused on Bowler, back to being the usual realist he was, but no less animated. "Because unless you want to end up like The Beast—or like your best *buddy* Mark—then you need to just *accept* that, and stop thinking like Mary Poppins!"

Hart snapped out this last part, and they stood there in silence, breathing heavily and staring into each other's eyes. It was Bowler's move, this slightly newer Bowler that didn't back down so easily, and Hart found that he didn't want his companion to do so. There was something raw here, and it was like heroin. It was dangerous, but Hart wanted it. And if he'd been self-aware enough to notice in the moment, he'd have felt his left hand shaking gently.

But Bowler's next action surprised Hart very much indeed. He began to smile. And it wasn't a smile Hart had ever seen on his friend's face before. It was a cruel smile. And Hart suddenly realised that—somehow, he didn't know in what manner yet—Bowler now had him.

"Well, Hart," he said, actually taking a small step backwards, and folding his arms, talking with a slow confidence that was also totally new. "You've not really answered my questions, and what you're saying isn't making too much sense. You see ... we can't influence change? But what was it you said to me? *'I never thought that it'd work,'* or that it hadn't *'been tried before'*? Or that I'm *'the luckiest Check-in there's ever been'*? Who was it that made those things happen, Hart? Who made that change? You ... or at least, the man you were a year ago." The smile widened, turned into a grin. "But then, that's how *people* sometimes change, isn't it? Nothing for years, and then all at once ... you just change. Things build up, then they fall over, all at once. And you end up different. You end up afraid."

Hart said nothing, but had gone slightly white. Silent from confusion and surprise, and from what Bowler was saying. Who was this before him? Where was Bowler?

"Or maybe it was me. Maybe I made you lazy. Maybe it was the other way round; fear was motivating you, and then you got me. And *then* you got lazy, and then you got scared. I don't know. But anyway; here's another question for you." He unfolded his arms, and pointed a finger upwards. The grin was now a smirk, and it looked no better on Bowler than it did on Hart. "If the Flyers, as you say, are going on to another frequency—another Foyer, if you like, the next one across, as you've said—why do they go up, and disappear from sight? The Foyers wouldn't be on different ... I dunno ... planes, is that the word? We know that, as *this* one is on earth. It's in Coventry, for God's sake. We walk the floor of The Foyer and we're bound to

43

this planet. So there's not going to be another Foyer in space, it's not going to be *above* this Foyer, is it? It'd be next door, wouldn't it? Especially if you're planning on hopping from one to another."

He stepped in close to Hart again, closer than before, while Hart just stayed silent, lips tight and white. Bowler spoke gently now, and slowly. He was feeling it too. That rush. Bowler had never had it in The Foyer before—in fact had always avoided confrontation—and this was his first taste of what it felt like in a world without communication, without true excitement, without common change. He revelled in it, and it took him away much faster than it did Hart. "So why do they go up, *hmm*? They'd just go across, wouldn't you say? But they don't. They go *up*." He punctuated this last point with a mocking finger point to the sky, then didn't move for a few seconds. Neither did Hart.

Bowler slowly raised his arms into an exaggerated shrug.

"Let's say I do believe in fairies, Hart. Fine. So ... you tell me. Why do they go *up*?"

Hart whispered something.

"Didn't catch that, Hart. What?"

"I said 'fuck you,'" repeated Hart through gritted teeth, now glaring at Bowler through eyes that were moist.

Bowler blinked—he had never heard Hart say the F word, not once in all the time he'd been there, it just sounded so awkward and wrong coming from the older—and then burst into gales of laughter, doubling over at the waist and roaring.

And Hart turned and walked away without a word, through the Ikea coffee table and the DFS settee and the plasterboard wall, and left Bowler alone in The Polish Guy's flat, hysterically laughing and slapping his thighs. Meanwhile, the Polish Guy looked at his watch, stood, and headed for his secret box, the one hidden behind the boiler.

***

Taken from *Hart's Imaginary Guide to Being Dead, 'Sleep'*

One has to look for the blessings. They can be found everywhere, if you really look. For example: what are the positives of never being able to sleep?

1. You can't have nightmares if you don't sleep.

2. You can't miss anything if you don't sleep. And that's important. One doesn't have to "sleep with one eye open" when one cannot sleep at all. Therein lies a major blessing. You can never be—quite literally—caught napping by The Beast. A worse awakening I cannot imagine. To see his immense face upon opening your eyes, and knowing what is to come ... that does, perhaps, slightly nullify positive number one in this case.

You don't *need* nightmares when there is always the possibility that The Beast could catch you.

***

"That was my Granny's favourite bench, you know," says Bowler, pointing at a metal construction across the street. They are standing opposite the Godiva statue outside Cathedral Lanes Mall, where, in a few years' time, the public will no longer be overshadowed by the plastic canopy currently above their heads. The locals will decide that it is an eyesore, and demand that it be taken down. Bowler has always thought it one of the city's more interesting features, but apparently everyone else will think otherwise. "She used to people watch, she said. Even though she had cataracts."

It's the first thing he's said since they left the train station, the first thing he's said since he let the Train doors slide shut in front of him. Since he watched the Train rumble and begin to move, a huge metal mass gathering speed and pulling away. Since he watched it leave, clenching his fists and his jaw and screaming to the heavens, since he turned and walked off the platform without a word.

Hart couldn't blame him. Hart thinks that maybe he shouldn't have warned Bowler—because Bowler NEEDS to go through it, needs to know—but at the same time, he just couldn't let anyone go through that without prior knowledge.

"Whenever I took her shopping, she always insisted we sat on that bench," says Bowler. "She used to say it was her knees hurting, but they were fine the rest of the time. I knew she just wanted an excuse to make me sit there for an hour. I never minded." He falls silent again.

Hart thinks for something to say, and the best he can come up with is:

"Do you want to sit on it now?" Bowler doesn't look at Hart; he keeps staring at the bench.

"Yeah," he says, after a while. "Okay."

They cross the street, waiting first at the zebra crossing with the other people—partly out of habit, and partly because being in the path of a car is something that Bowler still instinctively avoids after a lifetime of doing so—and fortunately, as it is a weekday afternoon and not a Saturday, there is still no one sat on the bench, no other old ladies, no other gangs of seventeen-year-old goths or chavs to take it. They stand in front of it for a moment—Hart not wanting to sit first—and then Bowler sits, suddenly flopping down in it as if his strings have been cut. Hart gently follows. Bowler is struggling more than Hart hoped.

You've been here a week. Let's see what you think in a year, *Hart thinks, and this is one of the incidents that makes him think he's made a mistake with Bowler. Because if he ever needs to get away—if Bowler really becomes unhinged, Loose—Bowler would always follow Hart. The thought is deeply disturbing.*

Bowler mutters something, and Hart has to ask him to repeat it. It turns out Bowler had said two words.

"Heart attack."

Hart is understandably confused.

"Pardon?"

"Heart attack. My Granny. Just behind there," he says, pointing at Cathedral Lanes without looking up, meaning the cobbled alleys around the cathedral itself. There isn't much Hart can really say in reply.

"I wasn't there," Bowler said. *"She'd gone shopping with one of her friends. Apparently she'd been fine before, laughing. She was a very giggly woman. Very friendly, not one of these nasty, bitter old ladies. Good laugh. I suppose it might have even been the laughing, at the time, you know. Either way, down she went."* And he accompanies this part with a surprisingly blunt effect; he slaps his hand hard on his thigh, like he's overcompensating, covering his pain.

"Heart went, down she goes. Nothing they could do. Dead before the ambulance got there." He pauses a moment, and then turns his red eyes to Hart. *"So, see, this is the thing for me, Hart. She died* right there. *Well within The Foyer."*

Hart sighs, not unkindly, and settles back while Bowler talks.

"So," continues Bowler, turning farther, to stay looking into Hart's eyes now he has moved backwards, his hands turned upward into cups, waiting to receive. *"Where is she, Hart? Don't get me wrong; I'm* glad *she's not here. That she's not stuck with ... all this. But she died here,* here. *So where's* she *gone?"* He isn't angry. He's after answers, pleading. And worse, he knows Hart doesn't have them.

Hart laces his fingers together and looks at them. These are questions he used to ask, used to need to know. But he knows now that they don't matter, in the long run. They are here, and surviving and getting out are the priorities, not the things that can't be changed. But Bowler needs something.

"Perhaps ... perhaps she is *here,"* says Hart. *"Perhaps she's here, but on a different frequency. In the way that everyone in our Foyer is roughly on one*

frequency—*close, but not close enough to be able to communicate like us—and we're all loosely on it, not totally fixed, which explains why we can fade in and out with George sometimes, for example ... and your grandmother, and others like her, are on another frequency altogether. Except we can't see them or even be aware of them, the same way the living can't see us."*

He falls silent, not knowing whether to go on as Bowler hasn't even looked at him throughout this speech. Hart thinks this must be the worst week of Bowler's existence, living or otherwise. Hart is wrong. So far, it is only the second worst, and although this week will end horrifically—almost bad enough to make it number one—the next four weeks will shunt this today firmly into third place. For this day will end with Bowler riding the Train, and all that comes after for Bowler in The Foyer will, in one way or another, be a result of that experience.

"You want to know what I think?" he says, and Hart does want to know, though he thinks Bowler will be wrong. He wants to know Bowler's thinking. "You want to know why I think we're here and she's not?" He takes Hart's silence as confirmation to continue. "I think we're here because we wasted our lives. I think we had the potential to be anything, and do anything, and we did exactly nothing. Born here. Died here. Let me guess; you were born here too, yeah?" Hart nods, quietly. He has a reply immediately, but he has to let Bowler speak.

"Granny did something. She travelled, at least. She did missionary work, you know. Built stuff, over there. She's in a better place. And I fucking hope Mum and Dad go the same way. They will. Man, they did all sorts of shit. Dad started a business, gave hundreds of people jobs. Factory. Mum was a full-time teacher, full time; God knows how many lives she had an impact on. Me, I've done sweet fuck all." He sits back, letting his head flop backwards with the motion so he is looking at the sky. "This is a punishment," he says, talking to the clouds, as if he resents their freedom as they drift effortlessly above. Above and away. "Not the worst one, but one that gives us what we deserve.

Monotony. Just like our lives." Hart notes this rare use of vocabulary for Bowler. Monotony. "And we're being forced to think, to act, for the first time, to get out of here. It's to see how much we want it. This is what it's here for."

"Bowler—"

Bowler smiles a little, and turns his head, still hanging backwards, to look at Hart.

"I know, I know exactly what you think. But let's look at it scientifically, then. It still adds up the same."

Hart is suddenly intrigued, despite himself. In the near distance he sees Churchill (Bowler's came up with the nickname; apparently the Guest they call Churchill looks like some bulldog character on the TV) come out of the building behind Bowler, talking silently and frantically to himself, scratching at his face. As usual, like all of the others, he sees them and pretends he hasn't, immediately falling silent and turning around. He heads back inside the building. Hart notes all of this without interest, and continues listening to Bowler.

"You wanna hear this, Hart. I'm no scientist, but get ready for Dr Frank Bowler's big scientific"—he searches for the word—"bullshit."

"Dr who?"

"Heh, you just said it."

"What?"

"Never mind. You talk about energies, and frequencies and shit, right?" says Bowler, looking up again now, his broad shoulders spread on the back of the bench and his arms moving lazily about as he makes his point. If Hart didn't know better, he'd think Bowler was basking in the sun's rays, even though they are passing straight through him, and he will never again have to worry about sunburn.

"Well, how about this," Bowler goes on. "How about if you live a really good, active life, and you really live, and love, and do things ... what if that builds up an energy? Every adventure, every kiss, every rush you get builds up

THE PHYSICS OF THE DEAD

something we can't even see? Like a, a, a store *of energy. What if that sets your frequency, if you like, and when you die, because you're* on *that frequency, you get to go somewhere the frequency you're on means you can do more in your Foyer, than we can." He sits up, waving his hands rapidly now. "One that means you can walk straight through The Foyer wall, or can talk to the other Guests, or even ... I dunno, even fucking fly if you like. Like ..." he pauses, blowing out his cheeks as he thinks. "Well ... like angels."*

Hart is silent.

"And if you were just ... look, bad, *for want of a better word ... that just kills your energy dead. And when you die, you don't even get to come here, you don't even get a chance, you just flat* die. *Nothing. And on the other end of the scale, if you live a life of, of ... like, you're happy, and do good stuff and just* live, *and help other people live, maybe your frequency, your energy, is so full and high that you go somewhere opposite. Somewhere your frequency is of a type where you can do anything, a Foyer that isn't really a Foyer." Bowler snaps his fingers as another idea occurs to him, and lifts his head up properly now, holding an open palm to Hart as he offers his idea.*

"Like if you fill your energy up like that, you go to a Foyer far better, far more free and loving than the real world because everyone that gets to go there are the good, adventurous, kind people. And they can all fly, and be happy. Where The Foyer has no wall. Jesus. Hart ... does that not sound like heaven to you? A free world full of all the good people?" He looks off into space for a second, shaking his head, getting around his own thinking.

"And when people die and come back, those out of body people you hear about," Bowler eventually continues, "maybe they've seen a glimpse of it, all these people that die and talk about how they saw their families and how it just felt so good and warm ... or these people that wrote the Bible, and talk about heaven and that, maybe they saw that world somehow ..." He is passionate now, lips wet, hands out in front of him, shaping in the air what he is seeing in his mind.

"Maybe it's not decided by a god or whatever, whether you get to go to a good place or a bad place. Maybe the energy from the way we live our lives chooses it." Bowler then pauses, considering something, then says it.

"Maybe the Flyers are the ones that lived that way. Maybe they're the ones that get to go to that top place."

Hart holds up a hand. Bowler has spoken more in one sitting than Hart has ever heard, and it is now time to have his say, because Bowler is missing one important, vital thing.

The one thing that Hart knows that means Bowler is wrong.

"All right. So tell me, Bowler. What do you know about my life?"

Bowler opens his mouth, and stops. He doesn't have an answer, but also sees that Hart is slightly angry. Hart is trying to contain it—Bowler thinks this is because Hart doesn't want to be angry—but he is angry nonetheless.

"So I have touched no lives? Helped no one? Well, did you know I pretty much single-handedly kept a school open?" says Hart.

Bowler is stunned.

"Getty-Hart Primary School. Ring any bells?"

It does. Half of his childhood friends went there, for God's sake. The connection was obvious and yet not obvious. He has heard the name so many times in his life that the idea it was named AFTER someone has never occurred to him, the same way that Rolls-Royce was just Rolls-Royce. That the name came from actual people was something you never thought about.

"Your mother was a teacher. Fine," says Hart. "That place was going under until I stepped in. That was a big sacrifice for me, Bowler. A lot of money, even back then. They changed the sodding name out of gratitude. I kept something going that helped children get their start for the last, what, seventy odd years? And it's still doing it. I visited, and taught, all the time; and guess what? Every time, I felt that 'rush,' as you call it, of satisfaction, and was aware of what I'd started, what it was doing, making a difference. I saw it,

and felt it. Takes a lot of money to keep a school from going under, Bowler. Do you know what I did for a living? You still don't know, do you?"

Bowler, silent now, shakes his head, red faced. Hart's expression has softened slightly, but the anger is still there.

"I was a barrister. Fought the good fight every day, pretty much. And unlike most, I made sure I was selective in my clients. And helped the right clients. And made it so they could afford it. So again, I helped a lot of people. It was my job. And I felt good about it. And yes, it paid well. Well enough to start a school. And see the world."

Hart leans forward, looking stern, and speaks slowly. "I stayed in Coventry because it's my home, and I liked it here. Not because I didn't have the imagination to leave. So please, Bowler ... don't judge me because you feel you wasted your life. It's a nice theory, but I'm proof that it doesn't hold any water." And Hart sits back suddenly, folding his arms. He doesn't like making himself into a window. He shouldn't have snapped, he knows. It wasn't Bowler's fault; he was just thinking aloud, while he was in pain.

They sit in silence. Hart will not apologise, but he needs to make it better.

"Although the fact that I once got a chap off an arson charge who then went on to burn down a carpet warehouse might have some effect," he says,

The silence continues, but it is now better. Eventually, Bowler's curiosity gets the better of his own embarrassment.

"Did you ... did you ever get mar—" and he cuts off, as he's had the realisation that caps this week as the second worst of Frank Bowler's existence so far, and the bottom falls out of his world.

He passes straight through the bench and onto the floor, where he keels over and curls into a ball, wide eyed and open mouthed. Hart leaps off the bench and crouches next to him, grabbing him without thought and shouting.

"Bowler! Bowler! What is it? What? Bowler!"

And Bowler doesn't look at him as he is still in total shock, doesn't even hear the questions. He has realised that which will destroy him here, and as he gasps out the words, Hart knows it, and despairs.

"I have ... a wife ... I have a wife, Hart ... it just came to me," and he wails, an open, soul-hurt cry that comes out as a ragged screech.

"Ah ... aahaa ... Hart ... her place ... her flat ... our home ... it's inside The Foyer, Hart ..."

Hart lets go.

"She ... she lives here ..." and then he is lost in hysterical tears.

Hart sits and rubs his temples with his fingers.

***

Part Two:

Orientation

Chapter 4: In Which We See the First One In Sixty Years, Bowler Takes the Train, We Are Presented With the Irony of Running for Your Life, And Learn the Physics of the Dead

***

Taken from *Hart's Imaginary Guide to Being Dead, 'Solitude'*

It's of little wonder why the other Guests—the ones that stay alone—are lunatics. The only mystery regarding *them* is also the reason why they are as they are.

Why do they stay apart?

I can only imagine how terrible their existence must be. To be alone, here, always … when their minds finally collapsed, it must have been a blessing.

I do worry sometimes, however, that they know something we don't. Something that made it worth it.

***

Hart found Bowler on Granny's Bench, as he'd known he would. They hadn't seen each other for two weeks, although Hart knew throughout that time that he could have found Bowler here any day. If Bowler needed anything first and foremost, it was comfort, sadly. And this place was as close as he would get to it.

The time in between had been tough on Hart, but he dreaded to think what it would have been like for Bowler. In all the time Bowler had been here, he had never been on his own for more than an hour or two. Yes, there were people like George and Sarah that he could spend time with, but it wouldn't be like anything he was used to. Hart only hoped that Mark had not found him and been in his ear, and that Bowler had been smart enough to stay out of the way of The Beast. He was pretty sure of the latter, but he was greatly concerned nonetheless; he had inadvertently made it so Bowler would always have to fear being alone more than anyone in The Foyer, by forming their bond. Bowler only knew an existence there with Hart, experiencing it through the protective filter of a companion.

Hart had died, and come into a second world, then gone through the hell of adjusting. Bowler had adjusted with a crutch. Being alone would mean he would have to do it all over again.

Hart didn't know if Bowler could hold onto his sanity after adjusting a second time (*and after the toll the Train took, don't forget that,* the voice in Hart's head told him).

It had taken Hart this long to admit to himself that he had picked the fight at the Polish Guy's house, or at least escalated it to levels that it should not have reached. He had mocked Bowler on a level that was totally unnecessary, and Bowler had responded in kind, hurt and angry. Hart didn't agree with what Bowler had said—he would *never* agree with Bowler on *that* issue—but knew that he shouldn't have reacted the way he did, letting anger take hold of him. Hart had learned to lock such things down long ago, and had taken a great deal of trouble over doing so over many years. Hart knew that he had escalated the argument. He was to blame. Such thoughts did not come easily to him, but two weeks was a long time in The Foyer.

He approached the bench from behind, seeing Bowler's stocky shoulders slouched above the back of the seat (Hart was always nagging Bowler about his poor posture) and not seeing his friend's face. Hart wondered what madness would be written in Bowler's expression.

Bowler's face was blank. Not the utterly vacant emptiness of the Loose Guests, but there was no thought there at the moment. Although Bowler hadn't had anywhere near enough time for lunacy to set in—and therefore for his hands to shake or his face to change—he had clearly brushed up against it, and come away feeling the effects. Hart hoped it wasn't permanent. Maybe he'd even started to adapt to it like Hart had. Maybe being connected with Hart hadn't made it worse for him after all. Bowler's breathing looked easy, and he at least looked relaxed … but at the same time, *aware* in a way Hart hadn't seen before.

"Hello, Bowler," said Hart, and felt a sudden, nasty little bite of satisfaction—despite himself—as Bowler jumped.

"Hart …" Bowler said, putting a hand to his chest. Bowler hated himself for it, but he felt an enormous rush of warmth as he saw Hart standing there. Relief. He'd handled the worst of it over the last fortnight, but things would be so much *easier* now. The unending loneliness, without even the blessed relief of sleep, the constant burden of relentless thought … Bowler would never be able to put words to these feelings—he didn't really think reflectively—but he understood exactly why things had been tough, knew it in his own way.

Even so, he wouldn't run back. He'd sworn that over and over again. That was what had gotten him through the dark nights by himself. *If he thinks he can just waltz up, and expect me to rush back, in his stupid* suit, *he can go fuck himself.* Hart didn't look ruffled in the slightest. He looked like he'd laughed his way through the last two weeks. But then, Hart never liked to look ruffled.

"Are you … all right?" asked Hart, genuine concern on his face.

Bowler stared at him for a long time.

"Been better."

There was more silence. It was very early—maybe 7am—and there were few people about in town, and even fewer cars. Those that did walk past had frost for breath. It was one of the few things that Hart liked about being dead; no cold. But they both hated The Foyer during these quiet times. It made the place feel—it was a pun they'd both made so many times that it had become a serious phrase to them—like a ghost town. Like there was no life even outside of The Foyer. It was a thought far too unpleasant to even consider.

Hart took a deep breath.

"I'm sorry, Bowler ... I'll get that out of the way right now. Though you know I hate you going on about that sort of stuff, I gave you permission to do so, and ... anyway, I went too far. And I forgive you for what you said back, I goaded you into it, and ... look, it's my fault," he finished, and folded his arms.

Bowler just continued to look at him. Hart felt that this was not the appropriate response.

"This isn't something that is easy for me to say, Bowler."

Bowler gently shrugged.

"I appreciate that," he said, crossing one leg awkwardly over the other in his seat "But I'm sick of you just brushing off what I say. That's bullshit." His face was pinched, as if he was trying to prove something. It made him look older.

Hart bit his tongue, and sucked back his sudden rise of anger; he had to sort this out.

"Bowler," he said with as little sigh in his voice as he could manage, "you know I don't agree with you on *that* issue, and you also know I never will. But I don't want to be ..." Hart tightened his hands by his sides, pushing the word out, "... dismissive. You are ... you're my friend, after all." Hart's hands relaxed. As with most difficult conversations, getting the words out was hard, but made everything infinitely easier once they were voiced. And he meant it, after all. "So let's just … let's just agree that we'll … I don't know, we'll try each other's ways of getting out, yes? And not discuss the whys and wherefores. They don't really matter. As long as we remember not to … you know. *Believe* too much. Dangerous, here, doing that."

Hart held up his hands and cast his gaze up the street, squinting in the morning light with a whimsical sigh.

"Anyway, let's be honest …" he added. "It's not like we have many better things to do."

Hart thought it was a fair apology, and honest. It had been even harder to give than he had expected, but there was relief now. And even more when Bowler finally smiled in response, faintly.

"You must be kidding," he said. "Bert and Sammy are on their way over for cocktails, and they're bringing some smokin' hot bitches with 'em too." Hart smirked, and Bowler waved a hand loosely over the seat next to him and shifted sideways. With that, everything was back to normal, and they both knew it.

Hart sat, and for a few minutes they watched the birds, milling about on the floor of the mini plaza. Hart used to love birds when he was alive. Now he hated them with a passion that he knew stemmed from jealousy. He'd never told Bowler.

"So … I have to ask, Bowler," Hart said eventually, trying to make it sound casual. He had to know. In The Foyer, you had to try and get the *real* curiosity out. "What was it like for you?"

Bowler watched the birds pecking about, and considered the question. Thought about the sense of loss, of utter helplessness. Of having so little direction that it was scary. Feeling the pull of the perimeter, even of the Train, anything, because *some*thing had to work … and the nights. Of Mark clearly trying to tell him he had all the answers, and realising without much surprise that Hart was right; Mark was going Loose. Of communicating with Mark and George here and there and it being like a poor substitute for a drug; he wasn't used to this, he needed to talk, to hear another voice responding to what he had to say. Of once hearing the cry of The Beast, sudden and deafening and terrible, and from nowhere. The sound suddenly cutting in halfway through, like someone had taken their finger off a mute button. Not being able to tell how far away he was, not knowing whether to run and risk being seen, or to hide. And worst of all, during that one, really bad night; that slowly growing feeling of his mind being levered up from its moorings, starting off so small like a splinter, then building up to a crowbar, that terrible pressure building up in his head. Almost a physical pain, and realising with great terror that he liked the idea of what was happening. That maybe this *was* the only way out, the only way to deal with it, and knowing how easy it would be to just ... *snap*. It was that realisation that made him focus most of all, made him pick something to use to get through it.

If that bastard could do it, I can bloody do it.

What Bowler actually said in reply was:

"I can't lie, Hart. You know what it was like. You must have been through it. And without knowing you could come back to me if you wanted. Before now, I mean. It was ... it was bad. But I've been through worse."

Hart nodded, and was about to tell him he knew, but it was at that moment—for the first time in sixty years, not seen remotely on a TV but in the actual flesh and close enough to touch—that a Bluey walked right by in front of them.

After a second of shell-shocked silence, Hart whipped around to tell Bowler to come on—not that it would have done any good, as he suddenly couldn't speak—but Bowler wasn't there. He was already up and running after the Bluey.

***

"I'll find you ... after," says Hart, though he knows Bowler isn't listening. He's gone, staring along the length of carriage C through eyes that no longer wish to see.

Hart's impulse, unusually, is to grab Bowler. He wants to reach in through the wall of the Train and pull Bowler out, to make him stand on the platform beside him while the Train pulls away, to keep him safe. But Hart doesn't. He looks at his friend through the scratched glass window and tries to find the right words to send him on his way.

Bowler's jaw is set firm, though his bottom lip is working up and down, twisting into a grimace, then falling loose as his head rolls back on his shoulders to stare at the ceiling, eyes closed, forehead raised in despair ... then the determination sets in and the whole process begins again. It's like watching an animatronic dummy.

Hart looks up the platform, seeing the station masters (were they still called station masters?) checking with one another. The Train will be setting off soon. Hart isn't happy; this is not a good time to be doing this. Grief was the worst kind of motivation for it. The pain after will be bad enough, but to go in with such turmoil in the mind ... is bad. Hart looks at the figure partially covered from view by a NO SMOKING sticker and worries that he won't come back. Not that Bowler could break The Foyer—Hart knows that won't happen—but that Bowler will not come through this as himself.

No. He'll make sure Bowler is all right.

And it occurs to Hart that he might as well start walking now. If he's not going to stop Bowler, he actually needs to start walking now. It'll take a good fifteen minutes minimum, and Bowler will be done a lot quicker than that; Hart needs to be there as soon as Bowler finishes, and he has a good idea of where he needs to be.

He hesitates for a moment, struck by a sudden stab of pity. Bowler doesn't deserve any of this; and it was about to get so much worse. Infinitely so.

"I'm going to get going then, Bowler," Hart says, uncertain. Bowler doesn't turn his head.

"Bowler? Okay?" Still nothing. Tears rolling down cheeks that tremble slightly. "Can … can you hear me, Bowler?" Is that a nod? Yes, it's a nod. Hart raises a hand, begins to lift it towards the carriage wall, and then draws it away. "Good luck, then. Just … well, I'll see you in a little bit."

But then the whistle blows, and Hart curses himself for leaving it this late. He'll have to run the whole way now to get there, and it won't really be soon enough. Idiot.

As the doors begin to slide noisily shut, Bowler suddenly looks at Hart through the window, fear briefly breaking through his grief. What he's looking for Hart doesn't know, as, in a moment he will return to in his mind for years to come, he can't meet Bowler's gaze. Hart looks at the platform edge until the carriage begins to move.

What happens next, Bowler will never fully remember; he will recall brief flashes, and there will be one particular part that he can never forget, no matter how much he wishes to.

But what actually happens is this: the Train begins to move, and to his surprise, Bowler's mind goes blank. Whether it's from his determination, or his focus to keep himself anchored in his seat, or a combination of the two, he forgets about everything else, about all of the pain, and it's a blessing. He looks through the window of carriage C and sees the wall of the station bridge slope away, sees the grass of the embankment begin to run past faster and faster, and for a bizarre moment he feels like he's just another passenger. He feels like leaving The Foyer will be as easy as taking a daytrip to London. Supersaver return, of course.

He can hear the conversations around him, the metallic rat-a-tat of the drum and bass music in the kid's headphones two seats away. He can hear the two West Indian women behind him talking about the price of the tickets. He can hear a man explaining to someone that he's probably going to lose signal in a second because the Train is moving. A woman coughing. He's just another person going to the NEC, to Birmingham International, to Birmingham New Street. He's going to try looking around the Bull Ring for a new pair of jeans, to see if he can find a little something new, going to buy a present for ... and his focus wobbles, and he pushes thoughts away.

He can't feel anything different, though, and after a minute of nothing, he almost relaxes slightly. They must have hit The Wall by now, surely? The Train has now reached high speed, and the frighteningly quiet feeling of pace, *the tiny bumps as it shoots forward over the tracks, the slight rocking of the other passengers ... these things, along with his own nerves, make him feel like the Train is moving at two hundred miles an hour, when he knows it's really probably only something like sixty this early in the journey. But even so ... it's been a while ... and The Foyer isn't that big ... could there be something different with him after all? He knows Hart said everyone thinks that, but they think that* before *they get on the Train, and here Bowler is. He's on it, and he's fine.*

He's waiting for a tug, a pull, an impact, anything, and it's not coming. He looks out of the window for a landmark he recognises, but it's all embankment and hedges, a wall of random greenery. He actually sits back in his seat for a second, not relaxing, just perplexed. This is easy.

Something isn't right.

He hears a kid screech in the seat behind, and in a moment of utter shock, he feels the kid kick the back of his seat, and his current confusion is so intense that it's not until he hears the mother telling the child to sit still that he realises he felt the kid kick the back of the seat.

What? He felt *that? How did he feel the kid kick the seat? What the hell is happening? And how did the kid kick it so hard that he's bent the seat out of shape—it has a solid plastic back—but he must have done, because he can feel it all different against his back, and that is when he looks down and sees that his stomach and buttocks have actually pulled back into the seat itself, and the pressure on his chest that he hadn't noticed—it wasn't as sharp or sudden as the one in his lower back—begins to increase, and he sees his whole torso descend into the seat back.*

All his senses kick into overdrive as he realises he's hit the edge of The Wall, has done a while ago, and didn't even feel it. But now he does. His hands begin to shake rapidly, but, thinking quickly, Bowler closes his eyes and wills *his torso out of the seat. It's not too hard, as the resistance isn't enormous, but almost as soon as he gets his form under control, he feels the pushing sensation building up rapidly.*

He's thinking too fast to be truly scared now, despite the realisation (I'M IN IT, I'M IN THE FUCKING WALL, I'M IN THE WALL, THIS IS WHAT HART WAS TALKING ABOUT, I'M GOING TO BE HURT, I'M GOING TO BE HURT SO MUCH, OH GOD) that he's in The Wall now, that this is where the fight begins, and with that realisation all Bowler's thoughts turn to locking this in. This is what he thought when he boarded the Train, what he thought when he decided to even attempt this; that he is going to be able to push through, because he will *be able to take it farther than anyone else. He'll do it for her, for himself and for her, and he grits his teeth and feels the push settle in.*

It's now enormous, suddenly enormous *(OH GOD HOW IS IT GETTING THIS STRONG SO FAST) before he has time to comprehend it. It's a wall of solid force all around him. It's more than gravity, more than a feeling of g-force or weight, it's actually* there, *it actually has a physical presence now. He can feel it pushing against his features. It feels like a blanket of fine fibres, like a blanket stretched across the entire carriage, and it feels so solid that he knows that if he were to lift his hand he would be able to stroke its surface, to feel the fibres under his skin. It's tightest on his knees, but feels the worst on his nose—pushing the tip slightly flat—and now Bowler realises that he is unable to move or stand if he wanted to. To do so would mean a shift of focus, and at this level of pressure he can't do that at all; he would be pushed straight through the seat and out of the back of train, which even now is picking up speed and forcing him harder,* harder *against The Wall.*

All that's keeping him in it now is his own will, keeping him locked in the Train as it thunders forward, and for the first time he fully doubts himself as the pain begins at his nose. He feels it and just has time to realise with horror that this is where it gets really bad as his nose starts to flatten, spreading the pain outwards across his eyes, and round to his temples, round the back of his head and suddenly his whole head is on fire, then his neck, chest, stomach, legs. It's a burning pain, like each individual fibre of The Wall, the super fine cables that surely must make it up, are slicing their way into his skin and squeezing him flat, like the solid wall of some enormous, terrible, fibrous hydraulic press. And still Bowler pushes.

If he could see himself, Bowler would see his entire body flattening smoothly, and to the thickness of a magazine. He eyes feel like they are boiling now, and he can no longer see through pain and pressure. He would be screaming but he can't; it's like trying to make your hand work once your arm's gone to sleep. And there's a sudden thundering in his ears, rapidly rising to a deafening roar, like bubbles rushing past your eardrum underwater, only louder, and now it's agonisingly loud. The pain reaches a crescendo as his body flattens and his skin begins to split, peeling backwards on his arms and flying out behind him like streamers on a kid's bicycle handle.

And still he pushes. It's all he can think to do.

And suddenly, Bowler feels something snap.

And the pain stops.

For a moment, the relief is so complete, total, and indescribably wonderful that Bowler bursts into hysterical tears.

He then stops almost immediately as he realises that he can't. He can't because the pressure is still there, only pain free. It's an impossible weight on his entire body, but it's like he's aware of it on a different level. No pain means it's comprehension only; Bowler knows there is huge pressure, and he cannot move, and that is all he is aware of on the subject. His panicked mind can't grasp it, as well it shouldn't, for even his rational mind would struggle.

He opens his eyes, with difficulty—now the pain is gone he can see, but the sheer force makes it hard to get his eyes open—and looks to see what has happened. The Train is still moving—if anything, at its greatest pace yet— and the people are all still there, oblivious and reading magazines, listening to music, staring out of the window, talking to or ignoring the people they're sharing a seat with, not wishing to talk to a stranger.

Bowler watches for minute, squint-eyed, trying to get what's happening. What the fuck is going on? The thought slowly comes to his battered consciousness; did he make it, then? What happens now? Straining, juddering, his manages to work his forehead downwards, slowly craning his neck against the pressure to look down at his body. It's not down there.

His body, from the neck downwards, is spooled out along the length of the carriage behind him, like silly putty stretched thin. It continues all the way to The Wall and disappears through it. He can only assume that his legs are somewhere on the other side of the carriage divide, but it's hard to say where because his clothes have disappeared now (this realisation comes to him through his freshly returned terror). He's just one long stream of flesh, pale pink chewing gum, and he's stretching even farther. He can see the thin length of rubber that is his body drawing thinner and thinner, stretching out as the Train progresses, and he crazily thinks of that guy from the comics, the stretchy guy with the rock guy and the other ones, and he struggles to get his mind under control as he knows he has to make a decision; let go now or keep going. Is this another stage to get through, like before? Is it? Bowler frantically tries to get his head together, a feat near impossible while seeing

your body drawn out behind you like hot toffee.
WHERETHEHELLAREHISFEET

And the answer comes to him as the question is made; they are back where the pressure began, where he hit The Wall. He's stretching. But maybe, maybe, maybe, maybe if he holds on, he'll snap back, he'll stretch that far and pop through, maybe that's how you do it! How you make *it! But … he could pop back the other way. But so what? He'd only be back where he was bef—*

Suddenly there's something else. Something else that comes in as his body is now stretched so thin that the stream of flesh behind him is less than a foot wide. What is it? A feeling. A presence. A change in the air, the atmosphere, but it's something … it's in every fibre of his being, and it's growing. It's something big, something vast, something incomprehensibly enormous … something he's only just brushing against, getting a sense of, but it's growing, and he's more aware …

He looks around the carriage, and sees he's the only one feeling it. Of course he is, he knows *where he is, but it's still so weird to be feeling this and have no one around even bat an eyelid, and now his vision is changing. As that feeling grows in him—what the hell is it, he can't describe it—his vision starts to change, and everything seems a bit more … hazy. Harder to see. Like the contrast on a TV being turned down, slowly, and the colour just being that little bit less* there, *and then he realises what the feeling is.*

It's not something growing, it's something leaving. Everything is becoming less. The pressure on his body is still there, but it's going because the feeling in his body is as well, and his sight … his thoughts now, he realises, not words, just feelings, awareness, dimming to instinct, and now the lights are getting darker and it's only because his thoughts are simplifying, that there's nothing to look at because everything is going *that he finally understands what he's brushing up against.*

It's not something crazily big after all. It's the other end of the scale entirely. Every cell of his body, every instinct in his mind now knows *this, as certain as anything he has ever known in his life, and he knows this because he is rushing into it, stretching away into it. It's too big to comprehend, no, not too big, too not-big, too not there, it's a nothingness so all-encompassing that if he understood even a fraction of it then his mind would cease to exist.*

It's oblivion, and Bowler is on a speeding train heading straight toward it.

It's the worst thing he will ever know.

Bowler's eyes roll over and—with a horror that takes a piece of him that never will return—he unlocks, he lets go.

***

Hart caught up with Bowler in seconds, just as the Bluey stopped outside the newsagents next to the cobbler's, fiddling in her purse for something. She hadn't gotten far; the two had sat in shock for only milliseconds, and she hadn't been walking at any particular pace.

This Bluey was a woman in her mid-fifties, well dressed, probably on her way to work. Sensible skirt with black boots, matching a short black suede jacket. Dark, greying hair, worn short, revealing a pair of stud earrings. High features that, though still elegant and attractive, would have turned many more heads twenty years ago.

But neither man gave Shit One about any of that. All they cared about was the pale blue glow all around her. Seeing it up close was a breathless revelation for Hart. He could barely keep himself under control, for here was *change*, here was only the second new thing to happen to his world since he'd arrived, the first being tuning in permanently with Bowler. It was a hint, a clue, a way of *understanding*. It was the single most exciting thing he had ever seen. Had he looked down, he would have noticed that his self-control had disappeared so much that his feet had sunk into the concrete.

The blue aura was constant; there was no flicker, no parts where it was stronger than others. It was completely even, and though the colour itself was pale, it had strength, a thickness to it that was unmistakable. It made no sound, and to Hart it looked like it was made of some magic, solid plastic that could move in whatever manner the woman did. Aura wasn't even the right word; that was the first one that came to mind, the first word to describe light around a person. It wasn't a glow; it had an edge. A clear, definable edge, an *outline*. It was more like a blue *layer*, hovering just above her skin and clothes.

Both Hart and Bowler moved slowly and simultaneously, reaching out their right hands to touch it. They caught each other's eyes as they did so, and Bowler looked for approval, despite the fact that his hand kept going before he got an answer. Hart nodded, looking into Bowler's wide-eyed expression with a matching one of his own. Bowler was clearly shocked and excited, but despite this, Hart could see the younger man was taken aback by seeing Hart looking the same way. Understandable, thought Hart. There'd never been a moment when Hart had seen anything like this. He was so light-headed he thought he might faint—even though he knew it was impossible here—and as he looked back at the Bluey, seeing his hand about to touch one, to, *to touch an actual Bluey*, he thought he may finally go Loose when his fingers reached it.

Their hands met the blue edge and passed straight through, as if they'd misjudged the distance and it had only looked like they were close enough to touch. No resistance, not even a breeze. The blue layer didn't even colour their hands once they went through it; they seemed to be above it, even though Hart could clearly see his hand had gone inside the edge of the blueness. To Bowler, it was exactly the same as when you went to see a movie in 3D, and grabbed for whatever you saw. Your hand was in it, and yet over it at the same time. Touching the blue light was like a bizarre optical illusion.

Hart's disappointment was like a knife in his lungs. He didn't know what he'd expected—and hadn't *really* expected a revelation—but there was always that chance, that possibility that there would have been a shock, a vision, some sort of connection to something bigger. And in the end it was so insubstantial that the disappointment wasn't worth it. Without realising, Hart's hand dropped.

No, he thought. That was no way to be right now. Any second the Bluey might walk right out of The Foyer—there was no way she lived within it, she was old and Hart would have seen her before now if she did—and they had to make the most of this. Think objectively. Look for clues. Focus.

Bowler was still passing his hand in and out of the blue layer, watching it. He hadn't been here long enough to realise how incredible being this close to one was, and perhaps it was this that meant he was actually one step ahead of Hart in figuring out possibilities for learning.

We need to follow her to The Wall. See what happens when she passes through. And maybe we can communicate with her!

He assumed Hart was already thinking this. Bowler put his hand back in the blue and spoke.

"Lady! Hey, lady! Can you hear me?"

Hart almost slapped himself on the head. Of course! He did the same, using both hands after seeing Bowler get nothing from his one-handed effort. The Bluey finally found what she was rummaging for—a small black mobile phone—and began to dial.

"Miss! Miss! Hello!" yelled Hart. Nothing. Louder. "*Miss!! Miss!! Hello!!*" Bowler joined in, this time stepping bodily into the blue, half into the Bluey's body, ignoring the unpleasantness, and yelling at the top of his lungs into her head.

"*Aaaaah!! Lady!! Hey! Hey! Aaahhh!!!*" Hart dived in too, and now his and Bowler's foreheads were touching in the middle of the Bluey's skull.

"Miiiiss!! Miiiiisss!!! Yayayayayayayayayayayayayayayayayaya!!"

A horrible feeling of desperation overtook them as the shouting continued, both of them hoping they were shouting to be heard by anyone that might finally save them.

They stood there for the duration of the woman's conversation (all ten minutes of it, while she discussed what exactly to get Lisa for her birthday, as she didn't want to spoil her even though Lisa was Sarah's first, and not wanting to outshine whatever Sarah got her, as they've not been as flush since Steven lost his job) all the while unaware of the two screaming men inside her head. Men losing that little bit more of whatever hope they had left, and doing so with their eyes shut lest the other's gaze confirm that they both knew it.

Hart gave up first, stepping back and turning away so Bowler could not see the tears, nor the way he was screwing up his face painfully in an attempt to stop them. He bit his teeth together with vicious force.

Bowler stopped when Hart stopped, stepping back quietly, head down. He knew something had happened quickly there, and something had gotten out of hand. He was embarrassed and didn't really understand why. He knew Hart was too; that's why Hart was standing with his back to him, now with his hands on his hips, breathing heavily. Bowler was struck by the last time he'd felt that desperation. *Suzie, please, let's talk properly, I'll talk properly, I won't shout again,* please. He pushed the thought away as best he could; he was confused enough as it was.

Bowler decided to let Hart decide what to do next, unless the Bluey moved. This was still too precious to let go, and he knew Hart knew it too. This became more evident a split second later when, as they heard the Bluey close her phone with a snap, Hart whipped round, red-eyed, and pointed.

"We'll follow," he said, quietly. "Eventually, she'll reach The Wall." Bowler nodded, silently. Hart continued speaking, unconsciously adjusting his suit, composing himself as his mind searched for more ideas, more possibilities. They followed the Bluey as she walked through the small archway by the cobbler's place, into the tiny plaza beyond that led onto the Bull Yard, and an idea seized Hart.

We'll try and be inside *the blue when she passes through The Wall! Perhaps—*

And a terrible fear gripped him as he thought it. He'd been on the Train, just like Bowler. He'd felt what lay beyond The Wall. What if he was right, and by being in the blue they could get through ... and that was all that was there? That leaving The Foyer through The Wall meant that was what you got? That by breaking through The Wall and not by going some other way that you found yourself in oblivion, sucked away into that ultimate nothing? No matter how bad things ever were in here, that was just ... but then again, perhaps, if you went through with a Bluey, *in* the blue, you went somewhere else—

That was when Hart noticed Bowler had stopped dead behind the newsagents, slightly crouched, looking straight ahead. Even with his mind swirling with ideas and possibilities, he thought this annoyingly odd. What on earth was Bowler doing? Here they were, with the biggest potential breakthrough of Hart's entire afterlife, and not only was Bowler not following, he was actually just standing still like a dimwit! He opened his mouth to vent his frustration, and then saw a woman—a middle-aged early commuter in a thick black fleece—Pass Through Bowler without Bowler even trying to get out of the way.

What on earth?

As he looked at Bowler incredulously, he noticed the look in Bowler's eyes for the first time, and saw the terrified expression on his face. Bowler was scared; he was scared of the Bluey? Hart then properly noticed Bowler's body language. Not just standing still; frozen.

Bowler was trying not to move. Trying not to be seen.

What the blazes was going on? He took a step forward, and froze himself as Bowler's eyes widened almost comically and darted towards him, accompanied by an almost imperceptible shake of the head. At that moment—even before Bowler's darting, gesturing eyes told him to look behind him—the penny finally dropped, horribly, and Hart felt his scalp and testicles tighten with fear as he realised what was going on. Of course. They were in deep, deep, *deep* trouble. Nevertheless, Hart turned his head extremely slowly over his right shoulder. That would be where the danger was. To his right, and slightly behind. On the other side of the square; of *course* he would have been too busy watching the Bluey to see.

He looked across to the corner of the deserted plaza and found— terribly—that he was right. There, so big and dark as to look almost superimposed against the glass front of the cafe, *impossibly* huge, completely at odds with the mundane surroundings, stood The Beast.

He saw them.

***

Bowler awakes to an indescribable pain. So intense that all thought is blocked out. He cannot form coherent thoughts. All he is aware of is a few, basic things.

The pain.

He cannot feel his body.

He cannot see.

He cannot think properly.

And some part of his brain registers through the agony that he must be back in the cloud, but different, some sort of pain cloud. There was pain on the Train. The Train. He was on the Train. That hurt more than this. This is very bad, but the Train was worse.

"Hello, Bowler," says a voice. "Sorry it took me so long to get here. I don't know what I was thinking."

He doesn't recognise Hart's voice, doesn't assign a face to it. He can't. He endures the pain, and listens in darkness, lost.

"I know you can't see me. You will, eventually. It's just going to take a long time. A few weeks, normally."

Bowler listens, and somehow feels the white hot steel fibres of fire pushed through every piece of his skin even though it doesn't seem to be a part of him, and this time he can't understand these words.

"I call this being Broken ... It's hardest when your mind comes back just enough to be aware, and be conscious, and you're in the dark, and can't talk ... but you still can't think enough ..."

Silence for a long time. Bowler doesn't know it's only about four seconds, but it seems like an afternoon of pain to him.

"But for you, it's going to be easier. I'm going to sit with you. All the way through it. Just like in the beginning, do you remember? I'm going to talk to you again. I'm going to help you through. It won't be as bad. Okay? I'm ... I'm here."

Hart tries to think of something to say to pass the time. Nothing will help any more than anything else, so he thinks of a tale to tell.

"Did I ever tell you about the second time I tried to break The Wall? I know this sounds unbelievable, but I tried a second time. Not on the Train, obviously, but this was too good an opportunity to pass up. Plus, my thinking was, this time I knew when to let go, once I could tell it wasn't going to work. I'd already experienced what happens. But this had to be tried. You see, no one had ever tried going over The Wall before. And some promotional thing was going on in town with a helicopter. A helicopter, can you imagine? George was there too, this would have been oh, 1980 maybe. He didn't come with me though, thought it wouldn't work and I'd end up Broken again myself, and he wouldn't go through that again ... sorry," Hart added, checking himself.

"Anyway, I thought I'd be fine as I'd know when it wasn't going to work. I'd felt *what happens when you push against The Wall*, but I didn't know if *The Foyer* had a ceiling, *you see*.

Bowler hears Hart sigh, and wishes he could scream.

"Turns out it did. I had to jump out of the helicopter before I pushed too far. Unfortunately ... I hit the ground so hard that I went straight through it, and I mean completely *through it. Turns out The Foyer has its own floor, too. It's a little way down. We don't sink that far if we don't concentrate, but you can go down that far if you Pass Through the floor whilst falling at terminal velocity. The impact was unspeakable. I was Broken all over again. George saw roughly where I fell though, he came to help. Put me in someone's flat so that I could at least hear the TV. That helped some."*

The sun is beginning to dip in the sky, and on the section of railway where he knew he would find Bowler, at the very edge of The Wall—Bowler had pushed quite far, but he had sprang back no farther out than anyone else ever had, as Hart knew he wouldn't—shadows are lengthening, cast onto the gravel between the sleepers, and onto the grass on either side, hedges and fields beyond. They are not that far out from the station. Hart wishes he could make a fire. It would be nice.

He looks at Bowler's flattened out body. Stretched out, coiled up, skin torn and loosened. Broken. Eventually, he knows, it will start to reform as Bowler's mind does, but that is a long way away. And there will be times when he has to leave Bowler alone for a while, though he doesn't say that. Weeks out here, alone, talking to himself, will mean he needs to go back for TV or some kind of input, and go back regularly at that.

"It's not just hitting The Wall at speed that can do it, you know," he says, putting his arms around his knees and sitting forward. "I've seen it. The Guests ... obviously, you know we can touch each other. But that means—and you've probably thought about this—we can hurt each other."

He looks up to see a plane leaving trails across the sky, remembering. His brow furrows.

"We can Break each other, providing we hurt each other badly enough. It takes a lot though; a broken arm or something won't do it. It has to be injuries equivalent to, say, a car crash. That sort of thing. Like I say … I've seen it."

Screams. Roaring. Hell before his very eyes.

"That's why you have to fear The Beast."

Hart looks at his feet now, as he talks.

"Because if The Beast catches you, he'll hurt you very badly indeed. And … well, I've even seen The Beast hurt people so badly … they stay *Broken*. True, these were Guests that were already Loose or close to it, but they end up even worse. It is possible, you know. I saw them lying there for two months, reforming, in the same place, never moving. And when they eventually fully reform … they're gone. Broken so badly their mind never recovers."

He shudders.

"That's why, when you see The Beast—or hear him—you run. You run as fast as you can. Even though he's faster."

***

Chapter 5: In Which the Deal Is Still On, Everybody Loves George, The Hell Debate Occurs, We Learn How the Deal Was Made, And Discover the Horror of the Westward Room

***

The Beast focused his attention on the Bluey. He watched her as she walked away from him, oblivious to his presence.

Bowler and Hart were both frozen to the spot now, not sure what to do. The Beast had seen them, so running was probably a bad idea; depending on his mood, he would probably give chase. If he was in one of his lucid, more intelligent states, he might give chase and hurt them for fun. If he was angry, he definitely would. If they were extremely lucky, and he was in one of his dense and docile moods—which happened rarely—he might ignore them due to his own confusion.

Either way, this one was a terrifying conundrum. He *had* seen them, yes, but was temporarily distracted by the Bluey. If they ran and he gave chase, he would be on them in seconds. Hart's mind was racing; his terror was total. He desperately, desperately hoped The Beast would follow the Bluey, and they could slip away. He scarcely dared look at Bowler, but could see out of the corner of his eye that the younger man was frozen to the spot. He wouldn't move until Hart did. He'd never been this close to The Beast. Not many had, without being Broken.

The Beast was easily nine feet tall now, the biggest Hart had ever seen him. He remembered when The Beast had been about eight feet, back when Hart had first arrived. He'd been incredibly dangerous, even then, but hadn't attacked quite as much. And when he did, he would hurt people, then grow bored. Now, he didn't. It seemed his sadism had grown along with his size. Hart still wondered just how mad The Beast had gone to get to that point, how long he'd been here, how he'd even *gone* that crazy. Crazy enough to physically change.

The Beast's forehead was enormous, twice the size it should have been, and even more bulbous on the right-hand side, framed all around by a mane of wiry black hair. It came forward over his eyes like a coastal shelf, shadowing his eyes to the point where you could barely see them. His jaw was far wider than his head, with a slight under bite. His hands were disproportionately large too, enough to completely cover a man's face. Hart knew this for a fact. His shoulders hunched up higher than they should be, huge and wide, making him seem more like a bull than a human.

The Beast was the only one in The Foyer who—in Hart's time, at least—appeared in different clothes at different times. They seemed to be in a constant state of flux, flickering slightly on The Beast's frame, like they weren't sure what they were supposed to be. Today they consisted of a huge black donkey jacket buttoned up over a pair of white dress trousers, with incredibly well-polished black shoes. The buttoned-up jacket made him look even larger than normal.

His skin was so white it looked like he'd been painted. Against the black of his jacket, he'd never looked so terrifying.

"Bowler," muttered Hart, not moving a fraction. Bowler's eyes darted to Hart, but other than that the younger man made no other movement. They stood with more stillness than a living man could attain, fear lending them focus to stop their chests rising and falling, enough focus on staying still to remember that they didn't need to expand their lungs anymore.

"Sshhh …" replied Bowler, saying it gently and drawing it out to make it quieter.

The Beast's colossal head turned as the Bluey passed him by, considering her the way a big dog considers the flitting motions of a butterfly, mildly inquisitive and curious. A shovel-sized—no exaggeration— hand came out gently, slowly, and passed straight through her, the way someone will trail their hand through water.

He's going to follow, thought Hart, *the second he turns his back, we're running.*

But to Hart's shock, he saw The Beast smile at the Bluey, and chuckle lightly in his throat the way someone will smile at a private joke. *He* knows *something!* thought Hart. *He knows—*

The second realisation hit him just before The Beast turned his head and looked directly at them, the smile turning to a gleeful grin, the eyes bulging huge and white beneath that vast brow.

If he knows something, that means he's lucid. He's noticed us all along. He's playing with us—

He just had time to yell "*Bowler, run and don't st—*" but The Beast had already bent his hands to the floor like the world's biggest and most terrible gorilla, still grinning, and with a silent roar—which made it worse— dropped his head low and came for them, galloping across the small plaza, a huge black nightmare right before their eyes.

***

"*The worst time to get caught by him is when he's switched on, when he's aware. Because he's unbelievably cruel. He delights in hurting people, in breaking them. I think in some ways—and this is just my own, cod psychology—he wants other people to suffer like he does. Because he must be in terrible suffering, being stuck here and being like that. But I've no pity; I've*

80

seen what he does to people. The delight he has in watching them scream. I've seen him make it last for days.

And when he's self-aware, that's when he's hardest to lose. Because he's clever. *He can be* very *clever. At any other time—and if you're lucky—you might be able to lose him. But if he finds you after you've made him hunt for you, if he gets you then … then he's* desperate *to hurt you."*

***

The Beast fell upon them, catching them both in opposite hands. Its grip was unbreakably strong. Bowler was sure he felt the bones in his arm bend as The Beast squeezed, and as he did so he realised The Beast was laughing, silent to Bowler's ears, but The Beast's whole body was shaking with it. It was a big laugh, and it was pure malice. The Beast then lifted them by the arms and smashed them both bodily together the way a child would when making toys fight, his laughter and convulsions growing as Hart and Bowler cried out in pain.

He flung Bowler down and gripped his foot, squeezing it hard and fracturing several bones instantly. Bowler screamed again, and The Beast roared with laughter as he released Bowler and grabbed Hart by the nape of the neck, hefting him into the air and flinging him down to the street. This wouldn't have hurt in itself, but the force was enough for Hart to go all the way down to The Wall floor beneath the stone slabs of the courtyard. He hit it and bounced off, feeling something crack in his collarbone and shift again as his body instinctively settled itself on the concrete.

He opened his eyes to see Bowler come crashing down upon him, thrown down by The Beast, who was screaming with laughter now. Their heads collided and Hart's vision flashed white, making him think drunkenly, *I can't be knocked out here,* as Bowler was lifted up for a second throw.

He's just getting warmed up, thought Hart. *He's playing with us before the real torture begins.* Ignoring the pain in his shoulder, and powered by survival instinct, he struggled to his feet. The Beast towered over him, blocking out the light and casting a long shadow that made him look even bigger. He held Bowler aloft in his left hand by the back of the young man's top, inspecting him, and The Beast's massive chest shook with more uproarious silent laughter. Bowler was yelling in pain, his leg pulled up to his chest so he could hold his shattered foot. Hart struggled to stay standing in his fear.

The Beast drew Bowler back for another throw—he was enjoying this game—and an idea flashed through Hart's mind. He turned and looked across the plaza behind him. It led to a covered avenue of shops, a small statue of Peeping Tom at the top of the archway. About thirty or forty feet away this avenue split into a fork, a set of downward steps on the left leading to a lower level of shops, and a long downward slope on the right for wheelchairs and strollers and the like, lined by more shops. And both of these led onto ...

Hart whipped round to look at The Beast, who, Hart realised, was returning his gaze. The Beast was cocking his arm to fling Bowler at him, whose own eyes were screwed up as he screamed in pain. Hart saw all this and in a sudden flash of hope saw his idea might work; he might have seen a way to get out before The Beast's playtime warm-up ended and the proper Breaking started. That is, if The Beast was in the mood Hart thought he was.

Hart turned and started to run towards the steps, panic behind his eyes. The steps were better than the slope; it would give them more time before The Beast figured out what was going on. If it worked. He heard Bowler desperately scream his name as he ran, and he thought, or hoped (*PLEASE GOD PLEASE GOD PLEASE LET THIS WORK*) that he might actually get away with this. He braced himself for an impact that he didn't want to happen, but had to hope *would* happen. *Either way, I'm going to be hurt,* he thought. *It's just a question of how much.*

He thought he felt a rush of movement behind him and heard Bowler's screams get progressively louder, very quickly, as if he were approaching at great speed. He didn't dare look back, but he thought the rapidly increasing volume meant he knew what had just happened. *I hope I'm right,* Hart thought just as Bowler finished his flight through the air and hit him across the back, knocking them both clear over the top of the steps and dropping them the twelve feet to the street below.

Hart winced as they fell; they wouldn't hit the concrete fast enough or hard enough to go through to The Wall floor, but their bones would jar as they landed, and the two of them would collide as they hit the street. He was right to be worried. Bowler's knee caught Hart square in his kidney as they went over the steps, and somehow his other leg managed to slam straight into Hart's balls from behind. Hart cried out in pain, as he thought *how in the hell is that even possible,* but his panic dulled the worst of it. His kidney would hurt more later. His balls were hurting perfectly well right then.

On the plus side, as they fell over the edge, they separated in midair and landed two feet away from each other. Hart had been right; as their descent suddenly stopped, it re-jarred Hart's broken collarbone and Bowler's fractured foot. Bowler started screaming afresh, but Hart managed to block out the pain, motivated back into action by the thought of The Beast getting closer. Not quickly though; he'd guessed correctly that The Beast was toying with them, enjoying this, and was taking his time getting to the top of the steps. This was what Hart had been counting on, this time while they were on the ground floor below The Beast's upper level and therefore out of sight. This time unseen to get close enough to where they needed to be before The Beast realised and gave full chase. They had seconds before he saw them, seconds before he saw what Hart was doing and put two and two together.

Hart rushed over to the screaming Bowler and, gritting his teeth, picked him up.

Hart had a strength that greatly contradicted his wiry, thin frame, and was stronger than a casual observer would expect. Plus, bodies in The Foyer were less substantial than living ones. However, picking up Bowler and running with him on a broken collarbone was extremely painful, but fear lent Hart extra will. Hart's collarbone screamed louder than Bowler as he lifted the other man's body, and now Hart joined in the yelling as he straightened, cradling Bowler in his arms.

"What are you doing?" gasped Bowler, as Hart grimaced, bit down, and began to run.

"Shut *up!*" hissed Hart through gritted teeth, eyes narrowed. Above and behind them, he knew that The Beast had reached the top of the stairs. He winced, waiting for the pursuit that he knew would come. The Beast was in smart mode. He'd work it out. And as soon as he did, they'd have seconds. If that.

The Beast followed his prey. This was such fun for him, when they tried to escape. It made everything so sweet. He saw them as they emerged into sight, trying to flee, running forwards. He smelt their fear, and laughed even louder. Didn't they know they weren't fast enough? Didn't they know he could close the gap between them in seconds? He laughed, feeling the pulse inside him, feeling it throb, feeling the rage and passion that kept his confusion away, and it made him happy. Later, he would want the escape of the confusion. It was sometimes a refuge. But then he would get bored, and wake, and want to hunt, as he had done a few hours ago. He saw them run, and decided he'd given them enough hope of escape. It was always a delight to give them a chance, make them believe, and then see it die in their eyes as they looked over their shoulder and saw him rushing silently upon them, already at their heels and reaching out a hand to take them. He prepared to gallop after his quarry, and saw them heading for the road at the end of the row of shops. The dual carriageway. The road where the cars passed.

They were thirty feet from the edge of the road when Hart heard The Beast's roar of rage cut in, the sound suddenly filling the air with that uncanny switched-on-halfway-through sound. Tuned in. *Blast! He worked it out! He's charging! Shit!* Ahead of them, where the row of shops ended, the dual carriageway through town curved round to the left. The very early morning traffic was perfect, enough for there to be the odd car, but not so much that the roads would fill with traffic; moving fast enough to get away, and not enough cars for The Beast to take one too. He redoubled his efforts—even though he was already at full pelt—as fresh terror lent him a second wind. Twenty feet to go now, yet he felt the slam as The Beast landed on the lower level, leaping from the steps to give pursuit. Hart didn't dare look back. It would be terrible, and he couldn't afford for fear to drain his strength. They were ten feet away now, and Hart saw an approaching car, frantically checking the distance to it; would they meet at the right time? If the car was too late, it could be three or four feet too far away if they reached the kerb before it was there, giving The Beast that extra three or four feet to catch them. Appropriately, the oncoming vehicle was a taxi.

He could hear it already, the *slap thud slap thud* of The Beast's lolling, hands-and-feet gallop coming up behind him. He could hear how huge he was, how terrible. *Exactly like a bull. A charging, murderous bull.*

"He's coming!" gasped Bowler, looking over Hart's shoulder. His face was nearly as white as The Beast's, eyes wide.

"Shut *up!!*" Hart told him again, shouting, and now they were about three feet away from the kerb, as he realised that the taxi *was* going to come a good three feet short of where they needed it to be as he heard the snarl of The Beast right behind him. Rolling, gritty laughter, now rumbling way back in its throat.

"*Hart! Haaaarrrt!*" screamed Bowler, gripping Hart's broken collarbone with white knuckles as he saw what was about to fall upon them.

"*Fuck!!!*" screamed Hart for the first time in his existence, in pain and rage and fear, and his first instinct was to hurl Bowler away, to get him off his (*fucking*) collarbone, and in a flash of inspiration he realised that was exactly what he had to do to at least save one of them.

With a scream—not from effort, but from the pain of pulling Bowler's gripping hand from his collarbone as he did so—he hefted Bowler up, one hand behind the small of his back and the other behind his neck, and flung him at the oncoming taxi.

"*Lock in!!!*" he screamed at Bowler as he saw him pass into the back of the approaching car, not having time to see if Bowler came out of the other side as he was already turning on instinct, automatically preparing in terror to defend himself fruitlessly against The Beast who was now upon him. He saw the enormous head and grinning, wide-eyed face filling the world, and if there had been air in The Foyer, The Beast would have been blowing it right into Hart's eyes. Hart braced himself, and then he felt a terrible grip on his neck and was jerked backwards, seeing The Beast suddenly grow smaller, a surprised look on his face.

The grip wasn't terrible; it was beautiful. Bowler had leant right out and grabbed him as the taxi had passed.

He heard Bowler yelling with effort as he pulled, and then his grip was gone as Hart fell back onto the cab floor, legs still sticking out through the door. His collarbone protested at the impact. He scrambled fully inside, ignoring Bowler, and cast a quick glance out the front window— miraculously, *amazingly*, the lights ahead were on green—and then out the back window, where The Beast was roaring in rage by the roadside. At first he was growing smaller, but then he suddenly dropped into that terrible stance and gave pursuit. But the pair's taxi was already at the island at the top of the hill and rounding onto the ring road, and just before they turned off, The Beast was already slowing up. It knew it wouldn't catch them now. Hart saw it straighten, bellowing, and raise one hand. Hart thought he saw it extend a finger, to point after them and mark them, but he couldn't be sure.

He then collapsed onto the floor, pale and trembling, and moaned with relief, somewhere between tears and relieved laughter. He looked at Bowler, now laid out on the backseat, who *was* crying gently, but smiling, raising a hand and giving him the OK sign. And now Hart started to laugh, gasping. He winced as his collarbone moved, but this was too good a moment not to; they'd been caught by The Beast *and escaped!* They'd actually done it! It was inconceivable! Now Bowler was laughing too, and they both sat there, laughing and crying and raising their eyebrows at one another, shaking their heads in disbelief.

When Bowler said, "Hospital please, driver," they both went into hysterics, and even when the cab started to hit The Wall and they both quietly dropped out of the backseat, they laughed harder.

They lay there on Quinton Road, cars driving over them, as their laughter turned to giggles. After several minutes of this, Hart stood, wincing, and helped Bowler up.

"Thanks, man," said Bowler, as Hart helped him limp to the roadside. Neither of them really liked being run through by cars. Old habits, again. They sat down on the kerb, watching the cars go past for a few moments, as they got their breath back.

"We're going to need to lie low somewhere for a bit, aren't we?" said Bowler. "I mean, ideally, we'd keep moving, but with my foot, we'd be too, y'know ... vulnerable out in the open. I mean, I'll be all right in a day or two, right? That's how it works. I mean, I've never had anything other than the Train."

"Yes," said Hart, airily, still light-headed from what they'd just achieved. They'd actually gotten *away.* "You'll heal very fast here. And I'm hurt too, remember. I'd think at least a week, to be honest. So we'll need to hide out somewhere, just to be on the safe side. I'd better think of somewhere."

Bowler muttered something, and it took Hart a minute to realise what he'd said. The younger man was now inspecting his nails, that horrible shifty look back on his face. Hart waited.

"Well ..." said Bowler. "Look ... you don't have to come with me, if you've got a place you'd rather go. I mean, I know we have a deal and all, but that's a perfectly good place to lie low ..."

Hart managed to bite his anger down. They'd only just gotten things back on track after one horrendous row, and things were still delicate. He had to handle this one correctly.

"Bowler. I've just saved you from being Broken—"

"I saved you back—"

"*And* you are not to going where you're thinking about, because that debt you've just gotten into means the deal is on now more than ever. Do you understand? You are never to go there ever again. We agreed to this. Didn't we?"

Silence.

"Bowler?"

"Okay."

There was a pause. Cars continued to pass.

"It's the right thing for you. You do know that, don't you?"

"Yeah."

"Anyway ... I know a place we can go that's not far from here. It's right on the edge of The Wall; might make us harder to find. Come on. We'd better move."

***

It's coming to the end of Bowler's four terrible weeks. He's almost totally back in his body, and his mind is almost back together. His relief would be near total, if not for the fact that he knows he will not be the same now. He knows already something is different. But anything is better than what he has just been through.

He's back in Mary's flat; once he was physically together enough to be moved, and not a seemingly endless bundle of flesh, Hart carried him there. It was better for Hart too, the TV meaning that he could leave Bowler sometimes, get out, walk around, "talk" with Sarah and George and even Mark, if he could find him. The others, of course—the Loose Guests—wouldn't talk. If they even let themselves be seen.

Breaking through The Wall isn't allowed, *thinks Bowler.* You have to get out some other way.

The thought comforts him. And now he's nearing the end—he can feel it—he feels well enough to confront the new memories.

It's as if—before his mind was dislodged and abused and spread—his mind was like a drink in a glass with the flavour settled on the bottom. The Train changed that. It had stuck a swizzle stick in there and swirled that bastard up, and now the juicy bits were floating on the top, accessible. Not all of them ... but new ones.

Not good ones.

It had made the last three and a half weeks so, so much worse.

Bowler remembers.

***

1998:

Suzie is still up; he can see the light on in the bedroom window above. Every part of his rational mind is saying to leave it, to go back to the

nearest boozer and stay there until they kick him out. And when he comes home, Suzie will be asleep. *That* will be better.

But a night of boozing has put Bowler on a roll. His momentum is there, and with that, his courage. He's tired of the rows, of the self-recrimination, of looking in the mirror and hating himself. Of constantly having to think on his feet for answers. He *hates* that. It stresses him out. And it's all the time now.

These are the thoughts that have been rattling round in his head, as he sat in The Beer Engine, then Whitefriars, then The Oak, then Lloyds. He fucking hated it in Lloyds. Too noisy. Couldn't hear himself think. He draws his too-thin jacket in tight around him as he walks. The cold is intense tonight. He'd have bought a decent winter coat if he could have afforded it. What was Suzie's word? *Frivolous.* It would have been a *Frivolous* purchase. It doesn't seem so *Frivolous* now, as he stands behind the row of bus shelters freezing, the street and the shops behind him, looking up the narrow cobbled path toward the cathedral and the small flats to the right that contain his home.

He steps forward, and hesitates. Did he really want to do this? He takes a deep breath, lets it out.

Right. Fuck it. If there's enough in the pocket for another drink, I'm going twenty steps in the other *direction to the Weatherspoons.*

He fumbles in his pocket for his change, fingers grubbing to make sure he's got it all, then he pulls it all out and counts.

Not even close; £1.75.

He sighs again, blowing the air out forcefully now, turning the sigh into a psyche up, and starts to walk. He should never have stalled; his fear is greater now, but he pushes it back as best he can.

Then he's already inside, up the stairs, and putting the key into his front door. He feels cold inside. Hollow. Sick, and it's not the vodkas. He pushes the door open gently, delicately, and walks into the small hallway. It's dark, lit only by the thin halo of light around the closed living room door. He can hear the TV on. It's peaceful in the hallway, comforting. He's scared of the other side of that door, frightened by the possibility of a memory of warmth, frightened that it might take away his resolve or hurt him and make him think again.

But he knows it's gone too far. It's time to talk. He strides to the living room door and opens it without hesitation.

Suzie is sat on the settee, legs curled up alongside her. She's wearing a pair of his joggers, combined with a lazy, about-the-house jumper, her long blonde hair pulled loosely up on her head in a ponytail. It's her usual end of the week wear, the sort of thing she's always worn on a Friday night. It doesn't do justice to how pretty she is, yet at the same time it does because she's able to shine through it, proving how good she looks in it. And similarly, he loves it and hates it in the same breath. He loves it because it's just her, relaxed and low maintenance, warm and soft and loving. The way she always was with him. So much so—that level of dedication—that he sometimes felt awkward. It meant he would be that little bit more mean to her just because he could, would push her just to get her to stand up to him, would overreact over nothing just to get her to stand up for herself. And after she did, she would be hurt and things between them would be that little bit less. And he hates this reminder because she is *not* that way these days—that now-missing level of dedication—and it's a mockery. It's a disguise. It's a shell, a painted face. These thoughts are really of the way she *used* to be. That will never return, and just as he feared, it's *extremely* painful to know, made worse because he knows there's no turning back.

She has a glass of red wine in her hand, and on the floor is the bottle. It's nearly empty. And he realises she hasn't looked up at him yet. She was supposed to start shouting.

He feels anger starting to build, and it feels good, in a self-righteous way. She's being rude, and it gives him a leg to stand on. It gives him confidence.

He opens his mouth to speak, but she does before he gets the chance.

"Are you waiting for something?"

She's still looking at the TV, and she's caught him unawares. She turns to look at him now, a soft, patronising smile on her lips that makes his hand twitch, and he struggles to see any lingering affection in her eyes. Right now, in fact, there is none. And now it comes to it, he hasn't got anything to say. He doesn't know where to start.

"No," he says, resorting to flatness, curtness, in lieu of anything else. And he adds, dumbly, "Are you?" Inwardly, he winces.

She chuckles, and it's a sneer. She's drunk too.

"Very good, Frank. On top form, there." She takes a sip from her glass that becomes a gulp. "Unfortunately, how drunk you are isn't going to shock or impress me either, tonight," she says, scooping up the bottle and pouring the last of it into her glass. "Because as you can clearly see, I'm not too shabby myself. How was *your* night, Frank? Had a good time feeling sorry for yourself? But that's *all* you do these days, isn't it?" She points an unsteady finger at him. "That's your favourite pastime now, eh?" No shouting. Calm speech. That was worse. This was going wrong from the start. He had it scripted in his head, and it was supposed to start with her shouting when he walked in.

"Fuck off," Bowler says quietly, and walks into the kitchen, needing a chance to regroup. This isn't going how he'd anticipated an hour ago. He fumbles open the cupboard to get a pint glass, to get some water in him and help him focus, but she's gotten up and padded in behind him. Shortie Suzie, as he used to laugh with her, all 5'2" of her. She's still holding the glass, and the anger inside her is on her face now, the smug front dropping away.

"You think I should?" she says. "You think that's fair, do you?"

Bowler is at the sink, filling up the glass. This is clearly not the time for confrontation. He can't get his head together, and is suddenly very emotional and confused. She needs to be punished with silence, he decides. This is the best option. He's angry too, but he can't drop the bombshell now; he expected shouting, that would have made it easy. Best to get out of there, start again another time. It's all gone wrong.

"Do what you like, Suzie. I'm going to bed."

But she's barring the doorway now, and as he goes to leave, she doesn't move. He can't stop this now without calming down, *backing* down, and that isn't going to happen.

"Let me ask you something. You remember Glasgow? You remember all that?" Bowler rolls his eyes, but only for her benefit, to annoy her and to hide the fact that she had been successful with smashing him in the emotional balls. An incredibly hurtful, cruel question. How could she use that so casually? Who was this?

"Yeah, of course you do," she continues, voice shaking and eyes watering as she nods at her own statement. "*I'll* never forget it, as long as I live. You probably won't either. But here's the thing, Frank; how long did I wallow over that? Over something as, as, as *devastating* as that? Any ideas?"

Bowler folds his arms and sets his jaw. His own anger is building now as he realises she is turning Glasgow into a weapon, and also because he knows what her point is going to be, and knows already that she is right.

"And last year, Frank, when Corrigan gave you the boot? You remember that, when this ... this *bullshit* started?" Suzie never swears. The most she ever normally manages is a very quiet *Shit* when, and only when, she was near tears. There are no full tears here. Just watery eyes from her anger. Her face is red, and her eyes are accusing slits staring up into his face. "What was I always saying? *It'll be all right, it'll be all right, I make enough, I make enough.* But you went off into your own little world, and never came back. *You.* When I'd done nothing of the sort, I'd done nothing like that even when we'd lost ..." She stops herself, composes herself, swallows. She then goes on, mouth turned up into a hurt sneer. "And I kept trying, kept trying to keep everything nice, while all you wanted to do was make me feel guilty about something as shitty and pointless and *nothing* like money! Pushing me away, until the idea of everything being nice became a sick joke! Over money! *Money! Nothing!* When I was there for both of us after ..." She stops again and folds her own arms now, openly shaking her head at him, assessing him and finding him sorely lacking.

"So here's the thing," she continues, with a stiff, bitter smile. "Who do you think had the bigger thing to feel sorry for themselves about? Who had the bigger thing to overcome for the sake of us? Who cared enough?" And for a second she weakens, and the way she used to look at him flashes across her face, and then it's gone, replaced by near hate. It's the saddest thing he's ever seen. It's a tragedy.

"But you wouldn't, would you? A job, a ... a fucking job!" A bit of her spit catches him near his eye as she shouts. "Everything else I could handle, all the arguments, but that, *that* you couldn't even pull your head out of your arse to save *us* ..." She deflates now, quickly, sadness drawing her back in. "You'd rather go out and run away, and leave me alone. And that's when I started to think differently. It really surprised me at first, the very thought that we could ever end. The thought that I could find someone else who *would* try."

Bowler realises that she's been doing the exact same thing he has; drinking to prepare for this. And his skin has a cold rush, and he starts to panic a little. He doesn't want to hear this at all, because he can see that she's calming down, and fast, because she's leaving behind the thing she *is* upset by; the sad memories. And by catching up to the present, she's calming down. The distance is coming back.

"And I realised something else, Frank. I mean, I don't know if you were always like this and I didn't see it—I don't think so, you know, because before Glasgow you were just so ... *there*, always there—but I realised that now, at least ... you're a coward." And she says this last bit with so little emotion—she's bang up to date now, right back to where she was before the shouting started—that the contrast is stunning, her eyes gently examining his face, as if she was thinking *what did I ever see in this guy*. The woman who once said *I've never met anyone like you* and *Don't ever let me go* and *I love you so much, I'd be nothing without you* and *I'm gonna take care of you forever.*

And if there is one, tiny, helpless pinpoint of a chance to save this, the moment is now, but once again Bowler's anger—anger he has never felt as strongly with anyone else than the woman he loved—blasts it away, even as he knows what he is doing, something gives as he hears that word.

Coward.

And Bowler throws the pint glass full of water into the empty sink, where it shatters—*smashes*—with a bang, spraying glass fragments and water into the air, and he sees her jump, stung and scared, and for a moment he's back in control. This is the moment he will remember the most afterwards; seeing that little scared girl in her eyes, the little girl that would have done anything for him at one time. When he remembers it later, he will think that if he could pull out his own eyes to be able to go back and comfort her, to go back and protect her, he would have done it in a heartbeat.

"*Fuck* you, Suzie, *fuck* you! Coward? You know what's it's been like for me?" he roars, and she shrinks back slightly, and he knows this is how he takes control again, by scaring her into submission, even when he knows he should listen. The urge to destroy is too big to swallow.

"Being a fucking housewife to *my* wife? Being the bitch about the house, bringing in nothing? I work with my *hands,* my *hands,* Suzie!! Why don't you get it?! You throw Glasgow at me like it's something I don't care about?!" He's wrong, dead wrong, he knows it, but this is all he has. Well ... not all. He still has the bombshell. And he can see her blinking fast and swallowing, taking a deep breath, while looking at his feet, and this is something new. The emotions that normally would make this moment his victory are gone, and all she is doing is riding out the rage of a man that has become a stranger, and he sees it, but he can't stop now. Like an angry child, he needs a reaction, he needs to shock her, needs to *jolt* her into her old self.

"Where the fuck do you get off calling me a coward? Eh?" He needs to let the anger build, he knows, hit a climax. She's still breathing deeply, and now she even raises her eyes to meet his, face pale but set. No anger. Bravery. It scares him.

"This is the shit I have to deal with?" says Bowler. "The shit you give me. This is why I don't fucking bother coming home. Why would I, when my own *wife* calls me a fucking *coward*?!" He's shouting, but it's false. And she's shaking her head again, no smirk, no scowl, just cold appraisal. He's getting nothing, and he could almost weep with frustration and sadness. "Why else would I bother going out Saturday night to try and find some *fucking respect that I can't even get at home*?! Why else would I go out? And you know what, you know what I did? I *fucked* someone, some random *slag*!! *That's what you did! That's what you made me do*!!"

But it's empty, and instead of the satisfaction of shattering her exterior, he only has a horrible dying feeling inside, especially when her face doesn't falter even one bit.

She pauses, and then speaks very calmly, with no satisfaction or pleasure.

"I've been seeing Rob from accounts for the last three months. We've being sleeping together, and I've told him I love him and I'm going to live with him."

She takes a sip from her wine glass, and as she does it Bowler realises—not for the first time, not by a long way, but a million times worse—what he's done. When he sees he has no choice here—she's already decided that there's no coming back, and this is not his choice but hers and it's already made—she instantly, terribly becomes ten feet tall, a goddess, the best thing that ever happened to him, the single love of his life, and he would give anything to take the last year back. It's an instant, dramatic conversion in his eyes, and the plummeting feeling inside that it causes is impossible to describe.

But the other Bowler is still calling the shots, and even though he wants to beg, wants to drop to his knees and scream for forgiveness, he has to keep up the act, keep up the dance, and so he does scream, not in penitence but in rage, and puts his fist through the nearest cupboard door. His foot smashes through another one, the one under the sink, cutting his ankle badly, and he then proceeds to destroy everything in sight, cursing her name. And all she does is step backward slightly to avoid flying debris, looking at the floor. She has seen all his tricks, and this, his biggest one, has no more power to shock.

This rage will go on until she eventually feels she has shown him as much respect as she should for his pain, and when she feels she has put up with as much as is proper, she leaves. He does grab her arm once, on the stairs, but when she looks at him, he looks at his own hand holding her, and his rage finally breaks and turns to babbling terror and helpless begging as he gets a vision of how the future will be. For the first time her eyes show terrible, terrible pity. There is no going back.

As she gets in her car—he's begged her all the way—the rage returns. She's walking out on him, can't she see how crazy this is making him, the pain he's in, how can she *do* this, the woman who secretly learned to knit just so she could make him a jumper with his name on it for Christmas, how can the same woman from a memory so incredibly sweet and close and loving *do* this—and he screams at her again as she drives away, screaming to the night, weeping openly, and in his desperation he has the idea. To run back inside and check her sat nav, the one he knows will be there, because she's always leaving it inside, he's always telling her to stop it, it's useful, it's no good if she doesn't have it in the bloody *car*, is it (was *always telling her*), and he finds it, looks in it, looks to find any unfamiliar Favourite Destinations.

And he finds what he wants, and there are consequences.

***

"There's George," said Bowler, looking to his left.

Hart was holding Bowler up as they walked—being very careful to make sure Bowler's weight stayed on his good collarbone—and so he had to lean backwards to see around the back of Bowler's head.

"Hmm," said Hart, lips pursed. "Unfortunately, here also comes Mark. What do you want to do?"

Bowler dipped his head slightly. "I'd like to see George. I was trying to find him all the way through, you know … when I was on my own. It was weird, I didn't see him once. Anyway, do you mind?"

"Okay. All right," sighed Hart. "But let's try and make this pretty quick. You know Mark … it's never quick. Odd bastard."

"Careful," smiled Bowler with a wince, as they turned and he jogged his fractured foot slightly. "It'd be pretty embarrassing if he'd tuned in with us just now," he added. Hart smiled.

"Odd *bastard*," Hart repeated out of the corner of his mouth, and Bowler suppressed a giggle. Hart did as well, and it was good to have Bowler back, very good.

Bowler had spotted them just as they'd been heading into Hart's safe house, walking along Quinton Road on the edge of the city centre, parallel to the Train's tracks. Heading into the suburbs. Their destination was Joan Ward Street, and a terraced place in an estate on the edge of town. Here they were on the perimeter of The Foyer.

Much to Hart's delight, when he originally found this place some time ago, he'd also discovered that it had a basement den, replete with TV. He didn't come here often—it was a bit too much of a walk, and too often he got all the way here and the telly wasn't on—but he liked it because it was the sort of place he would have had for himself. A place for a smoke and to get away from … but he dragged himself back to the present, and their current journey.

After the elation of their escape had died down, both men had pretty much fallen silent as they'd remembered what they'd missed. The Bluey. Missed the chance to follow her to The Wall, missed their chance to TRY something. Neither Hart nor Bowler had truly believed it *would* have worked—thought it quite unlikely, in fact—but the point was that it *might* have, and they'd missed their chance to find out. Though neither man wanted to dwell on this fact (even Bowler knew after his far shorter time here that doing so was a very bad idea indeed) and both men had gotten very good at pushing away disappointment, it was still a heavy blow.

Neither wanted to talk about it, and neither would admit that they were thinking about it. They didn't have to.

And now here was Mark and George, half a pleasant surprise.

"Bloody hell, Hart, look at Mark's face. You see that twitch just then?" muttered Bowler.

Hart had. It was quite noticeable.

"Why the hell do you think George keeps hanging around with that guy?" asked Bowler. "He almost looks guilty, see what I mean?"

Hart wasn't sure if guilty was the right word, but Mark definitely looked nervous. His numerous tics, his permanently shifting gaze, even the way he stooped his head when he walked; Mark was definitely a man going Loose, and had been that way for some time. That said, Hart had never liked him beforehand. Though communication was, after all, highly difficult in The Foyer, and Hart was prepared to believe that any dislike would be a matter of miscommunication, he didn't really think it was the case with Mark. Everything he ever said was negative, or a challenge, or an attempt to prove something. Very abrasive, and unpleasant, but only when he felt he could be. Only when he spotted a chink in someone's armour would Mark speak up, which was exactly why Hart didn't like him. Weak, but opportunistic. Typical, Hart thought, that of the handful of people in The Foyer that "talked," they had to get *this* imbecile. At that moment he was quiet, almost sullen, which Hart took as more proof of his downward spiral. Soon he would stop "talking" altogether. Soon he would be like the others. And then it would only be a matter of time before he was completely Loose.

He was a big man, too—not at all the kind you would want going mad on you—standing at around 6'2", and broad. Big hands, thickset shoulders, even broader than Bowler. His Foyer wear was a button-down white shirt and black trousers, the most common theme amongst men in The Foyer (Hart would have truly loved to be able to put some time into finding why this was so, but with the others being the way they were, this was next to an impossibility) which, combined with his thinning black hair, made him look like an oversized accountant. It was unusual to see a man of his build with such a nervous, shifty air, like he would be more comfortable being a foot shorter. That way it would be easier to shrink into the background when he wanted to, easier to observe without being observed.

Hart sometimes came close to berating himself for judging him so harshly. The Foyer was tough on its Guests, and he occasionally felt mean for being uncharitable towards a man upon which it had taken its toll, a man whose pomposity and bombast had been sucked out, leaving this coward who occasionally found the guts to be unpleasant. The fact was, however, that The Foyer has simply amplified the negative traits that were already there. Put simply, Mark just made Hart too damn uncomfortable, and had done so even before his more recent changes. Bowler felt the same way. Even in the face of eternity, some people were just unbearable.

The only reason he could think of for George associating with him at all—friendly George, open and jovial and completely at ease, contrasting with this unpleasant, awkward chap—was that George liked to talk. It was George's system; George moved from talking Guest to talking Guest, leaving only when the discomfort that came with lengthy physical proximity to another Guest became too much to bear. From Hart and Bowler to Sarah to Mark and back again, the hunt for the next person on the days in between giving him a focus, a purpose. It was a great system; Sarah did the same, or, Hart noted with an inward sigh, used to until recently.

But George loved to talk. He *loved* it. Hart and Bowler had developed a vast appreciation for human contact since coming to The Foyer, but Hart thought George had always been that way, and that—as with Mark—The Foyer had simply amplified that which was already there in spades. All the talkers needed it, but for George it was, seemingly, life's greatest pleasure. Hart could see the fascination it held for him, the way he rationed out company like a favourite food. For example, there was no way George would stay any longer than a few minutes with them when he was with Mark; this might mean that the physical discomfort might start with all of them, and he may have to spend a week by himself. But this wasn't needy desperation on George's part, nor was he some bumbling idiot that was oblivious to the living nightmare he was in. It was about finding the best in a bad situation. It was finding what you enjoyed within times of difficulty. It was classic British spirit, and Hart thought it was wonderful.

And here George was, his clear delight in seeing them both turning to open concern as he drew closer. He'd seen Hart holding Bowler up, and was now pointing—even before he was within ten feet—with a questioning look on his face, wanting to know immediately what had happened. Mark simply raised his eyebrows and "said" nothing.

Bowler was waving the concern away, wincing as he did so, and so Hart did the same. Mark looked at Bowler's foot, then scanned the area around them, trying to hide his obvious concern. George turned to Hart and shrugged theatrically, eyes wide, searching.

Hart started to gesticulate, and then thought better of it; one look at Bowler told him so. The small smile that played around Bowler's mouth had proved it to him, and when Bowler caught his eye it turned into an embarrassed grin that Hart couldn't help but laugh at. They were both like excited kids with a breathless story to tell.

The fact was that Bowler's injury was the more serious one, and so it was his fishing story to tell. Bowler was proud of it. Hell ... Hart was proud of it, dammit, and in a place where there was very little news of any kind, this was enormous. So enormous, in fact, that even with George, it would be hard to get an audience to believe it.

Bowler pointed between himself and Hart, a blatantly false, modest smile on his face, and then shook his arms in a mimed run, mimed a few punches, then bared his teeth and made his hands into claws.

The effect was immediate on both men. George's eyes became the size of baseballs and Mark actually broke from his grumpy reverie and burst into laughter, which was a reaction as shocking as it was inaudible.

Everyone turned to Mark and watched. His laughter was almost hysterical, and not even forced. The reaction was so extreme that Hart realised Mark must have been even further down the line than they'd thought. He felt a chill, and looked at George, trying to catch his eye, but even George was shocked enough to be staring at Mark.

Mark, through bursts of silent laughter, made mock claws in the air above his head, followed by comedic punches thrown floppily in front of himself, then pointed at the pair of them. The sarcasm and disdain was obvious. *The Beast? Really? You?* To accentuate the gag he gritted his teeth, Beast-like, and mimed punching himself in the mouth, his eyes rolling. This managed to set him off all over again, doubling over at the waist and pointing. Bowler, annoyed and in a lot of pain from his ankle, was suddenly in no mood for this.

"Listen, you crazy bastard, for starters, you're not even funny, you fucking freak—"

"He can't hear you, Bowler," interrupted Hart, coolly. He was too concerned by the realisation of Mark's encroaching lunacy to be offended. Could Mark be dangerous? A man of his size was not someone to take lightly. Were he to get hold of Bowler, it could be bad news indeed, even though Bowler was not a small man by any means.

But Bowler wasn't listening. He pulled free of Hart—who let him go without a struggle—and dropped his weight onto his good foot, taking a large, clumsy, limping step closer to Mark, whom he poked firmly in the chest, forcing Mark to take a small step backwards.

The shock on Mark's face was evident; he hadn't noticed Bowler step so close during his laughter, but the transformation in his demeanour was still striking. He seemed to almost physically shrink, like a big, dopey, family dog caught doing something it shouldn't. His hands came up to the centre of his chest, his shoulders sloping inward, everything about his posture showing deference and fear. His eyes became wide and almost watery.

Even Bowler took a step backward, feeling slightly guilty, his anger instantly gone. It was like Mark had become a child all of a sudden, although that was not enough to make Bowler fully let his anger go; he held up an uncertain finger, looking Mark in the eyes. Bowler clearly didn't really know what to do next. How to mime his point, and how forcefully to make it? It was all just so damned *odd*.

In the end, Bowler seemed to come to a conclusion. He raised his finger higher, and pointed to Mark, then to his own mouth. He then pointed to Hart and himself, then did his Beast claws, then pointed very firmly back at Mark. He concluded by raising his eyebrows. *Got it?*

Mark stared at the floor like a scolded child. George was pretending to be interested in something in the distance. And Hart continued to watch Mark, wondering what was next. Was that all?

It wasn't. Something shifted inside Mark again, and he straightened up, though still not looking at Bowler. His gaze remained on the floor, but not just in whipped puppy mode anymore. With the instant emotional shift of a madman, his face suddenly twisted into a petulant scowl. With a dismissive flap of his right hand, and a turn that was more of a flounce, he quickly spun on his heel and began to stomp in the opposite direction.

Bowler turned to Hart, his mouth open.

"What the fuck ..."

Hart stepped up and gently grasped George's shoulder, who was already turning to follow. George turned to Hart with a concerned expression, almost apologetic. *I have to go.* Hart held up one finger with a theatrical *Hold on a second* smile. George sighed with a smile of his own and rolled his hands over one another, looking again in the direction of the slowly disappearing Mark. *Okay, but hurry up.* Hart nodded, and gestured disdainfully after Mark, then back to George. Then a shrug and a screwed up face. *What on earth are you doing with him?*

And then a very unexpected thing happened. George opened his mouth and raised his hands to reply, and then stopped. Hart watched as George's hands returned to his waist, and his eyes slowly dropped, like he was thinking. Hart started to raise a hand to touch him, to reengage, but George did it first, straightening and placing a hand firmly on Hart's shoulder, looking him firmly in the face again.

Bowler stared. This was *George,* for goodness' sake ... what the hell was going on?

George continued to look into Hart's eyes, smiling warmly, but not like he was trying to keep Hart's attention, or even as if he recognised the other man was really there. It was like he was *considering* Hart.

And then George patted Hart on the shoulder, winked, and tapped the side of his nose with one finger.

Hart was so stunned for a second that he didn't react as George spun on one foot and jogged after Mark, with a friendly wave over his shoulder back in Hart's direction. Hart went to shout after him—old habits again— and realised it was pointless. He turned back to Bowler and put his good-side arm back under the other man's shoulder, which Bowler sank onto gratefully. He was blissfully unaware of many things in that moment. Including, of course, the terrible events that lay in his own future.

But most immediate was that he'd just had the last conversation with George that he'd ever have.

"That was just weird," said Bowler. "I knew Mark was a bit loopy, but not *that* loopy. And I mean, George ... what do you think that's all about?"

"I don't know," said Hart. "Logically, it can only be one of two things. Either Mark's been speaking about some doolally nonsense and old George—not the most cynical person—has bought into it a bit, or ... well ...

he knows something we don't. D'you think Mark and George know something we don't, Bowler?"

Bowler chuckled slightly.

"Anything's possible, but I find it hard to believe. Plus I'd be *really* fucked off if that arsehole had worked out something that we hadn't. Mark, I mean."

"Though I don't agree with the language, I do agree with the sentiment," nodded Hart. "Let's get a move on anyway. We need to get you off that foot, and we certainly don't want to be out in the open right now. He might be looking for us, and we certainly don't want to make his job any easier."

For a moment Bowler nearly asked who Hart meant, then suppressed a shudder as he remembered. The incident with Mark and George had made him forget briefly, but the pain in his ankle was there to remind him.

***

"This is hell. It's hell. Hart, we're in hell." It's the first time Bowler has said anything lucid today. During the entire first week—after his lungs and larynx, or his memory of them, knotted themselves back together, since he was able to make a sound—was just unintelligible noises and wails, or guttural half words.

After that he could form sentences, but nonsense ones, unconnected phrases as he tried to remember how to get his brain to tell his mouth to say the things that were actually on his mind, the pain making it near impossible. But now he knows he can do it, now he knows he can talk correctly at will, he prefers to stay silent. He knows it makes things harder for Hart, but fuck it, he just wants to get everything finally fixed together now. Wants to concentrate on movement, not talk. His mind is back, even though he knows something small has changed about him, probably for good.

106

Hart, startled slightly by Bowler's words, turns in his seat. Normally, he dismisses this kind of talk offhand, refusing to be drawn, but Bowler needs to talk now. Needs to start getting things back to normal, conversing, laughing, anything.

He looks to where Bowler stands by Mary's window, looking out at the city below. He's paused in his pacing, in his faltering, staggered steps as he teaches himself how to walk again. He's almost there. He no longer needs Hart to hold him up, progressing from there to holding his hand, to Hart's hand on his back, to going totally solo. In a day or two he'll be walking almost completely normally.

It's a Friday, and Hart can hear the dull whump—whump—whump from the cars and bars as what passes for a nightlife in their city starts. He can hear the drunken shouts of the men (and women, he thinks, we never had anything like that, women brawling in the street, just unthinkable) the boozy songs, the abuse. Mary has the window open. A lifelong smoker, she seemed to be wary of letting her flat smell of cigarettes for when her real guests arrive. That was always Hart and Bowler's favourite time, both sitting in silence as Mary—and themselves—caught up with whatever Eric or Iris or Pat had been up to. Hart especially; these people were HIS kind of people. People of a different time.

But no visitors today; Mary asleep in the chair again, the TV quiet in the background, and the pulse from outside like a faint heartbeat, like a city trying to stay alive. The table lamp by Mary's chair casting a warm, faint orange light that makes the room feel safe by comparison, the chaos outside unable to penetrate.

Hart sighs and stares at the ceiling for a second. Bowler's words have given him pause. Not because they bring a new idea, but because they've cast his mind back. Back to his own early days, alone, wandering the streets. At first trying to find someone else like him at all, then, once he found many, trying to find one that would either talk back to him, or one that wasn't a gibbering wreck. Wailing. Coming to the edge of madness himself after the first two months, and discovering—out of the blue—Simon.

Funny, excitable Simon. Far too small a man physically to match his ebullient personality, the man who saved Hart. The man who found Hart screaming in an alleyway, pulling at his own skin. Simon who was shocked by Hart's grateful tears at his touch, and who burst into fresh tears of his own as they fell upon each other in a painfully joyful and wretched embrace, found and still hopelessly, profoundly lost. Hart had never been as physically close to a man before or since, never embraced like that. But unusual circumstances create unusual responses.

Simon who'd kept Hart going. Hart who kept Simon going, even though they could do no more than gesticulate at each other. Simon who'd convinced Hart that something lay outside of The Foyer, purely through the sheer force of his own unshakable belief. He was infectious like that. Simon who taught Hart the saving grace here that was the wireless, and years later—once it came along—Simon who had raved about the similar benefits of television, though Hart had been cynical at first to say the least. How could something that did all the work for you be as good for the mind as the radio? But Simon had been adamant, and Hart had finally realised his point; the whole point was you didn't *have to think. A way to, dear sweet lord, switch your mind off completely in The Foyer.*

Simon, the former butcher. Simon who was the only Guest Hart would ever know who could remember what it was like to be hungry, but only when he was confronted with choice meats. You could see the longing and the pain in his eyes. The only Guest Hart had ever seen whose Foyer wear was his former work uniform; a butcher's apron and hat. Hart had once asked Simon if he could take his hat off. Simon had looked at him like he was crazy and said of course. Hart had asked Simon what he would do if he lost it somewhere. Simon had thought about it, shrugged, and said maybe he should *lose it, as finding it would give them something to do.*

A stronger man than Hart was, even though he was a younger man; Simon only being thirty-eight to the best of his knowledge. Without Simon, Hart never would have been able to support Bowler, to be the leader here that Bowler needed. Without Simon first showing him, he wouldn't have known how.

And terribly, in the end, it was Simon who saw The Beast break another Guest. Saw it happen before his eyes, purely by chance, and was never the same afterwards.

Hart remembers Simon coming to him, looking—ironically—like the walking dead. He remembers questioning Simon, gently at first, then forcefully, shaking the zombielike figure before him, this thing wearing Simon's form, with no trace of his friend to be seen.

Simon eventually tried to mime it, but with his shaking hands and zero focus, he just kept repeating himself. The Beast. Breaking. The Beast. Breaking. *Eventually, he calmed down, and appeared to be like his normal self again. He'd explained how it happened, how he'd been looking for Hart and had heard the screams coming from behind a pub, cutting in and cutting out (the Guest tuning in during his pain, going through the different frequencies as he was Broken). How Simon had gone to investigate despite knowing better ... but even then he couldn't go any further with his story. He'd apologised and excused himself, saying that with the stress and the proximity to Hart he just had to get away. The physical discomfort had apparently kicked in, though Hart hadn't felt it.*

Hart had said he understood, and let him go. Simon had walked slowly away, all his energy completely absent, and Hart can remember clearly *how, for one brief moment, he'd paused. He'd been a few feet away, and Hart had seen Simon's shoulders slump, heard Simon give a visible, weary sigh. Simon had* started *to turn back.*

But he didn't. After a few seconds, he'd suddenly picked his feet up and walked away, slightly faster and more forcefully than before, but nowhere near his usual brisk stride.

And Hart would always wish he'd stopped him, and asked him why he paused, because that was the last conversation they would ever have.

Yes, Hart would see him around; of course, the very next time he did, he went to talk to him but Simon, to Hart's shock, had run away. Hart was sure Simon had been crying. For a year, finding Simon became Hart's obsession. He found him, many times, but Simon always saw him coming. They'd even had a chase through The Foyer, Hart uselessly screaming Simon's name, screaming through manic tears for him to come back, that he needed him, that he couldn't survive without him, that he couldn't be like the others, that he didn't want Simon to end up like the others.

But Hart had always lost him. And eventually, as Hart had given up on Simon, the madness had started to come back. Slower this time, as Hart's time with Simon had made him a lot stronger, and taught him many ways to get by alone. But still, of course, it came, and if it hadn't been for the timely arrival of George in The Foyer, Hart didn't know how things would have turned out.

He did see Simon again after George arrived, on just two occasions. Some would say that only seeing someone twice inside such a small area over fifty years was unlikely, but the first time explained why. Five years after their last conversation, Simon had been in the middle of Gosford Street, right by the edge of The Foyer, his hand tracing the edge of The Wall. Pushing ... testing. Hart had rushed forward, his arms outstretched to embrace him, hope and joy temporarily blocking out what he already knew to be true.

Simon hadn't turned when Hart touched his shoulder. He'd just kept muttering something, his lips forming the same shape over and over. Hart watched in silent horror, tears streaming down his face. Simon, his eyes bulging in his sockets, his hat, apron, and shirt all gone, stripped to the waist. Barefoot. He'd rocked gently as he pawed at The Wall, muttering, muttering.

Hart, through his tears, had tried to read what he was saying. He got it, eventually.

"It's true it's true it's true it's true ..."

It was only when Simon had reached up to his face with one hand to gouge a four-inch-long groove in his cheek, tearing his own skin, that Hart had touched him again, grabbing his wrist to stop him. Simon had jumped away like Hart's hand burned, blood flicking from his face with the movement. He'd looked Hart up and down like an animal, crouching away and staring. He'd then bared his teeth— actually bared his teeth like a dog—and spat some phrase at him that Hart couldn't read in time. Hart could then only watch as Simon had suddenly sprinted away up the street with astonishing speed, bent at the waist.

The second time Hart saw him was from afar six years later. He'd had no desire to approach him, to see how much worse he had become. He'd seen that Simon was completely naked.

From time to time, when Hart allowed himself, he would think of Simon, and in the main it was about the good times together; of course, to think of what Simon became was too painful. But other times, he would think of those two words.

"It's true."

On the rare occasions Hart saw a Guest, it wasn't uncommon for them to be talking to themselves, rambling away to invisible companions. Sometimes conversationally, sometimes in a full blown chaotic verbal explosion. So, for the most part, Hart would dismiss Simon's words as the same, during those sad, quiet times when he thought of his former friend and saviour.

But at the same time ... Simon had been a strong person. Hart just couldn't believe that what Simon had seen The Beast do would send him crazy enough to go off alone. No ... Hart often thought that there had been something else. Not something that had made him go Loose, but it was enough to make him live by himself like the others, and his time alone had been too long. Simon had known the dangers of being alone in The Foyer more than anyone, but whatever he'd found out—or what he'd thought he'd found out—had been enough to make him risk it. Enough to make him never come back.

It was all a question of that very careful balance of hope and inaction. And Hart thought he had an idea of what Simon had meant; Simon had always had a lot of theories, and one in particular had always intrigued Hart. But that was far, far too risky to think about without proof. So dangerous, and not just because of the risks of belief and pursuit ...

"No, Bowler. I don't think this is hell," says Hart now, with a faint sigh, not of annoyance but of immense tiredness. Even Bowler notices it. The weight of sixty years. Bowler turns from the window, eyes alive. He's never heard Hart speak about this before, not so freely at least, without anger.

"How many were here, Hart? When you came here? How many Guests?"

Hart blows air from his cheeks, even though there was is no air to blow.

"About twenty-six, I think. Obviously, I can never really count, but the only Check-ins I've ever known of are you, Sarah, George, and Mark. Anyone else I've ever seen has been mad, or a hiding Guest I've caught out. Obviously every time I've seen a fresh face I remember it. You can tell a Check-in, obviously, from a normal Guest. You can tell straight away. Obviously, I've not been here the longest. Nowhere near. I think that dubious honour would go to The Beast. He's certainly the most Loose. Which might explain why he's so ... distorted. Physically."

Bowler shudders slightly, and there is a moment of silence in the room, apart from Mary's gentle breathing. Not raising his eyes from the floor, Bowler speaks quietly.

"Do you think anyone has ever gotten out? Ever?"

Hart shrugs gently.

"Ever? How could I say? But during my time here ... I don't think so, although I can never be certain. I still catch faces I saw here sixty years ago, so

I think not, but ... who knows? I don't keep track of everyone. There could be several. I can't say. I can't say."

Bowler turns back to the window.

"So ... so what keeps you going then?" he asks. "You've been here so long ... and you don't know of anyone that's ever gotten out. How do you ... y'know ..." He trails off, and there is silence again. Hart thinks to himself, Balance, Bowler. It's all about balance.

"I keep myself safe, Bowler. Hope is good, but as that black gentleman said in that film, it's also dangerous. Look for escape, go mad with frustration. Don't look, and resign yourself to ... well ..." He gestures out of the window. "I keep my eyes open and get on with things," Hart continues, eyes misting as he warms to his theme. Bowler knows that Hart's looking through him, seeing something only Hart can see. "You keep your hope, Bowler, but you ration it very, very carefully. And you tell yourself you have *to keep going, as the alternative is unacceptable. And you keep. Your eyes. Open."*

Bowler continues to stare out of the window, and Hart cannot see his expression.

***

Before Mark turned up—with the news that meant the beginning of the end of Hart and Bowler's time together—the pair had been watching TV.

"Oh, I've seen this one before—"

"Ssssh!! I haven't."

Hart had come back from a brief walk. It was several days after they'd holed up in the "safe house," and even though Hart thought the coast wasn't entirely clear with The Beast yet, he didn't like to stay in one place so long. If there was one thing all of the Guests shared, it was restlessness, although Bowler didn't seem to have it as badly as the others. Give him something to amuse himself with—a good programme, a group of people conversing, a film, a radio show, a football match—and he seemed able to lose himself in it and forget his situation in a way that Hart never could. Bowler would never understand how much Hart envied him that.

Still, Hart had been careful and watchful as he walked, and had made it back in one piece to find Bowler sat with the house's true resident, the person they'd first dubbed The Fat Man, although observation of his mail when it came through the door revealed his name to be Terry. Bowler still called him The Fat Man. Terry was in Hart and Bowler's favourite part of the house, the den. Terry—or someone—had done a good job of converting the basement, so much so you wouldn't know it hadn't originally been a room, despite its cramped size and fairly low ceiling. As far as dens go there wasn't much to it, though given its dimensions there wasn't a lot you *could* do. White plastered walls, a few wooden shelves adorned with novelty pint glasses and holiday souvenirs (stuffed animals with T-shirts saying SAN ANTONIO, little men with googly eyes made out of sea shells) and small photo frames of Terry, his wife, and various friends arranged next to a few small pub trophies. The single bulb in the ceiling lit a brown carpet, mostly covered by two armchairs, a mini beer fridge and a large flat-screen TV in the corner.

The flat-screen TV was currently showing Millionaire, and although Hart would of course normally be glad to see this, he was disappointed that, as he'd previously stated, he'd seen this one, and even more so that there was still a good half an hour of the show to go. Bowler was engrossed as usual, and so would be no good for conversation until the ad break. Fortunately, though, Bowler had taken the floor for some reason, leaving the second armchair free next to Terry himself, who was sat in his work shirt and trousers. Home early today, thought Hart.

Hart settled himself into the empty chair, and was quiet. He was happy to be patient until the break; he didn't particularly feel like taking Bowler out of his release right now; let him be lost in it. Plus ... Bowler's distant demeanour seemed to be from more than just the usual engrossing effect of the TV. Hart could tell these things.

The ads came, and Bowler turned around.

"All right?" he asked, not particularly brightly.

"Yes. Better for that."

A pause.

"No trouble then."

"No. Only other Guest I saw was actually Bella Emberg. She was pushing away at The Wall as usual."

He'd hoped to get a smirk out of Bowler at the mention of his favourite Guest lookalike, something that never failed to raise a smile normally (even Hart had to admit the resemblance was uncanny), but there was none. Hart continued.

"We're probably all right to move tomorrow, possibly the day after, I would have thought," Hart finished.

"Whatever you say. I'm easy." He stopped and looked around the room for a moment. "We should come back here more, you know. I like it."

"Yes, it's nice. I saw Sarah, you know. Just now. Doing her perimeter walk."

"Oh, right. Did she apologise? For before?"

"No, I'm afraid not. To be perfectly honest, she didn't even really acknowledge it."

"Well … I guess she's always been a bit stubborn, right?"

"Yes, but … it was like she didn't even remember it. I've said it before, Bowler … I'm worried about her."

Bowler chuckled, humourlessly.

"At least she didn't try and spark you out again. She gets any worse, she'll try and throttle you." He stopped for a moment, and turned to Hart. "But you'd 'survive,' wouldn't you?" he asked, making the air quotes with his fingers, "I mean, I've been bad. After the Train, but you can't like … 'die' again here that way, can you? We always heal?"

"Of course. Remember my helicopter story?"

"Right. So if I ever had enough and wanted out, you couldn't just, like, strangle me?" said Bowler, looking back at the TV. He was wearing a smile that wasn't really a smile. Hart decided to play along.

"No, that wouldn't work, I'm afraid."

Bowler chuckled again, that flat, gentle guffaw that didn't reach his eyes.

"No, I know that. Plus … you'd be stuck then, wouldn't you?"

"How's that?"

"Well. There'd be no one here to strangle you."

There was a long pause. Hart began to suspect strongly that leaving Bowler alone—even briefly—after his injuries had been a bad thing. Was it just that? Before he could divert the subject, Bowler turned back to the TV and continued.

"Yep … you'd be all alone. Like before."

Something stirred inside Hart, and he moved closer behind Bowler, who turned at the sound.

"No matter how bad this place is, Bowler, no matter how sick you get … remember that feeling on the Train. How oblivion felt. And think about whether that's any kind of alternative at all."

There was a very long pause while both men regarded each other, Hart expressionless, Bowler admonished. Eventually, Bowler dropped his eyes.

There was another long pause, until Hart spoke.

"Watch your programme," he said, quietly.

Bowler turned back to the TV for the last time, not even looking at the screen, but immediately whipped back around in his chair as Mark suddenly passed through the door and burst into the room.

"What in God's name—" started Hart, but Mark was grabbing Hart's sleeve and dragging him towards the stairs, gesturing frantically for Bowler to do the same, mouth working hysterically.

***

Taken from *Hart's Imaginary Guide to Being Dead, 'Vices'*

It's easy to find oneself with a whole new set of vices here. And most of them, fortunately, are healthy; it's good to be occupied.

But if the unobtainable becomes your vice, you have just became Loose without even realising it.

***

Hart can hear Bowler before he sees him, and it is a surprise. He hasn't seen Bowler for two days, and has been looking fearfully; fear not just for Bowler, but for himself, for there is an undeniable current of selfishness on Hart's side of their relationship, and he is all too aware of it. Bowler had simply announced he was going for a walk to help settle his now-fixed legs back in, and Hart, engrossed in a Richard Burton film, had been happy for him to do so. Bowler hadn't come back, and that had been forty-eight hours ago.

Were it daytime, Hart probably would have missed it under the street noise, but now it is dark, late, and quiet, and so it is easy to hear Bowler's moans, echoing clearly down to him from inside a second-floor flat. Sounds of the Guests travelled much more easily through concrete and stone than they would in their previous lives, although, strangely, not quite as clearly as they would were there no concrete at all.

Bowler's disappearance isn't entirely unexpected; yes, Hart hadn't expected him to go off for so long, but Hart had suspected that there would be some psychological, post-traumatic aspect to Bowler's recovery from the Train. Hart listens and picks whereabouts in the building he needs to enter to gain access to the correct stairwell. Of course, he could just pass through each wall until he finds the right one, but Hart would like to avoid that as much as possible. Better to get it right first time, and only pass through once.

It's quite a modern building, one of the many new metropolitan-style blocks that have gone up in the city centre in recent years. Hart approves of these new-build places in his city. Its heavy scars are finally starting to fully heal, long after the raids have become a part of history. Hart passes through the door and enters the hallway.

The sound of Bowler is louder here. He is clearly in great pain. Hart mounts the stairs and begins to climb; it sounds like his estimate of the second floor was correct. Another floor, and now Bowler is harder to hear. It isn't because Hart is in the wrong place, but because Bowler's moans have dropped to a low sobbing. Hart can still hear him. Bowler is two doors away.

Hart passes through the correct door to find himself in what he guesses the media would call a "fashionable" flat. The floors are laminate, the walls are an interesting mix of pastel shades—a different colour for each wall—with warm, art deco lighting attached to them (uplighters, but Hart wouldn't know the term). Various "ethnic" ornaments adorn many surfaces, and to Hart, the whole thing seems contrived rather than welcoming; the sort of place more mindful of impressing visitors than of being a warm living space.

The huge TV mounted on the wall is on, and a young couple sit in comfortable silence in front of it, watching a cooking programme. He's a large man in his early thirties, slightly tanned, slightly thinning on top, but handsome, dressed in home wear. T-shirt, jeans, barefoot. Possible traces of the Greek about him, thinks Hart. She has the back of her head resting on his lap, her slender frame stretched out along the settee. Because it is so large, and she is so small, her stockinged feet don't even reach the other armrest. Her face is elfin, her blonde hair very long, reaching halfway down her back, which is covered by a loose fitting vest tucked into her jogging bottoms. She too is barefoot. Her hand occasionally reaches up and absentmindedly strokes the man's arm. The couple have an air of contented comfort, happy to be silent, feeling no need to speak at that time. The image is completely at odds with that of Bowler, sat wretchedly cross-legged on the floor before them. His hands on his face muffle his cries.

Hart is too stunned to move, and for a moment, he doesn't. He has never seen Bowler this way. His hair is sticking out, like he has been pulling his hands through it, pulling on it. His entire face is red, and his cries are hoarse and grating, as if this has been going on for some time. Occasionally he will look up at them, raising his eyes pathetically, then wail painfully, and carry on moaning like a dying bird.

"Bowler."

The younger man looks around, seemingly unsurprised, and immediately turns back to the couple. His cries slow down and stop over the next few minutes, and although he is still highly distressed, the presence of another seems to have reduced the self-indulgence of his pain. Bowler takes a very big sniff.

"Hello, Hart. Sorry … sorry, I've been, ah … gone a while. I had to, ah …" He stops and wipes his mouth. "Had to … come here. I had to come here."

"That's all right, Bowler," replies Hart, gently, but awkwardly. "Do you … want to come with me? We can …" he searches for the right phrase, out of his element. He thinks of the American programmes. "We can talk about … whatever is upsetting you." It sounds unnatural coming from his mouth, and it's uncomfortable for him in the extreme, but even Hart can recognise the situation requires it.

Bowler immediately shakes his head.

"No. No, it's all right. I'll come in a bit. I just need to sit here a little while. I'll come in a bit, it's okay."

Hart hesitates, then quietly moves closer.

"Who are these people, Bowler? Why did you come here?" Hart then winces as, upon hearing this, Bowler is wailing again, openly wailing, and Hart can only stand there awkwardly playing with his cuffs and looking around the flat. He waits, and Bowler's sounds eventually reduce back to a quiet sob.

When he looks again, Bowler's eyes are on the floor, and he is pointing at the woman. He holds a shaking hand there for a moment, and opens his mouth, but the sobs overtake him at whatever thought he has. He can only point sharply away from her, back at himself. His head sinks, and he sobs despairingly at his own crossed ankles.

Hart feels like kicking himself. It should have been obvious, and although he feels for Bowler, Hart is already thinking, assessing. Survival. There is a vital, practical element to be avoided here. Again, not just for Bowler. This absolutely cannot continue. It cannot. He moves right over to Bowler's hunched form, and Bowler looks up almost in surprise, unfamiliar with Hart being this close. He looks up through red, moist eyes, squinting in the light from the ceiling bulb as he looks almost directly into it in order to see Hart's face.

"You shouldn't be here, Bowler. It's probably the very worst thing you can do. I …" Hart pauses and sighs. He doesn't like this. "You will gain nothing this way, Bowler. Do you understand? You'll only … it will hurt far too much. And in the end, there's only one way you'll go."

"Hart. I have to. I have to feel something. I have to feel something." *He looks up at her, fresh tears spilling down his cheeks. "She's all I have, Hart. Oh … look at her, Hart. That was …" he trails off. He drops his eyes again. "I have to feel something," he repeats, quietly.*

"Bowler, I can't let you do this. I know what will happen. You have to come away with me now …" and now Hart trails off, unable to say the truth, the words I Need You *physically unable to pass from his lips. He sighs again,*

and tries a different tack that is easier for him and harder for Bowler. More cruel. But Hart has a job to do for them both.

"She's not all you have, Bowler. She's not yours."

Instead of the angry tirade he expected, Bowler simply moans loudly, not looking up. This is a promising sign—one of acceptance—and Hart presses on.

"I don't know how long you're going to be here, Bowler, I don't how long I'm going to be here, but you know what this will do. You can't, you cannot tell me that this is how you want to spend your time here. And I can't watch this happen." It's a bluff, and he desperately hopes Bowler won't call it. "I can't. You don't get to do both. Imagine that, Bowler. Years and years and years of nothing but this. You're indulging it right now, Bowler. Indulging your own self-pity, feeling something and wrapping yourself up in it because you know that when you leave here, I'll be there. Well I won't, Bowler. You have to choose."

Bowler rocks back and forth, shaking his head with a pained expression, and Hart knows he has him.

"Because you'll go like the others, Bowler, and I won't be with you like that. You have to make a choice. You don't get to stay with me and get your fix of pain, and remorse, and seeing what the hell she's doing with another man." That is a lot, and Bowler actually lets out a yelp, but it was necessary. "You don't get to do both. You either stay here or come away with me."

Hart weighs up the gamble, and decides to go for broke. He turns and starts for the door.

"No ..." Bowler wails sharply, but Hart knows it's not enough; it's halfhearted. He keeps walking. There's a pause, and his hand is on the handle, and Hart begins to think that maybe he's pushed it too far, when Bowler screams at him.

"Hart!!" he cries, and half-dives towards Hart, a sloppy, grief-stricken effort that merely pitches himself over, still in his sitting position. His face and

shoulders flop onto the floor, his arm reaching out blindly towards Hart, who moves to Bowler and crouches down. He waits for Bowler to look up.

"Say it."

"Hart ..."

"It's your choice, Bowler, but you're making it now. We make a deal."

"..."

"I'll make it easy for you. Repeat after me. 'I agree' ..."

"I ... agree ..."

"'That if I am to stay with Hart ...'"

" ... that ... if I am to stay w—with Hart ..."

"' ... then I must never come here again.'"

"..."

"Last chance, Bowler." This is said as tenderly as Hart can ever manage.

"... I must never come here agai—hainnnn ... ." Bowler weeps quietly to himself after this, and Hart knows there is acceptance. He has been ruthless— and aren't his intentions nothing but good, good for them both?—but he has had the desired result, and thinks that perhaps something softer is now called for. He stands and speaks to the wall.

"I'll give you five minutes, Bowler. I think that's ... well, I think that's only fair. Give you time to ... compose yourself, and ... say your ... yes, time to compose yourself, yes?" He sniffs, hesitates. "I'll ... be outside, then. Five minutes, mind."

Bowler nods into the carpet, and Hart turns for the door. When Bowler joins him six minutes later, he has stopped crying.

***

"Where the hell is he taking us?" said Bowler for the fourth time, as they walked after a frustrated Mark. They'd set off at a jogging pace, keeping up with Mark as he continually looked over his shoulder and gestured them on, but even though The Foyer existence meant stamina and fitness was less of a concern than in their previous lives, they struggled to keep up. They didn't get tired, but they had caps on their levels of strength and speed, and some Guests were stronger and faster than others. And Mark was fast. This left Mark huffing and puffing in front of them, flouncing every now and then when he realised they had no intention of going any faster. Hart could have kept pace, but he hung back for Bowler, who could not.

Mark was more Loose looking than ever, his hair sticking up and out in a crazier manner than before, his eyes bugging out with his intense unrest, and—even Bowler noticed—strange red marks on his cheeks, like he'd been pulling at them. Hart had seen something like that before. Bowler had even wondered out loud if Mark had lost weight, and if that was even possible.

He'd led them back into the centre of town, with very little complaint from the pair. Bowler's repeated question had been one of curiosity rather than annoyance; here was a situation packed with excitement and the unknown. Yes, a lot of things were unknown to them in The Foyer, but this was a question with, they assumed, an answer for once. Mark wanted to show them something, was frantic about it, and they would shortly find out what. To say this was a rare and intense pleasure for Hart and Bowler was an understatement. Although it was coming from a Guest that neither man liked or trusted, it was still a game to be savoured greatly. After all, this was The Foyer, and both men knew that no matter how Loose Mark might be, he was no Beast, and there was two of them after all, so of course it went without saying that there was nowhere Mark could take them that would lead them into danger.

No chance at all.

They were heading along Gosford Street, and already the sun was halfway set; the streets were still reasonably busy in the increasing gloom.

Students and late commuters were milling about, and there was still a constant presence of traffic. Bowler loved this time of year. They couldn't feel the cold, of course, and so only experienced the positive parts; the winter night atmosphere, the fogged breath and the streetlights emitting a fuzzier glow in the gentle, otherwise invisible mist. Bowler almost smiled, not consciously realising just how much he was warmed by the sights. But there were couples standing close, hugged together as they walked to keep warm, wearing smiles of their own, and his faded.

Mark had stopped several feet ahead of them, now truly frantic, flapping his hands at them and waving. He actually stamped his feet in frustration and impatience. Bowler looked to see which building he'd stopped outside; Whitefriars Olde Ale House. A very old, timber-fronted building, at odds with the concrete city around it. What the hell was he taking them to a pub for? He caught Hart's eye, who screwed up his face, clearly thinking the same thing, but Mark was already heading through the door.

The pub was busy, and the atmosphere was pleasant and warm, but this meant difficulty for Hart and Bowler. This many people, combined with the cramped, narrow thoroughfare of the building, meant that avoiding unpleasant incidents of Passing Through people was problematic, especially while keeping an eye on Mark, who turned sharply right a few feet from the entrance to ascend the even more narrow, winding staircase.

The upstairs room was unusually empty compared to the bustle below. Hart briefly took in his new surroundings; the upper floor had high, oak beamed ceilings and timber laden walls, and was a warren of three smaller rooms, with uneven floors and mismatching, ageing bar furniture. It had a charm Hart liked. The tiny hallway they were standing in was now a kind of landing, with a back room full of tables and a dartboard on their right, and to their left, two sets of small steps leading up to the west and down to the east to reach the other two respective rooms.

Mark's demeanour had changed slightly; the nerves and tension were still there, but it was clear now that they'd reached their destination. He was no longer looking at them, but at the floor, and breathing slowly and deliberately, as if he were quietly psyching himself up for something. His body was pointed towards the westward room. Bowler and Hart looked at each other silently, thinking the same thing; whatever Mark had to show them, it was in there, and he could not bring himself to show them directly. He wanted them to take the hint.

Bowler shrugged, confused and excited, and flapped a hand at the left-hand room while looking at Hart. *I guess we get it done, then.* Hart nodded, turned, and then stopped. He'd had a sudden flash in his mind, from nowhere. He suddenly felt that going into that small room was a very bad idea. He had no idea where this feeling came from, and there was nothing they'd seen or heard to make him think this way, but suddenly he was convinced that it was a very bad idea indeed, that whatever was in there meant the end of what passed for a balanced existence for him in The Foyer. No, more than that; it was something terrible. *Look at Mark, for God's sake,* said the voice in Hart's head. Mark had one arm out, leaning himself on the wall now for support. *He's seen it, whatever it is—*

But Bowler sighed impatiently behind him, and pushed past Hart's right shoulder, and through Hart's uncertain attempt to hold him back. Mark didn't look up as Bowler passed, and even put his face in his right hand as Bowler rounded the corner. Hart caught himself starting to panic. Why would Mark do that? What the hell was in there? And why was he too scared to move all of a sudden?

That was when he heard Bowler scream in utter terror.

"Oh GOD!! Oh … oh … oh my GOD!! OH MY FUCKING GOD!! AAAAHH! AAAAAAHHHHHH!! Fuck!! FUCK!!"

Mark still hadn't moved—of course, he couldn't hear Bowler anyway—but the screams broke Hart's spell, and he bolted past the stationary Mark and up the small set of steps into the westward room.

Just like Bowler, it took him a few moments to realise what he was seeing. It was so unlike anything he'd ever seen in his previous life, yet alone in the unchanging monotony of The Foyer, that any recognition was slow indeed, and harder still as Bowler's hysterical screams were now right in his ear. But once Hart made the connection in his head between sight and understanding, the effect was the same on him as it had been on Bowler; a feeling of complete horror took hold of his mind. Hart began to scream.

In front of them both, on the floor, was George. The reason both Hart and Bowler had failed to recognise him at first is because he was, inexplicably, a corpse. Frozen, both arms outstretched as if to ward off an attack or to grab an assailant, fingers splayed. He didn't look like George at first because his face had an expression they had never seen on his face; shock, wide eyed, open mouthed, taken by surprise. There were no cuts, no breaks, no blood on his body, yet his eyes stared wide and empty against the ceiling, and it was clear that, somehow, their friend George was—for the second time and for good—dead.

Bowler had collapsed to his knees, still screaming, and gently reached out for George's face. Hart was screaming too, but now suddenly found himself overcome by a rage of grief, and balled his hands into fists and screwed them into his eyes. George had been a good, loyal friend, and a kind, happy man, and when you could only count three people in sixty years that had ever been any kind of a companion—that had been the only *possibilities* of being companions—that made the loss so, so much greater, however selfish that thought may be. Hart opened his mouth and sobbed loudly and plainly.

Bowler slowly stopped his own noise as he heard this, completely alien to anything he had known of Hart. His own pain stopped briefly by this

126

newer shock, and in that brief moment of clarity he realised the obvious questions to be asked of this situation. He whipped his head round and saw Mark sheepishly entering the room, and he suddenly *knew*; somehow, Mark had done this. Mark had made this terrible thing happen. He pointed a shaking, accusing finger.

"You did this. You did this, didn't you, you fucking crazy bastard. How the fuck did you do this. Why. *Why?!*" Bowler stood and advanced on Mark, who raised his hands in innocent protest, his mouth working silently and frantically. Bowler didn't try to work out what he was saying; it took a fair bit of effort and patience at the best of times, and this was not a moment of patience for Bowler. "What the fuck did he do to you? He was one of decent ones, the good ones, *and he didn't do anything!!*"

Bowler shoved Mark in the chest with both hands, hard, who staggered backwards several steps, ending up against the hallway wall. Mark's hands worked aggressively, more angrily now; pointing at George's corpse, then at himself, then hands up in the air—confusion, showing confusion—then a carrying motion, then a putting down motion, then pointing back at George, then Hart and Bowler.

Confusion set into Bowler's mind, halting his anger; Mark was saying he'd carried George here to show them, had been looking for them. Bowler made a connection; he and Hart spent most of their time around this area, so it made sense that Mark had come here to find them and failed, and then had put the body here and gone to look where he'd seen them last; out by the safe house. But carried the body here from where?

"Where from, you sick twat? Where from?" Blank stares from Mark. "Where did you find him, where"—Bowler made a rapid carrying motion—"*did you carry him from, dickhead?*" A blank stare from Mark in response, a small shake of the head. Bowler jumped over and grabbed Mark's collar. "*Tell me where you found him, you fucking crazy bastard, what the fuck did you do—*"

127

"*Bowler!*" shouted Hart, suddenly, from the westward room, and when Bowler halted in his shouting in surprise, Mark knocked Bowler's hands from his shirt. Hart turned his tear-stained face toward them, crouched as he was over George now. "He can't understand you. Just ... look, just let him go for now. Now's ... not the time. Eh?" It wasn't an order. It was a quiet plea.

There was a long, silent pause in the room, but then Bowler slowly stepped back from Mark. He didn't say anything, but pointed two fingers to his own eyes, and then sharply back to Mark. Mark gave Bowler the finger. He seemed about to say something else, and then shook his head and stomped away down the stairs.

"We need to tell Sarah," Hart said, standing, composure strapped on about himself now. Bowler found himself lowering his outstretched hand.

"Hart—"

"We need to tell Sarah," Hart repeated, crouching down again, his back to Bowler. "Be a good chap and see if you can find her, will you? It's probably best if we bring her here to see for herself."

"Do you think that's—"

"I think we don't have much time, either," interrupted Hart. "Look. He's crumbling." He pointed to George's left hand, where the skin looked hard and waxy, and at points like it was flaking heavily. There were small flakes on the floor. Hart took George's fingers gently in his own, and after a moment, snapped them. More flakes burst off as he did so, like those from a busted cream cracker.

"Hart!"

As the flakes hit the floor, they settled, then descended through it, gone forever. That would be how the whole body went, thought Bowler.

"We don't have much time, Bowler," Hart repeated quietly, in a smaller voice. "There's a good chap." He didn't look round again. Bowler muttered to himself, confused, hurt, shocked … and suddenly he wanted to get away. He left Hart, and went to find Sarah.

Hart sat and stroked George's face.

***

Part Three:

Checking Out

Chapter 6: Ten Years Later, We See Sarah On Her Way Out, The Dead Hold a Funeral; There Is Also an Incredible Discovery, And An Unexpected Outcome

✳✳✳

TEN YEARS PASS:

"No. No, I totally disagree."

"Look at the way he keeps touching his face—"

"You don't believe that rubbish, do you? Look at how fast he's responding."

"He's shifty as hell."

"That's total nonsense. *Shifty.* Pah. He's confident, assured, and look, look how he's looking him constantly in the eyes; that's an innocent man."

"You can't seriously tell me—"

"Let's just … agree to disagree, Bowler."

Hart fell silent, tired. He knew better, these days, to disagree with Bowler in these moods. It would only end in trouble. Mary's daughter seemed to watch nothing other than Court TV, and even though Bowler was a fan, Hart didn't like it. It was a different world to the one he knew, and not just the American system. The way these people talked, the way they addressed the court and each other. It was alien to him, and uncomfortable. But Bowler wanted to watch, so they pretty much *had* to watch, and for tradition and sentimentality's sake he was reasonably happy to come back to Mary's place. And, in a way, he felt like he was being respectful to her. Thanking her for all the nice times they'd had courtesy of her place, even if it wasn't as good as it used to be. Many things were different now, he thought, sadly.

He turned his attention to Mary's fat daughter, plonked on the settee eating, as usual. She'd wasted no time in moving into the flat as soon as Mary had died, and though she'd changed little about the place in the last FIVE years, it just … wasn't Mary's place any more. The amount of mess was far greater, for starters.

He tuned back in to Bowler, who had carried on talking about the defendant's body language some more regardless of Hart's request to leave it, holding his own court. Bowler's vision in The Foyer was now as good as anyone's, and—Hart had to admit, to himself at least—superior to Hart's. Bowler had come a long way in many respects. Hart sighed.

"What?" said Bowler. It was almost impatient.

"Just looking at the judge," Hart said, keeping his tone civil.

"What about him?"

"Oh, come on … he doesn't remind you of anyone?" Hart furthered, enjoying the superiority and trying to start a game..

"No. Just tell me."

"Someone that used to hang around … sadly no longer with us?"

Bowler scowled, irritated by the test, but his face relaxed as he remembered.

"Oh … George."

"That's right."

Pause.

"I don't see it," said Bowler, flatly.

"But he's the absolute spit of the man."

"He was a nice guy, George. Just … just a good, solid guy."

"Yes, he was."

"You remember I was the one that went and told Sarah?" said Bowler, his tone impossible to read.

"Yes, I remember."

"I saw her today. Sarah."

Hart stiffened slightly. He thought he might know where this was going, and wanted to get through just one day this year without an argument. But if Bowler wanted one, there tended to be one. So there was no point in tiptoeing.

"How is she? Did she talk to you?"

"Yeah, she did, for once. She's ... really bad. I could barely understand a word she was trying to tell me. I knew she'd gotten really bad, but ... she was *really* bad."

Hart nearly smiled. For a moment there, Bowler had actually sounded like Bowler.

"She just kept changing subjects, babbling away. It's her eyes, Hart. I've only ever seen them like that in ... well ... in Mark."

Hart didn't say anything.

"I said I've only ever seen them like that in Mark."

"Yes, yes I heard."

"Well, she looks like that now, but at least you could get sense out of Mark. Sarah's gone pretty much totally."

Hart still didn't pass comment.

"You don't have anything to say, do you?" said Bowler, staring at Hart now, head cocked lazily as he lounged in the chair.

That made Hart angry. He wasn't going on the back foot today. He'd heard this enough times, and wasn't in the mood to take it.

"Not really, Bowler. I think we've had this conversation enough times. I think you've said everything you have to say on this subject. I think you've made your feelings clear without doing it again."

"I'm glad you know, Hart," Bowler said as he leaned over in his chair, a smirk playing around his lips. "You always act like you don't, though. Like you don't know that it's your fault. Her going Loose."

"That's your opinion, Bowler, I tell you every time, and I'm bored of saying so," said Hart, turning back to the TV. Despite his anger, he just couldn't face another joust today. He might have not been able to sleep, but there were still ways for a Guest to be tired. Bowler leaned farther out, eager.

"Hardly, Hart. She stopped talking to us, hanging around with us—"

"Yes, yes—"

"—after what *you* did, Hart—"

"Yes, yes, yes ..."

"—which is just a cast-iron *fact*, really. So that not being related to her mental collapse seems pretty unlikely, wouldn't you say?"

"She made her choice—"

"And let's be honest, she wasn't exactly solid before that, was she? So going off by herself was pretty much a disastrous decision in here at the best of times—but after what you did, who can blame her—but doing it in the state *she* was in ... I think that's pretty likely that's what pushed her over the edge, I'd say."

Hart didn't reply. Given the same situation, he would do the same all over again. And he would not *admit* Bowler was right. *Bugger him*, thought Hart, and something occurred to him.

"Regardless, Bowler, if I were you, I'd stay away from Sarah. If she's gone Loose, she could be dangerous," Hart said. Bowler just scoffed, and then there was silence in the room.

After a few moments, Hart snuck a glance at Bowler. There it was again. He'd thought he'd seen it out of the corner of his eye a few times, but this time there was no mistaking it. Small, subtle, so much so no one other than Hart would ever notice it, but there it was. A sharp twitch in Bowler's left eye.

Before he could say anything—and Hart didn't really know what he *would* say—Bowler stood. He didn't look at Hart.

"I'm going out."

He remained there for a moment, then looked at Hart and paused for a second. Then he walked out, alone. Not for the first time, Hart felt relieved. Things were different now. Strangely, almost like she'd waited for Bowler to leave, Mary's daughter changed the channel. She flicked around, and Hart waited, watching intently. With Bowler gone, the choice of channel was of vital importance. Hart hoped that it would be a soap.

And then she picked a channel, and what Hart saw dropped the bottom out of his world.

***

"Do you want to go first?" asks Hart, though he already knows what the answer will be.

"Nah … you can."

Hart nods and tries to remember what he'd planned to say. Not having so much as a napkin to make notes on renders speech-making that much harder.

They're standing by the fountain in the lower precinct, solitary in the centre of town. The shops are all closed, and the winter midnight gives everything a sense of occasion; perfect. This was the idea. Exactly the right feeling for a funeral.

As Bowler had rightly pointed out, they couldn't bury George's body, even though for some reason, it didn't sink into the floor as they would have expected. When they'd tried to move it, they'd found out a possible reason why; it was so light, even for a Guest, feeling like a thin fibreglass shell. Only the flakes that broke off George's body as it rapidly disintegrated had sunk. It made no sense, but then there were so many things about the physics of The Foyer that didn't either, so they'd just accepted it without too much question. After all, how can they know how second-time-dead bodies worked here? They'd never seen one before.

And although it had looked very much like George's body would disintegrate entirely within a few days—the amount of flakes that had appeared around his body in the first hour alone had suggested that possibility—both Bowler and Hart had very much wanted to mark his passing with some kind of ceremony. George had been a good friend to the pair of them.

And so the idea had been hit upon to place the body in the fountain at midnight and say a few words. Not only, they had theorised, would the body slowly disappear as it crumbled, but it was a nice ceremonial idea. George always loved the precinct, and a water burial seemed as good as they could get anyway.

There are many, many questions raised by this—not least of all how it happened, who did it, and what it means for Bowler and Hart—but they can wait. Right now, they have a job to do. And here they are; Hart is to go first, as he looks at George's body resting on the edge of the fountain.

"George ..." he starts, and falters immediately, lost in a mental block and his own discomfort. "You will never be forgotten. You were ... much loved by Bowler and I; but it was more than that. In this place ... friends are ... vital. Absolutely vital. They are one's life blood. And to have a friend as kind and friendly and good as you in that situation, well ... you were an immense blessing, and your loss is incalculable ..."

Hart loses his train of thought again as Bowler starts to cry gently but helplessly beside him. He wonders how much more Bowler can take, and realises with a sinking feeling that it's just them now. Who else is there? *Hart thinks.* Mark? Loose. Sarah? On her way out. No one else now. Just us two.

How the hell will Bowler cope? Hart *pushes thoughts of a Loose Bowler away and continues his speech, and feels, when he's done, that he does as good a job as possible in the circumstances. Surprisingly for Hart, he feels no shame when his voice cracks and tears spill down his cheeks. When he finishes, he looks to Bowler, who nods tearfully, and steps forward. Bowler looks down at George's body resting on the edge of the fountain. It was effortlessly light to carry here, horribly so. He bites back anger, and begins his own fumbling speech.*

"I'm gonna miss you, George ..."

A few minutes later, he is finished. He gestures wordlessly to Hart, unable to meet his eye, and fumbles blindly to grip George's shoulders. Hart takes George's ankles, and they lower him into the water. He looks very, very still and cold in there.

"Good-bye, George," says Bowler.

They stand there looking into the water for a few minutes. A taxi drives past at the top of the precinct slope.

"We need to warn Sarah," says Bowler, quietly. He hadn't been able to find her after he set off to do so; this is the sixth time he's said it.

"We need to tell her, yes," says Hart, kindly, "but we don't know yet if we need to warn her. I know Mark is the most likely suspect," he adds quickly and firmly, not looking at Bowler but raising a hand to quieten his complaint. "But we can't go slandering him until we know for certain. He's alone here, like the rest of us. To decide this about him before we definitely know is to ... well ... to damn him. You know what I mean, Bowler."

Bowler nods but doesn't let it drop.

"You know what a weird, twitchy fucker he is, Hart. He did this. He fucking *did* this. *Look at George, Hart.* Look *at him."*

"I said I agree that he probably did. But you can't say so to Sarah. You can even tell her your suspicions, if you like. But you can't tell *her he did it. You understand why, Bowler, and you know it wouldn't be right, or proper."*

There is a pause.

"He sucked him in, Hart," says Bowler, his voice low and angry. "He was up to something. George knew *Mark was up to something, and Mark convinced him to be in on it. And whatever it was, George paid the price. You know I'm right, Hart. They were always slinking off together. We should've warned him ... he was always too, whatsit, too ... trusting."*

"But he was no one's fool, George. Don't forget that. I don't think Mark sucked him in, or tricked him. I think they tried something ..."

He thinks of the best way to put it.

"... and something went very badly wrong."

Bowler fumes quietly, staring at George and rocking back and forth on his heels. He looks at Hart in a way he never has before.

"No. No, Hart. You're *wrong."*

***

Hart fell backwards, his legs and bottom passing through the floor several inches. He didn't even notice. He wiped his face with a trembling hand in a pointless attempt to clear his vision, but of course what he saw didn't change. It was there, clear as a bell, undeniable, and devastating in its impact.

Good God in heaven, he thought. *It's* true ...

***

Bowler eventually finds Sarah walking, as he'd rightly assumed, along The Wall. It had just been a matter of circling the perimeter until eventually she showed up, and the small gamble has paid off sooner than he'd thought. He's found her as he headed towards the train station to start his lap. She'd been coming the other way, as if she was done for the day. This is totally contradictory to Bowler and Hart's behaviour; they like to wander and walk at night, trying to pass the time as best as possible until morning comes and people start turning on their TVs again. She'd seemed fairly relaxed when he'd seen her, meeting him at the edge of the ring road where the slip road headed up to the roundabout. She'd responded to his greeting warmly, and had moved agreeably enough onto the roundabout with him (Bowler, like Hart, was never totally happy standing in the road) but it becomes clear very quickly that all was not as well as he'd initially assumed, and it does so most clearly when he tries to tell her about George.

It's hard, especially at first when trying to even get her to realise who he's talking about, but after several repetitions of the motion for George's bald head and round stomach, she eventually twigs it with a smile. Bowler struggles to think of the right mimes at the best of times, first struggling to think of the best way to construct the sentence, then stumbling even more when it comes to thinking of the best visual representation. He reads this charade—speaks a lot better than he signs it. But this is toughness on a higher level; not only does he have to deliver bad news, and to warn her about Mark (regardless of what he'd told Hart, he's going to do just that), but he has to do it sensitively. He begins to wish he'd brought Hart with him ... but then Hart would have been there like always, editing and putting his own spin on it.

Bowler scowls. Hart. Always so ... distant. Even in here. When all they have is each other.

He looks at Sarah's face, looking way up at him (she's short, about 5'2" Bowler reckons) searching his own, waiting for him to finish whatever he has to say. She wants to be off. More coldness here, Bowler notes, and feels his shoulders sink that little bit further. When he tells her what has happened to George, it has taken several awkward repetitions of the fact he was dead. The concept was almost impossible to grasp here, let alone express by mime. How could someone die in the land of the dead? At first he thinks she is just in denial about it, but he very quickly realises that she simply doesn't understand. *After miming that he finds it confusing too, trying to get the idea over that this is a matter of* Somehow, It's Crazy But ... *and* then *doing the slit throat gesture, he sees the connection register in her face. But the worst thing is that even now, when she* does *realise what's happened, she barely seems to have an emotional response.*

Sarah's face just kind of twitches, and her shoulders move in a sigh. Then she nods firmly, as if to say, Okay, I get it. *And that's it.*

No shock. Then she wants to know how it happened, where he was. That at least was perfectly understandable, but this had all been so odd. Hart was right. Sarah was on shaky ground.

Bowler offers for her to come with him, but she shakes her head firmly, rolling her hand. She wants answers, and quickly, so she can get on with whatever she's up to. This feels so uncomfortable that Bowler just wants to be out of here, and decides the best thing to do is *just to get this done quickly.*

And so Bowler holds up a finger, and gestures Mark's big ears. Sarah gets it straight away, holding her hand up above her head. Big Mark. *Bowler nods, and holds up a warning finger. The ears again, then a no-no gesture with the finger. Sarah holds her hand up again, questioning, then slashes across her throat with her finger. Bowler nods emphatically. And Sarah laughs.*

Bowler gawps, and Sarah laughs heartily, and tries to gesture something to him, but she can't as she's convulsing too much, and it reminds Bowler of something he's seen only a few days ago. But now Sarah's gesture is becoming clearer; the ears and the hand, then the throat-slit, then George's belly, then suddenly all the laughter stops.

Staring into Bowler's eyes, blank faced, with tears now running down her cheeks, she does a double thumbs-up, then George's belly. If George Is Dead, Then Good For George.

She holds his gaze for a few seconds and then, now suddenly catatonic, all life and expression gone from her face, she turns and begins to shuffle away. Bowler wants to call out to her, but knows not only will she not hear him, but he won't have the words to comfort her anyway. With a twist in his gut, he thinks that Hart would have known.

It has been a hell of a day, Bowler reflects.

"Sarah ..." he mutters, now strangely calm. Shaking his head, almost amused by it all. "You are one craaaaazy bitch ..."

He sets off to find Hart.

***

It's all about energy. It really is! thought Hart, *About* force *... I was right in the first place!* He stayed sitting and watched for a few moments more, trying to gather the full implications in his mind. He realised one thing, clear as a bell; he'd waited long enough. The guessing games were over. No more fear; he would take the very next opportunity. But that would mean finding it. Searching. For the first time in seventy years, he could now begin to commit to hope, to searching, for he knew, once and for all, that the risks were worth it.

Consequences be damned.

***

Though he doesn't know it, Hart is not too far away from Bowler and Sarah's conversation. He is, in a rare moment, enjoying the solitude of a walk by himself, enjoying the chance to collect his thoughts in quiet. He makes his way through the Gosford Street car park, an easy feat given the late hour and the subsequent lack of vehicles stored there, creating several acres of concrete field. The ring road overpass above casts a shadow across the white parking bays, the few overnight cars in the open air expanse lit by the streetlights on

142

the road. Despite it being nearly 3am now, there's still the odd car passing by on the street, but otherwise town is fairly still.

Bowler's gone to find Sarah, and Hart doesn't believe for one second he's going to stick to the arrangement they've made. But this isn't the time to think about that. It's time to think about what on earth could have happened to George.

Does he believe Mark did it? That Mark found a way to murder George? No, Hart doesn't think that for a second; Mark is losing it badly, but he isn't Loose enough to want to do it, even if he did know a way. Plus he seemed so genuinely shocked at the accusation. But Hart doesn't think Mark just found George like that, either. Too convenient. Why bother bringing him all the way back into town to show them? No ... there's evidence of guilt there. He needed to show them ... to get their forgiveness? Hart relaxes into his stride, not realising he's flexing his old mental courtroom muscles, adding to his inappropriately good mood.

Something went wrong. Mark was up to something, and George knew about it, hell, he wanted to be a part of it. That much was clear. Bowler hadn't known George as long as Hart had. George gave off an air of being a good-natured, simple chap, but he wasn't simple at all. People often confused an easy-going nature with being easy to manipulate. It doesn't mean that. It just means they're more casual about the things they choose to do, if they choose to do them. No ... George wanted in on whatever Mark was up to, and something went wrong. And George paid the price. And Mark, not thinking straight, carries George's corpse back into town, panicking, to show them, to be told what to do. But he can't find them, so he stashes the body and goes looking properly. And that's—

A hand grabs Hart's shoulder and spins him round, surprising him. It's Mark, and he looks upset. More than upset; he looks furious. His large shoulders are rising and falling with each rapid imagined breath, his fists are clenched and his jaw is set, eyes thundering, and Hart feels a stab of concern.

All of the sheepishness of the other week is gone. In its place is rage, and Hart knows he needs to be very careful indeed. He has never seen anger like this is another Guest, The Beast excluded. Mark's eyes look ready to burst from his head, stark white against the redness of his face. Hart slowly raises his hands to his chest.

The placatory gesture does no good. Mark pokes him in the chest, hard.

Hart, unprepared, takes two steps backward with the force of it. Mark flaps his hands, and Hart can't understand what he's saying, but he doesn't say so. He just stares blankly at Mark, who takes this lack of response as an impertinent challenge and, head nodding slightly, takes shaking, dangerous steps right up into Hart's face, never moving his eyes. It's like watching a hungry predator advance upon prey, excited and nervous lest it should escape. If Guests could breathe—if there were air here—Hart would be inhaling mouthfuls of it as it rapidly pumped from Mark's mouth and nose. Mark thrusts his finger into the air by Hart's side, waves it, and throws his opposite hand up. Bowler. He wants to know where Bowler is.

This is very bad. Bowler is stocky, but Mark is the bigger man, and he is very angry. Earlier (was it earlier that day? The day before? Not sleeping makes it so hard to block time off into separate days) Mark had allowed Bowler to push him about, but that had been guilty Mark, sheepish Mark, a Mark in the throes of regret and pain over the loss of George. Here is a going Loose Mark who has had time to think about it, and to become insane with rage by the looks of it. Hart becomes very concerned for Bowler indeed.

Hart does a finger walking gesture, and points his hand away and flaps it, followed by an energetic shrug. Mark doesn't believe him, clearly, and squints his eyes nastily. There is a poison in Mark now, made far worse by his impending Looseness, and Hart knows for certain that if Mark finds his quarry, things will be very serious for Bowler. He backs up slightly, but Mark follows him step for step, his large hand forming a warning finger. Worse, there is now the trace of a slight smile on Mark's face. He can see the concern

144

in Hart's eyes, as the smile is spreading as Mark sees the situation as being cat and mouse. There is a horrible, sickening sinking feeling in Hart's stomach. This is someone enjoying seeing fear in another man. Pushing around an equal. A bully. Someone deciding to make Hart his own, through fear. And Hart is a proud man. So much worse for him.

Mark is saying something. Through much pointing and thrusting, Hart eventually gets his point; Bowler accused him of killing George, and Mark is now very angry about it. Also he is angry that Bowler pushed him and grabbed him. He says he didn't kill George.

But all of this is said with a wild-eyedness that tells Hart, with a horrified revelation, that Mark is actually happy about this. There is a relieved glee to his rage. This is something he has needed; an excuse. An outlet. A genuine reason to snap on someone. Is it George dying that's pushed him over the edge? Hart looks down, and sees that he has backed up all the way into one the remaining cars. His body from the chest down is now inside the vehicle's passenger side.

Hart tries the placatory gesture again, but Mark screws his face up and actually pushes Hart's hands out of the way. That smile again. He steps closer, and points to Hart's side once more. He then—Hart can barely believe he's seeing it—slowly purses his lips into a grotesque pout. Mocking Hart. Mark mimes stroking a puppy and patting it.

His face then turns to a bitter grimace, as he grits his teeth and mimes snapping the dog in two, and the grimace goes back to a bully's smirk as he leans right into Hart's face and keeps coming until their noses actually touch. Mark chuckles to himself.

The anger swells within Hart. The cruelty here, the desire to inflict pain on Bowler—but far worse than that, the desire to enjoy intimidating another human being, to enjoy taunting them and seeing their helpless pain ... Hart is not an overly kind man, but this is anathema to him. The opposite of what he believes to be right, Loose or not. His own rage comes flooding in, and he hasn't felt anything like it in a long, long time. It feels good. Consequences be damned, *he thinks, and restraint goes out of the window.*

He circles sideways, away from Mark (and out of the car), and does the walking finger gesture again with his right hand. With his left, he repeats the "away somewhere" gesture. Here we go, *thinks Hart. He then slowly turns the walking fingers on his right hand around to give Mark the "V" sign. The English* fuck you.

Mark's smile drops when he sees it. His lips curl, and Hart cracks a big smile of his own, beginning to laugh. It is desperate, breathy laughter, powered by anger and excitement and by the almost crazy sensation that comes with it. Belly laughs are so rare in The Foyer. He only hopes too much damage isn't being done as he lets this very Loose sounding laughter fly free.

Mark shakes his head gently in disbelief, still staring intently at Hart, trembling, but draws back his huge fist anyway. Hart doesn't move, and simply braces himself for the impact, quietly setting his jaw. Here come the consequences, *he thinks, and he laughs harder as this thought is followed by* Ah, but this feels good ...

And he feels a dull thud on the lower half of his face, but it is only gentle, like someone patting his face to get his attention. Hart opens his eyes to see Mark holding his hand, yelling soundlessly, and at this Hart's laughter intensifies, becoming light-headed and giddy. Mark, in his fury, is already swinging his left fist at Hart's stomach, and again Hart braces for the impact. He barely feels it, as he already knew would be the case, knew from the moment this confrontation began. Mark clearly does now, mouth wide open in a silent scream, holding his hand.

And Hart is laughing wildly as he steps forward and backhands Mark across the face, delirious now, as something has come Loose inside of him and is rushing out in glorious release. Hope and feeling compressed for sixty years. Mark is knocked back several feet by Hart's lazy blow, holding onto his face as his feet fail to keep up with his backward velocity and he falls to the floor. Still laughing, Hart advances on the fallen bigger man.

"So you'd hurt Bowler, would you? Break him?" Hart laughs, strolling eagerly towards a physically and mentally stunned Mark. "Threaten me, have your fun? Not going too well, is it?" says Hart with a mad grin, knowing Mark can't hear him and talking anyway. Part of him, the main part of him, is watching all of this unfold as if someone else is doing it. He knows this isn't him, but he can't stop it and doesn't want to; he won't stop until it's done. Mark has done something very bad; he deserves this. "Didn't you ever wonder to yourself why The Beast is so strong, Mark?" Hart says, and laughs wildly as he kicks Mark in the stomach, the force lifting Mark a foot off the floor and turning him in midair so that he comes down on his face. "Because he's crazy? That wouldn't work. There are lots of very crazy people here, and they're nowhere near as strong. After all, you're crazy now, Mark, and you're no stronger, are you? No. It's to do with time, Mark. And The Beast has been here longer than anyone. And who do you know, who do you talk to who's been here the longest after him? I'll give you a clue." Bursting into manic laughter again, Hart bends and grabs Mark's ankle, and as he rises he pulls, lifting Mark from his feet and then throwing him a good six feet away.

"Think about it, idiot," says Hart as he advances again on Mark's crawling and shaken form, Mark who is frantically trying to gather himself to escape. "Day one, you can barely see properly. Then you're sinking into the floor every two seconds. But you learn that control. After all, these bodies aren't real, these clothes aren't real. These are just what our minds pull together; we're just floating clouds of energy before this. You've seen them. And then that control becomes automatic, as unconscious as breathing used to be. And with time, we learn better control, conscious control. That's why I healed so much quicker the second time I tried to break The Wall. Of course, you could never have so much control that you could actually break The Wall, and I'm not even sure that would be the way you'd want to get out. But the *difference is, I've got about an extra thirty years on you, Mark. I have so much more control. But you didn't think about that, did you? You just thought"*—he *breaks off to kick Mark viciously in the head, which snaps back sharply on Mark's neck as he lets out a silent scream*—*"you'd bully the old man. Bad idea, wasn't it?"*

Mark is babbling something, hands out in the air to ward Hart off, to halt him. Mark's shirt is torn and bloodied from the flow that is bubbling from his mouth and nose, and Hart chuckles, with nothing but disgust and contempt in his eyes. This worm, *he thinks,* this crawling, babbling thing. *And the overwhelming desire to Break Mark fills him, rushes through him, and it is sweet.* The things I could do, *he thinks*, and I'd be right to do them, I'd be right. *Mark is still talking, blood flicking from his lips like spittle as he pleads frantically, staring up at Mark in terror.*

But there is restraint in Hart that does not come from compassion. Hart needs to know. Even now, lost, he needs to know.

"I have nothing but hate for people like you, Mark," he says, breathing heavily, trembling now, revelling in the delicious sensation, trying to remember if this was what it was like to live. "I didn't realise you'd gone this far, but now I see it. So I have no qualms whatsoever getting answers out of you, by whatever manner I feel is necessary. So tell me," Hart says, as a grin spreads across his face and his breathing becomes shakier. He crouches and seizes Mark's collarbone, causing the beaten man's mouth to open wider in an agonised silent scream, "What happened to George?"

*Instantly, in his terror, Mark responds, pointing vigorously at Hart, then tapping his forehead, and then repeating the two actions over and over. Incredibly, he looks confused, as if he doesn't understand why Hart is even asking. For a moment, Hart's madness intensifies, as he thinks Mark is being awkward, impertinent (*The worm is talking back, he's daring to talk *back) but then Mark's gestures make sense and Hart realises just what he means.*

You know, you know, you know.

Hart goes cold, his rage ending as suddenly as if a tap had been turned off.

He releases Mark's collarbone and asks the question in a trembling voice, even though suddenly, he knows the answer.

"What the hell are you on about?

Mark, wincing with pain, knows the question without being able to hear it. He grips where Hart had been holding him, holding the point of pain, and sits up slightly, breathing heavily. He glares at him reproachfully for a second—like a kicked dog—and then points at Hart, taps his head, twirls his fingers off and away. Points at Hart, yapping motion with the hand, fat belly gesture, yapping gesture, points to himself.

YOU *thought it up! You told George, George told me! Fat belly gesture, but then he stops. And George … he can't finish, flaps his hands in a sad shrug. Hart doesn't need that last bit explaining; George paid the price.*

Hart stands there blinking, stunned. He'd never thought that *theory up. It wasn't* his.

That had been Simon's *theory.*

It's been niggling away in his mind as a possibility since he saw George's body, but he'd never even considered it as a real possibility. Plus … that the theory would end up killing someone? Kill a dead person? That was never a possibility. That wasn't the idea, and it hadn't even been his in the first place. And anyway, it had been nothing when he told George, just passing conversation. That's why he'd never truly believed that it had anything to do with all this.

He remembers Simon's babbling, bloodied face. It's true it's true it's true ….

He'd told George Simon's idea casually, in a moment of boredom, in a rare conversation about Foyer Theory with the man. An idea of Simon's that was so laughable because it was so crazy, and ridiculously dangerous. But he remembers now how George's face had lit up, and how George had gotten him to repeat it. He'd thought George had just seized upon it because it was such a wild notion, something new and varied. But now it seemed that maybe he'd taken it a little too seriously. Maybe then, some years later ... he must have told Mark. Told Mark it was Hart's idea. And Mark had maybe done the legwork, and George had been the guinea pig, and George had been the victim when it all went wrong, reduced to a flaking, disintegrated corpse ... and it was Hart's fault.

Hart stumbles backwards, footing lost in his moment of terrible shock,, and Mark looks up at Hart with a mad grin, eyes suddenly wide with recognition. He points a shaking finger at Hart, still smiling like a madman, and turns the same finger into a knife across his throat. Then the fat belly. So really, *you* killed George. Hart shakes his head numbly, but he knows it's true. Mark is the one laughing now, rolling on the floor, holding his stomach, pointing at Hart and cutting his throat, cutting his throat.

"Shut up!" yells Hart, and grabs Mark's shoulders, shaking him, but Mark won't stop laughing. "Tell me what you did! Tell me what happened to George! Tell me what you two did together!! How did you do it!! Tell me! Tell me!!" But Mark won't stop laughing, and that thing is Loose inside Hart again, and, screaming, he shoots out a hand to Mark's neck and snaps his right collarbone.

Mark stops laughing, starts screaming, and Hart is filled with a comforting, icy cold calm. This man got his friend killed. This man encouraged George on a madman's errand.

"Tell me what you did, Mark," says Hart, and realises Mark can't hear him, so he pushes Mark flat on his back with his boot and pins it on his chest. He makes Mark look at him by pushing the heel into his sternum.

Hart gestures come hither, then points at Mark, then fat belly, then twirls his finger in a circle in the air, then come hither again. Mark shakes his head, wide-eyed, scared of the consequences, so Hart stamps on his left collarbone, breaking that too. Mark's mouth opens afresh, yelling.

And that is when Hart sees a movement out of the corner of his eye, and turns to see Sarah ten feet away, open mouthed and ashen faced. Of course, *he thinks.* We're near The Wall. *Where the hell was Bowler? But Sarah is already pointing, horrified, to Hart's feet. Hart looks down to see Mark, writhing and screaming beneath his boot, collarbones pointing sickeningly. The fear, the horror on Sarah's face (*Why is she looking at *me* like that? I'm the *good* one!*) makes something nudge at his mind, and he suddenly sees Mark's broken bones with fresh eyes. Sees what he has done to another human being.*

With a rush he comes back to himself, the monster instantly unconscious in his stomach, and a wash of sickness floods through him. He wonders what the hell he is becoming.

He frantically looks back to Sarah, to explain, to tell her he's doing it for George, but she is already backing away with wide eyes, shaking her head, and then breaks into a full run down the street, disappearing into the night.

Hart stands and watches her flee. As he watches, a numbness grows in his heart as he comes to understand what this means.

His existence—a possible eternity—has just gotten so much harder. He realises he has now lost two of his three only friends, and in this place, that is an indescribable loss. Were Sarah sane any more, perhaps he could have explained, if he could have gotten her to trust him. Even that would have been difficult, for she had seen the madness in him set free, seen the results of his uncontrolled rage. But to a Loose Sarah ... any hopes he had of bringing her back were now irrevocably gone.

He turns back to Mark, empty-minded, and there is a long, long pause, as he watches Mark's mouth move noiselessly in pain, watches him roll back and forth gently on the floor under Hart's boot, gripping at his snapped collarbones. Arms crossed like an Egyptian mummy. Hart doesn't move his foot.

After a moment, Hart does the come hither gesture again.

***

Hart nearly jumped into the ceiling when Bowler came straight back in the room. He wished he could turn the TV off, stop Bowler seeing what was onscreen. He moved his body quickly between Bowler's line of sight and the TV, desperately hoping that the movement wouldn't look too suspicious.

"What time did the film start again?" Bowler asked, flatly, not looking Hart in the eye. It took Hart a second or two to register the question, as his first concern was checking that Bowler couldn't see the TV.

"The film ... oh, was that where you were going?"

"Yeah."

"It was just that you didn't say."

Bowler shrugged.

"What time, anyway? I can't remember. You were the one that looked," he said, impatiently. Hart racked his brain, trying to keep his breathing level. He needed to get this answered quickly, needed to get Bowler out of the room. What was the damn start time?

"Nine, I think. Definitely not before."

"Right." Bowler paused, clearly knowing that he should invite Hart too, but wrestling with whether or not to do it, for whatever reason. There had been a time when an invite wouldn't have been necessary.

"Okay. I'll see you later then," Bowler concluded, turning and sweeping out of the room before an answer could come.

Hart let out a heavy breath. That had been close. Bowler couldn't know.

Not yet.

***

Chapter 7: In Which We See the Beginning of the End, We Learn What Hart Is Really Scared of, Sarah Boss Has Answers, And The Uninvited Guest Visits

***

Hart arrives back at Mary's some time later, still buzzing mentally from what had happened with Mark but disappointed in not finding Sarah. He'd had known it was pointless looking for Sarah, had known Sarah was gone for good. But still, he'd had to try, and he'd wanted the walk anyway. Bowler is waiting for him, and he isn't happy.

"What the hell did you do?" he asks from the window, whipping round and starting as soon as Hart passes through the closed door. The room is almost pitch-black, Mary long asleep in her bedroom. Bowler is a silhouette by the glass, a black shape against the outside streetlight around him. Hart can't see his face.

"What are you talking about, Bowler?" says Hart distractedly. He's returning more to himself now, and he does not feel comfortable for many reasons. Bowler shouting at him is not good.

"I've just had Sarah come screaming past me. I had to grab her, Hart, actually grab *her and try to get her to calm down, but she's totally gone! I could barely get what she was saying, but she was obviously talking about you." Bowler's silhouette moves animatedly in his anger. "You and Mark, you*

doing things to Mark! You told me to leave him alone, not to confront him, and you're off doing something yourself? What the hell were you doing?"

Hart screws up his face at this, and shakes his head slightly. He can't handle this, he just can't. He doesn't even know what to tell Bowler. He is only just processing what he'd learned himself

"Bowler ... look ... I'll answer your questions later. Just ... not now. I need a while."

Bowler throws up his hands up in exasperation.

"Bullshit! You tell me one thing and go off and do another, and then it's 'not now, Bowler, not now, Bowler.' It's always on your *fucking terms, Hart! Tell me what the hell is going on! Tell me, and you tell me right fucking now!" Hart says nothing and stays staring at the floor. Bowler's fists tighten. "It's always like this! Who the fuck do you think you are, Hart? It's just you and me now, do you know that? Do you know that? George is dead, Sarah's* never *coming back,* this *is it! You and me! And* you've *been here a* lot *longer than I have!"*

Hart looks up.

"What's that supposed to mean?" he asks.

"You know *what it means, Hart," hisses Bowler, wagging a finger. "You know. So show me some damn respect. You want to keep it to yourself, fine, but you* will *tell me eventually. When you want to open your mouth, come find me." He stands there a moment, shoulders moving, stunned a little by himself. It is a horrible moment, and both of them know something is different, but Bowler can't take anything back now. After a moment, he pushes past Hart and walks out where the other man had entered, leaving Hart to stare after him.*

Hart waits a while in silence. He sighs heavily, trying to get a grip on his thoughts in their confused, whirling fog.

Think of what's just happened, start there ... okay. Bowler will stop being silly eventually, and then I will tell him how Mark had threatened him, and that I'd taught him a lesson, and tried to get answers ... and that will be that. How Mark said nothing, told me nothing.

That will do for now as far as Hart is concerned. He needs time to think about it more first, before anything can be discussed with Bowler. Because what Mark and George did raises some very, very interesting and very, very dangerous questions. He has to decide what he thinks about them, and what he will do, if anything. Hart sinks into the settee, deeper and deeper in thought.

***

Hart and Bowler were outside the courthouse early, sat against the entrance wall. Once the court was in session, in an ideal world they'd sit in the jury box or the gallery, but obviously that might mean being sat on, so they preferred to play it safe and sit against the back wall. They hadn't meant to get there this early; Hart had read the clock wrong. So they were outside watching the world go by, waiting until the day's affairs began. Attending court wasn't something they did often, but it was an interesting change sometimes, and Hart liked to touch base. Bowler was happier to go along too since his exposure to Court TV, although the American system was quite different to the British in many ways.

They were sat in silence, both idly watching Kriss Akabusi making his way down the opposite side of the street in the distance. Hart didn't even know who the real Kriss Akabusi was, and understood the lookalike reference even less when Bowler told him in a past conversation, long ago, that the real Kriss Akabusi was black, even though this Guest was white. Bowler had explained that he thought they both had the exact same shape head. *A massive forehead,* he'd said. They were both wondering at what point Kriss would see them and turn around to head in the opposite direction. Once he was about a hundred metres away, he spotted them, then immediately ceased his silent rantings, put his head down, and crossed the street to walk the other way.

"D'you think it'll be a murder case today?" Bowler enquired. Hart started slightly in surprise, partly because he'd been completely lost in his own thoughts, and partly because Bowler rarely started conversations these days.

"Who knows," said Hart, happy to talk. "It's been so long since we've been here, I've no idea what's going on. Still … for all you can say about Coventry's crime rate, I don't think it's that high on the murder scale. Not like London, or even Nottingham. So I doubt we'll be in for anything with a high amount of, you know. Drama."

Bowler nodded silently.

"It's really not like TV, is it," he said. "Lawyers solving cases. They just want to get their clients off and look good so they can keep charging top whack." Hart bristled silently, not sure if this was a definite, clear jab in his direction or another one of Bowler's slowly increasing brand of passive aggressive comments. Bowler had become very good at those, and Hart hated him for it. There would only be a row if he bit, and Hart decided to win by not even acknowledging the barb.

"Well, that's their job," he said in a lighthearted tone, deliberately breezy. "Solving cases is for the police. Plus … well … look at me. Us, I mean. We're not much good at solving a murder mystery of our own. How many years has it been now?"

Bowler shrugged hastily in response like he wasn't bothered (though Hart knew this was one subject Bowler had great interest in), although he was clearly annoyed. This simultaneously proved both that his comment *had* been a veiled dig, and that he was annoyed it hadn't had an effect. Hart grinned to himself inside. *Up yours, Bowler.*

"Yes …" Hart continued. "Although, in all fairness to ourselves, it's hard to find clues or leads in a place where no one talks, where we don't leave any physical evidence behind—you remember the dissolving body, how those … crumbs, I suppose, disappeared into the floor?—and we certainly didn't have any witnesses. Holmes himself would have struggled." He leaned back and placed his hands behind his head. "Maybe it was just my theory, after all; maybe we each have a certain amount of time to get out, and his time was shorter than everyone else's. It's unlikely, but it's something."

"No," snapped Bowler, picking at his fingers in an annoyed manner. Hart thought he noticed a slight shake there. "You don't even believe that's a possibility. It doesn't even make any sense. Look at The Beast, how long he's been here. And the others that were here before you. Why would his be any shorter?"

"But it can't be totally dismissed offhand, because he wasn't—"

"Yeah, yeah, you've said it before, but I'm sorry, that's just not enough, there's too much against it and you know it." Bowler was looking at him now, finger wagging. Now it was Hart's turn to shrug, but a lot more casually. A slow, deliberate, lazy shrug. He was enjoying this. He didn't really believe it, no—though there *was* evidence to support it—but it was bloody good to goose Bowler for a change.

He was about to give him a bit more when a Check-in suddenly and effortlessly floated into view from the west, appearing from behind a cloud.

Hart's hand shot out and grabbed Bowler's shoulder, his eyes locked on it. Bowler actually slapped it away, not seeing the Check-in at first, but looked reflexively where Hart was staring. Bowler froze.

"Is that—"

And Hart couldn't answer; at this range, it was hard to tell. It *looked* like a Check-in, but it could just as easily be a Flyer. *Dammit, get closer! Oh please God, please, please,* please—

"*Hart*, which one is it? I've not seen enough of them! Hart! Hart! For fuck's sake—" And Bowler was on his feet, shielding his eyes. It was like the strangest cinematic effect made real, seeing the shimmering object gliding over the city centre. With the people walking below oblivious to its presence, it sailed gracefully over the buildings, hanging impossibly in the air. Hart was on his feet too, willing, *willing* it to begin a graceful downward slide. The sun (*the bloody* sun!) was making it too hard to look straight at it, to tell what type it was or where it was going. Where had all the bloody clouds gone?

"*Hart—*"

"*I don't know Bowler, I can't bloody well see!!*" yelled Hart, and Bowler snorted in frustration, but then let out a little pained noise—as did Hart—as they both saw the floating shape begin to clearly head upwards, arcing freely towards the blue sky and sun.

"No ..." said Bowler quietly, and actually reached up a hand towards it as it began to disappear from view.

Hart's shoulders dropped, and after a moment, he wiped his face with his hand. They stood in silence for two minutes as it rose, watching it become a little dot in the sky, and then vanishing entirely. As they did so, Hart reached a depressing insight; they'd seen Flyers before, but had never been as affected by them as this. He realised how much they both needed it now. How much they were both aware of how different things were. He sat down, unable to suppress a sigh. He found himself thinking that he'd really like a drink. Booze ... he'd *really* missed it the first ten years. He didn't so much these days, but at moments like this ...

"You all right?" he asked, staring at his feet.

"Yeah," said Bowler, kicking at a stone. His foot passed through it silently.

"So ... a Flyer, eh? Gone on to ... well ..." he suddenly felt a strong urge to get Bowler back on side, to make up for the ribbing. He needed it. "... to wherever we're getting to eventually, eh?"

"Shut up, Hart," said Bowler, quietly but sternly. "You don't even believe in it." He still hadn't turned around. He was still looking at the sky. "You felt what was on the other side of The Wall," he said. "You don't believe in anywhere else because you're *scared* to believe in it. You think you'll go loopy if you do. You don't have the ... *guts* to believe because of what might happen to your head. You've quit and you don't even know it."

Oh, Bowler, thought Hart, *yesterday I'd have screamed at you for that, and maybe because you were half right, but now ... I really pity you, my friend. And I'm so sorry, but I have done my time and then some.*

"Scared? I'm definitely scared, Bowler." He stood, taking his eyes off Bowler and stretching his back out of habit. He then fiddled with his suit as he continued speaking. "You were right earlier. I don't really believe that it's a case of time running out. But I thought of something else, and I didn't want to worry you at the time." He looked up, to where the Flyer had disappeared, and sighed heavily. "You say that because The Beast and the other Guests that were before me have been here longer, therefore it's unlikely to be a case of each Guest's time running out individually. And I think you're probably right there."

Bowler stared at him, blinking occasionally in a dim-faced manner. He didn't like this. Something in Hart's voice worried him. Did he know something? What was this? Suddenly it didn't seem like Hart at all.

"But what if it wasn't each Guest's time running out? What if it was The *Foyer's* time running out?"

"What ... what the hell d'you—"

"I mean, what if this place was only meant to last a certain amount of time? What if it was only supposed to be here for a while as ... as some kind of last chance saloon; get sent here for whatever reason, and you only have as long as the place lasts to work out a way out and ... I don't know ... *win* yourself a place outside?"

"That's crazy—"

160

"The logistics of it don't matter, but the basic idea does. What if this is the start of the place closing down? Guests dying? Think about it; the city is here," said Hart, spreading his arms out and turning lazily left and right, taking in all of his surroundings. He turned to Bowler, palms out, face unreadable. "The city isn't The Foyer. The *city* is inconsequential. We walk straight through it. It's a backdrop to us. So what *is* real, and physical here? What is The Foyer?"

Bowler said nothing.

"The Foyer is the Guests and The Wall, and that's it. Nothing else. So say you were whoever or whatever set up The Foyer ... how would you shut it down? Go through the options. Destroy The Wall? You couldn't. The Guests would get out. So how would you do it?"

Still nothing from Bowler. He really, really didn't like where this was going.

"You'd have to start by *killing the Guests.*"

Bowler laughed in a forced way.

"This is utter bollocks, Hart—"

"You know what, Bowler? Maybe it is. Maybe it's just another theory. But the reason you can't dismiss it is this; we know it's impossible for a Guest to murder another Guest. Impossible."

"As far as we know."

"As far as we know, yes. But regardless, George was killed. And as we were talking about not ten minutes ago, as we know, he wasn't the *only* one." He paused, remembering the second time, before continuing.

"George wasn't the only one that got killed."

"But they were five years apart! George was killed ten years ago, and it wasn't 'til five years later—"

"Who says it has to be a quick process? In fact, doesn't that sound like a fair way of doing it? One every five years? Give a bit of time to everyone to figure out what's going on?"

161

"But ... but ..."

And Hart knew he had him. He knew his plan—his lie—had worked. Hart really did pity him, but Bowler was making it easy to swallow any guilt.

Bowler scared Hart these days. The way he shook.

"First George was killed, in a way we cannot possibly know about," Hart continued, watching Bowler's worried eyes drop to the floor; he felt a pang in his heart as he saw in this a glimpse of his old friend, if only briefly. "And—maybe it was for the same reasons, maybe they'd both worked out what was going on, I don't know, because they'd both definitely been up to something—five years later, Mark was killed as well."

He waited until Bowler looked up.

"Which was five years ago this year."

***

2005:

Dealing with a madwoman would be hard enough at the best of times, Hart assumes, but when you can't hear her speak it's extremely difficult, not to mention unpleasant.

He wishes Bowler were here; it really should be his turn, even though Hart is better at this, but Bowler is off by himself again. This is the case more and more these days, but, Hart reminds himself, at least he comes back.

Sarah has spotted him on his way into the cinema, treating himself to a juicily rationed movie; Harry Potter and the Prisoner of Azkaban. Having heard so much about the books and, of course, not being able to read them, he's very glad they've finally made the films. He finds them enjoyable, but imagines the books would be better. He misses reading, misses it a lot. Always has here, from day one. Hart was always very well read.

She'd spotted him heading into the SkyDome, and he'd made the mistake of catching her eye through the huge glass doors once he was inside. He couldn't pretend he hadn't seen her; he'd looked directly at her as she flapped her scrawny arms to get his attention. A mistake … it saddens him as he realises he thinks like that. A few years ago he would have welcomed the opportunity to check up on her, see how she was doing, to just talk *to her. It's been so long since she saw him dealing with Mark—five years—and for the last four, he'd never been able to speak to her. She'd always run straight away upon seeing Hart, waving him away as she did so. She'd been close to the edge even then, but with George now gone and with Mark nearly Loose himself, as well as her refusal to come near Bowler or Hart, she has of course rapidly deteriorated in her time alone. Now she is pretty much fully Loose, and he knows he can't bring her back. Her wild eyes, her incoherent rantings, her embarrassing state of near undress—she is barely covered now—it always makes for a very painful, awkward, and saddening conversation. Plus, it's frightening. Like looking into a mirror of one's own dark future.*

And here she is, standing at the foot of the escalator in the middle of the entertainment complex, in between the false wood front of Jumpin Jak's nightclub and the glass side entrance of Old Orleans, two venues Hart has a strong suspicion of being part of a larger corporate chain. He'd long lamented the passing of privately owned venues, on principle more than anything else. He'd visited Jumpin Jak's in the early days when it first opened, in order to people watch, and had quickly learned that the patrons weren't people he particularly liked to watch.

*Sarah is grabbing his collar now and looking up at him, babbling away, alternately serious, laughing, then scared. Hart follows his usual policy of indulging her until she goes away. She looks worse up close; her eyes have dark rings underneath them (*How is that even possible? No one can be physically tired here, they don't need to sleep*) and her hair is dirty. The latter was less surprising. He'd seen other Guests lose their hair as they went*

Loose, so dirt and disrepair were just another manifestation of the change in her clothes and appearance, he guessed. As usual, he doesn't understand a word she's saying, and he stands there nodding and smiling in the places he thinks are necessary. She's not even trying to sign, just talking like he can hear her—it's what she does now—but suddenly her hands make a familiar movement, and it takes Hart a moment to place it.

He holds up a hand, and she stops, surprised, her expression comical. He does the "back up" motion with one finger, and she seems to realise that she needs to be signing. The interruption seems to have made her a bit more lucid. Her eyes flicker for a second, then she comes back to herself and does it again.

She means Mark; the mannerisms are actually uncanny.

Hart shrugs dramatically for her: Mark? So what? *The effect is instant, she's pointing frantically off in the direction of the precinct, pulling him by his sleeve. Hart goes cold, or as cold as one can go here. He's seen this before. He doesn't want to go.*

He takes Sarah by the shoulders, gently. She's not here anymore, his friend, but when he cuts her off these days, avoids her, it isn't because he doesn't care. It's because it hurts. It's because he failed her; he made her go away.

He does the tell-me-more gesture, and she rolls her eyes—which stop twitching briefly as she does so—and starts to pull again, and now he grasps her firmly , shaking his head, and roots her to the spot. He does the gesture again, bigger and slower.

Sarah does the Mark gesture, and runs her finger across her throat.

Hart pauses. He does nothing for a moment. He then points his finger firmly at Sarah and raises his eyebrows. Are you sure? *She scowls, and knocks his hands away, and nods, throwing her own hands up. Hart gives her the calm down gesture, one hand to his chest—*I'm only checking—*but she is off now, ranting with her mouth as if Hart can hear every spittle-laden word. Hart waits it out, thinking.*

First George. Now Mark. Five years apart.

Hart lets out a heavy imaginary breath. So was it Mark getting the guts up to try Simon's idea again, or was it … but that was a stupid theory. Time limits …

But he suddenly realises Sarah is giggling to herself. She knows *something. And Hart is frightened. He puts on a smile, drawing her out;* share the joke, Sarah. *But she turns from him like a playful dog with a stick, and the giggles continue, head bent right into her hand. But there are also tears running down her cheeks and her eyes are greatly distressed. The split in her mind is visible. She knows what she is.*

Hart forces another smile, and slowly shrugs. He has to keep this as gentle as possible, but the question is there; What do you know? *Suddenly she grips* his *wrists now, hard, all laughter gone, staring pleadingly into his eyes. Her grip is tight, and painful, and she is trembling all over, biting her bottom lip. As Hart watches, blood begins to bead underneath her two front teeth. Slowly, she releases one of his wrists, and points a shaking finger towards her chest.*

Hart doesn't react on his first conclusion. He holds himself back with enormous effort, and waits for her to finish.

The same hand travels up towards her face, becoming a fist, and then two fingers extending out in a V towards her eyes.

Hart lets out a sigh of relief. He nods to her quickly, wanting to get what he can before this time of lucidity ends. He nods again, and rolls his finger.

Okay. Tell me what you saw.

Sarah does. And almost as soon as she starts, she drops back into Looseness, so much so that Hart can only piece her story together later. And because of this, he cannot set anything by it, even though it backs up his own suspicions almost totally. He needs to be certain of what she meant. These are the words of a madwoman, after all.

Hope is far too dangerous. Giving in to it, searching, is far too dangerous.

He won't know for another five years—won't know for certain—that she was telling the truth.

***

2010:

"Tenerife?"

"Umm ... no. I was thinking more ... southern ..." A giggle.

"Aaaah ... Aus*trah*-leyah again. In your dreams, I'm afraid."

"Ah, come *on* ..."

"Noooo, unless you fancy getting into even *more* debt ..."

"You could flog one of your kidneys."

"Or you could flog one of yours."

"No, *you* need to drink less, so one kidney would help you cut back ..."

"Says she with the large glass of red ..."

"Doctors say to drink a glass a *day*!"

"A glass, not a bucket."

She let out a mock gasp, placed her wine glass down on the expensive carpet, and then dove onto him, tickling and grabbing. He laughed and rolled her over easily—she was tiny—and pinned her beneath him, kneeling on her upper arms gently, taking her wrists and making her slap herself softly in her face, as she laughs hysterically.

"You know, you should really—"

"*Rob*! Stoppit, ha ha—"

"—stop hitting yourself—"

"Aaaah, ha ha, get, ha, get *off*—"

"—in the face, you know, it just looks silly—"

"*Right*, you're getting—" She struggled underneath him, staging a doomed comeback, and he leaned his head back and laughed out loud as she failed. She flounced back, out of breath, mock pouting up at him.

"Have we learned our lesson? Hmmmmmm?"

"*No!*"

"Ah well, in *that* case—" But she was saved more tickle torture by a wailing from the other room. Both their shoulders slumped down with a smile, looking at each other.

"*Your* fault, gobby."

"*Your* name was called, missy."

"Well get *off* me then," she said, slapping his thigh as he rose up off her and stood. She still paused to slap him again on the other leg as he rolled over on the settee, placing his hands behind his head and letting out a melodramatic sigh of overacted comfort, a smug smile on his face. She stuck out her tongue as she left the room, and he waved her away with his fingertips, eyes closed, smile wider.

She walked down the hallway with a genuine smile of her own, shaking her head, and entering the room at the end of the corridor, wishing again that the sale would hurry up and go through. They'd been in this place two years too long as it was, and it had been too small even then. They'd only moved into their current flat for work convenience, plus both of their former places had been with previous spouses. Rob hadn't wanted to move into the place she'd shared with Frank, and Rob's ex-wife had gotten their fantastic house after the divorce.

She opened the door, the room lit by the blue glow of the night-light. Saw the SpongeBob wallpaper, the small bed, the toys still strewn on the floor (but now was the not the time for a nag) and the small lump under the covers. Sleepy eyes peered out from a blonde head surrounded by a faded Ben 10 pillow. She didn't see her dead husband look up at her, wide-eyed, from his kneeling position by the bed as she came in; face red and streaked with tears, hands balled into fists on his thighs in an attempt to stop the damn *shaking*. Didn't hear him call her name, didn't hear him frantically apologising at a manic pitch, didn't hear him saying the boy was just like theirs would have been, would have been if not for Glasgow, how he was beautiful. She sat quietly on the bed and smiled at her five-year-old, the woman and the boy beautiful together in the blue light.

"Hey ... did we wake you up, sweetie?"

"Yersss ..."

"Oh, I'm sorry sweetheart ..." And she gathered him in her arms, pulling him into a sitting position. He clung to her, eyes already puffing over, closing with a gentle breath. "Were you scared?"

"Didden know ... waddit was ..."

The woman chuckled.

"Ah, it was just Daddy and me playing. We didn't mean to be so noisy, sweetie, I'm sorry."

"S'okay ..."

"D'you want me to sing to you? Sing the cloudy song?"

"..."

And she held him for a minute longer to make sure he was asleep, sitting on the bed. Not seeing the shaking arms attempting to wrap around them both, not hearing the constant stream of breathless apologies spewing forth like a madman's mantra. She laid her son down on the bed, watching him for a moment, before pulling the duvet up to his chin and cinching it in along his sides, leaving him cocooned. She tiptoed to the door and closed it behind her, smiling again to herself as she tiptoed back down the corridor, not seeing the mumbling, weeping figure that followed her all the way.

***

Chapter 8: In Which We See the Flames That Made a Lesser Phoenix, A Painful Good-bye, The Death of Frank Bowler, And Hear Whispers In the Dark

***

"Helen?"

"Mmmf."

"Helen. Helen. Wake up. It's the sirens. The sirens are going off."

"Sirens ..."

"Listen! It's the bloody sirens."

She's asleep on the settee, by the wireless, of course; she always naps in the evening at this time of year. The winters have just always seemed to have that effect. They'd used to call it Helen's Hibernations. Richard had always let her; it was nice, the dark outside, with the comforting voice of the World Service as he got his paperwork done by lamplight. He loves it, in fact. Except they'd broken the radio a few weeks ago—he hadn't gotten round to getting a new one—and now he'd been working by the light of a single candle since the blackout was ordered. He'd huffed about it at first, but since the summer, he believed in it wholeheartedly. Anstу had been close enough; Hillfields, far too close. So now Richard's windows were covered up without question, and even if the radio had been working, hell, he'd have turned it off.

Helen had talked of leaving, of course; she wasn't normally that kind of woman, but seeing the ruins of the Rex had really shaken her up. But they'd talked about it (he'd talked her down, of course), and they'd both agreed in the end. This was their city. They supported it. And he'd put too much work into it to let the Germans chase them from their own homes through fear.

Besides, what was the Home Guard for if it wasn't going to keep them safe, darling? In the end, he'd convinced her.

And now Richard is frightened, and almost—almost—wishing he'd listened to her. The sirens have started, and he's certain he can hear something else, something behind them, closer. Or maybe he's imagining it. Either way, he wants her awake, wants her to be able to react if need be. Plus, he needs *her awake.*

"Whattumizzit …"

He looks at his watch; it's gone seven. Dark now, winter time. Cover of darkness, bastards.

"It's seven, darling. Come on now, up you get, quickly now." He puts an arm around her shoulder and pulls her upright.

"Richard …"

"Please don't argue, darling. Can't you hear them?"

And she can now, and concern penetrates sleepiness. She looks at him, and her face catches the candlelight; past fifty, and still with that round-faced beauty that the lines and looseness of age can't dampen. He catches his breath, and in spite of the situation, he smiles. She smiles back, confused, wondering why, and there are too many reasons to say. Twenty-five happy years, no badgering him over work, always understanding the long hours and the passion, always supportive, no self-pity over her inability to bear the children he knew she always wanted so badly, her childlike appreciation of all the little things he ever did … he sees it in that darkened room. He strokes her face, and she touches his hand.

"We'd better get in the cellar, Helen."

"The cellar? You romantic brute, you. Be still, my beating heart. Take me on the tins of paint …"

"Hel-en …"

"All right, all right, I know. Can I get more clothes? It'll be freezing cold in there."

"Yes, but quickly. The blankets are down there, though."

"Yes, yes, I know ..." She stands and runs a hand across Richard's back as she leaves the room. He listens again; there's definitely something else behind the sirens. Louder. Engines. Of course, he can't look out of the window because of the taped covering, but he's certain. The usual paranoia, Helen would say, but he doesn't think she'd be right this time.

He picks up the plate with the candle on it, puts on his shoes—the cellar will be dusty—and makes his way into the back of the house while he waits. Might as well check the cellar door. Anything to take his mind off the steadily growing fear. It's not a fear of dying (the concept is too unthinkable; it's an air raid and he knows no one personally who has been killed so far. What was the total for June and August, about twenty deaths?) but fear of losing everything they'd earned. They'd have each other, but getting where he is has taken work. *They won't come here anyway, he's certain, but his heart is still racing ... is it excitement? He's not sure.*

He crouches under the stairs and pulls on the rope for the trapdoor. It sticks a bit, but it comes up with a creak of wood upon wood. He leans in, holding the candle out ahead of him; he doesn't think there will be rats, but it's not an idea he's particularly happy about, and Helen would be terrified. The light reveals the tiny room, its bare floor and walls, the cobwebs and tea chests containing Helen's keepsakes and his certificates. In a cleaner corner he sees the recently laid pile of blankets and tins of food. He knows people that have done more, but they are a lot more fearful of the raids, even more so than Richard.

He hears her feet on the stairs above him, and he rises. She's put on her old coat and her thick slippers. She's got it wrapped tight around her, prepared, even though the house isn't cold. She flashes him a brief smile.

"Come on then, Clark Gable," she says with a forced smile. "Let's get down there." She sighs, and stops and looks at him, face slightly scrunched, feeling guilty about what she was going to say. "I hate this," she says.

"I know. It's horrible. But we'll get down there, get comfy, have a cuddle, and wait for the all clear. We'll make it nice, yes?"

She curls her lip briefly, a joking acquiescence, but looks around the room for a moment, taking in her things, her ornaments, her pictures, as if trying to preserve the scene in her memory. He stops her—he loves her—and puts his arm around her.

"Don't be silly," he says, smiling. "We were fine before, weren't we? Every time?" She nods, a gentle shrug in her thin shoulders, thinner than on their wedding day. And he leads her by her shoulders towards the trapdoor, and they enter the basement. She goes in first, gingerly, and as he begins to descend he realises that he can hear the engines now, clearly. Richard looks down to her, lit by her own candle, already rearranging blankets and making a little den for them, like they used to make on Sunday afternoons in bed together. Papers and toast and making love. They don't do the latter so much anymore, but to focus on this would be to suggest things have cooled between them, and they have not.

"Helen," he says, stage whispering, though he doesn't know why. She looks up to him, her eyes shining in the dim light. "I have to go and see. The engines are getting louder."

"Richard—"

"Two minutes, I'll be two minutes."

"No, don't—"

"Look, I'll be so quick you won't even know I'm gone, but I have to see. Two minutes, I promise." She isn't complaining now—she's known him long enough to know when it's pointless—but her hands are on her hips, and her face is pleading. He closes the trapdoor anyway to block the candlelight, and heads to the front door.

The noise is all around, and Richard isn't the only one looking out of a pitch-black doorway. One hundred yards up the terraced street, with moonlight shining on the road in lieu of the darkened streetlamps, he can see

John Strutter peering into the sky. Farther up the road there are others doing the same. One leg inside their houses, the other sticking out onto the street, as if somehow this keeps them safe. None look his way, and all eyes are fixed firmly on the skies. He isn't surprised, because out here the prominent noise filling the air is now the drone of the aircraft engines. He joins the upturned eyes, and to his horror he can see black shapes moving across the stars, blocking them out, emerging from over the roofs at the other end of the street. Other people have seen them, and are pointing, but now it's suddenly pointless as they are blocked out by dazzling white light that draws the eye. What on earth are they?

It's a harsh light that makes it hard to see the shapes above, hanging in the air like ghosts. Richard's heart leaps into his throat in panic. He's never seen anything like this in his life. These aren't bombs. They aren't falling. They're floating *there, hanging above the city, casting their iridescent light onto the streets. But then he sees they* are *falling after all, just very, very slowly, and his mind solves the problem for him, with a sudden combination of logic and sight. How do you find your targets in a city smothered in a blackout?*

You bring the light to them.

And now, his shock and confusion behind him, he can see them for what they are. Great parachutes, flare-like, many of them hanging above the city. He can see them, floating like great white Christmas decorations. But it's November, part of his mind adds crazily.

It feels like seconds, but it's really been several minutes, many more than the two he promised his wife, who sits in their cellar wrapped in a blanket and torn in terrible indecision whether to go after her husband or to sit and wait as he asked. She has her hands over her ears.

Some of the people in the street are calling to each other, but Richard can't hear what they're saying over the noise, and that's when the first incendiary hits. It hits the roof of a house about seven hundred yards away, which goes up immediately with a truly deafening bang and a blinding flash of phosphorous. There are screams from the watchers, and they scurry back inside like rabbits, as Richard can see more dropping in the distance, more about to drop his way. The night lights up even more than before, hellish and alive. Just before he dashes back inside his own house, he thinks wildly Markers, they're putting down MARKERS, *but then he's already slamming the door shut and fleeing for the cellar.*

He yanks open the trapdoor and sees the relief flash across his wife's face, replaced immediately by fear when she sees the look on his. He's down the steps in a flash and has his arms around her immediately, unsure of what to say, not knowing how to reassure her when he is terrified himself. Everything is at risk. Everything.

"It's close, isn't it! I heard a bang. I didn't hear those before," she says into his chest. He can't lie to her.

"It's close. I don't ... I don't think they're aiming for us, this street, I mean. They'll be after the factories. Not us. Anything that hits us will be an accident."

She doesn't say anything, and after a moment her grip tightens. He continues:

"I mean ... I don't think they're meaning *to hit here, so we should be safe, if we're lucky. Do you see what I mean? They're* not *trying* to hit us."

"Yes, yes, I understand. Let's be quiet, though. I'm dreadfully scared, Richard."

He is too. And the guilt ... he took her away from London, took her to his city. He brought her here. Was more than happy to get her away from her swine of a father. But wouldn't London be even more dangerous now? But he'd had his work, hadn't he? In the end, would that cost ... and he stops himself, and holds her tightly.

"It's all right, Hel. We're safe here," he tells her.

Ten minutes pass in the dark, in the silence. Ten minutes listening to the muffled booms, the muffled yells. Can he hear vehicles? He doesn't know. Seeing those hellish lights means he will not go up there again until the all clear is given. He is beginning to feel hopeful now—although uncertainty means he won't give into it—but he thinks the dull drone has gone from the noise above. No planes. No bombers. His wife is breathing closely against his chest. He thinks she might have dozed off again, and he wants this to be true, doesn't want her to be scared and doesn't want to risk waking her by checking. He will wait a few more minutes until he's more certain the planes have gone, and then he will wake her.

But a minute later his blood begins to run cold in his veins, as a horrible growing certainty begins, growing as he listens. The engines again, coming back. He again thinks it's his imagination, the encroaching dark around him making the mind spring to the worst assumptions, but another minute passes and now he is sure. A second wave.

And his spine turns to ice as he realises that these bombers will be following the markers.

He grips his sleeping wife tightly, while he considers the lunacy of running. They're under the floor, he thinks, where nothing can fall on them, under the foundations. Even if the house were to collapse, they would be safe, and with that thought Richard realises that he was an idiot. He'd give it all up, the life they'd worked so hard to build, all of the oh-so trivial things he feared losing, all of it sacrificed in a heartbeat in exchange for the guarantee that he could come out of this with Helen safe, with the two of them together.

Richard Hart kisses his wife's forehead and starts to say I love you *to her unconscious, lined face, when there is the loudest noise he can imagine and he doesn't remember anything until the hospital.*

Where they tell him what happened. Where he discovers the full extent of his loss. Afterwards, when he is discharged, he staggers out into the city, stunned and led only by a primitive, thoughtless, instinctive curiosity to see what is left of the place in which he built his life.

He sees what is left in its place, and he follows the only course of action he believes is left to him.

He wrongly believes that he is going to join his wife.

***

Bowler headed downstairs, pulling at his hands. It was so frustrating, the way his hands kept moving like that. He'd felt a lot worse than this, he was sure. He always got emotional seeing the pair of them, but that was only normal, for God's sake. He just wanted to make sure they were okay, and yes, it was upsetting, who wouldn't be upset by that, for God's sake. But he'd put up with it, to know they were all doing all right. He just couldn't keep his hands still. What was wrong with them, *for God's sake.* He wondered where Hart was, and then immediately thought of what he would say if he knew where Bowler had been. Hell, Hart probably *did* know where Bowler'd been, it wasn't like he made a particularly great effort to keep it secret these days. He used to, back at the start, back when he didn't want to upset the Great Leader, bless his Hart.

This set him off into a fit of giggles that went on longer than they should have done, and this caused Bowler a minor bit of concern, but they passed and he forgot about it. Jesus, he could hear Hart now, moaning at him about *danger, danger;* well, he'd been coming here for a long time and yes, there'd been tears, and yes, it was upsetting, but who wouldn't be upset by it, for God's sake? Yeah, he was a bit shaky, but he'd been here twelve fucking years, for God's sake. Twelve fucking years. This made Bowler suddenly angry, and he swung a fist at the nearest wall, which it of course passed through harmlessly. Look at it! Look at that! Can't even punch a fucking wall, *for God's sake!*

No, Hart wasn't shaky, of course he wasn't, he'd come from a time where being bored and doing fuck all was what you did all day for fun. A time when their idea of great entertainment was Chester Fucking Chuckles tap dancing to "I'm A Yankee Doodle Dandy" and playing the fucking banjo with his cock. Move over Michael Jackson. A time when a fucking radio was the pinnacle of entertainment, and a wild night out was drinking stout in a shitty old boozer. This whole thing was probably like a fucking holiday to Hart, fucking hi de hi fucking hi de fucking ho, and this set him off laughing again, his anger cutting off like a flicked switch. Ah, fuck Hart ... he'd go and find him and probably tell him where he'd been for once—Hart knew already, he had no doubt—and show him how everything was just fine in Bowlerland. It'd be good to see the look on his face. Then they could go and watch some telly or something and forget all about it. He suddenly really wanted to watch telly, suddenly *needed* to.

He reached the foot of the stairs, passed through the door, and found Hart outside, sitting on the floor. He turned when Bowler appeared.

"Hello," Hart said, standing. Bowler felt a once-familiar stab of panic. Caught. He nearly switched to the defensive, but realised in a rare moment of clarity that the best policy was to simply ignore the situation and play dumb. They both knew the score. Why even discuss it?

"Hi," said Bowler, straight-faced. Hart didn't respond, and looked up at the building that Bowler had just left. Bowler stiffened. No hiding it, then. It was all coming out. He felt the blood rush into his head.

"Bowler. I'm not ..." Hart put his hands forward, looking at the floor. He blew out his cheeks, dropped his hands and looked Bowler in the eye. "How long since you started coming here again?" Bowler was ready for the question, and had his response all ready.

"That's none of your business, Hart," he said. That was good. Confident sounding, solid, well put. And Hart couldn't come back from that. There was no way Hart could claim that it *was* his business. And Bowler decided that if

178

Hart *did* try and say that, Bowler was going to hit Hart as hard as he could. The arrival of this thought didn't surprise him.

"Bowler ... Frank. Please. I'm not trying to argue with you here. I'm asking out of concern, all right? Actually, let me change the question. How many times have you been here this week? Seriously?"

That fucker! Picks a fight and then tries to turn it on me, like he's the one being reasonable! Talking down to me like an arsehole! Like I need to be treated with kid gloves, for God's sake!

Bowler took a deep breath.

That's what he wants you to do. Get mad. Make a fool of yourself. Show *him, Bowler.*

"Hart ... it's *none* ... of your fucking ... business." Bowler punctuated each word with a point of his finger. Unfortunately he left his finger held out in the air for too long, and his hand visibly shook, right in between their faces.

They both saw it. Bowler snapped his hand back quickly and looked at Hart, red-faced and set-jawed, daring him to say anything. Hart sighed, heavily, and rubbed his forehead with his right hand.

"Look at you, Bowler. You're as red as a tomato, the veins are out in your forehead; you're ready to blow right now. Look at how little it takes these days. Your temper is ready to snap at any point, just look at your ha—" Hart stopped himself, changed the word. "Look at the way you're looking at me now. Look ..." Hart sighed again and dropped his hands to his sides. "I didn't come to argue with you, or tell you not to do what you're doing, or to tell you off, or anything like that. I simply ... I came to say I'm going to go off by myself for a few days. Not long, I just don't know when I'll be back. But I have to have some time by myself."

Why? Why? What the fuck are you up *to? What have you got? What's going on? First this shit at the courthouse, and now this! You're* up *to something, Hart. It's obvious, for God's sake!*

"Fine," Bowler said and shrugged. He looked like a petulant child. There was a drawn out pause. Bowler thought that Hart seemed to be assessing him. He didn't like it.

"I just wanted to make sure ... I just wanted to say this," said Hart. "And don't get angry, Bowler, it's just my opinion, and you can do what you like with it. Don't come here anymore. Never again." Bowler laughed a quiet false laugh at this and shook his head, but said nothing as Hart continued.

"This place, and The Foyer together ..." Hart said, "I don't think you were built to handle The Foyer in the first place, Bowler, and that isn't an insult, but I'm not sure it wouldn't have had the same effect all by itself, in the end. But add this into the situation—coming here all the time—and Bowler ... I don't think you'll last much longer. I've ... tried to help you as much as I can."

Bowler scoffed loudly here, and at this Hart's restraint finally snapped. His face twisted in anger.

"Where did he go?" Hart asked.

"Who are you on about?"

"The nice, quiet chap that first came here. All I see now is an angry thug. Maybe that's my fault, I don't know—" His words were cut off as Bowler hit him in the face, as hard as possible.

It didn't hurt, of course, but the emotional impact was as great as the force of the blow would have been. Hart turned his head back, sadly, looking at a shocked Bowler—Hart had barely even flinched—and slowly shook his head. Bowler thought he could see tears coming but didn't stop to acknowledge them as he was already throwing another punch. It landed again, but this time as it did Hart stepped forward and grabbed Bowler's shoulder, pushing him to the floor and pinning him there. There was no anger on Hart's face. He looked miserable. Bowler screamed incoherently at him, enraged, throwing more punches into his sides, but Hart didn't register them.

"I'll tell you something, Bowler, and you need to listen," said Hart, looking down into Bowler's furious eyes, and when Bowler carried on screaming, Hart sighed heavily, not wanting to do it, and twisted Bowler's shoulder until he stopped his ranting and listened. "I'm sorry, I really am, but this is extremely important. You need to hear this, and I need to know you heard it. I'll come clean. I'm not a very good liar, Bowler. I think you can guess what's going on, even though you don't know how it's happening, and unfortunately I need to make sure it stays that way. But listen to me now. The others go mad through loneliness. That's not what's doing it to you here, though. It's the other part of it that's getting you the most; it's the frustration that's making you go mad. It's sending you Loose, Bowler. You can't walk away, and by God you need to. And that ..." he trailed off, and the tension left his body. When he spoke again, the words were quiet, soft. "That's all I can say, really. I'm pretty sure you'll figure out the rest by yourself. I'll come and leave you a big clue before ... well. Just enough for you to work it out, but not so much that you could beat me to it."

He sighed and dropped his head.

"I can't *risk* it," he said. "That's the problem. I can't risk telling you fully. I think ... I think I've done my duty by you, Bowler. And if I *have* let you down ... then I'm sorry, Frank. I tried. I really did." He released Bowler's shoulder and stood looking down at him for a second, still fumbling with all the old Hart inhibitions, then took a deep breath. He opened his mouth to say something, faltered, stopped, shook his head ... and then turned and began to walk away.

Bowler flipped over onto his stomach, red-faced to bursting point, confused, enraged, desperate, and screamed after him.

"So the experiment's over then?! Yes?! You fucking bastard!"

Hart paused, mid-stride, then resumed walking, but stopped a few steps later and turned around, shaking his head. Annoyed, perhaps, at his own damned curiosity.

"Experiment, Bowler?"

"You fucking know. Get yourself a little eternity buddy to see if it'll help make sure you don't end up like the others. Get yourself nice and *safe*, you fucking coward. That's always been your problem, Hart, you're a big fucking *chicken*! But, what, you're done now, are you?! You know something, yeah? You think you're getting out?! You think you're getting *out*?!"

Bowler's white eyes bulged in his red face, neck thick and swollen with rage.

"You've got *nothing*! You've got *nothing! Tell me!! Tell me!!* Tell *me!!* What have you got? What have you *got?*"

Hart stood and watched Bowler writhe. He didn't speak, and he looked thinner than usual, lessened.

"You've got *nothing*," said Bowler again, this time with a mad grin, raising one accusatory finger. "You're stuck here, Hart, and you know what's *really* bad for you, Hart, I'll tell you, Hart, I'll *tell you*, Hart, and I've wanted to say this for five years, five *years!*"

Bowler's grin became a dark chuckle as his eyes blazed at Hart from the floor.

"You see, I *know*, Hart, and I've known this for a long time. *You* need *me* ... more than I need *you*. Because as hard as it is being alone here, I'm not *scared* of it like you are. You ..." Bowler's finger, that hadn't dropped throughout this rant, jabbed in Hart's direction. "You're *fucked* without me. *Fucked!*"

Hart didn't even blink. Despite his current mental state, Bowler recognised that this should not have been the response to what he'd just said. He'd just taken the elephant in the room and shone a 1000-megawatt spotlight on it, and Hart was just standing there, slack faced and impassive. Bowler's laughter died.

182

"Not so long ago, Bowler," said Hart, and Bowler realised that it worse than indifference. Hart was genuinely pitying him, and this raised a dim memory in Bowler's mind, one he couldn't grasp. "You'd have been fairly right about that. But not anymore. It might not make any difference to you, but ... I'm really sorry to do this. I've ..." He broke off, and huffed in a huge amount of imaginary air and blew it out heavily. With it came seventy years of stiff-upper-lippedness, and when he looked up, Bowler could definitely see moistness in Hart's eyes. It was horrible.

"I can't risk missing this, and I have no idea when ..." another sigh, another pause, and longer this time, an average man at the end of what little resources he had in the first place. "I've paid my dues, Bowler. I'll make sure you get your chance, I'll think of something. Though I have no idea how long it will be until you ..." Another pause, and he shook his head at himself—it was clear where it was directed—but this time it concluded with Hart balling his fists until the knuckles whitened, guilt dismissed and replaced by anger.

"This is *mine*, and I've earned it. Seventy years, Bowler, seventy-god-awful-*years* ..." Hart looked around himself for a second, and Bowler saw his jaw harden and nostrils flare. Disgust. "And at the same time, Bowler, regardless ... you keep up what you're doing and it's all academic. But me ..." Another look around. "I'm done. Don't follow me, Bowler. I don't want to hurt you ... and I hope you realise I really do mean that," he added, quietly. It was clear now that his restraint was at breaking point, and so Bowler wasn't surprised when Hart wiped his mouth with his hand and, after a last glance at his former friend, turned and began to walk away.

Bowler felt intense panic wash through him. All previous thoughts went with it, and all he knew was that he needed to stop Hart. He scrambled back up to his knees on the concrete street.

"Hart! *Hart!! Look—I'm sorry! I, I ... I won't come here anymore! I promise! We can make it like before, I promise, I promise!*" Hart didn't stop this time. He kept walking down the street, and Bowler knew that in about thirty seconds he would be gone from view and that he would be alone amongst the dead, without even George or any of the others. How had he not seen this? What the hell was going on?

"*I'm promising you, for God's sake!! Listen! Listen to me! I'm promising! I'm promissiiiing!!*" Hart kept walking, now action figure-sized in Bowler's view. "*Hart! Haaaart! Please! Oh God, please! I can't be alone here, Hart! I can't be alone here!! Hart!! Hart!! I need you, please, oh, oh please!!*" But Hart kept going, and Bowler's shifting mind changed gear at the sight, that Hart was *leaving* him, that Hart *could* leave him. How could he *do this?*

"*You think I don't know how you figured it out?! I've always known, you motherfucker!! Ever since Mark went as well, it was all so simple! Funny how, once you had me all locked in, that George died, isn't it?! Then Mark? Because you could gamble once you had me, couldn't you?!?*" Bowler began to pound his fists into the floor with every syllable, giving him the appearance of a child throwing a tantrum. Hart continued to walk. "*You could try things out, or even smarter, plant the ideas in their heads and let* them *try them out, right?! More experiments!! And if they went wrong, you'd always have me, right? And now you've got it!! You've finally worked it out!! Well, well done, you fucking bastard!! I know what you did! I know you got them killed!! I know you got them kiiiiillllledd!!*" This last was a guttural, hysterical shriek, and Bowler rolled onto his back and continued to scream to the sky. Hart finally rounded the corner without turning to look back, travelling to his destination.

Bowler never saw him again.

***

The bottle has helped take the edge off the pain of the black eye, but it hasn't killed the rest of the pain in his face and won't even come close to killing the real pain, the soul-hurt, that fills his whole brain and makes him feel cold—literally, physically cold—all over.

*He's in his living room—*their *living room, a voice in his head throws at him, and he corrects it—and there is a lot of mess covering the floor, made worse by his own blood spread everywhere. That part wasn't intentional, although the systematic destruction of the TV, the shelves, the living room door, the lamp, the coffee table, the small dining table, and the pictures was. Every picture apart from the one he holds in his hands right now, the one that is giving him his current dilemma.*

It has been, looking back, the worst evening he can imagine, though that makes it sound far, far too light, like an awkward dinner party. He shifts on the blood-soaked sofa, and that jolts the other physical *pain. The worst one, much worse than the black eye, and the JD has helped with it a lot less than he thought it would. He thought that's what they did in films, used the booze, but he supposes it should have been pretty obvious it wouldn't work in real life. He grits his teeth and waits for it to die off.*

While he does, he is—for the first time that night—able to separate himself from the situation and see it as an outsider would. He's drunkenly aware of that internal shift, and realises that at least the booze is doing something. This makes him smile, and he smiles more because he is smiling. It's good to know she left him with one thing. He can still smile, although he knows it will be brief. Even with his current positive shift of perspective, reflecting—for the hundredth time in the last hour and a half—the rest of the evening's events will be ...

Well ... just look at yourself, Frank, and see what it's all done to you.

But it's not just tonight, is it? *the voice continues.* She was right, she was totally right, and you even had a chance to fix everything and you FUCKED it, fucked US, fucked YOURSELF, and left yourself with NOTHING, you fucking—*but Bowler clamps down on it and yet cannot stop himself from going back to a time about two hours past, outside a big house in Allesley, the house he'd followed her to. Big place. Money. Money man. Big earner. Not a no-job fuck like Frank Bowler. Nononono. Sees her car parked outside, and amazingly, she's still standing on the doorstep in the arms of the other guy, a lengthy intense comfort session. Him comforting her because of her experiences with Bowler. Another man telling his wife, his* wife, *that it's okay because she's away from Bowler now, that she's with a good man, a better man, and that her* husband *is the cause of her pain.*

Of course, Bowler is already out of the car and crossing the road, though neither of the pair has seen him yet. Part of his mind is assessing his rival; a little bit taller than he, but slimmer. He doesn't think this consciously. Instinct is doing it for him. Conscious, rational thought is not occurring in Bowler right now. Were anyone who knew Bowler to see him, they would not recognise him. This rage, this anger, this is not Frank Bowler. But whoever it is, he's striding across the road and the other guy sees him—Rob From Accounts, Bowler remembers—sees him, and to fuel Bowler's fire, he says something in Suzie's ear, and she turns to see him. She starts to say something, possibly in shock or anger—"Frank!"—but Rob From Accounts has stepped in front of her and is ushering her into the house. She hesitates, but she GOES, she actually GOES INSIDE.

Then Rob From Accounts is stepping forward himself, crossing the distance between them over his lengthy gravel driveway, passing his Beemer in the twilight. His hands are raised, saying something about the police, and that he doesn't want things to get out of hand. Bowler isn't listening to his words—they're just noise, noise meant to distract him from what he wants to do, and there is nothing that will stop him—and is already swinging a heavy fist at Richard's head, who somehow isn't on the end of it like he should be, he's suddenly off to the side, and now his voice is raised too. That feels better to Bowler, though Rob From Accounts is saying something about not being an idiot, how the police are on their way, for God's sake, but Bowler is already turning and swinging again, and this time something hits the inside of his forearm, meaning the punch is stopped and it doesn't go where it's supposed to, and immediately after that something explodes on his left temple and everything goes white. He feels, far away, the gravel drive crunching against his back, and another white flash as the back of his head hits it, too, a split second after. He tries to spring back up, but his body isn't responding, and pain is exploding in his skull.

He's lost his bearings totally, but he can hear Rob From Accounts' heavy breathing, and then hears him speak.

"Don't get up. The police are on their way. Stay down."

Then crunching gravel as he heads back to the house. Bowler turns towards the sound, and horribly sees Suzie at the window, looking out, having seen the whole thing. She doesn't have her hand over her mouth, no tear in her eye, not even the opposite, not even a malicious grin, just that awful inexpressive face. Then she drops the curtain back as the door slams, and Rob From Accounts has entered the house.

Bowler lies there, defeated—he is very aware of the sensation, if not the word—and staring at the sky, numbed and distant, like someone has hit the pause button on his fury. He is not aware of the logic consciously, but in his mind it is unquestioned.

This is of his own making. How can he complain? After all, after everything he's done, doesn't he deserve this? These thoughts are not clearly spoken in his mind; they are abstract, a feeling rather than a cognitive process.

He feels unfillable. He thinks of holidays, he thinks of Christmas, he thinks of nights out with the boys, and in this very strange, whirling moment, they all seem black and white, sucked dry, and these are the things that should fill this hollow pit inside him, but they seem to be like adverts for insurance, boiled potatoes, junk mail. They stimulate nothing.

Part of him is aware of the need to leave. Police. *The thought connects; devastated, traumatised, and now humiliated (*And it's all your fault, *the voice* *says), that would be too much for a man who has already* had *too much. Dragged away in handcuffs? He may have brought this on himself, but he can't give them that on top of everything else. Please God no, not that. He needs to get up.*

Struggling, and on very shaky legs, he manages to half walk, half crawl back to the car. He sees a wash of extra light flood the driveway around him— they've opened the curtains to see what's going on—but it drops away. She'd let him drive like this? Of course she would. She wants you gone.

He fumbles with the door lock, gets in the passenger seat. He chances a look in the rearview mirror. Already red and swollen, the left-hand side of his face is a mess, and it will get a lot worse. He's been hit very hard and very well, by a man who knows how to do it properly. He somehow gets the car home.

Once there—once he has collapsed helplessly in the hallway, once he has cried himself totally dry, rolling and wailing like a pathetic child—all he can think of is drinking. The thoughts in his head are too much to deal with, and thank God he has a bottle of JD in the kitchen as he'd be fucked without it. After fumbling the cupboard open blindly, he gropes for it, finds it, opens it.

And as he breaks their *table,* their *TV,* their *things, unaware of his own screams, unaware of his neighbours sitting up in their beds discussing whether they should phone the police, unaware of himself repeating her name, and that empty feeling inside him grows until he can't imagine a time where it will ever be full. He sees a future that stretches out the same way every day, and it terrifies him beyond belief, and he doesn't want it, can't take it.*

And he thinks how he can fix both, fix the fear and make sure *she finally reacts to* something.

And so here he is now, swigging occasionally from the bottle in his hand, the settee getting wetter and wetter around him. Although there is a growing sense of fear—a different fear—he feels a lot of relief. Not just from the physical pain; now more time has passed, it's finally ebbing, the booze doing something after all as it combines now with his slowly dimming senses, his slowly dimming awareness. But no, the relief is in his head as well.

He's escaping that terrible, terrible emptiness, and all the confusion is gone because none of it matters *now. Everything is outside of his control, his choice, and it's wonderful. As his vision begins to cloud over, he thinks he can hear a knocking at the door. Something dimly flickers in his head, but he can hear an authoritative male voice saying something, though Bowler realises it's nothing to get worked up about. Still, for a second there, as the thought of possible concern had flashed across his mind, it triggered another one; is he sure he's not made a mistake?* Well … too late now if you have, son, *the voice in his head says, and Bowler smiles faintly (his facial muscles are losing their ability to respond) although he can't seem to get his arm to bring the bottle to his mouth as he'd like now; his arm lies twitching slightly in his blood-soaked lap.*

The knocking is starting up again at the door, louder, and the authoritative voice outside is speaking more forcefully, but he ignores it and lets his eyes close fully. That's even better, and although the fear is there now, stronger, in another part of his mind, that easy feeling talks to it, soothes it, helps it to accept what's happening.

Come on, *it says.* Whatever comes next … it can't be any worse than this.

***

Many hours later, Bowler stopped looking. He sat down in the sloping walkway outside Primark, which was now closed (it had long been dark out). He was all cried out, numb, and confused, unaware of his twitching hands (and, now, feet). He was just so damn *messed up*. Did Hart really say something about getting out? Had Bowler made that bit up? Bowler *thought* he had. Had they even had that conversation? No … they'd had it. They definitely had. He just remembered being so certain that Hart was off, leaving him, but at the same time ... he didn't seem to remember him actually saying so. Bowler just needed to talk to him, he was sure, so they could clear it all up. He remembered being angry, ridiculously angry, but now he just wanted to talk. If Hart wanted to him to say sorry, he'd say sorry. He just needed it explained, for God's sake. But he couldn't find Hart anywhere.

He sighed heavily, trying to piece the day's events together, and looked up and down the walkway, lit by ceiling lights. The closed chemists and bakery opposite were darkened holes, which seemed appropriate; nothing they sold would ever be of any use to him ever again. He ran his hands through his hair and thought about going back over to Suzie's. Just a little bit. Being alone today ... he wasn't sure he could handle it.

"Bowler."

Bowler nearly jumped clean off the floor. *Hart!* He was here! But he couldn't see him ... Bowler looked up and down the street and behind him.

"Hart? Where are you? I, I ... look, I'm really glad you're here," Bowler said, raising his voice, and turning as he talked, looking all around him, desperate for Hart to hear him.

"I don't know what's going on with me, and ... I'm scared, Hart, I'm really scared. I know I've been a bit funny lately, but my *hands*, Hart, I can't stop my *hands*—"

"I'm inside the clothing shop, Bowler. Come inside the clothing shop."

Bowler turned around to the wall of Primark he'd been leaning against. So that was where Hart's voice was coming from. Now he'd heard more, he could tell Hart was raising his voice. He must be quite a way inside the building. Bowler couldn't see him because he was inside. Of course. Why didn't Hart come out, though? Before now, that question would have given him pause, but this was a different time, and Bowler was a different man.

Breathlessly, eagerly, Bowler passed through the wall and entered the building.

"I'm coming, Hart! Yes!"

Inside the huge, cavernous building, it was extremely dark. The light from the entranceway gave some illumination, but other than that, the first floor stretched away into gloom. There was an initial set of steps that led down to the shop floor, and Bowler stood at the top of these and called.

"Where are you, Hart? I can't see you."

Bowler's head turned when the response, surprisingly, came from the left.

"I'm over here. Come and see this."

It was farther back than before, right in the middle of the shop floor, suggesting that Hart had moved farther back into the dark once he knew Bowler was coming in. Hart has now moved somewhere amongst the standing racks of clothes that spread expansively across the enormous room. Standing farther back, amongst the maze of cheaply made, affordable garments that were creating black hedges and obstacles in the gloom.

In the daytime, this place would have been a bustling, packed, bright centre of consumerism, full of people taking advantage of the prices. But now, in the heavy dark, it looked something like an Egyptian tomb; foreboding, abandoned, and full of indistinguishable relics. Silent.

Even Bowler, in his hope and relief, noted that something was odd about Hart seeming to deliberately move farther into the room, even worrying perhaps, but it was quashed by the overriding need for *contact*. He jumped down the steps and began to make his way through the darkened store, even now going round the objects in his path out of habit. Twelve years, and still some things didn't change. He was peering through the gloom as he picked his way along, eyes adjusting slightly, but still couldn't see Hart. Hart was taller than these clothing racks, wasn't he?

Bowler should be able to at least make out his figure. Maybe he was crouching, looking at whatever he wanted to show Bowler.

Maybe he's hiding, a voice said in his head, and this time it penetrated properly. Bowler stopped in the dark.

"Hart?"

"Over here, Bowler. Come quickly. You need to see what it is I have to show you."

Bowler jumped slightly. The voice was now a lot closer than Bowler thought it would be. And now he stopped to think about it; Hart's voice sounded odd. He'd been so relieved to hear his name that he'd taken it as read that it was normal (and hell, who else talked to him here? A voice saying "Bowler" meant Hart, and always had) but now it seemed like Hart sounded different. Where was he? He'd thought Hart would be ten feet or so farther away. Had he overestimated how far away Hart was, the darkness inside the store affecting his perception? It sounded now like Hart had actually moved past him, like Hart was now slightly behind and to his left, hidden by the nearest rack of clothes. *Or he moved in the dark,* said the voice again. *He called you from over there, and while you moved towards him, he moved around behind you, behind the clothes, where you couldn't see, to put himself behind you. Between you and the way you came in.*

"Come over here, Bowler."

The voice spoke again—firmer—from behind the nearest black shape, from behind him, and *now* when Bowler heard it, now he was ready to consider the possibility, he heard the voice and knew with an icy chill that whoever or whatever was talking to him in the dark, it was not Hart. Worse still, it was a voice that wasn't Hart's and *somehow he could still hear it.*

And whoever, or whatever it was, Bowler thought, it was hiding between him and the way out.

Crouching and waiting for *him*. Bowler realised, far too late, that he had walked blindly into a spider's parlour. He stood still in the blackness, while his hands spasmed violently and fear froze him to the spot, listening desperately for any sound and knowing with dread that he was not alone in the dark. He could think of nothing but the way George's dead body had crumbled in his hands.

***

Chapter 9: In Which Bowler Discovers—The Hard Way—How George and Mark Died, And Other Questions Are Answered.

***

Elsewhere, while Bowler was experiencing the terror of the abandoned store, Hart made his way slowly up Starley Road. Being so close to the ring road meant he could hear traffic every now and then; passing cars were not a constant sound this late at night. He had to admit, he'd always liked this, and in the past (though the appeal had worn off a long, long time ago) in his madder (*Looser*) moments he used to walk out into the middle of the ring road, at times like this, on nights like this. Standing in the streetlit dark with cars coming intermittently, and letting the cars "hit" him. Letting them Pass Through. As he was standing—and the vehicles' passengers were sat—he didn't have to go through the eyes of anyone, so it was mainly the thrill of putting himself in the path of what his instinct thought was imminent danger. Over the years, it had become something his mind had pretty much learned to ignore, though he still tended to avoid cars. Bowler would never have believed he ever did anything like that, he thought with a smile, but the smile quickly faded.

He reached the right house, and paused for a moment. It was possibly an extremely momentous occasion, one the biggest, if not *the* biggest of his existence—after all, his time in The Foyer was longer than his time alive on earth—and so it required a moment of reflection. Though, not too much, as his information was at best unreliable. But he didn't think so. Now he was this close, he thought he could even physically *feel* something. Feel something different in the surroundings, here in this place, leaking into him.

His information ... Sarah. What she'd told him a week ago, lying broken at his feet. It had been deeply unpleasant for them both, but she'd told him what he'd needed to know. That was the main thing right now.

Sarah, George, Mark, Bowler ... Simon. Poor, poor Simon. Simon who was absolutely right all along, but never got the chance Hart had right now. Simon who abandoned him, and who paid the price in the end. Hart couldn't blame him. Wasn't he doing the same thing to Bowler? But he'd sort it so Bowler at least knew how to get out, how to at least have some chance, whenever it may come, and however many years it might take. Bowler would just have to make sure he stayed sane, and it wasn't Hart's responsibility anymore. Dammit, hadn't he looked after Bowler enough? The boy would have gone Loose in a week. No. Seventy years was more than enough, and more than he'd deserved.

He'd blamed Simon for such a long, long time ... but now he understood. And for once, instead of hating him, he pitied Simon for being doomed to become the mad, creeping thing that he undoubtedly now was.

***

Bowler still hadn't moved for over a minute, and the voice hadn't spoken again from behind the clothing rack. The silence was deafening. Bowler's ears strained to hear for more movement, to hear any possible manoeuvres going on in the dark, but he heard nothing. He looked back to the entrance steps. Twenty feet away. It was possible he might make it, but he could hear Hart's real voice in his head. *Five years since Mark was killed.* And he knew that whatever was in here with him was something very deadly indeed.

He looked back to the coatrack, gauging distance as his imaginary heart pounded in his chest, and the voice finally spoke again, physically jolting him. It was lower this time, deeper, more resonant. Now any attempt to imitate Hart's nasal pitch had been dropped entirely, like it knew that there was no point continuing the pretence. It was a creeping voice, a cruel voice, with a crack to it that left Bowler in no doubt that the speaker was entirely insane.

"You are wondering if you can get out in time. If you can get away," it said. It sounded as if it were smiling broadly now, it's trap sprung beautifully, pleasingly. Bowler's eyes were wide and terrified in the dark.

"Bowler ..." it continued.

The pause went on, as if the speaker was enjoying it.

"*You cannot.*"

And the speaker stood, and as he did so Bowler realised the large dark shape he'd been looking at wasn't a coatrack at all, it *was* the speaker, huge and crouched and hunched, the near total blackness and surrounding obstacles and unlit promotional boards meaning the difference was undetectable. As it stood, its vast size expanding fully, Bowler realised just how much peril he was in.

Before him, filling the space between Bowler and his escape, stood The Beast.

His immense grin was visible even in the darkness, and his black eyes were shadowed even further by his enormous brow. And Bowler realised the situation was even worse, the intense terror of the moment blanking out the question *How the hell can I hear him* and replacing it with *Please God let me get away from here, let me out of the parlour* because he finally realised that The Beast had been talking, The Beast had been *cunning*, and that meant he was fully, totally lucid, and *that* meant there would be no escape this time. The Beast had Bowler all to himself.

"Hello, Bowler," he said, speaking in a voice like seawater over jagged pebbles, and grinning wider as he did so. "I am afraid you have made a terrible, terrible *mistake.*"

***

Hart straightened up with a slight shiver, turned, and—after checking up and down the street for other Guests, of course—he entered the house.

The stairs greeted him, heading upwards directly from the entrance hall, and to the right was the living room. He looked into it. As he expected, there were quite a few people there; what looked to be an extended family, ten or eleven people in the small room. The older ones filled the three-piece suite, the younger members sitting cross-legged on the floor. No one was talking, and the adults that were clearly couples were holding hands, or had their arms around one another. The TV wasn't on, there wasn't even any music playing, and all of that was to be expected. The silence was oppressive, the lack of TV noise notable, and this triggered the memory in Hart's mind.

What he'd seen, and what he hadn't told Bowler ...

***

The Beast lazily spread himself as wide as he could, planting his feet far apart and filling Bowler's path utterly, looking down at him. The Beast cocked his head to one side very slowly, taking nearly thirty seconds to move it to one side. Still grinning, as if regarding his prey. He was silhouetted almost totally now, as the only light was now coming from directly behind him. Bowler couldn't see what he was wearing fully, but from the shape of it, it looked like he was still in his enormous donkey jacket and trousers. His vast hands caressed each other in front of his chest.

"I know what Hart *says* about me, Bowler," he said, his head not moving in the dark. "About my ... changes. My *moods.* You are wondering what you have in *front* of you now. Which mood am I in? Is this right? Is this what you are thinking? In there?"

No, Bowler thought. *I already know that. You're at your most dangerous, and I'm wondering how the hell I can get out of here alive without ending up like the others. Without becoming a dead statue, however you do it. If I can stop shitting myself and think straight, which isn't fucking easy even when I'm not trying to get away from monsters. Think. Talk!*

"Uh ….uh … uh …" said Bowler, and his hands rattled against his sides like freshly caught fish. The Beast spotted it, and that horrible, liquid, bubbling voice gave a gentle gargling laugh.

"Bowler, you are on your way, yes you are. Hart was not enough to keep you *safe*, was he? You were never going to be one to last long here, I think so, *yes*, I think so. I think you would have lost yourself soon, *yes*, another few years, or perhaps a little less, and you would have lost yourself, Hart or no Hart." He edged slightly closer, glacier-like, and Bowler equally moved away. There was roughly three feet of space between them, and Bowler could see no opportunity for escape here. The Beast would cover three feet in a nanosecond.

"But Hart is leaving now, yes he is," The Beast continued. "And you will be lost a lot quicker, I think so. Poor Bowler." Bowler could hear in The Beast's voice that the grin had spread, and realised that his only choice right now was to spin this conversation out. He wasn't having any ideas, and he needed time to think—he just couldn't switch *on*—and he needed to get The Beast talking so he could get it. Talking. *He's talking.*

"I … I can … h—hear you … *constantly* … you're talking …"

The Beast let out a pleased noise that sounded like water draining out of a bath.

"Oh yes, you can. You can hear. You can hear because I can make you hear. It is a matter of *projection*. That is the word. Pro. Ject. *Tion*. I send the sounds into you, into your head. I like how you and Hart managed it though.

Clever. But my way is simpler. It just takes a long, long, long, long, long, long time to learn. Very long."

Bowler had a second to be amazed by this, but then The Beast suddenly jabbed both hands at him, like a parent scaring a child playfully, his head and shoulders dropping as he did so and lunging with his upper body. There was a sound like a snorting bull. Bowler jumped several feet back, and perhaps would have had a moment to make a run for it, had he not stumbled and fallen onto his back. He scrambled to his feet to run, but by the time he had done so, The Beast was already moving close again, was already *too* close, chuckling way back in his throat with a low rumbling sound.

"Very long," he said again. "Far, far longer than you. Far, far longer than Hart. Far, far longer than anyone. Yes ..."

Through his fear, curiosity—no more than that, a need to know—pulled at Bowler. Here were answers, and he wouldn't die without them.

"How ... how long? How long have you been here?"

The Beast's laughter stopped. In the dark, he saw the shape of the great head with its vast brow cock to the side slightly. The Beast went silent. His hands wavered slightly in the air, and, for a moment, he seemed utterly distracted. It was like he'd been switched off. There was total silence.

He's thinking, said a voice in Bowler's head. *He's gone. That's how much it takes for him. Move! Move* now, *now*— But the chuckle started up again as if it had simply been taken off pause, and The Beast was back online again. The moment was gone, but Bowler thought he had seen a faint glimmer of hope in the darkness. With The Beast in this lucid frame of mind, this devilishly cunning and *thinking* frame of mind, he had a chance. He'd seen a weakness. It obviously took more effort for The Beast to stay in this state, and as a result he perhaps could be closed down, if only briefly? Bowler dared not believe it, but it was *something*, and as the sense of doom lifted slightly, so did his fear, his mind—though still racing and as fractured as it had become even before now—got a grip on hope and told him *if we're smart … there's a chance we can get out of this.*

"There is no way to be completely certain, Bowler, as you know, but it is at least six hundred years. I think that it is perhaps more than this. Can you imagine? Can you *imagine*? No, you cannot." He stopped for a moment, and his head shook like he was being electrocuted. His shoulders joined in, and there was a growling noise. Then he stopped, and all was quiet again. "I am … still with you," The Beast said, in a voice that was almost a sigh, like a man speaking after a great physical effort. "I choose to be. It is not as enjoyable when I am … other. You understand."

Bowler did. *You want to be fully aware of just how much you enjoy killing me. But how the hell do you do it? Did you develop that as well? How? Keep him TALKING.* The natural next question came easily, because he so desperately wanted to know.

"So Hart was wrong? If you've been here six hundred years, I mean, people's time here doesn't run out? Mark and George were killed … and you killed them …"

The Beast suddenly roared with laughter, clapping his hands rapidly, like a delighted child. But he never took his gaze off Bowler, who could feel it upon him like a steel trap.

"Ah, yes, yes, Hart's 'theory,' yes? I did like that. I listened, you know. Sometimes … when I try very, very hard, and I am not … other. When I am as I am now … I can listen. Listen from far away. I can listen to anyone here, you know. I can listen like I talk. I have learned so many things. Like your friend learned to be stronger. That was the first thing I learned. And I learned to be stronger still. Then bigger. Then many more things."

"But we hid from you that time—"

"When you escaped from me once? I remember this. I was … other, then. I could not … listen, properly. To find you. Alas, even when I am as I am now, I cannot always listen. And even then, I become … other, and get …

distracted, you see. So I very, very, very, very rarely hunt that way. But I *am* getting better with this. Over time. Getting quicker. And I have so much time. Soon I will be able to hunt this way whenever I like." That low, low chuckle again, dark and sinister.

Bowler pushed the idea from his mind, and tried to focus on his only course of action; to keep asking the questions that came naturally, and wait for another lockdown. He opened his mouth without knowing what he was going to say, but then The Beast continued talking.

"But as for Hart's *theory?* This place ending, people dying ... You actually believed that, did you not? Yes, you did."

Bowler just stared at him, stunned. Was this just crazy talk?

"He did a good job, I thought so. When I practised, practised my listening, a long way away, and listened to you many times. Many times. I thought Hart did a perfect balancing act. Keeping you off the ... *scent* ... of the truth ... but making sure his companion was still there, still with him, but not a threat. Very clever. Clever Hart."

"But ... the truth is ... you killed them. Why would he want to—"

"I have learned many, many things in my time here," said The Beast, and it was almost a sigh. "But I have not found a way to kill what you call Guests. No. I have never learned this. Why would I kill my own toys? How can you kill what is already dead? There is no way to kill a Guest. You *cannot* kill a ghost."

"But Mark and George—"

"They were never killed. They got what they wanted."

***

What he'd seen, and what he hadn't told Bowler ...
It lasts about ten seconds, and it means everything.

It is a news feature about a government initiative for poorer families, or something like that; Hart hasn't seen the start of it, so he can't get the whole story. It doesn't matter. He does know that it's being trialled in Leeds. Far away from Coventry. That in itself will be fascinating to Hart later. A reveal of more potential layers, and another piece of how it all works. But right now what does *matter is the woman on the screen. The woman being interviewed in her living room as part of one of those "voices of the public" montages. The woman sat in her living room with her son. The woman's son. The woman's* son. *The ten-year-old boy sat surrounded in a blue glow.*

A Bluey, yes, but a different Bluey than ever before. A Bluey Hart recognises.

A Bluey that is clearly George as a ten-year-old boy.

Not only can Hart recognise George, but he can feel *that it's George. The ten-year-old boy sits awkwardly by his mother in a hoodie and jeans, clearly not wanting to be filmed, red with embarrassment, looking anywhere but at the camera.* That boy is George. *It radiates from the screen at Hart, and he doesn't know how, but he can* feel *it in every fibre of his being, which would be more than enough even if the kid wasn't the spitting image of Hart's old friend. Plus his mannerisms, the way he sits, the way he occasionally fiddles with his right ear ... it is* George.

He wasn't killed, *thinks Hart. He wasn't* killed! He got out, he got another go around! He got out. He got out!! Simon was right! I was right! And he not only got out ... he got to live again!! *And Hart falls backwards, onto the floor, his legs giving out.*

His mind whirls. George heard the theory, tried it first. Mark saw it ... Mark must have been there ... but only saw what was left behind. Saw George's ... corpse? Shell? Skin? Who knew what it was, who knew what the Guests were actually comprised of? After all, they could touch other, couldn't they? So no matter what, be it on a different plane to the living, they had a physical presence, and George had left his behind when he moved on. Fine. But how would you react to that?

How would you react if you were Mark, trying your theory for escape, and seeing what looked for all the world like a dead body as a result? Seeing that crumbling, powdery corpse, but with no proof that anything had happened other than George being wiped out? No … it wouldn't be enough. Not after feeling the oblivion of the Train … you wouldn't risk that after seeing a corpse, for goodness' sake. No, Mark wouldn't dare, and neither would Hart. But after a while … five years, in fact … after more years of it, of going that much more Loose, and then finding a chance, a potential door … you wouldn't risk waiting for another exit. Mark took it, out of desperation and fear.

And now Hart would take his chance, now he knows—*finally*—*that it works, that he has nothing to fear. This means not only can he get out, but he finally knows that he* can *take it safely. Because Hart's fear has held him prisoner for seventy years, and for all of his qualities, Hart is a coward. Especially after touching oblivion, and knowing—from the Flyers—that there must be some alternatives. Bowler has come to realise this about Hart, and this is why things have changed. That and Bowler's own mind.*

But Bowler cannot know this truth, must be led down a path of thought that will ensure he never reaches the theory that Simon did. Bowler must be told lies. Bowler must be kept away from stumbling upon this idea at all costs. For when Hart gets his chance, when he finds it, there may only be one *chance, and Bowler* must not know. *There must be no chance of Bowler taking it. Bowler must not be there when it is time to take the exit. When the time is right, Hart must leave Bowler alone. If anyone is to get out, it is to be Hart.*

***

"You have never met Simon, have you?" asked The Beast. It sounded strangely like a genuine question. Bowler didn't have a clue what he was on about. Was this the beginning of some sort of sick game? Was Simon some sort of term for ... something else? *Sweet Jesus, I hope not,* thought Bowler. *That would really be the icing on the fucking cake.*

"I ... can't say I have ..."

"Yes, yes, I know you have not. Sometimes I ... do not remember things, but they always come in the end. He got here a year before Hart did, you know. They were easily the two arrivals that came closest together. Easily. I think in Hart's time, there have only been four, you know, including yourself. Your friends George, Mark, and Sarah. Did it ever strike you as *odd*, so *odd*, that these ones are the only ones to spend time together, to go to each other, even if it hurts you a bit after a while? That unlike the others, you get together, despite the fact you get that *discomfort* ... what do they know that you don't?"

Think, Bowler, talk!

"Is that why the others—the other Guests—is that why they go off alone? The discomfort?" asked Bowler, in the voice of a scared child.

"No, no, no no no no *no.* Of course not. You all need it, the talk, the endless ..." The Beast waved one hand in the air, both searching for the word and dismissing the concept. "The endless *talk,* don't you? No. No. No. They simply made their choice, and off they went. They decide the risk is too great. They take their chances. They think they won't go Loose. But of course, beautifully, they always do."

"But ... but *why*?" Bowler asked, not expecting an answer ... but what the hell did he have to lose? "The risk of what? What do they risk by being together? Surely a bigger risk is going off alone, going Loose?" Bowler was torn inside; he wanted this question to shut The Beast down again, give him a window, but crazily, he needed to know, *had* to know.

There was a pause from The Beast—was he locking down?—but then a chuckle came from the huge silhouette.

"Because then someone else might *take* it," The Beast said. "The partner, the friend, might take it. The opportunities are rare, so very rare ... and when it comes to a choice between an eternity here and ... *aheh* ... the *politeness* of friendship, one may easily trick another, turn on another. Would *you* risk it, Bowler, if you knew?"

The Beast grinned, and shuffled an inch or two closer.

"Faced with forever, and finding yourself standing with your friend before an exit that only one of you can take ... would you expect them to say *after you?*"

Bowler had no answer.

"And they've all been here so very long, the others ..." said The Beast. "A very long time. It cycles, Bowler. They come, they get together, and one by one they work it out—they work out how to leave, though some take longer than others ... and then they go off, desperate, to search alone ... and then when more come, new arrivals, they arrive in a world where no one associates with one another."

That chuckle again, that rumbling, terrible chuckle.

"And they either go Loose themselves, or—rarely—they manage to wait for other new arrivals, and form friends, and then they work it out and one by one ... you understand, yes? Yes. It's a wonderful, unending circle." The Beast straightened upright in the dark, and Bowler could see the outline of one enormous arm scratching the Neanderthal head.

"Yes ... and sometimes, sometimes I help out, Bowler," said The Beast, wistfully. "I prefer them Loose, you see. I just find them so much fun to *Break*, as you would say. The Loose ones. Ah, I love your phrases ... Loose ... no matter how many times I Break someone, that alone cannot make them Loose. They always cling on. No, they have to go that way themselves. But even if I could, I would prefer to *help* them on their way. More fun. Like

Simon. I made sure he heard me, that day. He thought he'd *over*heard me, but it was meant for him to hear. I made *sure* he found out how to do it. I could have waited, but he and Hart were together. I did not like that. I made sure he heard me so that he would go off alone."

The Beast clapped his hands together.

"So he would leave Hart because of the risk, and then they would both sweetly, so *sweetly*, lose themselves. I sit, far away, and listen to them, *feel* them turning. And it's so ... ah, so *good* ... to know I was the voice in their ear that made them turn. They think it is good news, when they find out, or work it out." There was a hissing, inward, rattling breath, like an old smoker's, as The Beast savoured the idea.

"But ... then you came along," said The Beast, holding up a finger and then turning it towards Bowler like a gun. "And Hart did something new, and you pair have intrigued me so ever since ..."

And then The Beast started to advance suddenly, and Bowler blurted out the first thing that came to mind.

"But how are you not like the others?" he yelped, scurrying out of reach. "They've been here so long, longer than Hart! Why aren't more of them more like you, rather than just crazy? Half the time you're a monster, but now you're thinking, talking, learning, and they're just Loose all the time!"

The Beast answered this with pride in his voice.

"Because, Bowler, they cannot stand this place. They cannot stand not sleeping. The frustration, the loneliness, the inability to shut off and take solace in company ... it turns them, and they cannot develop *anything*. But me ..." A low, pleased, rotten growl in The Beast's throat. "I *love* it here. I am more free in this place than I have ever been, Bowler."

The Beast actually sighed whimsically, and Bowler flinched instinctively from breath he didn't want in his face, although of course there was none.

"Unlike the others, I think I was quite, quite Loose when I already arrived," The Beast said, with a clear tone of pride in his voice. "I could have left a long time ago, and I have no intention of *ever* doing so. Here I can hunt a prey that never fully dies. It's *wonderful.* A-ha ... a-ha-ha ..." He spread his arms wide, and moved from side to side, hinting an attack, and Bowler tensed up. The Beast paused, suddenly jerked towards Bowler again, paused, suddenly moved again, watching Bowler squirm. He then laughed again, relaxing.

"It is amusing sometimes, how things work out," The Beast chuckled. "A lot of the time, I *move the goalposts* for them, as you would say, Bowler. They find an exit, and if I hear them finding it—if I can get there quick enough—I stop them. Break them. That is what I *exist* for, Bowler, those moments, to deny them like that. To deny them with one foot out of the door ..." The Beast let out a gasp that sounded almost sensual in its delight. "Ha ... it's so *good.* And they just get *worse* ... I did that to your friend Sarah just a few days ago. You know."

Bowler felt cold. So casual. The Beast telling him this fact like he was saying *I just went to the shops.*

"That one was easy," The Beast crowed. "That exit wasn't even *ready* at the time. But I am afraid I was lazy, I was so *lazy*, and played it *safe*, got her stopped *early*. But you know what? It worked out so well. She passed on the information to someone. She told someone where the exit was." He paused, and let Bowler work out who that person was.

"Hart ..." Bowler said, and felt the full sting of betrayal.

"*Yesss,*" said The Beast. "And you know what else? *I am not going to stop him.* I have something different in mind, here, Bowler. You two ... keeping each other steady ... and him knowing how to make more like you ... I want him gone. It's just better. Easier. But of course, I could never just ... let him go. It would eat at me so, Bowler. I have a much, much better idea."

The Beast moved closer, and Bowler realised in a terror-inspired flash, a wonderful, brilliant moment of insight—how could he have been so fucking *stupid?*—that he didn't need to reach the fucking exit at all.

The Beast had relied upon Bowler's fear and growing Looseness to cloud his mind, and it had worked. This was the reason for the stalking, the hiding, the intimidation; all of it was to create this false sense of a *trap.* The Beast wanted Bowler so scared because he didn't want Bowler to realise he could just run through the fucking wall behind him. So *cunning.* Bowler was a fucking *ghost,* for crying out loud! He didn't *need* to use the goddamn exit!

But with The Beast this close ... Bowler knew that he couldn't get away quick enough anyway. The Beast was faster. A lot faster, quick enough to catch him even if Bowler were at a greater distance away than he currently was. Still ... with The Beast occasionally shutting down the way he seemed to be ... it gave Bowler more hope, more of a fighting chance, and he began to think more clearly, earnestly.

***

Hart entered the upstairs bedroom. He knew now wasn't the time. Now wasn't quite time to go, it wasn't quite *ready* just yet—he could feel it at this close range—but even so, it was only sensible to check. To check it was there. Even now, he needed to be sure it was true, and believing after all these years of carefully avoiding hope was especially hard.

Of course, Hart needed to *know* it was real so, so badly. But still, even thinking all of this, he wasn't prepared. How could he have been? It was like nothing he'd experienced before, and so few people ever had.

Though he could feel it already from the hallway (his fear and excitement and sense of refusal to believe it until he'd *seen* it had been blasted away), it was nothing compared to when he walked into the room itself. Hart walked physically into bliss, into joy made touchable, *tangible.*

As he stepped through the closed door, it blasted him. Blasted *through* him. He was bathed in it, bathed in energy. Bathed in the blue light that filled the room, feeling it enter him, and call to him, gently pull him. Different to before; the Bluey they'd met wasn't a part of The Foyer, wasn't on their level. They couldn't touch it.

Of course we couldn't. It wasn't for *us.*

But this … this was all-encompassing.

No wonder Mark had taken the plunge in the end when actually confronted with it, no wonder he'd overcome his fear, once he'd dared to come inside this aura … how could he not? And even now—Hart could feel it all through his being—it wasn't quite time yet. But it would be soon, and then … *good lord, good merciful God almighty above* (though even now Hart did not believe, did not believe in a God that would be cruel enough to let The Foyer exist, these words still blazed in his mind) Hart would be free. Not just free … given another chance, another chance to end it differently, with different energy, for of course Hart now remembered how it had ended. It had taken many, many years, but they all did, eventually.

Sarah, he thought, with tears pouring unnoticed down his cheeks. *Thank you, oh* God, *thank you, Sarah.*

***

"Sarah! Sarah! Oh no, Sarah …" Hart rushes to her side, seeing her flattened frame in a crumpled bundle, half in and half out of the back wall of Waller's. Another bar, another body; it is a horrible symmetry. He can hear her voice. He doesn't notice this fact at first.

He passes through and finds himself in a beer cellar, metal barrels, clear pipes, and thrumming, rattling machinery all around. It is very noisy, and that's why at first, when he looks at her—relief flooding through him to find she isn't a shell like George, that she is "only" Broken, that she is crushed and bloodied and flattened but she is still here—that he realises she is saying his name, and that he can hear her.

Her voice is weak, barely there at all, but he can hear her clearly. Her voice is grating, torn, and he doesn't think it is from whatever has done this to her. Sarah has been pretty much Loose for some time. He isn't surprised to hear her sound this way, but his mind is rushing trying to think of possibilities. Was it just coincidence? Has she just happened to have "Tuned In" now, like George sometimes did? She's Broken, *he thinks.* Like the Check-ins are when they first get here, like you were and Bowler was. And she's recalibrating, just like Bowler did, as she heals. All this time … you could have saved her if you knew … you *idiot …*

"Hart …" *she says again, and he bends to listen. He knows it will only be more mad ramble, but he can at least comfort her. He has time; Bowler is off again right now, and at least here he can be of some use, can do something for someone he had previously decided he cannot help.*

"I'm here, Sarah. We're talking, isn't that good?" *Maybe it's not too late, he thinks.* Maybe I can bring her back, over time …

"Yes, talking like a pair of owls. Talking little owls," *she says, and Hart realises his last thought was utterly foolish. There is nothing that can be done for her now. And he wonders if madness can be a little contagious. This must be the last time he talks to her. But right now, he will do what he can.*

"Yes. Owls. Does it hurt?"

"Hurt, pain, you mean sadness, Hart, we're all sad here, aren't we? Sad little people. I … my body … sad … everything is sad. Hurts. I'm hurt. But it goes away, and we carry on looking, always looking, forever and ever, all we do. Do you miss chicken? I miss chicken. And beef stew, and Victoria sponge. We had it on birthdays. I miss birthdays. When's my birthday? Is it soon?" *Her eyes look through him.*

"It's really soon. Sarah … who did this?"

"The man. The birthday man. He's the ..." Her brow furrows, trying to get it right, and then says, "The ... birthday man!! Ha ha!!" and laughs at her inability to get it right. This goes on for some time, and Hart cradles her head and patiently waits it out, listening to the rattle of the pumps all around them.

"Sarah."

"Mmm. It hurts. Oh, it hurts."

"I know. It'll be all right. Sarah, who did this?"

"Beast."

It is as Hart suspected. Attacks by other Guests that were worse than a stay-away scratch or punch were unheard of.

"Okay. Well he's not here now. He'll have gone off somewhere, calming down. Just relax, and heal. I'll have to go in a bit, but I can sit with you for a whi—"

"Starley Road—"

"Mmm-hmm. Is that where he did it, is it?"

"Exit."

Hart freezes. Don't even consider it, he tells himself. This woman is mad.

"... how do you mean ..."

"Finally, finally, finally. That's where it is. Beast doesn't like that though ... keeps me here, keeps me here ... so pretty ... but I'm a woman, a girly ... wouldn't have worked anyway, you know, I could feel it was all wrong for me ... Like Betamax, ha ha, video, you remember videos? I could feel it ... I could feel the exit was wrong for me. Wrong ... type."

"Sarah, what on earth are you ..."

Her eyes open wide, not seeing him, and she points in the wrong place, but she is earnest.

"But you could use it. You or the other one, yes ..."

It takes some time, but Hart gets his answers. She tells him what he needs to know. And it is clear that this part, at least, is not the rantings of a *lunatic. He kisses her good-bye after a while, after he sits with her a short time longer—he owes her at least that, but is desperate to be off, breathless with fear and excitement—and then heads to Bowler's wife's home where he will find his friend, and they will part company.*

***

"Why not Hart, then? Why not stop him from going? Why let him leave?"

"Ah, Hart," said The Beast, putting a hand into the darkness where his chin would be, rubbing it. "I already told you why, but then he is the clever one. He found such a nice solution to a difficult problem. Find a companion, and keep them in the dark. Until he's *sure*. Until he *knows*. *Then* look for the exit. But in the end, he didn't even have the courage to do that. Was far too scared, scared little Hart. He had to wait until it was given to him on a plate … and now look. He has left you, Bowler. Left you for good."

Bowler took a silent imaginary breath, steeled himself.

"You didn't answer my question."

The Beast seemed to stand up straighter, and Bowler prepared for an all-or-nothing run; he knew he couldn't outrun The Beast, and could only make a break for it while there was a window in The Beast's awareness rather than when under attack … but Bowler refused to stand still and be Broken. Yet The Beast did not attack.

"He *disrupts* things," said The Beast, "He has connected with you already; he will connect with others when they arrive. And that means more people not being Loose, or taking so much longer. And I don't like that. Less toys. I can break him, yes, but I cannot stop him completely. Too hard to watch him all the time, too hard to watch to make sure he stays away from any new arrivals. It is better that he goes, it is just much *easier*. For example, once he is gone, and you are Broken, you will be Loose very quickly. Yes,

212

quick *quick* ..." The Beast hissed, held the sound. "It means that I can just play and prey and play without having to keep an *eye* on things. I like it better that way. And as he is on his way out—although I much, much, *much* prefer to play with the Loose ones—this time I will make an exception, Bowler. I can't Break you into Looseness, no, but you are *already going.* And with Hart gone, after I Break you, you will have no one there. And then I will find you, and Break you again. And find you again, and Break you again, with no Hart to help you ... *balance* inside. I will have you Loose within two months, much quicker, much better, and better to start *now*, yes?" The Beast now began to crouch slowly, and Bowler saw his arms begin to spread wide again. It was now or never. The Beast was winding up to attack, this was clear. Ending his speeches, ending the opening ritual.

Get him thinking!!

"But how ... how does it work? How does he escape?"

"Do you really think that I would tell you, Bowler? Really?" And The Beast began to advance.

"But ... what ... what ..."

NOW, do it NOW!! Something, he's not thinking about right now, something to shift his mind, he's coming, he's COMING, DO IT!!

"What ... what ... is your name!"

That's it! Something stuck way back in his head, something totally unexpected!!

"Your name! What is your *name!!*" yelled Bowler, as loud as he could, hands out in desperation and shoulders half turned for a desperate, doomed run.

And The Beast stopped dead in his tracks, his arms falling by his sides, slack and limp. All Bowler could hear was the sound of his enormous, imaginary breathing.

That's IT! Now fucking RUUUNNNN!!

And without any hesitation, Bowler turned to sprint full pelt through the back wall, and had not gone as much as a single step when The Beast's hand whipped out and snatched him up by the leg in an iron grip. He was trapped utterly, and all hope died in Bowler's heart.

There was no escape; he was doomed.

He looked back along his leg, saw the vast shape of The Beast's shovel hand gripped around his calf, and looked along to the now crouching, hulking mass connected to it, sprung from his worst nightmares. Bowler heard the low chuckle begin, signalling the pain that was to come.

"That is an easy one, Bowler," The Beast said. "You should have picked something harder. Because there *is* no answer. I no longer remember. I have been The Monster, The Hunter, and now The Beast for so long. And I prefer them, for they are more *right* than any other name could ever be." And The Beast began to drag Bowler along the floor towards him, and Bowler began to scream as he kicked ineffectually against the huge hand clamped on his leg, a fly drawn by the cruellest spider. The dark shape began to fill Bowler's vision, seeming to swallow him whole. As The Beast drew Bowler in, he spoke, in a hissing, horribly *keen*, horribly *hungry* voice that he had not yet used. Becoming more breathless, more excited.

"The worst thing is, Bowler, is that this place could not be much more cruel!" The Beast breathed, rapturous in his delight. "*To be so close to a hospital!* To have a hospital *just* outside The Wall—SO close—and yet not close enough. So many exits in there, so many every day! But here ... what do YOU think the chance is of one of the living people dying within the boundaries of this place? In the street or in their home, with you being there to see it? So cruel! So cruel! *So cruel!!*" And The Beast began to laugh, a desperate, horrible laugh, beginning to hand over control to his very worst side now that he had Bowler in his grip, now that he knew Bowler was his. In his complete terror, struggling helplessly and pitifully like a worm on a hook, Bowler understood nothing of what had been said. He could only think of the coming pain.

"*Ohhhhhh, Bowler!*" cried The Beast as he stood over Bowler now, snatching his captive's wrist in his other hand as Bowler desperately swung one last futile punch at The Beast's knee, hoping against hope to stagger him. "*You must have* something *to say. This is the last day of hope you will ever know, after all! After all! After ALL!*"

And all Bowler could think to say in his fear and confusion was:

"Why … why are you doing this?"

But The Beast's response was a guttural, animal snarl that signalled the end of his lucidity, and began the Breaking by tearing Bowler's hand off at the wrist.

***

Hart looked down at the dying man on the bed. Unsurprisingly, he didn't recognise him. Even if it had been a living face that Hart had known from the streets, from the pub, anywhere, he probably wouldn't have been able to place it now. Not just for the haggard, yellowing, sunken skin, and hollow cheeks, but for the oxygen mask that covered most of the man's face and aided his slowly weakening breathing. Add this to the blue light that filled the room—filled Hart as well—emanating from the dying man's body, and shining so brightly at the source that Hart had to squint just to make out the figure beneath.

There was a drip connected to the man, and other machines Hart didn't recognise, but he knew that this kind of home care did not come cheap; just as he could tell that the family downstairs—and the handful of people upstairs, the middle-aged children, their spouses, and the dying man's nurse—were not affluent enough to have this kind of private help as standard. This was costing them more than they could afford. This was a man who was much-loved.

Somehow, Hart could feel the time left. The light would intensify, and then ... as the dying man went on ...

Hart would go with him. Hart would ... finally ... leave. It was so *clear*.

Although how exactly it would work, Hart didn't yet know, but he knew he would understand when the time came. And he was quite happy, more than happy, to stand here bathing in the blue light until it did. It spoke to him, called to him, but not in words, just in a pull that seemed to tug at his very being. It felt like ... peace. And Hart had not known peace—not even the release of sleep—in such a very, very long time.

He wondered if he'd have thought of this on his own. He thought he probably would have eventually, but even so, until confronted with it like this—and when would he have been in the presence of a dying person, without actively looking, and going Loose in the process of trying to find one—would he have believed it? No. He'd never believed, even when Simon thought of it.

He moved closer to the dying man, listening to the beep of the machine, the gentle rattle of his breathing, the quiet sobs of the family members behind him. He wondered who'd been at *his* funeral. He wondered what Helen would think. *Helen, where are you,* he thought for the billionth time, and for the *first* time, he was not afraid to hold on to the thought, to let it stab viciously into his heart.

He stretched his hands out towards the heart of the glow, wanting more, eager to feel it at its most powerful; it would be a rush, he knew. But then there was something else. Something else was growing, another energy, slowly but clearly. Hart flinched, concerned, but then realised what it was.

The dying man was beginning to *truly* die. It was the final stretch. Hart could feel something coming from him, pairing with the blue glow, very slowly beginning to fill it. At this stage, Hart thought, if he'd been on the other side of the room, he wouldn't have been aware, but here, at the heart of it, he could sense it beginning.

So that was how it would work. The dying man would fill the blue, *become* the blue, and Hart would do the same; there would be just room for one passenger. He knew this, could feel the strength of it, knew there would be just enough. The old man would then take the blue with him, wear it unseen for his next time around. Ironic that, at the end, everything he'd learned about walking on the ground, staying solid, would be the opposite of what he had to do here. He had to let everything *go* ...

He thought of Bowler.

You were right. I'm a coward, Bowler, but I'm stronger than you. I should have been a better friend. I should have given you this chance, because you need it more than I do. But I can't. I can't take any more, and I'm so, so scared. Good-bye, my friend.

And he stood, and waited, and felt the blue continue to fill up, and felt the old man's memories, the old man's *life*, begin to come through him.

***

Bowler lay broken and alone, and all he knew was pain.

Unending, total, all-consuming, agonising pain.

He couldn't see anything—like before—but he could just about hear. He thought The Beast was gone, and that was the only good thing he knew. That the endless, endless pain and torture (The Beast knew so, so many ways to hurt, had learned so many in his time here, ways that simply weren't possible in the living world. This was a fact he had gleefully repeated over and over as he had carried them all out on Bowler, one by one) was done, but that was immediately followed by the knowledge that it was only a matter of time until it happened all over again. That as soon as he was healed and well, he would have to run, always, and do it alone.

You could find someone. A Check-in. Like Hart did. That would help, wouldn't it? If one came? Could you hang on that long, if it took years before another one?

The thought was vague, and brief, but Bowler couldn't think straight enough through the pain to consider it. *Could I? What? Running?* Then it was gone, and the broken glass feeling all over him blotted out everything again. And Hart. Where was Hart? Why wasn't he here, talking to him, helping him?

But Hart was gone, of course. He had no idea where to, but he remembered that Hart had left, left some time ago, and that he would be long arrived at wherever it was that he had gone to. He remembered being angry. So angry. But now, lost in his Broken cloud, he couldn't find it in himself to blame Hart. Couldn't blame Hart for leaving him. Although, the thing that saddened him the most was, if Hart had just *asked,* Bowler would have *let* him take the exit, wouldn't have needed to abandon him.

Are you sure that's true? Would you have let him take it, when it came right down to it? When the doorway was right in front of you?

He didn't have an answer. And a fresh wave hit him, and he went under again.

When he became aware once more, his hearing was better. He could hear slight sounds, a rhythmic noise. And he could tell someone was close by.

"Hello, Bowler. Can you hear me?"

"*Hart ...*" Bowler couldn't believe it. Relief washed over him; if only his eyes would work! He could see his old friend, know he was back! But he couldn't see. He would never see Hart again, although Bowler did not know this. "*Eyes ...*"

"Yes, yes, your vision will be shot for a bit, you know that. Oh ... goodness me, Bowler, I leave you alone for five minutes, and look what happens. What the hell were you doing, tangling with The Beast? I swear, I do nothing but waste my breath on you. Stupid boy."

"Hart?"

"All right, yes, I suppose it doesn't matter now. But you'll be okay, that's the main thing, although I know it's ... well, it's clearly very bad right now."

It took so much effort, but Bowler *had* to say it.

"M ... m'sorry ... Hart ..."

He heard Hart pause, and then sigh heavily.

"Goodness me, Bowler. After ... you're apologising to *me*? After I ... you never cease to amaze me, young man. Look ... please don't apologise. All right? This is hard enough as it is."

"We ... 'gether ... 'gain?"

Another pause, longer this time, and another, heavier sigh.

"I'm afraid not, Bowler. I'm afraid ... this is simply good-bye. There was time enough for this, I could tell. I can feel how long. Time to find you— you're easy, you never go far from the very centre—and I couldn't ... well, I had to say good-bye."

For a moment, the sinking feeling in Bowler, the comedown from the euphoria of Hart's return, was worse than the pain.

Then you shouldn't have come back, don't you know how cruel that was?

Bowler heard Hart shuffle, like he was getting himself into a more comfortable position.

"The thing is," Hart continued, "if I'm to be totally honest, this is along the same lines of what I'd planned. Obviously, nowhere near this bad, but ... I was going to go and check, make sure the exit was there, then come and say good-bye, and tell you how to get out once I'm gone ... but break your leg or something, just to make sure you couldn't follow, thus avoiding the risk of you jumping in first. Because I wanted you to know, you understand," he added, wanting to make sure Bowler got it. "I couldn't leave without giving you a chance to get out yourself, without you knowing how. Although ... well, when that chance might be, who knows ..." He sighed again, and after the longest pause yet he continued speaking, but more heavily, wearily, and Bowler was amazed to hear Hart crying. Bowler was suddenly glad he couldn't see.

"I know I could overpower you," Hart said, "if you tried to, I don't know ... muscle me out of there or something, but you never know with these things. If you were closer at the right second ... so I'd just planned to make sure that you couldn't follow me. Just a little break to your leg, not a Break, if you know what I mean. But ... I never wanted this ..."

Hart broke off, and there were muffled sniffs. Bowler knew that his friend was still, even now, trying to maintain the old Hart dignity. And Bowler decided to abandon his completely. Here was his only chance.

"Hart ... please ... I can't ... make it ...mmm ... nnnn ... need ... you ... ."

"Bowler ... please ..." said Hart with a wavering voice. "Just ... don't, all right? I came to ... ahh ... to say good-bye, and this is very, very difficult, so just ..." He suddenly broke off, and Bowler heard him catch an imaginary breath. When he spoke again, he was breath*less.*

"Oh, God," Hart whispered. "I ... I can feel it. It's now. It's time already. I thought there was longer ... *I might have missed it?* I can't ... can you imagine? I can't believe I ... oh God ... *Helen* ..."

Who's Helen? thought Bowler, crazily. Something was going on. This was it. Hart was leaving. Hart was *leaving.*

"HART ... please. Need ... .you ..."

"Shut *up,* Bowler!" snapped Hart, "This is important! This ... can you feel it? It's very important, *can you feel it?"*

Feel what? All I can feel is pain, thought Bowler. *Please, just stay, and we'll talk about whatever you want, anything.*

"Nnnn … .."

"Damn … shit! Then maybe … ah, the pain, maybe that's blocking … closer, you need to be closer … okay, okay, tell me if this makes a difference."

And Hart lifted Bowler's Broken body from the floor of the dying man's upstairs room and held him above the blue, right in the heart of the energy, and all the pain went away.

All Bowler could feel was warmth and peace. He became suddenly even more intangible in Hart's arms. Incredibly, Bowler's entire weight vanished, and he began to float. Hart, stunned to find Bowler suspended in midair now, backed away to let Bowler hover there, held in the warmth of the blue.

Bowler was flooded with the old man's life, memories buffeting him, filling him, his mind clearing and healing but cramming with images of things he'd never done, and with sheer will he pulled his own thoughts free and managed to focus just enough to speak aloud—blind eyes filled with nothing but blue, blue, *blue*—building to a desperate scream.

"Hart! What … no … not me! Not me! We'll stay together! I haven't *earned* this! Hart, you *earned* this! Seventy *years*! You don't need to do this! *Hart!! Please!!*"

And Hart stood there, tears streaming down his face, and smiling at the same time, remembering the dying memories of Christopher Phelps:

… lung cancer, but at ninety-two he'd had a damned good innings, and no one he'd ever known had managed to become a great-grandfather …

… retiring with tears in his eyes, his loved ones around him from the shop floor, a beautiful, beautiful gold watch they'd all chipped in for, and he's so happy, all that would be needed to make it perfect would be for his Iris to be here …

… it's actually twins, double Granddad, a boy and a girl, and we're calling the boy Chris …

… exactly what they wanted, a little girl, even though little Steve had wanted a baby brother, but his face when they brought her home, and Christopher didn't have his camera, dammit …

… promotion, but in the end he'd gone back to the floor, he didn't like the suit, he preferred to work with his hands, and they'd never been hard up …

… first day on the job, and Iris had put that letter and that saucy photo in his lunchbox, and although he's over moon he instantly thinks, I wonder where she got it developed, I can never show my face again in there wherever it is …

… the happiest day of his life, that's what they'd said it would be, and they weren't bloody wrong, not at all, and he can see it in her eyes that she's the same …

… pulling Trevor up off the beach as the bullets whicker around them, because he owes *Trevor, owes him his life, and so he drags the man him behind him—he'll always wonder how he managed it—and they head towards the gun turrets—*

… a bike on his sixteenth—

—And Hart opens his eyes and pulls himself free, his course of action changed irrevocably, and runs out the door for Bowler, praying there is enough time …

"Please. Bowler. Don't make me change my mind. I … owe *you* everything. You bought me the time to find out the truth. And you … yes, I might want this, Bowler. I might want it so, so badly. But you … you *need* it. And I owe you. I know this now."

Desperation, sheer desperation rattled around the blue in Bowler's mind, even though it was soothing him, warming him, like coming home, but he knew was abandoning his friend.

"Hart!! No!! Haaaaaart!!"

"And … I'm sorry I wasn't a better friend. I think … this is the best gratitude, and apology, I can show you. Good-bye. I will …" and Hart hesitated, struggling with his words. "I will miss you, my friend."

"Haaaaaaart!! I—I—I … I love—"

And there was a flash, and all the blue in the room wrapped itself around Bowler, formed a cocoon around his body, hiding him from view and cutting off his voice.

And despite his choice, Hart let out a pained gasp, an animal moan, as he watched the exit close. Watched it close around his friend.

The cocoon started to brighten—at first to a brighter blue, then to a turquoise, then changing to a glowing, fuzzy white light—and began to rise, slowly, towards the ceiling. Something large fell from it, and Hart was not surprised to see it was Bowler's frozen body—his discarded shell—fall to the bed. Even in the moment, Hart noted that it didn't pass through. He had time to notice the expression, same as George's; eyes wide, mouth open, hands raised, but Hart now knew it wasn't to protect himself, and that the expression wasn't fear; it was to reach for the blue, embrace it, with a look of sheer amazement, just as he realised that the now white cocoon containing the energies of Christopher Phelps and Frank Bowler was beginning to rise. It was going to pass through the ceiling, over the heads of the people in the room that were now standing up and moving towards the bed, some with small cries of "Dad?" and "Granddad Chris?" and fresh, silent tears springing from the eyes of others. *It's all right!* Hart wanted to tell them, *He's fine!* But the more urgent issue was following Bowler.

Hart turned and ran for the door, passing through it and into the street, moving way back into the road to look up over the roof, waiting for a glimpse. Nothing at first, and then *yes* … there it was, that inexplicable airborne cocoon, shining like a miniature sun in the night sky. It started to angle upwards and across, beginning its journey out, and Hart's tears turned into sudden laughter, sheer joy.

Bowler was getting out, out of The *Foyer*, out of the *prison*, and as it suddenly struck him what Bowler had become—*He's a Flyer. He's a bloody FLYER!!*—Hart let out of a whoop of joy, jumping up and down in the middle of the street as Bowler began to float away.

"Go *on!*" yelled Hart, deliriously, laughing with sheer delight. "Get *out* of here, fly!! Write me a postcard, you lucky bastard!! *Go!!!* Go, go, go, *go!!!*" Still laughing, tears streaming, he ran after the Flyer through the darkened streets as it travelled across the sky, waving and whooping like a child chasing an aeroplane. For the time being, the future was forgotten, replaced by the unfamiliar sensation of joy in his heart.

***

Epilogue: In Which We See That Which Hart Did Next

***

Four Years Later:

Hart sat in the lower precinct. It was Saturday, so it was always the best day to people watch. Today was particularly busy, being the second to last one before Christmas. For once he'd actually sat on a bench; he felt like it, and decided that if anyone came along to sit on him, he'd move. It was midday, and the atmosphere was more one of mania than one of Christmas cheer. So many people, so many shoppers, and even the couples seemed to be missing the occasion around them, bustling along, stern faced, with those foolish enough to go out without several layers of clothing looking even more so, eager to get to wherever their next destination was and hoping that it held heat. The children looked happy, though. Electrified was more the word; _Christmas._ Cocaine for children. They'd waited for this all year. Hart grinned as one particularly wide-eyed chubby boy walked past, clinging onto his mother's hand and trying to take in all the Christmas finery around him.

Admittedly, for Hart, Christmas was more difficult with Bowler gone. It had been a more difficult time even when Bowler had been here—seeing warmth and happiness that they could appreciate but not truly share—but the feelings of isolation and loneliness were even more acute now. George gone, Bowler gone, Sarah … well, he hadn't seen Sarah for a good few months, and the time before that had been … unpleasant. But even so, he'd have expected to have seen her more recently than that. Maybe she found a female Exit and got out. Maybe she'd been Broken again … but Hart thought

226

that highly unlikely now, after what had happened to The Beast. Hart smiled grimly at the thought. It couldn't have happened to a nicer person.

As he idly watched, a wall of TVs caught his eye. It was a full window display, and all of the TVs were set to the same channel. In a moment summing up a large part of the season, the commercial onscreen was advertising *another* shop advertising all the options this one was selling, but at *discount prices*. It would have been a cynical moment, but Hart wasn't thinking about that; he was thinking of the benefit of TV to his life here, now so more than ever.

He wondered how anyone who came here before him—before TV was as widespread and all permeating as it was now—survived more than a month without going Loose. Certainly, before Bowler, it had been hard indeed. The wireless set and pub conversations only provided so much help, but as TVs made their way into every home over the years it had been a godsend. He had come to rely on it more and more now, had been forced to—before Bowler, he'd had George and Sarah around, and here was another reminder that now there was no one—but he'd discovered that life was bearable with TV alone to help.

It wouldn't be, though, without the knowledge he had now; the knowledge of the possibility of escape. Before, the idea of searching for a way out had seemed like a cruel tease. No answers, just fruitless search against inevitable failure, a quest destined to do nothing but send one mad with desperation and loneliness. Yes, others before him had worked it out and gone searching, but *they didn't know for certain*, and that made all the difference. No self-doubt. No frustration, no fear that it might all be for nothing if you were wrong. For the others, if your day's search ended—as it always did—in nothing, the thought that followed wasn't *maybe tomorrow* but *this is pointless anyway, I'm stuck here,* and you took another step down the Loose path. But now—for Hart—this wasn't the case. Now, every day had possibilities.

Now there was the constant chance that today might be the day, and when he didn't find an exit he could shrug his shoulders and take a break with *Deal or No Deal*, and just look again later, *because he knew he wasn't wasting his time and driving himself crazy.* Work and reward; it was a hard existence—and some days were much, much harder than others—but it was better, and the two factors of Knowledge and Entertainment together made everything so, so much different.

Plus, obviously there were the other things. The other possibilities he'd discovered since. Things he was only just beginning to explore.

He leaned his head back, feeling good for a moment, thinking that everything was okay right now. He looked up at the winter sky, clear for once, rain free, with the sun shining dimly, and felt fine. Purposeful.

He thought about Check-ins. Not another one yet. If one came, he knew he wouldn't bond with him like he had with Bowler. Bowler had gotten him what he needed; and Hart had returned the favour, though some days, every now and then, it pained him greatly, but even in those moments he never wished he'd done it differently. No, Hart wouldn't bond again, as it would not be fair to whoever it was. He'd made Bowler weaker than he'd already been on arrival. Made him dependent on Hart. Denied him the chance to go through it, to evolve to be what he needed to exist in there, like George had. He would *befriend* the Check-ins, and that would be that.

He still didn't know if he would tell them how to get out. He had sacrificed once, and would not again. That was only fair. But he was still undecided about sharing the information; if he could find a safe way of telling them without them stealing it, he might. Although, there *were* the other things, as The Beast had discovered.

Yes. The Beast had discovered that Hart was ... different now.

There was no doubting what had caused it, although Hart, ever cynical, had tried to do so at first. The Beast had hunted him, found him, caught him. He hadn't been fully lucid, but The Beast—talking incoherently, but audible, to Hart's then-great surprise—had been furious, asking why he hadn't gone, why Bowler had gone instead, crazily asking why Hart had to *ruin* things and talking like a petulant child. And then The Beast had attacked.

And then … Hart still didn't know exactly what had happened, but what had played a part was clear. The Beast had gripped him, gone to tear him limb from limb, and Hart's fear had reached a crescendo inside him. And as his emotion boiled over, as his attention was focused into one single pinpoint of terror, something moved inside him, and The Beast …

… The Beast is screaming, in pain and confusion and surprise. Something is happening to him, and he is afraid. Afraid! *His eyes are wide in fear, and his words are gibberish, just guttural, pleading cries. Somehow, Hart is hurting The Beast.*

Very badly.

Hart watches in amazement as The Beast's arms work, as if he were trying to pull his hands away from Hart's wrists, but it appears The Beast's hands are somehow glued to Hart's skin. And horribly, The Beast's flesh starts to distort, bubble, and begin to run, running down off its wrists.

It runs off into thin air and disappears, but there is no skeleton beneath, just an outline of where The Beast's arms were. It is an incredible sight, and Hart can only goggle at it, as locked in as The Beast is. In wild fear, Hart looks at his own arms to see if the same thing is happening, but he is fine. What on earth is going on??

The Beast's cries become louder as the effect spreads like toxic water breaking on a beach, the flesh streaming off The Beast's arms, and now the flow is spreading away from his chest and neck, flowing from his stomach, working down to his legs. That terrible, terrible thin outline is appearing where his body once stood, and now only The Beast's shaking bellowing head is left. Hart looks at his wrists and can see nothing holding them save for this wire-thin outline on the air, though he can still feel a monstrous pair of hands holding him. He looks up in wonder to see the flesh begin to pour from The Beast's head, which is now moving in a frantic, gibbering, expression. Hart sees with intense, grim satisfaction that tears are streaming from The Beast's bulging, terrified eyes, which too bubble and then pour into nothingness. The last thing to trickle away is the yowling mouth, and then it is silent forever.

All that is left now of The Beast's outline, Hart needs to squint to see it. But no, it is becoming easier to see, as it is filling, filling, and Hart is not at all surprised to see that—though faint at first, and strengthening—that he recognises the colour.

The Beast's outline is filling with blue.

Hart looks down to his wrists, and sees that the colour is flowing out of him, *for it is strongest at his wrists, and when he looks back up, the huge outline of The Beast is now completely full of the blue. The blue is flowing out of Hart. Flowing from* inside *him. It is strong but translucent at the same time, moving and swirling, an incredible display of impossible colour. And just as quickly as it has filled up, the outline itself dissolves and the blue inside of it begins to disappear from the outside inwards. Hart wants to touch it, but he does not dare; he has seen one person take a ride in the blue, and though he knows this is different—there is no ride here, there is just an ending, a dissolving—he isn't taking any chances. Just as Hart does not believe in a God, he does not believe that the blue has any sense of justice. Extremely faintly, as if from very far away, he can hear The Beast screaming. The sound fades with the colour, the shop wall behind the vanishing blueness slowly being revealed in its normal grey, until finally it were as if The Beast were never there ...*

Yes, even if it weren't for the new possibilities to explore here—to explore what he had taken away from his brief time inside the blue, how it had changed him, what he seemed to now carry *inside* him ... and what it could do—life was more bearable, thought Hart. *A little knowledge may be a dangerous thing ... but it can also be a blessing.* Hart smiled slightly and was about to return to his practice, when the most miraculous thing that had happened so far in Hart's entire existence occurred.

His attention was caught by the out of place sound of American accents. A couple were coming Hart's way through the precinct, both in their early thirties and quite well-to-do by the look of their clothes. Apart from their accents, the other thing that singled them out were their smiles. *Had to be on holiday, visiting friends,* thought Hart with detached delirium in the back of his mind, while the vast majority of Hart's attention was yelling to him, *screaming* to him about the four-year-old boy that held onto his father's hand, oblivious to the bright blue glow all around him.

There are coincidences, and there are coincidences, and then there are statistical impossibilities, thought Hart. *There are things that are so far out of the realms of actual possibility that they simply cannot be true. This is not chance. This is not chance. This is something else. This is ... lunacy.*

But it was true. The four-year-old Bluey was Bowler.

Sporting a grin even bigger than that of his parents, wrapped in a Sky Blues fleece, hat, and scarf, Bowler babbled excitably in his American accent.

"Mom! *Mom!* SpongeBob!"

"Yep. See the fountain, honey? You see the fountain there?"

"Yes ..."

"Wanna balloon? You wanna balloon from the man?"

"*Aaaah,* yeah, can I?"

"Waddayou say?"

"Pleeeease!"

American, thought Hart as he watched, frozen. *Coming here from another bloody country, being here, Coventry of all places, and in the same part of Coventry that I'm in at this moment.* At this very moment.

As he watched them pass, heading towards the helium balloon seller by the fountain—George's fountain, as it would always be in his mind,

George's body long since vanished—every instinct said to get up and follow them, but Hart did not. There were no answers there, only more questions that simply could *not* be answered. It was Bowler's second chance. That was all. It just happened to be wrapped up in a coincidence so incredibly huge and ridiculous that it was almost mind blowing.

Calm down, Hart, he thought as he watched. *Is this any bigger than what you've already seen? No, so stop thinking so ridiculously. It is just coincidence … albeit an absolutely impossible one.* He took an imaginary breath, relaxed, shaking his head, and smiled at his next thought. *Though, of course, Bowler—if he were here (which he is)—would say it was more proof, more proof that there was something behind all this. Another point towards his religious claptrap. A sign, a message.* He chuckled slightly to himself and watched as the trio, complete with new helium accessory clutched tightly in the fist of a skipping Bowler, headed away up the precinct.

Once they'd left, Hart turned his attention back to the newspaper on the bench next to him. Practice time. He held his hand over it, took a deep breath, and tried to focus, hoping—as he did every time—to get at least the same minuscule, tiny result that he did before, that one time in a hundred. But his mind kept going back to the old debate with Bowler. Although he tutted at himself, the small smile didn't leave his face.

Bowler, you idiot, he thought, *it was always about energy. I'm telling you—*And then he was distracted by the newspaper beneath his hand.

Wait, was that a movement again? Was it?

Uncertain, Hart carried on, but his thoughts drifted again, back to his previous statement. He mulled it over, and after a moment's consideration, he shrugged and added to it.

And hope. Of course, it was all about hope as well.

IF YOU ENJOYED THIS BOOK, *PLEASE* LEAVE A STAR RATING ON AMAZON :-) THE FEEDBACK I'VE HAD IS NOT ONLY THE THING THAT KEEPS ME WRITING, BUT ALSO MEANS MORE PEOPLE ARE LIKELY TO BUY MY BOOKS (WHICH MEANS I MIGHT ACTUALLY MAKE SOME DECENT MONEY OUT OF THIS ONE DAY ...). YOU CAN ALSO FIND OUT ABOUT MY OTHER AVAILABLE BOOKS WHILE YOU'RE THERE. TO KNOW WHEN FUTURE BOOKS ARE RELEASED, VISIT www.lukesmitherd.com AND SIGN UP FOR THE SPAM-FREE BOOK RELEASE NEWSLETTER, OR FOLLOW ME ON TWITTER @travellingluke OR ADD ME ON FACEBOOK UNDER "LUKE SMITHERD BOOK STUFF." NOW READ ON PAST THE AUTHOR'S AFTERWORD FOR AN EXCLUSIVE EXTRACT FROM MY BOOK, *THE STONE MAN*, OUT NOW ON THE KINDLE STORE————————————————
Luke

Author's Afterword:

(Note: at the time of writing, any comments made in this afterword about the number of other available books written by me are all true. However, since writing this, many more books might be out! The best way to find out is to search Amazon for Luke Smitherd or visit www.lukesmitherd.com ...)

Personally, I always like it when a writer puts a little section in the back of a book to say a few things about the story you've just read, and how it was written, etc.

Now before I go any further, however, two things should be made clear. One, I don't consider myself a "Writer" (at the time of writing, this bloody thing hasn't even been *published* yet, for God's sake. Anyone who says "I am a writer" without having anything published and/or bought, rather than "I like to write" is, in my book, a tit). Two, there's every possibility you've just finished ploughing through this, hating every page and only making it this far through dogged determination and/or passing loyalty to me, and are now thinking "Jesus, Luke! I've just finally finished *reading* the bloody thing! I'm desperate to get back to *Confessions of a Window Cleaner*, and you're giving me even *more* crap to slog through? What's wrong with you?!?"

So listen, this isn't intended to be some pretentious self-back-slapping section, nor do I consider it a part of the story. Hell, you might be of the mindset that you don't *want* to know what I think of it, or what went on behind the scenes. Or you thought it was crap. If any of the above is you, thank you very much for reading; I'm sincerely grateful for your time either way.

However, if you're still with me, here's where it all came from.

The idea for the basic plot—trapped dead people learning to get out of the afterlife by using the dying energy of the living—was thought up about twenty years ago in a cinema in Derby, at ten years old.

You may or may not remember a scene in the Patrick Swayze film *Ghost* where, shortly after realising he's died, Sam observes another soul ascending to heaven, doing so by stepping into a beam of light that's sent for him from the sky. (Y'know, I always think that film gets written off as a chick flick, when it's actually excellent. If you haven't seen it recently, go and watch it; you'll be pleasantly surprised. Although I was surprised myself to hear Whoopi Goldberg won an Oscar for it. I'm not sure if that's true. I just checked Wikipedia; it's true. I did like her in that though.) I remember vividly thinking at the time—and all the way home—*why the hell didn't he jump into that light as well, and hijack himself a lift to heaven?*

Obviously, two things are clear here, one being the answer (*because there wouldn't have been a film then, dumbass*) and that I could be a surprisingly cunning and mercenary child. The idea stayed with me for a long time, and it was only about halfway through writing this book that I realised where the germ of the story had come from.

Fast forward to the winter of 2002, when I'd decided that what I needed was to saddle myself with a few years' worth of debt and went travelling through Australia and Thailand for two months. During that time, the idea to make a story out of it came from somewhere, and I put together the rough parts of it, but never found myself sitting down for any length of time to draft a plot. I did, however, start filling a little notebook with any ideas I had that I wanted to fit in. That notebook was an invaluable source of information, and so naturally I lost it at some point during the last eight years. For all I know some sod found it and now there's already a book out there about exactly the same bloody thing.

Fast forward again to early 2009, and I finally sit down with my laptop in a pub in Leeds. After driving along idly thinking about the ideas for the story for the umpteenth time, I decided enough was enough and thrashed out a plot and structure. The reason it had been nagging at me so much for several years was probably that I couldn't figure out how I wanted it all to fit together; but as soon as I sat down to actually *do* it, the whole thing just flowed out effortlessly, and I was pretty pleased with what I had in front of me. But some things were different than I'd originally planned.

Bowler was always supposed to be Bowler—the same characteristics and appearance—but he was originally supposed to be the "main" voice of the story. Though the book takes both characters' perspectives, I think Hart ended up being the driving force of the book (you might disagree; in fact, whatever you think, e-mail me at lukesmitherd@hotmail.co.uk and let me know) and this may be because I took more interest in him due to his turning out so differently than planned. For those of you that watch *Shameless* (I never have, though I hear it's pretty good), in my mind I always saw Hart as being like the Dad Gallagher character from what I gather of him, especially in terms of appearance. Someone rough and geezer-like, a bit of a wideboy, with Bowler being more naïve. But somewhere down the line Hart became this stiff, stern, old school gent, and I prefer him that way.

There was never a wall around The Foyer when I first thought of it, but it struck me that life in there wouldn't be anywhere near as difficult if you could go where you wanted. So I took the rather cruel step of trapping them within a mile.

And it was never supposed to be set in Coventry, my adopted second home. I just did that originally because I thought it'd be nicer to use real street names, and I know enough of them in Cov to make it easy. Plus it helps to visualise a story when you can *see* the places you imagine things happening in, because you've been there. Then I had the idea of how the Blitz could play a part in Hart's journey to The Foyer, and that seemed to fit nicely. I apologise for any historical inaccuracies, but I'm going to blame my research sources if there are any. I would like to add that, if in any way, I've sounded like I'm talking Coventry down, then I'd like to assure people I'm not. Like any city, it has its flaws, its tack, and its thugs, but it also has its good points and its good people. It's been my home for a long time, and when I'm away, I do miss it.

And that's it really; I hope you're happy with the way it all turned out. For myself, I'm pretty pleased with it. It's funny, as Glen Duncan says—or rather, his character does—in the excellent *I, Lucifer* (well worth a read), writers don't start a book wanting to write about a theme or a concept, they come up with a plot idea first and then decide what it's really about as they're writing. To an extent, I agree with that. Though I don't, as I just said, put myself in that group, I think it's still true here; I thought I was writing a book about being trapped, about the human spirit, and about hope, and I'd like to think I succeeded in that to an extent. But it wasn't until I'd finished it that I realised I'd written a book mainly about taking people for granted, and about people needing people. And so I changed the title from *If I Could Only Sleep* to what you now hold in your hands.

So thanks again to you, whoever you are, for choosing to read this, and I sincerely hope you enjoyed it. But here comes the part where I ask you do me a small, teeny-tiny favour in return; my approach here is to distribute this book for as little cost as possible, or even free. I don't know yet by which method this tale has ended up in your grubby hands—and I can guarantee you I will have done my best to get it there for as minimal a cost as possible—but the idea was to just get this out to as many people as I can rather than to make money, in the possibly misguided hope that I could then ask people to join my mailing list.

See, what I want to do is get a list of people who actually liked this book enough to—hopefully—spend a couple of quid/bucks on whatever I write next. If you don't want to, it doesn't change the fact that I love you dearly for reading this, and that I think of you often. Naked.

But if you *do* want to … please just drop me an e-mail at lukesmitherd@hotmail.co.uk (**author's note from the future, i.e. 2015: or visit lukesmitherd.com to sign up to the Spam Free Book Release Newsletter, which only *ever* e-mails you when a new book comes out and not before)** and, if you're feeling REALLY generous, add me on Facebook under Luke Smitherd Book Stuff, or on twitter by following @travellingluke .

But *most* importantly, please leave a star rating on whichever outlet site you got this from, as that stuff really helps. That is so freakin' important you wouldn't believe it. IT HELPS SO MUCH. (Especially Amazon or Goodreads.com.)

Ahem. Enough shouting. It's just that I can't stress how important word of mouth is to a struggling indie wannabe hack such as myself. Spread the word to your friends, send them the link … it's a revolution, baby! I'm not gonna clog up your inbox 'cos I hate getting that myself, but if you've enjoyed this and passed it on to someone else you'd be doing me a very, very big favour. And hey … don't you WANT to read more?

What the fuck do you mean, no?

And don't worry about Hart; I'm sure he'll be all right. I have to say how much I'm actually going to miss having this project to work on. The book was written in various pubs in Leeds, Newcastle, and of course Coventry; though the plus side of being finished is that I'm going to save money, as I no longer have to buy pub lunches to justify using the boozer's power supply. It just struck me today when I woke up and thought, "Ah, I'll put a few hours in with the dead guys," and realised it was all done. I'm going to miss spending time in their company. So much so, that—probably relying on the Light Bites part of the menu this time—I think I'm going to fire straight into another book about something else. I'd forgotten how much I enjoyed doing it.

Take care, and Stay Hungry.

—Luke Smitherd
Earlsdon, Coventry
March 30, 2011

NOW READ ON FOR THAT EXCLUSIVE EXTRACT FROM *THE STONE MAN*, THE HIT #1 AMAZON UK BESTSELLING NOVEL FROM LUKE SMITHERD

Chapter One: Andy at the End, The Stone Man Arrives, A Long Journey Begins On Foot, And the Eyes of the World Fall Upon England

***

The TV is on in the room next door; the volume is up, the news is on, and I can hear some Scottish reporter saying that it's about to happen all over again. I already knew that, of course, just like everyone watching already knows that 'The Lottery Question' is being asked by people up and down the country, and around the world. *Who will it be this time?*

That was my job, of course, although I won't be doing it anymore. That's why I'm recording this, into the handheld digi—dicta—doodad that Paul sent me after the first lot of business that we dealt with. *To get it all out if you need to,* he'd said (he knows I find it hard to talk to people. He thought talking to the machine might be easier. Plus, *getting it all out* now gives me an excuse to use it after all; feels strange holding one again, as if my newspaper days were decades ago instead of just a year or so).

I didn't really know what he was talking about, back then. It had hit him a lot harder than me, so I didn't really understand why I'd need to talk about it. Eventually I got it, of course ... after the *second* time.

That was worse. Much worse.

This room is nice anyway, better than the outside of the hotel would suggest. I actually feel guilty about smoking in here, but at this stage I can be forgiven, I'm sure. Helps me relax, and naturally, I've got the entire contents of the mini bar spread out in front of me. I haven't actually touched any of it yet, but rest assured, I expect I shall have consumed most of it by the time I finish talking.

I just thought that I should get the real version down while I still have time. Not the only—partially—true, Home Office approved version that made me a household name around the world. I'm not really recording this for anyone else to hear, as daft as that may sound. I just think that doing so will help me put it all in perspective. I might delete it afterwards, I might not ... I think I will. Too dangerous for it to get out, for now at least.

I'd obviously had to come here in disguise (amazing how much a pair of subtle sunglasses and a baseball cap let you get away with in summer) and it's a good job that I did. They'd already be up here, banging on the door, screaming about the news and telling me what I already know. Thanks to my disguise, I can sit quietly in this designer—upholstered, soft—glow, up—lit, beige yuppie hidey—hole, with Steely Dan playing in the background on my phone's speakers (sorry if you aren't a fan) and remain undisturbed, until ... well, until I'm done. And it's time.

This is for you as well, Paul; for you more than anyone. You were there for all of it, and you're a key player, not that you'll ever actually get to hear this.

Well, *actually*, you weren't there at the start, were you? I often forget that. Which, of course, would be the best place to begin. Heh, would you look at that; I just did an automatic segue. Still got all the old newsman moves. Slick ...

Sorry, I was miles away for a moment there. Remembering the first day. How *excited* those people were. Everybody knew it was something big.

Nobody was frightened. Not at first.

***

It was summer. Summer meant more people out shopping, eyeing up the opposite sex, browsing, meeting friends, having outdoor coffees and watered—down beer. In Coventry, the chance to do this (with the sun out, and not a single cloud visible in the sky on a *weekend* no less) was as rare as rocking—horse shit, and so there were more people out and about in the city centre than at pretty much any other time of the year. I sometimes wonder if this was the reason that particular day was picked; attracted to the mass of people perhaps? Or maybe it was just sheer chance. The day certainly couldn't have been more different the second time; smack in the middle of October, with the streets abandoned by every living soul due to heavy rain. But that first day, you couldn't really have had any more people in the surrounding vicinity without there being some kind of riot.

I was stuck indoors for the earlier part of that day, and that was just fine by me. One, because I've never been a person who enjoys being out in harsh sunlight (makes me squint, I sweat easily, I burn easily, I can't stand it when my clothes stick to me ... need I go on? Sun worshippers doing nothing but sitting in sunlight; I'll never understand them) and two, because I was interviewing a local girl group ('Heroine Chic'; I shit you not) who were just about to release their debut piece—of—crap single. And it was *awful*, truly awful (I don't mean to come across as someone's dad, but it really was an assault on the ear drums. Middle—class white girls talking in urban patois. Exactly as bad as it sounds) but, at the time, I was still just on the right side of thirty—five, and so considered myself in with a chance of charming at least one of the trio; a stunning—looking blonde, brunette and redhead combo in their early twenties whose management were clearly banking on their looks to get them by, rather than their output. None of us knew it back then, but even that wouldn't be enough to help 'Get Into Me' (again, I shit you not) crack the top forty. Two more non—charting efforts later, Heroine Chic would find themselves back in obscurity before fame had found them; of the six of us in that room, including their enormous security guard and their wet—behind—the—ears looking manager, only one of us was destined to be known worldwide. None of us could have ever guessed that it would be me.

Not that I didn't have high hopes of my own in those days, lazy—but earnest—dreams of a glorious career in my chosen field. Obviously, the likes of Charli, Kel and Suze weren't going to land me a job at *Rolling Stone*, but I was starting to get good feedback on freelance pieces that I'd written for the *Observer* and the *Times*, and was listed as a contributor at the *Guardian*; I'd finally started to believe that in a year or two, I'd leave behind the features department at the local rag and then make my way to London to start shaking things up. I actually said that to colleagues as well: *I'm gonna shake things up.* That's how I often find myself talking to people, using sound bites and stagey lines to make an impression. Not only does it make small talk more bearable—having a backlog of canned material ready to go at any point—but I used to think that it would help me make an impression. I now know that the impression it gave would have been that I was a dick ... but I still do it out of habit. I can't help myself.

As the interview drew to a close, and their manager started making 'wrap it up' signals while looking nervously at his smartphone, the girls and I posed together for a brief photo by the office window. They pouted, and I grinned honestly, enjoying the moment despite receiving zero interest from any of them. I'd had high hopes for the brunette, but any attempts at smart banter that I'd made were met with a polite but confused smile. It appeared that Suze was the brains of the trio, but, ah ... blondes. Not my thing. To be fair, it appeared that I was not Heroine Chic's thing either. I made myself feel better by putting it down to the age gap.

They left with an all—too—casual goodbye, their bouncer blocking them all from view as they made their way to the escalator. I pocketed my Dictaphone and texted my friend Kevin, telling him how I'd gotten both a phone number and the promise of a date from Charli. I'd even considered adding that she'd silently licked her lips over her shoulder at me as she'd left, but decided that'd be too much, and the wind—up would be blown. Kevin was gullible, but not *that* gullible.

I was done for the day—I'd only come in for the late afternoon interview, with it being a weekend—and it was approaching five, so the temperature would soon be dropping nicely into that relaxing summer evening feel that I actually like. I had no plans, and flatmate Phil had his brother over for the weekend. He was a good guy, and his brother a good guest, but I didn't particularly want to be stuck at home listening to the two of them endlessly discussing rugby. I decided that I'd maybe find a beer garden and have a read for an hour or so.

Once upon a time, this would have been that magical exciting hour where you'd text around and find out who was available for an impromptu session. Nowadays, everyone was either married and booked up for the weekend, or starting to think about getting the kids fed, bathed, and in bed for seven. Being single at thirty—five and living with a thirty—nine—year—old divorced university lecturer could sometimes get lonely, and I'd been forced to find ways to adapt. Fortunately, there were still a lot of people who were up for doing stuff, but getting schedules to meet was difficult. I got through a lot of books back then; nowadays I can't remember the last time I read a book.

I grabbed my bag and headed out of the building, thinking about possibly getting a bite to eat as well—although I intended to have something healthy, as lately the gym hadn't really been graced with my presence, and it was starting to show—and for some reason, I decided to stroll towards Millennium Place.

It used to be a big open—air space, a modern plaza designed for concerts and shows of all kinds. This would have been excellent for the city, were it not for the fact that it had a built—in Achilles' heel in the form of a raised series of lighting strips in the floor. These looked fantastic at night, but technical issues created by this unusual flooring meant that none of the imagined concerts could ever happen (genius). None of it's there anymore, of course; after the Second Arrival they dug it all up and put a small lake in its place, to see if it made any difference.

For some reason I was in a good mood and—in the words of the song—having 'no particular place to go', I thought I'd take a look at the summer crowds at Millennium Place, and then decide my destination from there, giving me time to work up an appetite. I people—watched as I went, passing barely dressed young couples who made me feel old and think about past opportunities of my own. I was not the settling—down kind then, nor am I now—just as well, really—but I still think about those opportunities and what might have been. I found myself humming a tune I didn't recognise, and pondered what it was as I rolled the short sleeves of my shirt up farther, wishing I'd opted for shorts and flip—flops instead of jeans and on—trend boots. As I gently cursed myself for dressing that way, for making such a middle—aged and futile attempt to impress the Heroine Chic girls, thought triggered memory and I realised that I was humming 'Get Into Me'. I laughed out loud—I remember that distinctly—as I turned the corner and saw Millennium Place fully. When I saw what was going on, the laughter trailed off in my throat.

I suppose that I must have heard the commotion as I'd drawn closer; I'd been so lost in thought that somehow it didn't really register, or possibly I just subconsciously wrote it off as the usual summer crowd sound. But this was different. Around two hundred people were gathered in a cluster near the centre of Millennium Place, and there was an excited, confused buzz coming from them, their mobiles held out and snapping away at something in their midst. Other people were hanging back from them, getting footage of the crowd itself. That was the other reason I wanted to get into the big leagues, of course; *everyone* was a reporter in the digital age, and local print was shrinking fast.

I couldn't make out what was in the centre of the crowd, standing at a distance as I was, but I could see other people on the outskirts of the plaza having the same response as me; *what's going on, whatever it is I want to see it.* Don't misunderstand me, at this stage it was surprising and intriguing, but nothing really more than that; a chance for hopeful people to capture some footage that might go viral. You have to remember, none of us knew what it really was at that point. I assumed that it was somebody maybe doing some kind of street art, or perhaps a performance piece. That in itself was rare in Coventry, so in my mind I already had one hand on my phone to give Rich Bell—the staff photographer—a call, to see if he was available to get some proper photos if this turned out to be worth it. Either way, I walked towards the hubbub. As I got closer I could hear two people shouting frantically, almost hysterically, sounding as though they were trying to explain something.

The voices belonged to a man and a woman, and while I couldn't yet make out what they were saying, I could hear laughter from some listeners and questions from others; my vision was still mainly blocked by the medium—sized mass of bodies, but I could see that there was something fairly large in the middle of them all, rising just slightly above the heads of the gathered crowd and standing perfectly still.

I reached the cluster of people, now large enough to make it difficult to get through (to the point where I had to go on tiptoe to get a clear view) and that was the moment that I became one of the first few hundred people on Earth to get a look at the Stone Man.

Of course, it didn't have a name then. I'd like to tell you that I was the one who came up with it, but I'm afraid that would be a lie. As you may know, I was one of the people who *really* brought it into the common parlance worldwide, but I'd actually overheard it being used on a random local radio station as Paul and I raced through Sheffield later on (obviously, more on that to come) and thought it perfect, but I'd never actually intended to rip it off. By the point I was in front of the cameras, I'd used it so often that I'd forgotten that it wasn't a common term at the time.

It stood at around eight feet tall (to my eyes at least; the Home Office can give you the exact measurements) and it made me think then, as it does now, of the 'Man' logo on a toilet door, if someone were to make one out of rough, dark, greyish—brown stone and then mutate it so the arms were too long, and the head were more of an oval than a circle. The top half of its body was bent slightly forward as well, but the biggest departure from the toilet picture was that this figure had hands, of a sort; its arms tapered out at the ends, reminding me of the tip of a lipstick.

The most intriguing thing was, there was also an extremely quiet sound emanating from it. The best way I can describe it is as a bass note so low as to be almost inaudible. They still haven't figured that one out.

Now that I was closer, I could hear what one of the ranting people was saying. It was the woman, standing about ten feet away from me on the inside of the circle of gathered people. Based on the distance between the crowd, herself, and the Stone Man, it looked to me as if she was the reason they were hanging back from the hulking figure, and not swarming forward to touch and prod it.

She was patrolling back and forth in front of the Stone Man, wide—eyed and breathing heavily. If she wasn't keeping the people around her at bay deliberately, she was still doing a damn good job of it. The mass of bodies on the other side of the Stone Man seemed to be getting an identical treatment from someone else; I couldn't see them clearly around the bodies of the woman and the Stone Man itself, nor could I hear what they were saying over the general noise, but it sounded like a man.

The woman was about fifty, well—dressed, and clearly at the end of her rope. She was very red—faced from her efforts, and sweating. Her smart white summer blouse and beige skirt were in sharp contrast to her flustered appearance, giving her a temporary air of great visibility. The people on the very inside of the circle looked uncertain, wondering if this was some kind of show (which was probably another reason that they were hanging back, not wanting to either spoil or become part of a public performance) and some of them were smiling nervously at each other. As I drew within clear—hearing range, she was taking a moment to try and get her air back. She'd obviously just finished her rant, and was now struggling to compose herself before continuing, deciding that an attempt at a more rational demeanour might better help her cause.

She closed her eyes slowly, and took a deep breath, lifting her chin. She reminded me slightly, in that moment, of Yoda, just before he tries to lift Luke's X—Wing out of the swamp. When she started speaking again, her eyes remained shut.

"I'm not crazy," she said, quietly but decisively, her voice shaking slightly. "I'm not making it up. I'm not some loony, and I'm not the only one here that's saying it. This isn't a, a ... I don't know, some kind of bloody *play* or anything, this is what's happened. It's real. Any of you who were here earlier, did you see anyone bring this thing over? Look, look how much it *weighs*, for God's sake!" she suddenly cried, shouting this last part as her composure gave way and she struck at the Stone Man, first with her purse and then with her balled up fists. She moved up close to it and began to push against it with her shoulders and full body weight. It didn't move a millimetre. I always remember the crowd's seemingly subconscious reaction when she first hit it; everyone responded in the exact same manner, without really noticing that they'd done it. They'd all flinched away slightly.

I think at that point someone might have moved in to calm her down, but I didn't see if they actually managed it because that was when the young guy—the one who'd still been shouting at the people on the other side of the circle—suddenly flung his arms in the air and pushed his way out of the crowd. I could see him clearly now, dressed in a dark hooded top and overly baggy jeans. The people parted to let him out, perhaps relieved—the human urge to treat public displays of volume as if they were contagious coming into full effect—and I broke away from my side of the circle to pursue him. I'd seen enough for now, and I wanted to find out what the shouting was about without having to deal with any interference. More and more people were arriving and joining the circle, and I knew that if I was going to speak to him, it would have to be now if I were ever to stand a chance of getting back into the crowd and regaining a decent vantage point.

I dashed around to the opposite side of the pack and saw that he hadn't gone far, stomping along with clenched fists and shaking head. He'd pulled the hood of his top up over his head as well, so I couldn't get an idea of his facial appearance from the angle that I was approaching at, but it was clear by his body language that he wasn't happy. I could at least see that he was shorter than myself, and of slight build. I decided to open a dialogue by appealing to his righteous anger; in my experience, angry people warm to you very quickly if you agree with them. Running around him so that I was several feet ahead, I stopped, looking past him to the crowd, pretending that an idea had just occurred to me. Waiting until he drew near, I tutted loudly.

"What the hell is wrong with all those idiots, eh?" I asked him, speaking as if I was just making conversation. I probably wasn't very convincing; small talk has never been something that I'm comfortable with, as I say.

"Fuck 'em," he muttered, not looking at me as he went to walk past. From this new angle I could see that he was in his early twenties at most, with crew cut hair and a face that was only just seeing off the last ravages of acne. His cheekbones stood out, giving him a drawn, wiry look. He started to fish a packet of cigarettes out of his pocket, and seeing the opening I pulled out my lighter to accommodate. I don't smoke myself, but I often find that carrying a lighter has its uses, especially in this job. He stopped—still not looking at me—and clearly wasn't really thinking about what he was doing, still lost in his fury as he fumbled out a cigarette and put it in his mouth. I flicked the wheel and a plume of flame appeared. Lowering his head towards it, he gave a non—committal grunt of thanks as he took a drag on the cigarette and let out a sigh that was more of a hiss. Straightening, he clenched his jaw and looked back at the crowd, still shaking his head. Whatever they'd done, they'd really managed to offend him.

"Ah saw it. Ah fuckin' *seen* it, man," he said, staring angrily at the crowd, shaking his head gently. He paused to take another drag, let it out. "*Twats*," he said, drawing out the *s* longer than was necessary.

"What, the statue thing?" I asked, pointing at it, the head still slightly visible above the growing crowd of people. He nodded, not turning around to look, inhaling again instead. The cigarette was calming him, steadying him, soothing his ego. I decided it was safe to press on. "But … haven't they all seen it as well?"

He suddenly whirled round to face the same direction as me, face screwed up in disgust at my stupidity. He looked like a rat that had smelt something it didn't like.

"No, ya fuckin' …" His words trailed off, as he realised that not only did he not know me well enough to talk to me in such a manner, but also that I could probably pound him fairly comfortably. I'm not a big guy, or even a tough guy by any stretch, but it was clear that taking down this spindly specimen wouldn't prove to be too much of a challenge. He looked me up and down quickly, and his angry eyes dropped slightly, although his expression didn't change. "No … all those arseholes *seen* the fucker, man. Ah saw it *first*." He stared at me, waiting for me to comprehend. I shrugged slightly, confirming that comprehension wasn't coming anytime soon. His face screwed up further.

"*Ah* saw it *turn up*. No one else was looking. Nah, ac'shully, dat woman was looking, she was looking, but she fuckin' …" He paused for a moment, waving his hand in the air dismissively. "She fuckin' *blah blah blah* and no—

one give a fuck, but ah was *tellin'* them that ah *fuckin'* seen it, and they all just standin' there like *errrrrrrrrr* and ah'm tellin' 'em and *tellin'* 'em and they don't fuckin' *geddit*. Fuckin' jokers, bruv, jokers." He took another drag, and wagged a finger at the crowd. "And some of 'em start *laughin'*, man, fuckin' bitches ... fuckin' nearly *battered* 'em, man, *boom*," he finished emphatically, punctuating the word with a short, aggressive air punch that said that he meant it, unaware of how ineffective he probably would have been. His anger was so genuine that I suddenly wanted to know what he had to say, despite my normal loathing for this kind of chavvy little twat.

"Look," I said, reaching into my bag for my Dictaphone, "tell me. I want to know, I'll listen." He saw the Dictaphone and started to back away, staring at it.

"Fuckin' *what?*" he said, drawing out the *t* in the same way he'd done with the *s*. Though my first instinct was to smash him over the head with the Dictaphone, I merely waved it dismissively, smiling.

"I write for the paper. Just want to get an idea of what happened. Won't even use your name if you don't want me to."

He didn't reply at first, just carried on staring at the Dictaphone with that screwed up face of his, smoking. He turned to look at the crowd for a moment, and then faced me again with a snort and a little shake of the head, gesturing me towards him. I bet Straub still has the recording. I'll never forgive her for taking that Dictaphone off me. I bet it's valuable, too; it's probably the first eyewitness account of the first human sighting.

***

(Faint sound of crowd noise. By now, there are around three hundred people in the background, plus constant traffic sounds from the cars driving past Millennium Place. The first sound is a large post—exhale intake of breath

from the interviewee. I can be heard telling him that it's now recording, and then asking if he wants to give his name.)

"Nah, bruv, nah ..."

(There is a long pause while he possibly considers what he's doing, but then thinks better of it, clearly keen to be heard. He's smarting, still angry and feeling humiliated with that brand of indignation that only the young can muster.)

"Ah was on da phone, like, just talkin' an' that, and dere, over dere like?"

(The sound fades as he turns away to gesture to where the crowd is standing.)

"There were no one dere, right, and maybe like ... some people dere, and dere, and over dere, and dat's it—"

("How many people?")

"... thirty ... 'bout thirty innit, like spread out? But ah was the only one near dere 'cos ah was on me phone, like. So ah fuckin' saw. Dey's like, like ..."

(He pauses, holding his hands apart, seeing it again.)

"Right next to me ... it was like, cold, like fuckin' freezin'. And ah'm like, fuckin', shiverin' an' dat, and everyone else is like la la la, fuckin' warm, and it's all sunny but ah'm lookin' round tryin'a see where the fuckin' cold's comin' from, but dey's just ... nuthin."

(He breaks off and takes another drag on his cigarette. His hand is shaking.)

"And then ma phone is just like WEEEEEEEEE in ma fuckin' ear! Like ah can hear Donna and then it's just this fuckin' ... noise, like the speaker's fucked, and ah'm like fuck dis an' hang up like, and then ah look and just like, dere—"

(He gestures to a spot about two feet in front of himself, implying distance.)

"—it's dere, and it weren't dere before, man, it weren't—fucking—dere, but it's not dere properly, like ah can see troo the fucker."

(Another pause as he stares at me, almost daring me to say anything. I don't respond at first, not understanding. He continues.)

"Ah mean, like, it was fast, man, like ah could see troo it for like, a second, then brap, it's there totally, and ah'm all 'ot again innit, and it's dere, but it's just fuckin', just ..."

(His eyes are wide, his expression manic, looking into space with his hands splayed as he sees it again.)

"... bing! DERE. *Outta fuckin'* nowhere. *And ah'm looking at this fuckin' stone thing dat's just fuckin' poofed, appeared like, and ah'm lookin' and* no—one's noticed, *and ah just ... ah just ...*"

(He searches for the words.)

"... ah fuckin' ... man ..."

(There is a long pause as he almost visibly deflates, shaking his head. I think he is starting to feel sorry for himself. When he continues, I think that he has forgotten who he is talking to, this adult stranger with a Dictaphone, an adult who thinks he might just be interviewing a smackhead. I almost turn it off and put it away. Later, I will know that he would have been genuinely traumatised by seeing the impossible, the materialisation of a solid physical object out of thin air, and was simply having an emotional release. But now, I just think he's off his tits. I carry on recording anyway.)

"... I just, like ... ah dunno ... ah just started fuckin' ... like...shouting, or somethin', and then ah can't fuckin' breathe an' ah'm shakin' and ah fall on ma arse, but ah'm still shoutin' an' pointin' at it, 'cos ... 'cos ... it shouldn't fuckin' BE dere, y'know? An' then ah fuckin' honk up a bit, and other people are comin' over an' ah'm tryin' to tell 'em but den dey's walkin' away quick, but den dat old woman come over an' she's shoutin' too like AH SAW IT AH SAW IT TOO and some people are stayin' and some are fuckin' off and some fuckin' pricks are laughin' ... but it's still fuckin' right dere and then ah go all ... like, fucked, like whoaoahah ..."

(He puts his arms out and mimes being dizzy.)

"An' ah have to just fuckin' sit down a sec and then ah can hear people talkin' about it an' deres more people, and some of 'um are talking about me and dat woman is shoutin' 'er fuckin' 'ead off man, she sounds fuckin' ... fucked, an' ah can hear people saying it's a statue, it's a fuckin' ..."

(He waves his hand, searching for the word. "Sculpture?" I say, offering it up.)

"Yeah, scupter. Dat. And I'm like, it's not a fuckin' scupter! An' ah stand up and start fuckin' shoutin' an' that, an' ah'm fuckin' shoutin' at 'em for ages, then ah just ... ah fuck off out of it."

(There's a long pause, and a faint sound as the cigarette is flicked away into the gutter. "So the woman saw this too?" I say.)

"Musta done. She said the same stuff. 'Ohhhh, it was see troo and then it fuckin' popped up ...'"

(I mentally register this statement in particular, as it is the first time I feel some real confusion. The woman had looked too well—dressed to be a crazy person jumping on the bandwagon. She'd looked like a teacher, or someone's Mum. Another long pause, as he stands looking back at the crowd, shaking his head. I don't speak either, rather bewildered at this point as to what the hell is going on. He suddenly speaks.)

"Right, fuck it, the end. Safe."

(He turns to leave, finished just like that, and holds out his knuckles for me to put mine against. I do so. "Are you all right?" I ask. He responds without turning around, still hurriedly walking away and not even looking at the crowd.)

"Yeah, safe, man. Safe."

***

I remained standing there for a moment, watching him go, and starting to think that maybe this really was some kind of annoying performance piece. I turned back to the crowd, looking for the woman and thinking that I'd try and have a word with her as well, maybe get a few crowd reactions for an opinion piece or something, but I suddenly realised that the woman couldn't be heard anymore. That was when the first of the police cars arrived. They didn't have the sirens or lights going; they just quietly turned up, presumably to check that there wasn't some kind of trouble occurring, or maybe brought there by somebody reporting the shouters. Either way, they'd arrived, and so I headed back over to the source of the hubbub. I don't really remember what I was thinking at this point; I was more intrigued than anything else, I think. I certainly didn't believe what the chav had just been saying, but it was all interesting regardless.

As I was walking over, everyone in the crowd suddenly let out cries of varying volumes—there were several screams—and jumped back a foot or two. I stopped walking and started running. So did the police.

I reached the crowd about as quickly as the cops did, and snuck in with them, following in their wake as they pushed to the front while asking people politely to back up and let them through. I was looking at the Stone Man and the crowd, trying to see what the hell had happened to make everyone jump at once like that. Most people were now giggling nervously, embarrassed at their reaction, but I couldn't tell what they had reacted to; a quick inspection of the Stone Man didn't give anything away. As far as I could tell, nothing was any different. The police were talking to some people at the opposite side of the inner circle, too far away for me to hear, so I tried to pick up on the conversations of people around me. I didn't get any clues at first.

God, feel my heart!

I was like, oh shit!

You elbowed me in the ribs when you jumped!

I was just about to ask the couple to my right what had happened, when I suddenly saw the evidence for myself; I'd been wrong. There *was* a difference to the Stone Man.

It was no longer bent forward. It had straightened up, and its head was now tipped backwards towards the sky. The arms seemed to be held out at a slightly wider angle than before as well. Everyone must have jumped when it switched position, but were simply excited now that it was perfectly still; already the police were smiling again and talking to the people, most of whom were now looking amused and expectant, phones out once more. It seemed that the general consensus was that this was definitely some kind of unusual, intentional show, and everyone was waiting for whatever was going to happen next.

I, however, kept seeing the teacherish woman in my mind as she leant on the Stone Man, as she struck at it. I hadn't seen any movement from it in the slightest. There was clearly real *weight* to the Stone Man, real solidity. I couldn't see any hinge or break in the rough stone surface, any point of articulation. So how the hell had it now straightened up like that? I looked around for the teacherish woman; she appeared to have left, just like her chav counterpart. One of the police was on his radio, sounding as though he was calling in more officers or support of some kind—there were still people turning up to see what was going on—but he looked more amused than anything. I decided to stick around. I wasn't massively hungry yet, the temperature was just nice now in the late afternoon, and there looked like there would be further developments.

As the next hour passed, police barriers arrived, along with two more officers who good—naturedly spread the now four—hundred—strong crowd back a few feet—receiving a chorus of playful boos as a result—and set up a low retractable tape barrier at a radius of about eight feet from the Stone Man. A gentleman from the council turned up at one point, asked the police a few questions, and then moved back to the outside of the crowd, where he remained on his phone for the rest of the time that I was there. It filtered back through the crowd that he was trying to find out who was responsible for it, if they had a permit, and so on. Eventually, he apparently moved on to trying to sort out its removal.

I'd gotten a few bits of audio from the people around me, a lot of them all too eager to talk into the Dictaphone, describing how it had suddenly moved without a sound (the silence of it was confirmed by all of them, which again struck a chord with me. How could something with so much weight move silently? Unless the teacher woman had been an excellent mime) and a few opinions (*I think it's representing the death of Coventry's industry/I think it's a marketing stunt/I think it's shit*) but was starting to grow a bit bored, to be honest. Rich Bell wasn't answering his phone either, so all I had image—wise were a few shots I'd managed to grab on the digital camera that I kept in my bag; my phone's own camera was far too primitive. Most of the new people that had turned up had hung around for a while, and, not having seen it move in the first place, didn't have the level of invested intrigue to make them stick around. Eventually, hunger and boredom would draw them towards their homes. Even those who had been there all along were starting to look at their watches and think about dinner.

I couldn't blame them. I would have liked to have sacked it off myself by then, if not for the fact that the teacher woman's story corroborated the impossible account of the chav ... it made me think twice, or at least give me enough desire for an explanation to warrant me staying longer. My stomach rumbled, and I began to think about where the nearest chippy was that I could dash to—even though it meant I would lose my place at the front of the crowd—when the temperature suddenly dropped by about twenty degrees.

Everyone there suddenly started chattering, and looking at the sky, even though the sun above was still blazing down. It was *freezing*, impossibly cold under that still—blue sky, and I was more covered than most of the other people due to my jeans. I hate to think how cold the summer—dressed people there would have been. Goose bumps covered my entire body, and I saw couples and friends suddenly and instinctively huddling together for warmth, some laughing, some looking confused. Even the cops shared a concerned look. I found myself remembering what the chav had said about the cold, how the temperature around him had inexplicably dropped, and suddenly I had a brief flash of belief; *he was right.* I tried to remind myself that this was the age of people like David Blaine, street performers who prided themselves on their ability to freak people out by making them believe the impossible, and took a deep breath. I noticed that my heart rate had still picked up dramatically, though.

Then the cold suddenly cut off just as quickly, and almost unnoticed in the moment of relief—everyone around me breathed an audible sigh and started to laugh, delighted that the heat was back again—the Stone Man took two steps forward and stopped.

Everyone who was directly in front of it, albeit eight feet away, shrieked and leapt backwards. One or two people at the back fell over. The steps had not been quick, or slow; they were about normal walking pace. The Stone Man had come to a stop with its feet side by side, like it had only meant to take two steps and no more. It was now completely still again, and nervously giggling people had already started to step back into their original position. The police inside the barrier had backed away, but one had already gathered his wits and was politely taking charge, telling people to calm down. The council man was impotently demanding to be let back through the crowd, but no one was paying any attention.

Then the Stone Man began to walk.

***

CONTINUED IN *THE STONE MAN,* AVAILABLE NOW ON AMAZON

LUKE SMITHERD

@travellingluke ON TWITTER

lukesmitherd@hotmail.co.uk

www.lukesmitherd.com

The Stone Man

The #1 Amazon Horror Bestseller

Two-bit reporter Andy Pointer had always been unsuccessful (and antisocial) until he got the scoop of his career; the day a man made of stone appeared in the middle of his city.

This is his account of everything that came afterwards and what it all cost him, along with the rest of his country.

The destruction, the visions … the dying.

Available now on the Amazon Kindle Store, and soon in traditional book format

Also By Luke Smitherd:

An Unusual Novella for the Kindle

THE MAN ON TABLE TEN

It's a story that he hasn't told anyone for fifty years; a secret that he's kept ever since he grew tired of the disbelieving faces and doctors' reports advising medication But then, he hasn't touched a single drop of booze in all of that time either, and alcohol loosens bar room lips at the best of times; so on this fateful day, his decision to have three drinks will change the life of bright young waitress Lisa Willoughby forever ... because now, the The Man On Table Ten wants to share his incredible tale.

It's afterwards when she has to worry; afterwards, when she knows the unbelievable burden that The Man On Table Ten has had to carry throughout the years. When she knows the truth, and is left powerless to do anything except watch for the signs ...

An unusual short story for the Kindle, The Man On Table Ten is the latest novella from Luke Smitherd, the author of the Amazon UK number one horror bestseller *The Stone Man*. Original and compelling, *The Man On Table Ten* will leave you breathless and listening carefully, wondering if that sound you can hear might just be *pouring sand that grows louder with every second ...*

Available now on the Amazon Kindle Store

Also By Luke Smitherd:

The Physics of the Dead

What do the dead do when they can't leave … and don't know why?

The afterlife doesn't come with a manual. In fact, Hart and Bowler (two ordinary, but dead men) have had to work out the rules of their new existence for themselves. It's that fact—along with being unable to leave the boundaries of their city centre, unable to communicate with the other lost souls, unable to rest in case The Beast should catch up to them, unable to even sleep—that makes getting out of their situation a priority.

But Hart and Bowler don't know why they're there in the first place, and if they ever want to leave, they will have to find all the answers in order to understand the physics of the dead: What are the strange, glowing objects that pass across the sky? Who are the living people surrounded by a blue glow? What are their physical limitations in that place, and have they fully explored the possibilities of what they can do?

Time is running out; their afterlife was never supposed to be this way, and if they don't make it out soon, they're destined to end up like the others.

Insane, and alone forever …

Available now on the Amazon Kindle Store, and soon in traditional book format

Also By Luke Smitherd:

IN THE DARKNESS, THAT'S WHERE
I'LL KNOW YOU

FROM THE AUTHOR OF THE AMAZON UK #1 HORROR BESTSELLER, 'THE STONE MAN', COMES A NEW MYSTERY TO UNRAVEL…

What Is The Black Room?

There are hangovers, there are bad hangovers, and then there's waking up inside someone else's head. Thirty-something bartender Charlie Wilkes is faced with this exact dilemma when he wakes to find finds himself trapped inside The Black Room; a space consisting of impenetrable darkness and a huge, ethereal screen floating in its centre. Through this screen he is shown the world of his female host, Minnie.

How did he get there? What has happened to his life? And how can he exist inside the mind of a troubled, fragile, but beautiful woman with secrets of her own? Uncertain whether he's even real or if he is just a figment of his host's imagination, Charlie must enlist Minnie's help if he is to find a way out of The Black Room, a place where even the light of the screen goes out every time Minnie closes her eyes…

IN THE DARKNESS, THAT'S WHERE I'LL KNOW YOU starts with a bang and doesn't let go. Each answer only leads to another mystery in a story guaranteed to keep the reader on the edge of their seat.

Also By Luke Smitherd:

A HEAD FULL OF KNIVES

THE LATEST NOVEL FROM BESTSELLING AUTHOR LUKE SMITHERD

Martin Hogan is being watched, all of the time. He just doesn't know it yet. It started a long time ago, too, even before his wife died. Before he started walking every day.

Before the walks became an attempt to find a release from the whirlwind that his brain has become. He never walks alone, of course, although his 18 month old son and his faithful dog, Scoffer, aren't the greatest conversationalists.

Then the walks become longer. Then the *other* dog starts showing up. The big white one, with the funny looking head. The one that sits and watches Martin and his family as they walk away.

All over the world, the first attacks begin. The Brotherhood of the Raid make their existence known; a leaderless group who randomly and inexplicably assault both strangers and loved ones without explanation.

Martin and the surviving members of his family are about to find that these events are connected. Caught at the center of the world as it changes beyond recognition, Martin will be faced with a series of impossible choices ... but how can an ordinary and broken man figure out the unthinkable? What can he possibly do with a head full of knives?

Luke Smitherd (author of the Amazon bestseller THE STONE MAN and THE BLACK ROOM series) asks you once again to consider what you would do in his latest unusual and original novel. A HEAD FULL OF KNIVES is a supernatural mystery that will not only change the way you look at your pets forever, but will force you to decide the fate of the world when it lies in your hands.

Available now in both paperback and Kindle formats on Amazon

Printed in Great Britain
by Amazon